CW00594957

'An absolutely stunning book fro[m]
Emotional, powerful, meticulous
wond[...]
Louise Swanson, au[thor]

'I was blown away not just by the gripping story, which had my heart
thumping at times, but the sheer eloquence of the writing. It is a story of
the strength of the human spirit, and of love which will not be defeated. I
know I will be recommending it to everyone'
Lesley Pearse, author of *Betrayal*

'An impressively researched, powerfully emotional tale of two women
surviving post-war Berlin . . . *Child of the Ruins* will have you gripped in
suspense from the first line to the last'
Louise Candlish, author of *Our House*

'In Kate's inimitable style we are immediately drawn into this impeccably
researched and terrifying period of history. Stunning from the very first
line, this is a masterclass in historical fiction writing. An absolute triumph!'
Dinah Jefferies author of *Daughters of War*

'There is only one word to describe *Child of the Ruins* and that is awesome.
It is compelling and evocative, thrilling and yet hugely touching. Kate
Furnivall has really steeped herself in the period and faced the horrors of
those times. I congratulate her'
Dilly Court, author of *The Lucky Penny*

'An extraordinarily tense and gripping story set in a city brought to its knees
in the aftermath of war, where life is cheap and crusts of bread are currency.
The plotting is ingenious and the writing beautifully atmospheric'
Gill Paul, author of *The Lost Daughter*

'Unforgettable characters negotiate desperate times in this vivid, brave and
suspenseful novel set in the chaos of war torn Berlin. The final twist made
me gasp!'
Rachel Hore, author of *A Beautiful Spy*

'Gripping from the very first page, *Child of the Ruins* is a powerful and
emotionally intense reminder that heartache and hardship linger long after
a war ends. Highly recommend!'
Teresa Driscoll, author of *Tell Me Lies*

About the author

Kate Furnivall is the author of thirteen novels, including *The Russian Concubine*, *The Liberation* and *The Guardian of Lie*s. Her books have been translated into more than twenty languages and have been on the *Sunday Times* and *New York Times* bestseller lists. Kate lives in Devon.

Child of the Ruins

Kate Furnivall

**HODDER &
STOUGHTON**

First published in Great Britain in 2023 by Hodder & Stoughton Limited
An Hachette UK company

This paperback edition published in 2024

1

A CIP catalogue record for this title is available from the British Library

Paperback ISBN 978 1 399 71361 0
ebook ISBN 978 1 399 71359 7

Typeset in Fournier MT Std by Manipal Technologies Limited

Printed and bound in Great Britain by Clays Ltd, Elcograf S.p.A.

Hodder & Stoughton policy is to use papers that are natural, renewable and
recyclable products and made from wood grown in sustainable forests. The logging
and manufacturing processes are expected to conform to the environmental
regulations of the country of origin.

Hodder & Stoughton Limited
Carmelite House
50 Victoria Embankment
London EC4Y 0DZ

www.hodder.co.uk

For Lilli and Pete
With all my love for you and your city

Sectors of Berlin, 1948

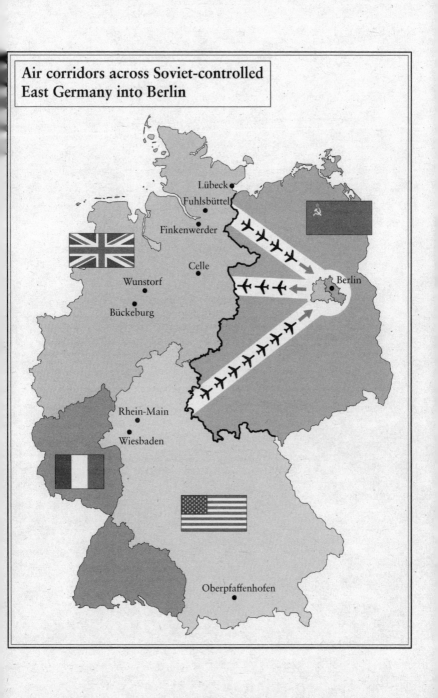

Air corridors across Soviet-controlled
East Germany into Berlin

CHAPTER ONE

◆ ◆ ◆

ANNA

There are only three people in Berlin who know I killed a man. And not just any man. A Russian, an officer in the Red Army. One with fancy boots and even fancier medals on his chest.

There are only three people in Berlin who know I killed a man. My mother. My friend Kristina. And Martha Dieleman. These are the three. They know that I didn't just shoot the bastard or even stick a knife between his ribs. They know I picked up a broken brick off the filthy ground in one of Berlin's back alleyways and pounded his head to a pulp till my hands were sticky with his blood and whatever he'd had for brains was trailing from my fingers. That's why I am here, alive, cycling up and down the grey and decimated streets of Berlin, and he is not.

The war is over. But the unspoken war of whispers, of midnight arrests and tortured body parts rages on unseen. I honestly believed I'd have learned to forget the killing by now, to roll the memory of his scream into a tight little wad and toss it away to rot among the piles of rubble that were stacked high in Berlin's streets.

Yet that killing still breathes deep inside me like a living thing. I feel it curled up behind my ribs, hidden away under my shabby brown coat where no one can see it. No one, that is, except me. Each morning I take my hard grey pumice stone and I scrub at a spot in the exact centre of my breastbone to rid myself of the stain of it. I scour it raw again and again.

Yes, I know the scrubbing is pointless because the killing has sunk too deep into the very bones and sinews of who I am. It is a part of me now.

But I say this, so you know: the Russian deserved to die.

'Where is he?'

I open my eyes. The darkness and the cold in the room are pressing down on me like something solid, trapping me. I can't breathe right. I drag in icy Berlin air but it feels as if it is packed full of tiny needle-sharp fishhooks that catch in my throat and snag on the inside of my lungs. I try to cough them up but it is like coughing up glass. I force myself to sit up. I spit out blood.

'Where is he?'

I begin to panic.

'Where is he? Where is he?'

Is that my voice? It sounds hoarse and scraped raw. My words hang unheard in my bedroom, and I can tell I am in my own narrow bed because my fingers are gripping the silky animal warmth of the sable coat that I throw over at night to fight the cold. A ribbon of ice-white moonlight unfurls across the floorboards where Felix's crib should stand. It is gone.

'Where is he?' This time I scream it.

I throw back the bedcover and am shocked by the effort it takes, my arm is shaking, and beneath me the sheet smells of stale sweat and vomit. It dawns on me that I am sick. And I am alone.

I get myself as far as the door of my room and am forced to lean against it, clinging to the doorknob to keep me on my feet. I ache. My whole body aches and my lungs are on fire, but none of it matters. It is fear that has dragged me from the depths of God-knows-where. It is fear that flares into an inferno, consuming the room. Consuming me. The fear that she has stolen my child.

I open the door. I listen. Silence.

It was the silence that had finally woken me. There were no cries, no sweet chuckles, no hungry whimpers. No snuffling snores. Nothing.

How long? How long had I lived in silence?

I don't know.

Hours? Days? Weeks? How long have I been sick?

I light the stub of the candle in an old candlestick that stands on a table by the door – we have no electricity supply at this hour. I make my way into what used to be the large drawing room of our apartment, before the Soviets came and carved it up into a pokey miserable living space. It lies in total darkness. I raise the candle to scour every corner of the room. The flame creates shadows that writhe away from me as though I am the one to fear, but I find nothing until a sudden swirl of light at the other end of the room sets my heart racing.

'Felix!' I whisper.

But it is a mirror, the moving light is a reflection of my own candle. For a moment I stand there, shaking, then I rush to my mother's bedroom door and throw it open. It slams against the wall behind and rebounds, almost knocking me to the ground.

'Mutti!' I shout and storm in.

Except the shout is more of a rasp and the storming is more of an unsteady hobble, but inside my head I shout and storm and demand the truth from my mother.

'Mutti, where is he?'

'Where is who?'

'Felix.'

She is sitting bolt upright in bed, startled, a picture of wide-eyed innocence. She wears a high-necked white silk nightdress and her long hair is scooped together by a white ribbon and hangs neatly over one shoulder in an immaculate braid. Her face is thin, her cheekbones jutting out under pearly skin, and her lips set tight with annoyance at this intrusion. My mother is a woman of fifty but in the swaying dim light of my candle she has the soft untouched appearance of a young girl, except for the look in the intense blue of her eyes. There you can see it. You can see exactly who she is.

'Get out, Anna,' she says.

I move forward past the stacks of furniture, avoiding the tottering footstool propped atop the carved Black Forest chairs that had once been my father's favourites. She is frightened that I will burn them for firewood, so she guards them in here. I reach my mother's bedside and look down on her, while I hold the candlestick high. Whenever I look at *her* eyes, I see *his*. Whenever I look at *her* mouth, I see *his*. I wonder now how she can face me and ask, *Where is who?*

'What have you done with my baby?' I demand. 'Where is my Felix?'

She blinks slowly. It has always been her way of making someone wait, even Papa if he was trying to hurry her. I can't wait.

I try not to shout. 'Mutti, Felix is only three months old. It is winter and he will die if he is out in the cold. Where is he?'

'He has gone.'

'Gone where?'

'Away.'

'What do you mean, *away*? Away where?'

'You were too ill with pneumonia to care for the little bastard and he wouldn't stop crying. I got rid of him. You know I never wanted him here, not from the very beginning. He was tainted. He brought shame on our name, we both know that. He's gone.'

'Where?'

I was shaking so hard the candle flame guttered and would have extinguished itself if my mother had not removed it from my grip and placed it on her bedside cabinet. With the same cold hand that had removed my son.

'You almost died, Anna.'

'Where?'

I lean down over her and it is only when I see a drop of moisture fall on her silk nightgown and spread tendrils through its fibres that I realise I am crying. The wind claws at the shutters and I think of Felix somewhere out there without me.

'Tell me, Mutti.' I seize her arm, nothing but bird bones, hollow and fragile. 'Tell me what you did with him?'

'I gave him away.'

'To whom?'

'To the first person who would take the brat.' She pushes me aside and swings herself out of bed. She stares glassy-eyed at the empty vodka bottle next to the candlestick instead of at me. 'He's gone, Anna. He's been gone more than a week and I have no idea where or with whom, so don't bother asking. Forget him. This city is crawling with unwanted children. You'll never see him again.'

'Is he still alive?'

I have visions of her lowering her pillow over his precious sleeping face and burying his limp body in the rubble of the city, while I lay burning with fever, soaking the sheets of my bed.

'I have no idea,' she says and I can hear the truth of it in her voice. 'He's gone. Accept it.'

Something breaks inside me, something vital that I had believed was unbreakable, and I know it cannot be mended.

'His crib? His toys?'

'I burned them,' she says. 'Like the Russians burned our city.'

I cannot bear to breathe the same air as her any more; rage is suffocating me and I leave the bedroom with images in my head that I cannot bear to look at. I am in the dark. Pitch dark. In our living space I cling to the icy window frame and press my forehead tight against its blackness as an ocean of grief sweeps through me and I recall the final terrifying Russian bombardment of Berlin. In April outside our city the Soviet Union assembled the largest force of military power ever seen, and Russian Marshal Zhukov inflicted enormous casualties and crippling damage to gain the glory of capturing the prize of Berlin. He grasped our poor city in a death grip. So now we live under Russian control, much of the time in darkness and in freezing cold because the winter is here. We have no lighting other than candles and oil lamps, or firelight if we're lucky, because oil is worth more than gold in Berlin. But right now none of this means a thing to me.

'Felix, my sweetest heart,' I whisper. 'Somewhere you are out there. Somewhere in this godforsaken city you are alive, I can feel your heart beating within mine.' I force myself to believe my own words. 'I love you and I will find you, my child, I swear it. Wait for me. I will come.'

CHAPTER TWO

◆ ◆ ◆

ANNA

'Halt!'
The shout made me jump. A harsh Russian voice.

I jammed on the brakes of my bicycle. My front wheel skidded across a cobweb of ice on the road, the threadbare tyre devoid of grip, and I had to slide my weight backwards to hold the rear end down. It was December and the sky hung low, laden with unspilled snow. Ice had gathered in the shadow of the massive columns of the Brandenburg Gate that dominated Pariser Platz at the junction of Unter den Linden and Ebertstrasse. Only one block to the north stood the obscene mangled wreckage of the Reichstag that had once housed our proud German parliament, but which now was a constant reminder of what we'd lost.

The bored Russian soldier at the checkpoint that marks one of the crossing points dividing East Berlin from West Berlin swaggered towards me in his grubby Red Amy uniform, and I felt the familiar twist of unease in my gut. It's what they like to see. The submission of the vanquished. Berlin's inhabitants were permitted to pass back and forth between the Soviet sector and the Allied sectors of the city, but not freely. Each time we were required to show our identity papers at the checkpoints and were prohibited from carrying forbidden items. So I settled one foot on the cobbles, lowered my eyes and halted.

I had learned to obey.

Berlin had learned to obey.

'Halt!' the voice at the checkpoint ordered again and addded in Russian, '*Bystro!*'

I'd heard the order clearly despite my woollen hat pulled down tight around my ears against the cold. Above me in the pot-bellied clouds the relentless drone of America's Skymaster planes and the British RAF's Yorks could be heard, as they continued to circle down in their all-day and all-night spiral into Berlin's Tempelhof and Gatow airports, bringing life-giving food and fuel to sustain the inhabitants of blockaded West Berlin.

This Russian guard was tall and cumbersome inside his thick brown winter greatcoat and *ushanka* hat with its cosy ear flaps. His boots crunched the ice underfoot and his eyes were half shut, as though he had no desire to open them wide enough to view Berliners in any detail.

'Wait,' he ordered.

I waited. I stood beside my bicycle, resting my hands on the rusty handlebars. I stood there, trying not to grip, trying to appear bored too, keeping any trace of panic off my face.

'Papers?' He stretched out his hand.

I obeyed. His gaze skimmed over my name but then flicked on to me and stayed there. Something pulsed into life in my gut. Give a man a uniform and a rifle and a reason to hate and it changes him, though this one looked as if even as a child his idea of fun would have been tearing heads off Moscow's pigeons.

'Where you going?' He spoke German but with a heavy Russian accent.

'To visit a friend.'

'Where?'

'On Ku'damm. That's the Kurfürstendamm boulevard in the western sector of Berlin.'

He frowned, his forehead creasing into well-worn grooves. 'Do you carry food into the western sector of the city for your friend?'

'No, of course not, that would be against the law.'

'Open your coat.'

I propped the bicycle saddle against my hip, fumbled with my buttons and held my coat wide open. The icy wind was bitter yet I could feel sweat gather in the notches of my spine. The Russian removed his gloves and his hands searched for hidden contraband under my armpits, between my breasts, tucked into my waistband. I stood still as stone. I am not brave. For good reason. During the three and a half years of the Soviet Union's occupation of the eastern sector of Berlin, I'd seen what happened to brave people. They were shot.

'I am carrying no forbidden contraband on my bicycle. No food. No lumps of coal. No candles,' I stated in a flat voice. 'I obey the law.'

I stepped back, keeping hold of my saddle, but the guard's hand followed me and gripped the handlebars.

'You call this piece of shit a bicycle?'

I minded that he called my Diamant bicycle shit. It grieved me to see the state of it now. But that was the point, the bald tyres and the rusting metalwork – to look like something that no one else would want. This checkpoint guard with the cavernous nostrils could smell something wrong though. Was it me? Was it the bicycle? Was it my fear?

His attention shifted to the leather saddlebag slung on the back of the bicycle. 'Open it,' he ordered.

I undid the buckle. Inside lay a bicycle spanner, a coiled spare chain and a puncture repair kit, because the city's ravaged roads shredded tyres. He prodded at the chain before raising the rear end of the bicycle a fraction off the ground, testing its weight. I held my breath. I knew if I ran now, he'd put a bullet in my back.

A thin wail of despair rose into the grimy air, startling us both. For a second I feared it had spilled out of my own mouth, but no, it came from the young woman standing a few metres away. She wore a bottle-green coat and peony-pink headscarf, and she was staring at a grey duck egg balanced on the palm of a second Soviet guard at the checkpoint.

'Please,' she begged. 'Please, don't take the egg from me. It's for my son.' Her voice was trembling. 'He's sick. He needs it … please …'

She held out her hand, her eyes pleading. Her face was thin but lovely, the way bone china is lovely, her features delicate, her skin taut and translucent. It was the kind of face people turned to look at, but here if you look too lovely, these men get greedy. Behind her a line of people had formed, people with stiff blank faces, trying to hide their eagerness to cross into the west if only for a few hours, patient figures well accustomed to queueing in the cold because in the Soviet sector we have to queue for everything.

A Russian military vehicle rumbled past, too close to a plodding horse and cart, and I saw the cart driver turn and swear silently, but otherwise the traffic across Pariser Platz was sparse except for the rattle of trams. Just ahead of us loomed Brandenburg Gate, a triumphal arch flanked by two gatehouses and crowned by a bronze Quadriga chariot driven by the goddess of victory. Ironically she was blown to bits in the war.

The other guard was older, his eyes kinder, but my bastard guard stalked over and jabbed his comrade's elbow so hard that the egg went spinning off his hand. It hit the ground with a smack and the shell shattered. The yolk slithered intact on to the cobbles, a bright splash of orange in this grey colourless world. Quick as a cat the young woman sank to her knees, scooped up the yolk between both hands and slipped it into her mouth. She jumped to her feet, her large blue eyes fixed warily on the soldiers.

We all knew she hadn't swallowed.

With a sour smile my guard swung out his arm and caught her hard across the throat. She recoiled, clutching her throat, a violent retching sound rising out of her because the blow had forced her to swallow. No one spoke as tears gathered in her eyes.

'Go now, *Fräulein*,' the older guard said.

She turned and ran with long angry strides that carried her across Pariser Platz, past the burnt-out Hotel Adlon, once the grandest hotel in all Berlin. The blackened remains were located in the heartland of the handsome government ministries and embassies, but like the Reichstag, it was a lesson about the fragility of life in the city. Nothing is safe. The young woman made her way out of the Soviet sector and into the British sector of Berlin, her green coat flapping behind her. The guards lost interest in me and waved my bicycle through with impatience to clear the line.

When you do something enough times you get hardened, don't you? Like layers of hard skin forming between the experience – whatever it may be – and the soft edges of yourself. So why didn't it happen to me? I'd waited and waited for it. Why didn't crossing the border from one half of the city to the other ever get easier, from the Russian eastern sector, where I lived, to the western sectors controlled by the Allies? Why did it feel as though I was walking on broken glass with bare feet? Why did I always look for a pair of dove-grey eyes that were never there?

I swung up on my saddle and cycled past the large sign that read *You Are Now Entering The British Sector*. I breathed. I was in West Berlin.

I caught up with the running figure in a side street, the peony-pink headscarf easy to spot. It was one of those streets where the tall elegant buildings on one side were still standing, admittedly with chunks knocked out of them, bullet holes scarring the walls, and most of the glass in the windows missing, but definitely still habitable. On the opposite side the landscape had been flattened to vermin-infested rubble, though someone must have been living among the ruins because a string of washing fluttered like a white flag between the outcrops of what had once been a staircase, its brass handrail long gone.

'Wait,' I shouted.

The peony headscarf stopped running. I braked alongside it, abandoned my bicycle and seized her narrow shoulders. It was like holding a skeleton, not a scrap of flesh on it, nothing but fragile bones. I gave her a shake.

'Kristina, what the hell do you think you were doing back there?' I demanded. 'You scared the life out of me.'

'You told me to distract the guards.'

'Yes, but I meant with your smile. With your charm. Not with a bloody egg in your pocket. You know it's against the law to carry food from the Soviet sector into the west of the city. You could have been arrested, you fool. You could have been shot.'

My fear for her tasted slick at the back of my throat. I drew her close and hugged her to me, then stepped back so that I could take a proper look at her.

'Is your throat okay?' I asked.

It didn't look okay. A dull claret bruise was already forming.

I heard Kristina sigh. 'You don't have to worry about me, you know,' she said.

'Yes, I do.'

She leaned forward, kissed my cheek and smiled. She was good at smiling. She used to practise in her mother's dressing-table mirror when we were young, trying different ones on her face for size. Kristina Fischer and I had gone through our school years together, arms linked, digging each other out of scrapes, watching each other's back. When I think about it, we were an odd pairing. I was the sporty type, living on my bicycle, swimming in the Wannsee or building secret hideouts in Tiergarten, my limbs the colour of honey. Whereas Kristina, well, ever since I could remember Kristina had yearned to be an actress. She'd dolled us both up in makeshift costumes at every chance, me hot and sweaty in my mother's mink coat, while she took the starring roles in the extravagant scarlet velvet opera cape she would sneak out of my mother's wardrobe.

But in 1939 the war came. We were sixteen. It sucked the oxygen out of our world. So instead of becoming an actress, Kristina went to work in a munitions factory and married a soldier who was a war camera-man. His name was Helmut and he was crushed to death by an American Sherman tank in the Battle of Aachen four years ago.

On the pavement with her now I waited while an old man hurried past, his head ducked against the grit that the wind snatched from the ruins and hurled in our faces. Grinding grit with our back molars had become a daily occupation for Berliners. I lowered my voice because

KATE FURNIVALL

even here in West Berlin walls listened, windows watched, doors opened a crack.

'How is Gerd?' I asked softly.

'Worse.'

'I'm sorry. Give him a kiss from me. And this too.'

I propped my bicycle against the wall and we both crowded round it, shielding the saddle from the view of any casual observer. Using the spanner from the saddlebag, I gave the screws under the seat a few twists, and the saddle came loose. I removed from inside it a roll of greaseproof paper and a small brown bottle of tablets, both of which I tucked into my friend's coat pocket.

'Thank you,' Kristina whispered.

'Aspirins,' I said. 'I wish there were more.'

'They'll help Gerd. They'll ease his pain.'

Gerd was her son, my godson, and I adored him. He had a broken wrist, poor kid. He was only six years old and though he was slight like his mother, he had a big heart beating in his skinny little chest, and golden curls that I couldn't keep my hands off. The two of them were living in a tiny one-bedroom apartment in the remnants of Müllerstrasse in West Berlin where you'd have to sell your grandmother to obtain even the simplest medication right now.

'Go home to Gerd,' I told her. 'Thanks for your help.'

Though Kristina lived in West Berlin, like many Berliners she worked as a maid most days at a smart hotel that had been taken over by the Soviets in East Berlin, which meant she had to pass through a checkpoint twice a day to get there and back. She was paid a pittance, but her luminous smile could earn her tips from the wealthy Soviet elite who now stayed in its luxurious rooms. They were pampered and petted, and savage as bears.

Instead of leaving, Kristina leaned against the wall and the dark circles under her eyes stood out against her flawless skin like grubby thumbprints.

'There are slices of *wurst* for you both rolled up in the greaseproof paper,' I told her.

A spark leapt into her blue eyes. 'Thank you,' she mouthed, though no sound emerged.

I stood her up straight, rubbed her arms to bring warmth back into them, rubbed them hard because I wanted to rub the sadness away. I took hold of my bicycle's handlebars again, but she wound her thin fingers around my wrist.

'Good luck,' she said.

'Thanks, I'll need it.'

Word had gone out that the Americans were hiring today for jobs out at Tempelhof airport.

'Don't forget there will be a load of people going for whatever jobs are on offer.' Kristina gave me a quick inspection and I saw her open her mouth to question my dowdy mouse-brown coat, but she shut it again and snatched the peony-pink scarf from her head. She tied it around my neck. 'That'll get you noticed,' she laughed, but then said uneasily, 'Be careful, Anna. Trust no one out there. We both know there are paid informers everywhere.'

'Oh, Kristina, you don't trust anybody.'

'I trust *you*,' she said and then she was gone. The green coat without the peony scarf was running away up the street.

Above my head the heavy aircraft engines continued to roar. The Russian blockade of West Berlin had turned the city into a prison.

CHAPTER THREE

◆ ◆ ◆

BERLIN, 1948

INGRID

A knife flew through the air. A brief blink of sunlight caught its blade as it slammed into the wood only a hair's breadth from Ingrid Keller's left cheek.

Go to hell, Fridolf. Too close. Far too close.

Another blade came at her.

A roaring started up in her ears like a mini whirlwind. She forced her face into a paper-thin smile but her stomach jammed in her throat. When you have an expertly honed metal tip tearing into the large circle of wood on which you're tied, you run out of smiles fast.

Another thud. Another. Missing her by no more than a sliver of spit. One slit her sleeve. The next nicked her buckskins. Her mind was now spinning so fast, her vision blurred and she no longer knew which way was up and which way was down as the knives flashed and streaked and raced towards her. *Scheisse!*

Fridolf. No.

One whirled flashily, haft over tip, and cut into the wood at a spot midway between her legs with such force that she felt the board vibrate.

Enough.

A drum roll. She held her breath. The final blade parted her hair.

Mein Gott!

It was that close.

The small crowd that had gathered to watch the performance in one of West Berlin's public squares whooped and clapped their appreciation. The ragged kids oohed and aahed wide-eyed and drew in their collective breath with gasps of amazement. That was always good. The more the audience gasped, the more they were happy to throw some money in the hat. The entertainment gave the onlookers a giddy pleasure because it wiped out, even for a few blessed minutes, the struggles of their day. It lifted the corner of the misery around them like the edge of a blanket and allowed them to forget. Allowed them to laugh. Ingrid was proud of that.

She knew that Fridolf was the best knife thrower in all of Germany, but her heart was still crawling around somewhere in her cowboy boots when he winked at her and brought the circus Wheel of Death to a halt. He loosened the rope loops that fastened her wrists and ankles to the gold-painted wheel that had been spinning her round and around while he hurled his knives at her. She slipped free. She stood on firm ground, swaying like a drunk, and took a bow with a showy flourish for the audience.

There *had* to be an easier way to earn a living.

They had set up that day – without a licence – in Breitscheidplatz, a huge public square right in the centre of West Berlin, one of the busiest stops on the U-Bahn. It sat at the southern tip of the Tiergarten park and the zoo, just off Kurfürstendamm, and was a great catch-all for shoppers crossing the square to queue with their ration books. The square had been decimated by bombing during the war, its life and soul pummelled to a stinking black dust until all that remained of its classy eighteenth-century buildings was the all-too-familiar heap of rat-ridden rubble piled high and the painful sight of the Kaiser Wilhelm Church at its centre. Except that now the church – an extravagantly Romanesque affair with five pointed spires – was no longer a church, it was a set of broken teeth.

Everyone loved a circus. It had always struck Ingrid as wonderful that people seemed to be born with a desire for its magic, and before the war Ingrid's father had owned one of the best circuses in the state of Brandenburg. Big top, aerialists, animals and clowns, yes, the whole star-spangled package – she'd been a highwire artiste herself – and she'd loved growing up among performers stinking of sawdust and greasepaint. Disbanded now. Gone. Ever since her father's death in one of Rommel's Panzer tanks in the African desert. But she still popped up in the city with snippets of what was left of the circus whenever she could get away with it. Berliners loved to watch the next best thing to a full-scale circus and that was a scary knife-throwing act.

The danger to Ingrid wasn't faked. Her heart rate was proof of that. But – for now – it was over. She breathed again and took another bow as the sky righted itself and settled back into its God-given place above her.

'One of these damn days you'll take my eye out, Fridolf,' she growled at him as they acknowledged the applause.

'One of these damn days you'll learn that I never miss my mark.' He grinned at her.

'To hell with you,' she grinned back. 'Those knives had my name on them today. I could hear them whispering to me.'

Fridolf chuckled. His thick tangle of black hair was worn tied back from his lined face, dark suspicious eyes as sharp as his blades. He was probably not far off fifty, small and wiry, and she couldn't remember a time in her life when Fridolf hadn't been around, utterly devoted to her father as well as to the circus animals. At the end of each day he'd never rolled himself up in his blanket without first rubbing heads with each of the big cats, and he'd wept like a newborn baby when there was no money left to feed them.

For the knife act, he and Ingrid always dressed in cowboy outfits for no good reason other than that audiences seemed to love to see her in tight, fringed buckskins. It got them excited. So now she grabbed her upturned Stetson and darted in and out of the crowd, collecting the few pfennigs they could spare. Novembers in Berlin were like the tremors that come with a dose of winter flu, they seeped into your bones, but Berliners were hardened. Standing around for hours on freezing cobbles outside sparsely stocked shops, clutching their ration books, was a daily pastime if you wanted to eat. Berlin could be cruel.

'You got something for me, soldier?' she urged.

. With her Stetson begging bowl in her outstretched hand, Ingrid made a beeline for a figure in US military uniform. The Americans were best. More generous than the Brits because they were paid more. This one was blond as the corn of Kansas and had wide farm-boy hands and a smile to match.

'That's one hell of an act you got going there, *Fräulein*,' he said and dropped one of the brand-new blue Deutschmark notes into her hat.

She'd been hoping for a dollar. It had more kick. All the scumbags who were selling black-market stuff would give the best deals for the all-powerful US dollar. But he backed it up with half a pack of Camel cigarettes, the universal unit of currency in Berlin, so she flipped him a smile. Just then a man's voice shouted out from the crowd to Fridolf.

'*Zigeuner!* Fucking gypsy! I thought that Hitler had got rid of all you filthy vermin for us.'

He was referring to the death camps.

Fridolf was still entertaining the straggling crowd by juggling five of his knives with an easy, focused rhythm, and despite the shout that must have sent chills down his spine, he didn't miss a beat. But Ingrid was hit by a burst of fury that raced to her cheeks and she moved fast. She snatched one of Fridolf's knives out of the air and launched herself into the crowd. They scattered, leaving the man with the loud mouth exposed. He turned at the sight of her coming at him and was striding away across the square in alarm when she ran up behind him and slid the tip of her blade into the soft hollow just under his earlobe. He froze.

'Halt, *mein Herr*, you've hurt my friend's feelings, do you realise that?' She spoke softly.

Ingrid was small and looked inoffensive, it would be easy to overlook her, whereas the man was big and brash with a pricey overcoat and hefty shoulder pads and he had that arrogant look of an ex-Nazi about him. It seemed no contest.

'*Verpiss dich!*' he spat. 'Piss off.'

She leaned on the knife and a trickle of blood spiked its way down into the collar of his nice smart coat. 'My friend is so upset,' she said, 'he'll need a bottle of schnapps to help him sleep tonight.'

The man hesitated. She could sense that he was the kind of person who had survived the widespread manhunts for Nazis that had gripped Germany after the war by knowing exactly when to back down. He pulled his wallet from his pocket and pushed a fifty-mark note at her. She took two and lowered the knife, but she saw the American soldier approaching at speed from her left.

'Move on,' he ordered the onlookers with military authority, breaking up her audience. He didn't mention the man with the shoulder pads, nor the knife half hidden in her hand. 'You got a licence for this here thing?' he gestured at the wheel.

'Yes,' she lied.

'You'd better shift it before the police turn up,' he told her. Then he lit a cigarette, glanced upwards to make sure that his country's transport planes were still streaming down through the clouds with their cargo and sauntered off to find a bar.

Ingrid tucked the two fifties into Fridolf's cowboy-shirt pocket and stared up at the planes for a long moment. From down here they looked like toys. Thrilling toys. The sound of their engines never ceased, steady and strong, a giant heartbeat in the sky.

She walked over to help dismantle the wooden Wheel of Death. There *had* to be an easier way to earn a living.

CHAPTER FOUR

◆ ◆ ◆

ANNA

Berlin was a city like no other. And though it lay in ruins now, I still loved it. I loved it as much as I loved to cycle. In summer its avenues – the broad carriageways of Unter den Linden and the magnificent Kurfürstendamm – smelled extravagantly of linden blossom, and every autumn, as a cherry-nosed child, I would tramp through its crisp mountains of leaves, kicking them up into a golden rainbow in the icy air.

That was back in the crazy years between the wars, when Berlin was the finest, the grandest, the leafiest and the bawdiest metropolis in all Europe. Maybe not as showy as Paris, nor as gracious as Vienna, but it vibrated with an energy that was intoxicating. It was irresistible. This was during the Weimar Republic, before Hitler's vile jackboots stomped into the Reichstag in 1933 and the war reached out in 1939 to rip Berlin's heart out. Before that, the city shimmered and shone and shocked in equal measure.

In those days people flocked here from all over the world to taste its delights and revel in its outrageously modern culture – Bauhaus designs, Fritz Lang's films, the sharp social satire of Brecht's plays and Kurt Weill's music. These all flourished alongside the hottest of hot jazz. My mother used to adore being a part of the extravagance of Berlin life, her lips a sweep of bright carmine red as she and Papa headed off to dance till dawn in glamorous venues. Their favourite was the Esplanade Hotel on Potsdamer Platz, where furs and diamonds came to be flaunted.

'If I'm lucky,' Mutti would whisper as she tucked me up in bed, 'I shall rub shoulders with Chaplin or Garbo tonight.'

'Be good, *schatzi*, sleep well,' Papa always said as he dropped a goodnight kiss on my dark curls, his gaze already bewitched by my mother in her latest Vionnet evening gown of ivory silk. Her limbs would trail their lingering fragrance of jasmine over the covers of my bed to keep me company at night. Mutti was happy in those carefree days. How things have changed.

But it wasn't just the smart places that pulsed with the spirit of the city in those days. The street cafés were brimming with it and it spilled out of the night-time haunts for which the city became infamous. Mutti used to tell me thrilling tales about the wild nightclubs. Ones like the Eldorado on Lutherstrasse that did a roaring trade in the Schöneberg area of Berlin. They oozed – yes, oozed – decadence.

Decadence. Just the smell of it. The taste of it. The pills bought and sold in unlit alleyways. At night this city of mine put on a darker mask. In underground caverns the lure of naked breasts on dance floors and men wearing vivid lipstick was addictive. Writers and poets and artists came to soak up the heady atmosphere in their quest for … for what? Inspiration, they called it. But it seems to me now that it was more like people came to stretch their human experience to the limit, to reach out and find release in being someone else. They'd lived through the horrors of the Great War and needed to escape those ghosts. To stand on the very edge of a cliff and laugh into the wind. Berlin was that cliff edge.

And now, here we were again. It was December 1948 and we were standing on a new cliff edge, gazing down into a new abyss. One that would mean the annihilation of all that it meant to be German. We were on the brink of being absorbed by communist Russia, the way Poland and Hungary had gone.

As I cycled, I looked around at the shattered remains of what had once been the handsome Königstrasse, with stylish shops and a magnificent domed station, and I had to remind myself that it was peacetime. Peacetime, for Christ's sake. The war was over. Yet it didn't look like peacetime. It didn't feel like peacetime. The streets were bristling with Russian soldiers brandishing their rifles and their hatred of Germans.

And I was aware that Berlin lay completely surrounded by thousands upon thousands of Red Army troops with their military tanks, holding us in their Russian bear-grip, ready to squeeze harder. Threatening us. Suffocating us. Starving us.

Yes, Berlin was in ruins, bombed almost out of existence and turned into an ugly savage wasteland, but it was still my city. My beloved city.

Jobs in Berlin were hard to come by. Too many offices, shops and factories had been obliterated, and those that managed to survive were being looted by the Russians as we looked on, helpless. So where in this godforsaken city were people supposed to find work?

On the coat-tails of the victorious Allies – the Americans, the British and the French – that's where.

After leaving Kristina, I cycled deeper into the American sector and breathed in great lungfuls of free western air. It tasted different every time and made me giddy with relief, even though I'd have to be back in the east tonight. I turned on to Königgrätzer Strasse in Kreuzberg district, a densely populated area of the city where on one day in February over a thousand wartime Allied bombers, accompanied by a barrage of Russian artillery, had been particularly efficient at reducing it to rubble. Here I came to a halt outside a large building that had managed to remain standing, its red-brick façade bristling with American military uniforms, and the Stars and Stripes flag snapping back and forth above its pillared entrance as though shouting out orders.

On each side of its scarred oak doors stood two guards in United States Army uniform, so round-cheeked and apple fresh in their warm winter greatcoats that I felt an urge to take a bite out of them. But my heart sank at the sight of the line of Berliners already there, stamping their boots to force blood back into their feet. The queue snaked right around the block inside which the job interviews were being held. We'd all hurtled over here, desperate to be the ones lucky enough to find work at the American airbase, and were now eyeing each other sideways, unobtrusively, assessing each other's chances.

I took my place in line behind three broad-backed men in navy overalls and waited. And waited.

The queue shuffled forward every now and again, sending a frisson of hope rippling through us, which was just as quickly snatched away when the line jerked to a halt once more. Word had spread fast that the Yanks were hiring. People kept coming, faces gaunt and garments frayed. But they were cheerful at the prospect of work, even if it meant labouring alongside the troops whose rifles they'd been on the wrong end of only a little over three years ago. We swallowed our pride, hid our shame and queued.

The work of unloading the cargo planes at the US airbase was said to be backbreaking, which was why the line consisted mainly of men, all shapes and sizes. The three in front of me were burly figures. Fists like shovels and thick bull necks with what looked like burn scars on them.

'We were sheet-metal workers in the Alkett factory out at Berlin-Borsigwalde on Breitenbackstrasse,' the tall bald one called Stefan informed me. 'Bombed to hell during the war. Well, we'd been building tanks for the Wehrmacht, so I can't say I blame them. We survived, but only just.'

These three were exactly what the Americans wanted today. Heavy lifters. Not young women wearing pink scarves.

'What about you?' asked the bald one's friend, the one with a shaggy moustache. 'What do you do?'

'I repair bicycles. I've owned my own workshop for years, but now ...' I shrugged.

Stefan roared with laughter and slapped me on the back so hard I nearly coughed up my lungs. 'Not much call for bicycle skills on an airbase.'

'I can shift heavy loads as well,' I insisted. 'I'm stronger than I look. Like a donkey. But no one has money for bicycle repairs any more,' I admitted.

Stefan nodded his big friendly head. 'Yes, I can see you're far too skinny, mädchen. You need to earn yourself some of the new Deutschmarks so you can eat.'

And search, I thought. So I can search. Searching costs money too. But I didn't say that.

Two hours later. Feet blocks of ice. My three metalworker and I were only a couple of metres from the entrance to the building, so we could, as my newly acquired friends put it, now see the whites of their eyes.

The queue had fallen silent, our faces pinched by the east wind off the River Spree, our tongues curbed by a listless hunger that sapped energy, but the tedium was spiced up a bit when a jeep roared up in front of the building with a screech of wheels. We watched, interested. An officer, in the distinctive seal-brown leather flight jacket of the United States Air Force and an officer's peaked cap pushed back at an angle, leapt out of the jeep and strode towards the entrance.

His black brows were drawn together in a frown and his footsteps were hurried, but Americans always seemed to be in a rush to get things done. He was in his early thirties, but with a tight jaw that was accustomed to command and a broad athletic frame, most likely developed by a lifetime of roping hogs or wrestling steers to the dirt with one hand, or whatever it was that all those steak-fed Americans got up to for fun. The two guards at the door saluted him smartly as he stepped up to the entrance.

'That man,' I muttered, 'is going to cause trouble.'

Stefan laughed. '*Scheisse*, I hope he does. At this rate it'll take days to process all these job hunters.'

I felt a sudden prickle of dread. It seemed to reach out like a thread of smoke, not from the officer but from the red-brick building itself, and wrap itself around me. I froze. Unnerved. I looked quickly around. No danger in sight. Nothing that shouldn't be there. Gaunt faces of Berliners, collars turned up against the wind, the American guards relaxed and smiling at a dog being made to dance on its hind legs in the hope of earning a few pfennigs from those in the queue. I am not someone prone to irrational fears. I'm not that kind of jittery person. But a thud-thud started up in my brain and I seized hold of Stefan's coat sleeve.

'Come,' I said.

'Where?'

The big man half closed his eyes into slits and studied me for a second, but when I started to race away from the queue, head ducked low, he let me drag him with me. His two companions, surprised, ran at his heels.

An explosion ripped the air apart, hurling us off our feet as it roared and raged out of the building. The blast came from behind and hit like a hammer blow as we ran, slamming the air out of my lungs. Punching me forward so that for a handful of heartbeats I was flying. My ears screeched. How can ears screech? Yet I swear they did and I landed in a jangled heap on the road while missiles of brick and timber shot through the air all around me. Pounding down on bones. Striking through flesh.

A drainpipe smacked into the tarmac with the force of a javelin. It landed right next to me, but left me untouched. Brick dust rained down on me. Plaster fragments turned my brown sleeves white, but I lay there unhurt. When I pushed myself up and looked back at where the red-brick building had stood a moment ago, there was nothing. Just a mass of rubble and blood.

In this city, violence was a language. It sent a message. The communists of East Berlin didn't want us working for the Americans in West Berlin and this was a warning.

How can people do this to each other? I can't understand. Their desire to kill was insatiable, even just after a war in which more than 50 million people had been slaughtered. When will enough be enough? But who am I to throw stones? Even one killing is ... inhuman.

I coughed out cement muck and looked for Stefan. I know I coughed because I felt my body shake and my lungs spasm, yet I heard no sound. Still my ears were shrieking fit to burst my head wide open. The air was thick with masonry grit and when I peered through the fog of it I saw that everywhere people were screaming. Mouths gaping. Lips moving. Frantic. But I heard none of it.

'Stefan,' I shouted and struggled to my feet.

He was lying behind me on his front, unmoving, blood streaming from a jagged gash on his bald head.

'Don't die on me,' I shouted — I think I shouted — and I knelt beside this man I scarcely knew but suddenly could not bear to lose. I turned his head sideways to free his airways, his nose was bleeding and I dug dirt from his mouth.

'Stefan!' I shouted again.

He shuddered, an earthquake tearing through his body, then dragged in breath. He opened one eye.

'I ain't ready for no angel wings yet,' he groaned, shook himself and let me help him sit up. 'Where are Walther and Jörg?' His words sounded blurred and slippery to my ears.

Just then Walther emerged through the thick cloud of dust like a grey ghost, face twisted with anger, followed by a limping Jörg, both bruised and battered but alive.

'Fucking communists!' Walther swore through his dirt-caked moustache and spat a tooth on to the ground.

I snatched Kristina's pink scarf from around my neck and pressed it hard against Stefan's scalp wound to stem the flow of blood, but already the military were taking control. Behind us lay a war zone of dead and injured, a heartbreaking sight, but from nowhere uniforms of all colours descended on us. Olive and khaki, dark blue and deep grey. Uniforms were what held Berlin together these days. They were the city's glue. Men with tired eyes in doctors' coats and women in nurses' whites with a gentle touch. They all came to clean up the human wreckage, these angels of mercy. I was dimly aware of being herded away and prodded for damage and of earnest faces leaning close to mine. Questioning me. Forcing my ears back into action.

'Why did you run?' they asked, again and again. 'What made you run from the queue?'

'A sudden sense of danger.'

'How did you know something was going to happen?'

'I didn't. It was just a feeling, that's all. I felt unsafe.'

'Had you heard any rumours about a communist attack today?'

I shook my head. They seemed to believe me because they moved on to the next person and the next, while I sat on the ground with others and listened to the thud-thud that continued in my brain like a drum. Trying to tell me something.

What had I seen that I didn't know I'd seen?

They stuck those of us who could walk unaided in a nearby yard. It took three minutes at most to walk there, trudging past what used to be the administrative offices of the Ministry of the Interior, while Stefan and his companions stayed tight at my side like guard dogs as if they thought I might still be in danger. Only three brief minutes. Yet in those three minutes I lost touch with the reality of where I was. Of who I was.

The wind had picked up, slapping at us in gusts, and as we moved along the pavement I averted my eyes from the ambulances racing away on their errands of mercy. But my heart tripped over itself at the sight of two young girls who squeezed past us and streaked up Königgrätzer Strasse. They raced past the blackened skeleton of the extravagant Excelsior Hotel, once the largest hotel in Europe with its enormous Greek portico. The girls were no more than ten years old, all legs and hair. They looked like twins, an identical flash of delicate features and golden locks streaming out behind them like a burst of sunlight amid the grime of the ruins. I couldn't stop staring. It wasn't just their young laughter that snared me, a sound so honest and free in a city that had forgotten what honesty and freedom meant. I couldn't look away because I'd seen what each girl held in her hand – a fat jar of pickled gherkins.

Gherkins. Instantly I was skidding back down a tunnel – a tunnel that was three and a half years long – to another hand, another jar of gherkins. I was standing inside a vast warehouse.

'Here,' the owner of the hand had said. 'Take it.'

I'd accepted the jar proffered to me.

'Thank you, Timur.'

I'd looked up into a pair of deep-set, dove-grey eyes and smiled my thanks. By then I'd become adept at blocking out the hated sludge-brown Red Army uniform that came with them, embellished by an officer's insignia and cap.

It was at a time of sickness. It was 1945. The war had just ended and there were so many people sick and starving in occupied Berlin that even waking up each morning felt like a miracle. My mother was sick. This man – this booted Russian bear – had helped us. He'd picked my mother's broken body up off the ground in a filthy alleyway where she lay injured, carried her to our cold cramped apartment and laid her on her bed. I didn't know why he'd chosen to help us – this enemy of Germany – and I didn't ask, but I thanked him softly with every breath while my mother cursed him over and over, long and loud, for being one of the bastard Russian invaders.

He brought morphine. He brought penicillin. He brought wood for our stove. He brought a doctor who set her broken leg. But still she cursed Major Timur Voronin. And despite the fact that she continued to voice her hatred of all things Russian, he was relentlessly kind to us and something from deep inside this man seemed to detach from him and attach itself to me. I could feel it pulsing inside me and I fell in love with him as easily and as unintentionally as falling off a cliff.

The day of the gherkin jar he had entered our pokey apartment with his usual courteous smile, his officer's cap tucked under his arm, his hand extended. An orange sat on his palm. It was as bright and vibrant as one of my mother's jewels, so that I laughed just to look at it. It sent a swirl of joy spinning through me. Oranges were up there with miracles in those barren days.

'For you,' he said, widening his smile.

'Thank you. It smells wonderful.'

Our skin touched, his and mine, my fingers surprised at the tendrils of warmth that curled from his. I had a fierce urge to grasp his hand instead of the orange and hold it tight. My hands were hungry for him, but I stepped back.

He stood awkwardly on the parquet floor and I could see he was uncertain whether to stay or go, having delivered his gift. Timur was a tall man, in his thirties with dark cropped hair and straight honest eyes, and he possessed an air of quiet certainty. I used to watch the shifting planes and angles of his face, as though I might find a crack in them somewhere that would let me in, and I knew that if I were a soldier facing enemy fire, I'd want this Russian officer, this Major Timur Voronin in command of my platoon. I cradled the orange in my hands and inhaled its fragrance, willing him to stay.

'How is your mother today?' he asked.

'Not good.'

'Still unable to leave her room?'

'She's too weak, she has no strength.'

He flipped his cap back on his head with a sudden burst of energy and took hold of my wrist. 'Come,' he said, 'I know what she needs. Come with me.'

Now I look back and I wonder at the way I went with Timur. At the way I trusted him so readily and believed in his kindness and in his decency. Which shows what a stupid fool I was back then. He hurried me out of the apartment and we ran down the four flights of stairs together, but the moment we stepped outside on to the pavement, he released his hold on me. We both knew that Berlin women who fraternised with Russians were spat on in the street. Or worse.

'*Hure!*' people yelled at any German woman who hung on a Red Army sleeve. 'Whore!'

He led me deep into Lichtenberg district up near the Tierpark, skirting the dreaded main office of the Soviet Military Administration in Berlin, and we came to a stop outside a factory with an arched entrance, wide enough for carts to pass through. Carved into the stone above the arch was the word *Klavierfabrik*.

'A piano factory?' I queried. 'We don't need a piano. It would never squeeze into our apartment and anyway —' I smiled at him — 'we can't eat a piano.'

He laughed. Such a nice laugh, a laugh that made my palms tingle. 'Come,' he said and hammered the imposing brass knocker. We entered a wide tiled hallway where Timur had to sign his name into an admissions book and only then were the big double doors thrown open to the interior space.

I gasped. I felt my jaw drop open like a child's.

A magical wonderland was spread out before me. Shelf after shelf sprawled from one end of the huge factory building to the other and every single shelf was crammed with food. Not a piano in sight. This had to be one of the select shops in East Berlin open only to the military elite and to the privileged politicians. I'd heard of these places, I'd even dreamed of them, my empty stomach growling through the night, but I'd never seen one before and it was utterly glorious. Quivering with lust, I stared at colourful pictures on cans of peaches and jars of scarlet berries – *Himbeeren* and *Erdbeeren* – and at images of grazing cows and happy-looking pigs on big square tins of preserved meat.

'*Verdammt!*' I exclaimed. 'This place would feed five thousand of Berlin's children for months.'

But Timur was already leading me towards a shelf in the far corner where he took down a jar of Kühne pickled gherkins. He placed it in my hand and a jar of pickled sauerkraut in my other.

'These will help your mother,' he said cheerfully. 'They are packed full of potassium and provide necessary traces of iron and vitamins. They'll give her a boost of energy.'

'How on earth do you know these things?'

'My father was a doctor.'

'A doctor?'

I wanted to pin him to the spot there and then, to learn more about his family, but off he strode, gathering tins and jars which he loaded into his long arms. I caught up with him.

'Why are you doing this?' I asked.

He smiled, tucked a packet of biscuits under my arm and kissed my mouth.

Even now as I watched the two girls running off down the street with their gherkins, I could remember the feel of those cold glass jars against my palms and the intense warmth of his lips on mine. I had an odd sense that the weight of the jars was the weight of his heart in my hands. I stood in the middle of the pavement staring after the girls until they were out of sight, every last golden scrap of them, because I couldn't bear to let the moment go.

Once in the yard I wanted to shout out to the crowd of battered and angry Berliners slumped alongside me that despite the unforgiving winds of hatred that scoured this city, not all communists wished us evil. Timur was proof of that. Yet even my Timur had gone, had abandoned me, and instead I kept seeing a man's hand in the yard where the explosion took place, a labourer's hand resting on a section of splintered door on the ground outside the ruins of the brick building, a hand wearing a good strong wedding band, a hand unattached to a body.

That was when the American pilot, the captain who had roared up in his jeep earlier, marched into my life. I was astonished he wasn't dead.

'Those of you who still want a job out at Tempelhof airbase remain here,' he announced. 'The rest of you can leave.'

No one moved a muscle. The captain was coated in dirt and filth like the rest of us, but I could spot no sign of injury on him except for a long tear in the shoulder of his leather flying jacket that revealed its creamy sheepskin lining. It hung off him like a dead animal. He must have had the luck of the devil.

He shuffled us into a line of sorts.

'You,' he said to a burly man with a jaw to match his own. 'Two paces forward.'

The man stepped forward eagerly. 'Yessir.'

'Wait here.'

The officer moved on, picking out men who were well-muscled, avoiding the elderly and injured and most of the women. My heart sank further. I watched him select only two women, both with the weathered skin of farmers' wives and broad capable hands. He came to a halt in front of my three companions, glancing at the professional medical dressing on Stefan's head.

'Is it bad?' the American asked.

'No, sir. Barely a scratch.'

'Two paces forward,' he ordered. 'You three look like strong workers.'

'Yessir.' Stefan grinned, revealing a set of teeth that were fine and straight, though yellowed by years of tobacco.

I took a deep breath and stepped forward with them. 'I am a strong worker too, sir.'

'Get back in line, *Fräulein*.' He was already moving on.

Stefan draped a heavy arm across my shoulders. 'I know she looks like a scrawny sparrow,' he said, 'but she has the muscles of a horse.' He squeezed my shoulder to demonstrate and my arm instantly went numb. 'She worked alongside us on Tiger tanks in Takt 2.'

The American regarded me with blatant scepticism. 'Is that so, *Fräulein*? What exactly did you do in the tank building process?' he asked in flawless German.

A flutter of panic. But tanks were machines, like bicycles were machines.

'I used to drill the holes for the drive sprockets.'

He considered calling my bluff, but instead asked, 'What is your name?'

'Anna Wolff.'

'You German women built tanks?'

'Of course. Our men were at the Front.' I shrugged. 'Unless they were employed in essential labour like my three friends here. I am a strong worker.' I stared directly into his seal-dark eyes. 'And tenacious.'

But the American was a man in a hurry. He was on the verge of dismissing me again, when his eyes lingered on Kristina's pink scarf, at my neck again despite Stefan's blood. I saw him hesitate. Something softened a fraction. Was it a memory of a comrade's blood? Or of his mother's scarf? Or a girl back home? He gave an abrupt nod and moved away down the line.

I was in.

'Listen up, Berliners. The hours are long, the work is tough. You might as well get that straight now, right?'

We nodded.

'I expect hard work from you.'

We nodded.

'It will be a night shift.'

We nodded.

'Good, then we should rub along okay. I'm Captain Noah Maynard of the 61st Troop Carrier Group of the United States Air Force and I'm in need of extra manpower over at Tempelhof airbase.' His impatient eyes flashed across to me at the edge of the group. 'And woman-power too, it seems. I need you all to start tomorrow. The paperwork can be filled out at the airbase. I need workers immediately, so I can't hang around while this atrocity –' he gave a grim nod in the direction of where the building had stood – 'is cleared up.'

Those of us selected had been herded like cows up one end of the courtyard, all thirty-five of us. The American captain was standing with hands on hips in the middle of the yard where the cobbles still held their skim of ice. He was inspecting us the way I inspect bicycles, hunting out the weak spots, noting the strong links, the reliable sections. Was I a weak spot in his eyes?

'Tomorrow at sixteen hundred hours – that's four o'clock to you – two trucks will collect you all from this yard,' he announced. 'Be here.' He straightened his cap, clearly proud of the winged badge on it, and I wondered where he'd learned to speak our language so expertly. 'The trucks will transport you to Tempelhof where you will work a twelve-hour shift unloading cargo from incoming aircraft. All night. It's hard work, I'm not sugar-coating it, but after six hours you will receive a half-hour break and that is when you can register your names and addresses at the personnel office.'

'Sir,' a bearded man in a patched overcoat called out, 'how much do we get paid?'

A murmur trickled through the group. We all wanted to know.

'To be honest, I have no idea. The personnel officer at the airfield will sort that out.'

We moaned, but under our breath.

'Make sure you're here tomorrow at four o'clock. Oh yes,' he added, 'I almost forgot. In your break you each get given a hot meal in the canteen.'

A *hot meal*.

And he almost forgot.

CHAPTER FIVE

◆ ◆ ◆

INGRID

Lions smell wonderful. Pungent and exotic. Unlike anything else on earth. Ingrid loved the stink of big cats even more than the sweet musty smell of horses, though it was a close-run thing. She had breathed in both scents since the day she was born and learned to ride on the animals' backs long before she could walk, clutching their manes between her small fingers and crowing with young laughter that set off their contented huffing and whinnying. Lions and horses. Horses and lions. They had been her first playmates, the ones she whispered her first secrets to, and their straw or sawdust had cushioned her falls.

Now there was only one fine Arab stallion left and Ingrid was at work in his stable. Named Vulcan for his fiery temper, fifteen hands high and officially termed a grey though his coat was as white as Ingrid's thighs. She was rubbing him down vigorously while Fridolf Grossheim cleaned out the four miniature ponies. Bright as monkeys and twice as naughty, but real stars at performing tricks in the ring. Audiences loved them. There used to be six of the wicked little things, as well as three more beautiful Arab horses, but those days were long gone.

The scraps that remained of Ingrid's father's circus had found refuge out on the fringe of Grunewald, the forest beloved by Berliners. It lay at the far western end of Kurfürstendamm in West Berlin. Only a hop and a jump from the expanse of barbed wire that announced the border with East Germany. The forest stretched along the east side of the Havel river in the district of Wilmersdorf, still inside West Berlin but in the British sector. The war had hit this quiet area hard. Air raids destroyed nearly half of all homes, and it was here among the ruins and within easy reach of the Grunewald's murmuring branches that Ingrid had chosen a spot in which to tuck away the last remnants of her father's beloved Circus Axmann.

It was a *Wanderzirkus*, a travelling circus. Shut down now, of course. When the war killed her father, the magnificent Max Axmann who, in her eyes, was the greatest circus strongman and lion tamer who ever drew breath, Ingrid had hunkered down in a group of deserted barns beside the river. They did their best. Gave performances when they could, but gradually and inexorably the money ran out. Berliners' pockets were empty. Audiences grew sparse. Her father's faithful crew had stayed as long as they could, but one by one they – and most of the animals – were forced to leave or starve. She couldn't blame them. But she nursed grand dreams of one day setting up the circus again with a great fanfare that would wake Berlin up and make its inhabitants take note.

As Ingrid wandered from barn to barn she breathed the smell of each one deep down into her lungs, the intoxicating stink of the circus animals. Powerful, insistent and fierce in its vitality. It was alive, it punched you in the face, it forced you to choose life instead of the stench of death that stalked so much of this wretched city.

Ingrid scooped an apple, wrinkled and fragrant, from a basket of them on a shelf and unbolted one of the larger barn doors.

'Hey there, Valentin,' she called as she stepped inside.

She held out the apple in the dim interior and out of a gigantic pile of straw lumbered a huge brown bear, its dense coat tipped with a rich golden russet that looked as though sunlight was trapped within its fur. It greeted her with a barrage of friendly grunts and low barks that delighted her and reared up on its hind legs, all nine feet of solid muscle, all forty-two teeth aimed in her direction. She laughed as it heaved its massive paws around her shoulders, towering over her and pulling her into its chest so that she inhaled its thick musky odour close up and heard the slow lazy thump of its heart. It was winter and the animal liked to sleep most of the day. She'd loved Valentin for as long as she could remember and she offered up the apple now with a hug.

'Ingrid?' It was Fridolf's voice. 'You there?'

He stepped into the barn and the wind whipped dead leaves inside along with him in a frenzy of activity.

'How's Otto?' Fridolf said.

Something in the way he asked the question sent fingers of alarm skittering up her spine. Otto Keller was her husband.

'The same as usual,' she said. 'Always busy, always hustling.' She dug a fist deep into the bear's dense fur. 'Why do you ask?'

They were both being casual, too casual.

Otto was addicted to risk. He used to be a flier in the circus, a breathtaking trapeze artist who leapt into space and held himself there by sheer force of will. Now that he was grounded he went looking for his thrills elsewhere.

'I heard a rumour,' Fridolf muttered.

He leaned against the oak planks of the door that looked as if they'd been stolen off a ship centuries ago. He took his time about rolling himself a skinny cigarette and lit it despite her rule about not smoking inside the barns because of the straw. It smelled foul, God only knew what was in it, certainly not tobacco.

'A rumour? About Otto?'

'Maybe.' He shrugged.

Rumours constantly dripped through Berlin like rainwater dripped through the barn's cracked shingles.

'What kind of rumour?' Ingrid asked, rubbing her cheek against the bear's luxuriously soft chest fur. She wanted to bury herself in it.

'Someone's been filching from the medical supplies that America is flying into Tempelhof.'

'Everyone out there is stealing, we all know that, Fridolf. Especially at night.'

'Not now. They've tightened security on the gates.'

'What on earth makes you think that Otto is involved? He doesn't work out there any more.'

He gave her a look, screwing up the creases on his face. 'He was sacked for thieving, remember?'

She remembered. Her husband was lucky. They didn't turn him over to the police.

'What kind of medical supplies are going missing?'

'Penicillin.'

She blinked. 'That's serious.'

Everyone knew there was a severe shortage of the drug.

'Otto's name is being mentioned.'

Her stomach lurched, the way it used to when Otto would pretend to almost drop her mid-air or catch her with just one hand, thirty feet up with no net, just to make the audience gasp. She knew the danger.

'Why Otto's name?'

Fridolf chuckled and breathed out his foul-smelling fumes. 'Because who else could scale a sheer three-storey wall to reach the window of the storeroom where it was kept?'

His chuckle came again, laced with respect.

Ingrid didn't chuckle. She pushed the bear down and it waddled back to its straw nest with a rumble in its chest that sounded like an echo of the distant aircraft in the sky. She noticed its hide looked as if it belonged on a larger bear.

'Otto wouldn't do anything so stupid,' she snapped.

'Wouldn't he?' His dark gypsy eyes fixed on her. 'He loves these animals. This morning he rolled up here in a van packed with horse feed, enough to see us through to the new year.'

'*Scheisse!*'

She'd kill him.

It was late afternoon and the sun had crept out from nowhere to spill along the horizon like a river of blood on which floated pillows of grey clouds. The air was raw and Ingrid Keller had her head down, key in hand, hurrying up the front step of her apartment block on Leibnizstrasse in the British sector when she found a man. It was not uncommon. In the ruins of Berlin she often saw people washed up on the street with nowhere to live. They skulked among the bombed buildings, their clothes and their skin rapidly taking on the same grey hue as the concrete dust of their hidden dens.

This man was tucked tight against the wall. He was huddled on the ground on the wide step in the shadow of her building, seeking shelter from the knife edge of the wind. His face was buried in his knees, arms locked around his shins, his limbs so thin his trousers flapped around his legs. He was not young, but neither was he old. She caught a glimpse of brown stubble and a few wisps of brown hair under a felt hat. But she didn't stop, she didn't disturb him. She let him sleep.

Yet as she put her key into the lock, something struck her as not right. She lifted her face from the folds of her scarf, releasing white coils of breath into the air, and turned to look back at the man. Ice was glinting on the brim of his hat but no surprise in that. No, it was something else that stopped her walking on. She stared down at the hunched figure and consciously took note of the way the ice gleamed in the early evening shadows, a rainbow of it, not just on the brim of his hat but also like specks of glass along the ridge of his cheek and down the side of his neck. Ice crystals do not belong on a man's skin. Not if he is alive.

The street was run-down and empty, except for a scrawny kid watching from further down, but you couldn't go anywhere these days without being spied on by feral children. Orphaned by the war, they ran in thieving wolf packs and stole anything that wasn't nailed down.

She touched the man. He was cold.

Her touch, though light, altered the delicate balance of his position and his head flopped sideways, toppling him off the step and on to the pavement in front of her. Ingrid gasped and knelt quickly. His body lay sprawled on its side, his veined eyelids frozen shut by crystals of ice, but the odd thing was that his cheeks were not sunken, they were puffed out wide.

She shuddered because she'd noticed the thing trailing out of his mouth. Between his bloodless lips lay the end of a piece of string. Ingrid took hold and pulled it to clear his airways, though it was too late, she knew that, of course she did. But still she pulled again, a quick sharp tug and the snake of string emerged, wet, draped with threads of mucus and curiously obscene. Longer than she expected. When it suddenly caught on his teeth she jerked harder and it flew out of his lifeless mouth.

It smacked against her own lower lip as she bent over him and for a moment she thought he had spat at her. But no. Dead men don't spit. She studied the coiled string in her hand with abhorrence. From the end of it hung a small pearl brooch shaped like a cross.

CHAPTER SIX

◆ ◆ ◆

ANNA

T he Blockade. You cannot comprehend the character of Berlin in 1948 if you do not understand the blockade. It changed our lives.

When the war ended in 1945, the British and American leaders sat with their big fat cigars and brandy glasses in hand and capitulated to Joseph Stalin, Marshal of the Soviet Union. First it was Churchill and Roosevelt at the Yalta Conference, and then Churchill and Truman at the Cecilienhof Palace in Potsdam. The whole of Germany was occupied by the Allies following the Berlin Declaration on 5 June 1945 and they cut up our country between them. Snip, snip, snip. The three leaders jostling and scheming and dealing. I give you this, you give me that. You take Pankow, I take Spandau. You take East Germany, we take West Germany. Bickering and bartering, and by the end of it Germany was crippled.

It was retribution. Retribution for the terrible suffering our country had inflicted during the war, and yes, I hang my head and admit with bitter shame in my heart that it was deserved. But that didn't make it any easier to bear. To raise your head and see Berlin's remaining buildings draped in scarlet Soviet flags. In Stars and Stripes. In the Union Jack. To watch the military uniforms of occupying forces strutting along the streets of our city as if they owned it. Which they did. Roosevelt and Truman, Stalin and Churchill all ensured that we had no power ever to inflict such suffering again.

This is what they did.

Germany was divided into four occupation zones: American, British, French and – I spit in the gutter – the Soviet zone. In horror Berliners blinked and woke up to find our city had turned into a fragile island of western values marooned deep within the communist Soviet zone. One hundred and sixty kilometres from West Germany. That meant one hundred and sixty kilometres from freedom.

The Allied Control Commission then took out their street maps and their red pens and sliced Berlin itself into four sectors as well. There were the American, British and French sectors. And then on the other side of a line drawn right down the middle of the city, north to south, lay the Soviet sector, East Berlin, all 403 square kilometres of it. Far larger than any of the other individual sectors. Across that line the two opposing political systems — capitalism and communism — faced off against each other, like knife fighters in a ring, each looking to sink a blade into the other's weak spot.

And Stalin was the first to strike. The first to draw blood.

In response to America introducing a new currency into the western-occupied zones of Germany — the replacement of the Reichsmark by the more stable Deutschmark — Stalin introduced the blockade.

The Russian leader had grown greedy. He was determined to force the western Allied powers out of Berlin. The blockade was to be a first step towards the taking over of the whole of Germany by Soviet forces. So overnight he took the city prisoner and severed its connections to the outside world. He proceeded to squeeze the life-blood out of it. We woke up on the morning of 24 June in the summer of this year, 1948, to find all road, rail and river links between the western Berlin sectors and the rest of the world were cut. No road access for transporting goods. No freight trains to bring food. No barges carrying coal.

'West Berlin will starve to death.' My mouth was dry with rage. Tears coursed down my cheeks.

'And when winter comes, any who are left will freeze to death,' Mutti had added as she stared sorrowfully down at the knitting needles flying between her fingers and considered the fate of the doomed western sectors.

'We must help our friends in West Berlin, poor Martha and Klaus Dieleman.'

'If you do,' my mother looked up at me with the kind of look you give a pup who is about to pee on a favourite Persian rug, 'you will be shot.'

We both knew the truth of her words.

But there were over 2 million inhabitants in West Berlin and those of us who lived in East Berlin wept for them. Yet Berliners were allowed to pass back and forth between the east and the west of the city every day, through designated checkpoints. They were allowed to live in one sector and work in another, passing freely between the two sides each day, as long as identity papers were shown at the checkpoints between the Allied and Soviet sectors and no illegal goods were hidden in pockets or tucked into the lining of caps.

So what counted as illegal goods? The Soviets permitted no food or medicines or coal to be smuggled into the Allied sectors. And no Deutschmarks or western newspapers to be carried into the Soviet sector. The penalties were harsh.

In the Soviet sector of Berlin most of us were already half-starved because the economy lay in ruins. Factories were being looted, food was scarce and there were no jobs to be had, but at least we had access to the black-market alleys. These were the bustling corners that required no ration books, where farmers lumbered in with their meagre produce from land in the outer Soviet zone that surrounded Berlin. We'd learned to barter our most precious possessions. For a potato. For an onion. Maybe for a thin scrape of stale cheese if we got lucky.

But the western sector, it had nothing. Stalin cut off food, fuel, electricity supplies, all the necessities of life. Gone. Then he sat back with a vulture's patience to watch those in the western half of the city starve to death under the stern gaze of his border guards. His blockade turned the Allied sectors of the city into a death pit.

It is this that you must understand. That Berlin was dying.

'They are angels,' my mother said.

I did not believe in angels. Not any more. Unless they lay in cribs and came with featherdown golden hair that twisted around my fingers and wide-set blue eyes that laughed when I tinkled my bicycle bell at them. Those angels I believed in.

My mother, wreathed in an old picnic blanket, was standing, as she so often did, at the window observing the dying of the day as the city withdrew its ruins from view behind a lilac veil of mist. She was watching intently, gripping the curve of the sill while ice formed in the corners of the pane. A steady stream of aircraft flowed down into the city, lit by a single beam of sunlight that had punched a hole through the dark clouds and was bathing their wings in a heavenly glow.

'Angels,' she said again.

'Brave men,' I corrected.

'Berlin's saviours,' she added.

I didn't argue with that. I joined her at the window. It was nearly six months since Stalin slammed shut all access to the city and these *angels* were accomplishing the impossible.

'It can't be done,' everyone had said. 'It is logistically unfeasible. You cannot feed more than two million hungry inhabitants or keep them warm throughout the winter using just a few aircraft to transport supplies. It will never be enough. Never. They will starve.'

'They are miracle workers,' my mother said.

I didn't argue with that either. They were superhuman, these western Allies and it was no wonder to me now that they won the war. With breathtaking optimism, the Berlin Airlift was launched to keep Berlin alive. The chief miracle worker was America's General Lucius Clay, the military governor of the US zone of occupied Germany. This man of genius, backed by President Truman, put Operation Vittles – that's what they called it – into action when it seemed an impossible feat. Never before had any nation mounted so ambitious a supply operation by air, saving so many desperate lives.

Now I would be working for them, unloading those angelic aircraft and funding my own 'operation'. I placed the flat of my hand on the chill glass of the window and swore to achieve my own miracle.

Operation Felix.

◆　◆　◆

That night we played cards, my mother and I. Just the two of us. It's what we did by candlelight most evenings, silence filling the cold spaces of the room, right up to the shadowy corners of the ceiling where spiders thought they were safe. But no one was ever safe in East Berlin, even though a strict curfew kept everyone indoors at night.

I didn't tell my mother about the explosion at the American building. I don't honestly know why not, but now I think about it I can see it was because something in me didn't want her to hate communists even more than she did already. She carried enough fear inside her. Enough hatred. Day and night she lived out her existence here inside our apartment, never leaving its four walls, never stepping over the threshold though she was fit enough to do so now. She wouldn't go *out there*. That's what we called the city. *Out there*. That's where evil prowled.

'I heard a joke today, Mutti.'

Her quick blue eyes looked up from the cards cradled in her hand and studied me, surprised. 'Is it funny?' she asked.

'Yes.'

'Let's hear it.'

'A poll was taken in three countries,' I told her. 'It wanted to know: what is your opinion of the recent shortage of meat? In America people asked, "What shortage?" In Poland they asked, "What is meat?" And in East Berlin they asked –' I paused to smile – '"What is an opinion?"'

I heard her snort, a thin whistle of air. Her gaze flicked over to the window where East Berlin breathed noisily on the glass, rattling the panes, reminding us of the dangers. 'What is an opinion?' she echoed softly and nodded. 'They believe in one system of living, we believe in another. And for that we kill each other.' She continued to stare at the black window.

It concerned me that I never knew what was going on inside her head.

'It's getting much colder,' my mother commented.

'Out there. And in here.'

We had no fire. No fuel. I would have burned one of Papa's chairs, but no, she hoarded them the way I hoarded my memories of little

Felix – the tiny hook of his finger around mine, the drum-tight curve of his little belly after a feed, the way his eyes turned a more vivid blue when he caught sight of my face. Yes, I hoarded these.

My mother and I sat huddled in our coats and in the multicoloured woollen scarves, hats and fingerless gloves that she had knitted from strands of old jerseys. Our breath trailed across the card table like candle smoke.

'*Mein Gott*, I'd sell my soul for a shot of vodka right now,' my mother stated. She said the same thing every night.

She raised one finely arched eyebrow and one half of her mouth. It was the nearest she cared to come to a smile. I stretched my lips in imitation of amusement. It was the best we could manage between us.

'Bed now,' my mother announced and folded her cards together.

She had won. Take that how you will.

The darkness made me invisible. In the early hours I opened the door to my mother's room, a thin crack, no more. I put my ear to the hairline of cold night air that drifted from it and listened hard. No sound, no soft breathing, no shout to get the hell out of her bedroom. Some nights she locked her door against me. She didn't trust me.

I didn't blame her. She had good reason.

I stood immobile for a full minute in my dressing gown, ears sharp for a sigh or for any intake of breath within the bedroom. None came. The brass doorknob was cold as ice in my hand and I peeled my fingers from it slowly, one by one, so that it wouldn't rattle. I knew each sound that this door could utter, every creak that the individual floorboards whispered.

I edged inside, into the darkness that was as solid as a wall. My mother kept the shutters closed day and night, tighter than prison doors. I steered a careful path around the piles of furniture, chairs balanced on top of chairs, boxes on top of boxes, to where a cheval mirror stood right in front of the honey-blonde dressing table where as a child, twenty years earlier, I'd been allowed to play with her lipsticks if I was good. She used to howl with laughter at my clown faces. Oh, but that carefree laugh has gone now, along with the lipsticks. One lipstick in exchange for bread. Another for potatoes. Her favourite Chanel one for a bag of coal at a grubby stall in Schönhauser Strasse. Priorities change.

I reached around the mirror, navigating by touch, and eased open a drawer. It let out the faintest murmur. I froze. The blackness remained silent. I waited for my pulse to slide down a notch and allowed my fingers to explore inside the drawer. They tracked down two small boxes covered in velvet and slipped them into the pocket of my dressing gown.

Would she notice their loss? No, I thought not. There was so much crammed into her room that two small boxes were nothing. Nothing.

That's what I told myself.

I squeezed past the escritoire, retreating quickly, but the sleeve of my nightdress caught on one of its swan-neck handles and the desk moved.

Don't let her wake. Please don't let her wake.

I stared blindly at the big double bed with its Black Forest scrollwork but could make out nothing. No rustle of sheets. I let myself believe she was fast asleep. I unhooked my sleeve and was reaching for the door knob when a dark figure loomed out from beside the mahogany wardrobe.

'Explain yourself, Anna.'

I had no explanation. But I had lies, smooth and shameless on my tongue.

'I heard you cry out, one of your nightmares, Mutti,' I said. 'I was worried. I came in to make sure you were alright.'

My mother couldn't see me, any more than I could see her in the darkness, couldn't spot the colour that rose to my cheeks or the lies that muddied my dark eyes. I reached out my hand to find her in the gloom. My fingers touched her arm, skin and bone under the silken material of her nightgown. It was fluttering.

'Get back to bed,' I urged. 'It's cold. You're shivering.'

'You know perfectly well that you are not allowed in my room. You interfere too much.'

'I'm trying to keep us alive. We have to live.'

'This isn't *living*. How can you call it that? Don't you remember what *living* was like?'

A taut spiky silence filled the bedroom, neither of us daring to breathe or blink while we recalled what it was like to be properly alive. Before the Russians marched into Berlin.

'You are a thief,' she said. Calm and cold.

'No, you are the thief.'

I sensed, rather than saw, her sudden movement. Her hand came out of the darkness and landed a slap on my cheek, sharp as the crack of a window pane. It was the shock more than the physical pain that shot a dart of white heat through me.

I gripped the spoils in my pocket and left the room.

'Let's go swimming,' he says.

I was lying in bed listening to the night wind drumming on the window, my mother's slap still branded on my cheek in the darkness. Yet I heard his voice, warm as summer sunshine in my room.

'Timur?' I whispered.

I heard the yearning in my voice and I closed my mouth tight. But I couldn't bar him from my mind however hard I tried. I put my hand on my heart to quieten it and felt an erratic drumming, as if that vital muscle was suddenly much larger and louder and eager to make itself heard above the wind. In my head I heard the scampering of squirrels in trees.

It came again, his voice. 'Let's go swimming.'

That day. It held me in its grip. It is July 1945 and Timur is waiting at the front door, a towel under his arm, his smile lighting up my day.

I laugh. I think he is joking. But no. So I bring bicycles from my workshop. We cycle south-east in the heat, through the battered district of Treptow to the beautiful Müggelberge where forests flank the emerald hillsides, and we swim naked in the chill waters of the Müggelsee. I recall how the sunlight floats like a sheet of satin on the lake's surface, and how I hold him close to me, jealous of the water's intimate touch on his skin. I press my breasts against his bare chest, a powerful bonding of bone and muscle, and we make love under the filigree canopy of a beech tree. A dart of slanting sunlight paints our damp skin golden, while red squirrels chitter, tufty ears twitching as they race along branches above our heads. Lacy patches of wild garlic cling to the earth. The air tastes as sweet as Eden that day.

Afterwards. We sit nestled together with our backs against a gnarly old tree stump and I ask, 'How do you speak such excellent German?'

'My grandfather was a fur trader in Siberia,' he says, looping an arm around my shoulders, 'and on a trading trip across the border to China he met a German missionary's daughter – out there to convert the heathens. They fell in love and married and she returned to Siberia with him.'

'That takes courage. Giving up her life to be with him in an unknown country.'

'My grandfather became a wealthy man from the fur trade, and when they had a child – my father – he was taught German, his mother's tongue, as well as Russian. He was sent to St Petersburg to study to be a doctor when he was old enough, but after he'd qualified he insisted on returning to his beloved Siberia. Times were hard. Under Stalin the further you were away from Moscow, the better.'

'So that means you are a quarter German.'

'I am.'

I think about that. 'Marching into Germany as part of the brutal invading Red Army must have been …' I pause. 'It must have torn you apart,' I finish softly.

He tucks a hand under my chin and turns my face to him. His grey eyes are brimming with emotion. 'It was like coming home,' he says.

CHAPTER SEVEN

· · ·

ANNA

People are disappearing.

Here. In East Berlin. I spoke to my neighbour yesterday, we laughed at some nonsense, and today he is gone. He was the one with the little dog and the fondness for bowing to the ladies he met on the stairs of our apartment building when the lift wasn't working, which was most of the time. We only discovered he was missing because the dog wouldn't stop howling and we all knew he would never leave his beloved pet. So I am careful, extremely careful.

The important thing to remember is that a static target is an easy target.

It's why I always rode a bicycle through the streets of the city, sliding in and out of alleyways and vanishing around corners, while others lingered on pavements under the linden trees or trudged slowly underground to the U-Bahn trains. I keep moving. It's why I'm still here.

Here is an icy kerb where Hochenstrasse crosses Alexanderplatz on the inner edge of East Berlin and it is killing me to stand exposed like this in the open. Waiting for someone.

I used to live on Prenzlauer Allee in Berlin.

Now I live on Prenzlauer Allee in *East* Berlin.

To many it may seem a difference scarcely worth mentioning, one small extra word added. *East Berlin* instead of *Berlin*. But to me it is the difference between night and day, between life and death. Believe me, I know.

I was waiting on the street corner, chilled to the bone by the morning's east wind, my eyes alert for patrols. Before the war a pharmacy used to stand on this spot in which Johann Neumeister dispensed pills, potions and kindness until a British bomb from a Lancaster scored a direct hit. Little white tablets and Johann Neumeister's body parts were scattered among the ruins like confetti. I missed him even now. He used to pop a soft pink sugary Turkish delight into my palm when as a child I did errands for him on my bicycle, delivering medication across the neighbourhood.

In those days we trusted people. Now they give the communist half of Berlin numerous names as if by doing so they can fool us into not noticing the line that divides our city: they call it the Soviet sector, or the Russian half, or plain old Ost Berlin or, more commonly, just the east. But call it what they will, it's still what it is. Half a city. Battered, bruised and shredded into ruins. Its people oppressed, their freedoms curtailed, their lips sealed in this rigidly controlled communist state.

In East Berlin no one trusts anybody any more.

I glanced around me, seeking out watchers, searching for a curious eye that lingered a moment too long or a head that turned away just as I lifted mine, but I spotted no one. And for once there were no Soviet military uniforms swaggering into sight, just the daily flow of busy Berliners hurrying to work, heads down, eyes averted. I breathed easier.

Where was he?

I glanced at my wrist, forgetting I had no watch. Of course I had no watch.

My gaze swept back and forth in search of a tall figure, one with a ski-slope of glossy scars down the left side of his face and a stillness in his eyes that at times frightened me, even though he was on my side. He would appear only when he was certain no one was watching, but it was with impatience that I stamped my boots, padded with newspaper against the cold, and felt the chill fog slide across my skin.

East Berliners are corralled into our half of the city by guarded checkpoints and watched relentlessly by the sharp eyes of the MVD. That's the repressive arm of the interior ministry of the Soviet Union. Ostensibly our half-city falls under the rule of the German Magistrate of Greater Berlin, but they might as well call it the Russian Magistrate of Stalin's Boot, because that's what it really was. Marshal Joseph Stalin stomps on us, his legs stretch all the way from Moscow.

So why do I live here?

Because it is my home. I am a Berliner, I've lived here all my life. That's twenty-five years of loving Berlin more fiercely than I care to say, despite its wartime devastation and its present Soviet overlords.

Then of course there's the other small point why I stay. The child.

A man appeared and set himself up on a spot on the pavement not ten metres from where my bicycle leaned against a crumbling wall. Not my man, not the one I was waiting for. This one was elderly and of military bearing, wearing a moth-eaten fur coat. He carried a violin case which he opened, removed a beautiful instrument the colour and sheen of fresh chestnuts, placed on the ground an upturned cap with a few pfennigs already in it and proceeded to play, tapping his foot. Something folksy and cheerful, at odds with his formal waxed moustache. His fingers were stiff, blue with cold, his knuckles knotted, and the music notes bumped into each other clumsily. He didn't glance at me.

I looked again to where my watch should have been but nothing had changed in the last ten minutes, I still had no watch. I parted with it months ago in exchange for a cabbage and a gnarled loaf of dense black bread, two candles and a sliver of soap no thicker than a communion wafer. I felt a tug of sorrow even now because it had been an exquisite Lange & Söhne, a gift from my father on my fifteenth birthday and I'd worn it every day for the next ten years. I could recall the exact moment when its elegant gold hands had pointed to 10.42 and I'd waved goodbye for the last time to Papa as he jumped up the steps of the train that would transport him to the front line. Even now I can smell the musty animal odour of his field-grey Wehrmacht tunic in the rain and the stink of hot engine oil on the crowded platform. From that moment on, the watch felt like his heartbeat kept safe on my wrist. Both gone now. I never saw him again.

The thin violin music paused but I continued to prowl. Where was he?

I knew my man as Herr Schmidt, though I doubted that Schmidt was his real name. I peered up to the far end of the street.

'Good morning, Fräulein Wolff.'

I swung round. 'Herr Schmidt.'

He stood at my elbow. How did he do that, materialise from nowhere? Schmidt was a stern, upright figure, his height emphasised by his long black overcoat which brushed his ankles. His hat was wide-brimmed and worn low, shadowing his face. I immediately focused on the large brown envelope in his hand.

'Herr Schmidt,' I repeated.

I held out my hand, not to shake his, but to take possession of the envelope, though I should have known better. He tucked it firmly under his arm and gave me what passed as a smile, a downward spasm of the damaged left side of his mouth, an upward twist of the right.

'Not so fast, *Fräulein*. Let's take our time.'

'I don't have time,' I told him.

'There is no one watching.'

I did a quick check past the violinist and down the street, skimming over the grey stream of hurrying pedestrians and a lumbering cart, until I spotted a man walking briskly in our direction. He was wearing very shiny black shoes. Only people who worked for those in power had access to boot polish. It was a luxury. I was tempted to retreat towards my bicycle but my desire for the envelope held me where I stood. The shiny shoes man walked straight past us with barely a glance. There was the smell of smoke in the air, not uncommon as buildings are slowly, very slowly, cleared.

'How can you be certain we aren't being watched?' I asked.

'Trust me.'

But could I? Should I?

Herr Schmidt used to be a *Kriminalkommissar*, an officer in the Kripo, Germany's criminal police, until nine years ago when he'd had some kind of disagreement with a Nazi SS officer. As a result the butt end of a Mauser rifle had been smashed into his face. That was all I knew about this man. Except that there was something hungry in him, a kind of hunger for truth, for facts, and that he now operated for hire in Berlin as a private investigator. You wanted information? Schmidt would do the digging for you. No questions asked. No job too dirty.

I studied him now. The damage to the left side of his face was appalling. The sunken facial bones, the slippery silvery scarring, the distorted eye socket. It was hard not to stare with pity, but I had trained myself not to. Herr Schmidt didn't want my pity, he wanted my money.

I removed a folded lace handkerchief from my pocket and rested it on the palm of my woollen glove, drawing Herr Schmidt's gaze. I flicked aside the top layer of it for half a second and a flash of gleaming scarlet flared between us. Gone in the blink of an eye as I swept the lace back into place, but its beauty lingered and Herr Schmidt knew an antique ruby ring when he saw one.

'I asked for American dollars,' he reminded me.

'I know. This is the best I can do.'

He paused and I held my breath, but he nodded. He passed the brown envelope to me and slid the lace handkerchief smoothly into his pocket. He would have made a good criminal. My heart was rattling against my ribs.

'Thank you,' I mumbled and took a few paces back towards my bicycle.

'Fräulein Wolff, wait.'

Herr Schmidt's hand touched my shoulder and I turned to find his face so close to mine that I could make out the neat rows of indentations where the sutures had tried to stitch the strips of his cheek back over the shattered bones. I couldn't tell whether his drooping left eye possessed any sight or not, and certainly I'd never ask, but his right eye was a clear quick-witted blue.

'What is it, Herr Schmidt?'

'I am concerned.'

I felt my stomach lurch.

'Why?' I asked.

'Because one of my operatives has gone missing.'

I knew what he was saying before he said it.

'The one working on my case, you mean?'

'Yes.'

'What happened?'

'I don't know yet. But I will find out.' The undamaged side of his face gathered itself into a frown. 'He was a good man. My best.'

I waited for more but none came.

'You think his disappearance and my case might be connected?'

His hand grew heavier on my shoulder.

'It's possible,' he said.

'Is this a warning?'

His sharp blue eye softened unexpectedly. 'It is a suggestion, *Fräulein*, that's all. That you drop your case. Give up your search.'

'No.' I stepped away from him, releasing my shoulder.

I heard his sigh. 'You know, don't you,' he said, 'that there are thousands of stray and orphaned kids running wild in Berlin, living like rats in the ruins? You haven't a hope in hell of finding this child.'

I brushed the fingertips of my glove over the rough brown envelope, back and forth, brushing his unwelcome words off its surface. Not a hope in hell? I wanted to tell this man that there is a world of difference between hope and expectation. Hope is a flimsy thing, as weightless as moonlight. Expectation has a backbone and muscle, it gets things done. I had expectation. Quickly I slid the envelope into the secret pocket inside the lining of my coat in case he decided to snatch it back from me.

'I'm very sorry about your operative's disappearance,' I said. I could see sadness etched into the grooves of his face. 'Let's hope he turns up with nothing worse than a hangover.'

'He's not that kind of person. Not one to give up on a job.'

'Neither am I.'

The twisted smile came again and I was oddly touched by it.

'So it seems,' he said. 'But how long before you run out of ruby rings and gold brooches?'

'That's my problem, not yours.'

'At the moment it's a problem we share.'

The unexpected softness was there again and I didn't know where it was coming from. It didn't match the rest of him. I was confused. The Soviet sector of Berlin was an unashamed police state and you had to be seen to obey the rules. We all kept up our guard because anybody could inform on you at any time, though what we were doing today was not exactly illegal. Unless you count stealing from your mother.

'The point is,' Herr Schmidt continued in his low voice, 'until I find out the reason why my operative has gone missing, we don't know whether his disappearance is connected to you or to your search in any way. We don't want any more disappearances, do we?'

He saw the shock. The way it ripped through me, though I tried to disguise it with a shiver in the wind, rubbing my hands together for warmth and seizing my bicycle's handlebars.

'Thank you, Herr Schmidt,' I muttered.

Though I was not certain what I was thanking him for. The envelope? Or the warning? Or was it the smile?

As I cycled away from him and the violin man, the envelope safely concealed, I heard Schmidt shout behind me, 'Watch your back.'

It was what lay ahead that worried me more.

CHAPTER EIGHT

• • •

ANNA

Bicycles are my passion, much to my mother's disgust. My workshop now was small and cramped, scarcely worthy of the name. Gone were the days when I had my own display window in Mollstrasse in Mitte district where I showed off my restored bicycles, the result of many hours of my labour. Sanding off rust and stripping clogged hubs. Replacing missing spokes, adjusting brake rods, spraying bare metal and fixing buckled wheels. I was meticulous. Bicycles were my business and I loved them all, every single one of them.

My father used to joke that I had bicycle oil in my veins. I was only sixteen when I set myself up in business doing repairs and resprays to Berlin's thousands of bicycles. Then the war hit us and I scavenged every rusting wreck on two wheels that I could lay my hands on – Kalkhoffs, Volkscycles, C&Vs, Kettlers, Brennabors, Diamants, Rixes, the list of fine German manufacturers went on and on. I would cannibalise one bicycle to repair another, a gear hub off one, a fork or callipers off another. Even an occasional stolen military bicycle would come my way under cover of darkness.

My Mitte workshop was blown to hell along with much of Mollstrasse. It wasn't America's Flying Fortresses that did for us, nor the nightly pounding by Britain's RAF Lancasters. In the end it was the Russian artillery bombardment that finished us off. *Boom*. Reduced to rubble.

It broke my heart, but I started again from scratch after the war. My new workshop was down steps to a dank cellar on Hinterstrasse in the east. A row of metal gratings at street level admitted a grey cold light into my underground world and I was forced to work in the gloom because kerosene for a lamp cost money I didn't have. Electricity was rationed to two hours only in the middle of the night. Rationed along with bread. And meat and fat and sugar and eggs and cooking oil and salt and just about everything else we needed to stay alive.

Except bicycles.

I hurried down the stone steps, trundling my bicycle alongside me, and entered my workroom, locking the door behind me. It was always cold in here, sometimes so cold it made my fingers clumsy with a spanner, which infuriated me, but at least it was dry. The long narrow underground space was more of a wide corridor than a room and the walls had once been painted sunshine yellow, but much of the paint had peeled away and just a scrap of sunshine remained here and there. I liked it.

I lifted Herr Schmidt's brown envelope out of the pocket within the lining of my coat and felt my expectation rise. My fingers tore it open with impatience. This time. This would be the end of my search. I had already convinced myself.

I tipped out its contents and a pile of photographs tied together with a length of blue ribbon fell on to my workbench. Each was the size of a small postcard, displaying an image of a child's face. I scooped them up and, breathing softly, I held them close against my cheek as if I could feel their tender young skin on mine. I tried to smell the warm scent of their hair, but a tremor ran through me and I made myself place them back down on the wooden surface. I untied the ribbon – Herr Schmidt always included that touch of silky blue ribbon – spread them out methodically in four straight rows and counted them. Thirty-one.

Thirty-one. Was that all?

I stepped back from the bench, but my gaze remained fixed on the thirty-one young faces that stared back at me. None jumped out. Not one. None leapt up and shouted, *Look at me first. I'm the one you're searching for.* I turned my own face away, blinked hard and waited for the threat of tears to pass. When I looked back, I smiled at them, my new set of boys, welcoming them into my life, and I picked up the magnifying glass that lay ready to hand on a shelf.

◆ ◆ ◆

I examined every photograph with meticulous care. The exact shape of each face, each head. The delicate sweep of each cheek, the rise of the brow, the set of the small chin, the width of forehead and the look in the eyes. Oh yes, the eyes above all else. The windows to the soul. Was one of these a picture of the little soul I sought?

Some scowled at the camera, angry at its lens, or were they angry at the world? At the hunger pains griping in their stomachs? Some grinned, flaunting bravado and dainty milk teeth, because none of these boys was more than three years old. The photographs were black and white, so their eyes all appeared grey, some darker, others lighter, but I knew they were in fact blue because that had been my first instruction to Herr Schmidt. Blue eyes. Fair hair. A slight wayward curl of hair at the nape, narrow delicate features and a pointed little chin whose tip I had loved to kiss. The darling face of a pixie.

I could see no pixie here.

What I saw were sharp unfamiliar bones. Dirty hair. Scabbed lips. Something raw, horribly raw, in their young eyes, something battered and bemused, and it tore me apart. There was a feral wariness about them, like a fox caught out in the open, and it sent tears dripping unchecked on to my magnifying glass as I leaned over the thirty-one photographs. One small boy with long rabbity ears looked as though he'd only just woken up, his eyes still encrusted with sleep, and I dropped a kiss on his forehead. He was not the one I sought.

I selected one. Only one. It was the closest to the image I carried in my head. I took it over to the light of the high window under the grating for a better view, though I knew I was clutching at straws and I could feel my hope slithering away through my fingers on to the concrete floor, just like all the other times. I twisted and turned it in the early morning light, first one way, then the other. I'm surprised my gaze didn't burn a hole right through the shiny paper, I studied the little face so fiercely, trying to work my way under his skin to the baby he had once been.

This one – with blond hair shaggy as a sheep over his forehead, his stare alert and curious – had my heart thumping because of his huge round eyes and the curve of his sweet full lips. Or was it because he was smiling? Was I so easily fooled by his smile?

Yes, I admit it. I was. Yet his boy's smile felt so … familiar.

I flipped the photograph over and on the back was written one word in Herr Schmidt's strong black hand. The boy's name. *Bernd*. It meant nothing to me.

'Hello, Bernd,' I whispered.

I needed to speak to this child, to discover from Herr Schmidt where and with whom he was living, but as always more information meant I needed more money.

I didn't have any more money but …

A knock on the door startled me.

My heart flipped. I was in no state for conversation, but it might be the knock of a potential customer and these days I couldn't afford to turn even one away.

'Just coming,' I yelled.

I grabbed an old dust sheet from under the bench and threw it over the rows of photographs. I unlocked the door and swung it open to find a warm hug waiting for me on the other side.

'Kristina.' I returned my friend's hug. 'Come on in.'

'I was worried about you, so I came to check you were okay. I heard there'd been an explosion and—'

'Oh, that.'

I didn't want to talk about it.

Kristina gave me a searching look from her observant blue eyes. 'They said it happened in the recruitment building and that's where you—'

'It missed me.' I found a smile and spread it over my face. 'As you can see.'

'Did it come close?'

'Close enough.'

She eyed my skinned hand. 'Tell me, Anna. No, don't turn away. Tell me what happened?'

So I told her. A potted version. No details. But I could feel my jaw muscles clenching and unclenching as I spoke, the mental images sending shivers through me, and she rocked my hand in hers. 'What was it,' she asked softly, 'that made you run?'

'I don't know. I've gone over and over it in my mind, replaying every minute in my head, but ...' I shook my head.

'Damn communists!' Kristina exclaimed. 'They do everything they can to try to sabotage the airlift. They don't give a damn how many they kill.' Anger washed through her, colouring her pale cheeks.

It reminded me of another day when I had seen that same anger in her, a day of warm bright sunlight. It was back in those early times when the war had only just finished and Timur had only just walked into my life. It was then that Kristina had come to me in my bicycle workshop. Her lovely limbs were all spiky and full of restless movement, jabbing holes in the air and pacing the length of my workbench. I'd glanced across at her, wary. She'd picked up a brake pad that lay on the bench and I would swear she was tempted to throw it at me.

I'd put aside my spanner, straightened up and said, 'Calm down, Kristina. What's happened?'

'You know damn well what's happened.'

'Tell me.'

'Major Timur Voronin has happened.'

My eyes flicked her a warning. I didn't want an argument.

'Timur Voronin is my friend, yes. If that's what you mean.'

She tossed back her flaxen braid, snatched off her straw hat and threw that at me instead of the brake pad. It slithered to the floor with the sound of mice under floorboards. 'Anna, how can you bear it? To be involved with a Russian. They are barbarians. They are killers. You of all people should know that. You will be despised. Everyone will turn against you.'

I'd looked at my friend and felt an ocean of sadness sway through me. 'Even you?'

Kristina's eyes glittered with unshed tears and she reached into her pocket, pulled out the rump end of a loaf of black bread and placed it on my workbench on top of the dust sheet as a peace offering. The hunt for food defined our day-to-day existence and she had probably queued for hours outside a *Bäckerei* for it.

She shook her head. 'No. Not me.'

I took her delicate spotless hands in my own oily fingers. 'I know you mean well, Kristina. But I will not let go of him. I cannot. Like I cannot let go of the air in my lungs or the blood in my veins.'

'But he knows you killed one of his comrades. You're not safe.'

I froze. So there it was. There was the nub. She'd voiced it. I stepped back and my gaze shot to my hands, expecting to see blood and brains trailing from my fingers.

'He won't betray me,' I murmured.

'Are you sure?'

'Yes.'

'He could have you shot. Whenever he chooses.'

'He won't betray me,' I said again. Louder.

'Is that why you're with him, Anna? To keep him quiet?'

I laughed, I couldn't help it. 'Oh, Kristina, you don't know Timur if you think that. If he is ever set on saying something, nothing on earth will stop him.'

'So why are you with him?'

I spread my arms as wide as I could, as though my answer was too huge to hold, and I gave her a smile to match. 'Because I love my big Russian bear.'

'Oh, Anna, that Russian will be the death of you.'

She left my workshop, but her words had hung there in the chill air that day. Sharp as bayonets.

Now there was no summer sunshine, no straw hat, but once again she was standing in front of me cursing communists and I knew that she included Major Timur Voronin among their number. I turned away and picked up a tyre pump to make it look as if I was working.

'Did you get the job?' Kristina asked suddenly.

'Yes, I start tonight.'

'Tonight?'

'Yes, it's the nightshift. I don't mind that. I can finish off these during the day.' I waved at the bicycles raised upside down on stands in the middle of the floor, awaiting repair.

'Take care out there, Anna. We hear so many tales of what goes on at Tempelhof. They are young men living on the very edge of danger, risking their lives every day in their planes, knowing the Russians could knock them out of the sky at any moment.' She smacked her hands together, startling me. 'And don't forget they are Americans and British, and both nations despise us Germans now.'

'Don't worry, Kristina.' I drew a deep breath. 'I am able to take care of myself.'

This time we both looked down at my hands but the only marks on them were streaks of oil. She nodded and turned to leave.

'Thank you, my friend,' I said and gave her a strong hug.

I locked the door after her, then listened to her footsteps outside, thin-soled shoes, too flimsy for a Berlin winter. I waited till they'd reached the top of the steps and had hurried away. The air in my workroom smelled of the street now, of lorry fumes and hunger and suspicion, instead of the sweet innocence of childhood. I inhaled quickly, trying to drag that sweet innocence back into my lungs, some faint trace of it, but the moment had gone. So I gathered the photographs up into a tidy pile with Bernd on top. I touched his pale forehead with my fingertips and a soft sound escaped my lips.

I wrapped the pile inside one of Papa's long cycling socks. It was knitted from leaf-green wool with narrow yellow stripes, and some days when my feet and my heart were feeling too cold to bear, I would pull them on over my own. Papa would have laughed that noisy laugh of his and told me to get outside on my bike to warm up because a bike ride solved all problems. For years I'd believed him. But I know better now.

CHAPTER NINE

◆ ◆ ◆

INGRID

A ll morning Ingrid Keller could not keep her mind off the dead body she'd seen on her return home yesterday, the way it had slumped on the steps. As her paintbrush swept back and forth hour after hour, the images of the man kept rising and imprinting themselves on the blank wall in front of her. She would blink and see the gleam of the ice on his skin. The blueness of his fingernails. She lost count of the number of times she tasted the sour bile on her lips where the pearl cross had taken a swipe at her.

Who was he?

But she hadn't reported him to the police. Was that the problem? Was that why she couldn't push him away?

No, the dead man was nothing to her. She didn't even know his name and Otto certainly wouldn't thank her for bringing the polizei banging on their door. That was too risky. She went back to work with renewed concentration, because she was not a woman to be panicked by the light tread of ghosts. She sprang up on to a plank that was suspended two metres in the air by a pair of stepladders. Her employer, Herr Kuznetsov – a Soviet bigwig of some sort – had instructed that the picture rail in this grand Soviet-sector apartment must be painted in gold flake. She shuddered. She loathed gold. And silver for that matter. She'd spent too many childhood years in the circus ring kitted out in outfits of glittering gold or shimmering silver that had prickled as she moved.

It was her husband who'd put her up for this job. 'My wife will redecorate your apartment for you,' Otto had promised Comrade Pavel Kuznetsov.

'Is she a fast worker?'

'She's good and she's fast. And she's cheap.'

Pimping her. Like a whore.

But she didn't mind because it meant proper paid work and anyway she liked this room. It was a spacious drawing room with elegant proportions and fine mouldings, and from her perch up here on the plank she could see out to the bomb-pitted lustgarten and to the burnt dome of the grandiose baroque cathedral, rimmed with glittering frost. The blackened streets around it were hidden from view by a thick white fist of fog that had wrapped itself around the wounded city like a bandage. But Ingrid didn't view the city's destruction as a catastrophe the way so many others did, she didn't whine and wail and beat her breast. She smiled quietly to herself. She saw it as an opportunity.

A noise startled her. Listening, she froze. It was the unmistakable sound of footsteps. But she was alone here, the apartment was empty. There could be no footsteps. The hairs on her neck rose and she rested her hand on the stubby sheath-knife that was always in her pocket. She was in the east here, and Russian soldiers had a reputation for molesting German women.

The drawing-room door swung open and in the doorway stood a straight-backed man in a smart black fedora and a well-tailored suit. Over his shoulders hung a long cape, damp from the fog, and she could smell his musky cologne. In his hand he carried an ebony walking cane but she suspected it wasn't just for show. Something about the way he handled it left Ingrid in no doubt that it was a weapon.

'Herr Kuznetsov,' she exclaimed, 'I wasn't expecting you.'

'So I see,' he said.

His eyes went unerringly to the vodka bottle and dirty glass on the window sill. *Scheisse*, she should have been more careful. She'd discovered them in the cocktail cabinet under one of the dust sheets that were draped over the furniture and taken a nip.

'It gets cold in here,' she said by way of explanation.

'Then work faster.'

'I've nearly finished, just this last section of gold flake to complete. I think you'll be pleased with it.'

The Russian strode further into the room. His ice-blue eyes skimmed the walls, checking her work, quick observant glances at the ceiling and cornices. He was a good-looking man, somewhere in his forties, who clearly cared about his clothes and wore them with style. Ingrid liked that. Not like most of the filthy Russians over here who looked as if they'd just rolled up from clearing out the pig sty at their dacha. Dear God, they smelled bad too. But Kuznetsov looked so incredibly clean. No one in Berlin was that clean because the water was frequently cut off for days. He possessed the kind of face you don't forget, angular, with strong cheekbones and an elegantly long nose. Only his mouth let it down. It was hard and inflexible. Like his voice.

'The apartment must be finished by the end of today,' he informed her. 'It must be perfect. I have two Politburo officials arriving from Moscow who will be staying here. They don't wish to be put in a hotel.'

Ingrid was interested. From the safety of her perch, she smiled down at him. 'Don't they trust the hotels? Too many ears listening?'

He gave her a cold silent stare and then turned his head away in disgust. 'You overstep yourself, Frau Keller. I don't appreci ...'

His last word trailed away and Ingrid realised he was staring for the first time at the wall behind him. She saw his fists grip the silver handle of his cane tight as though preparing to knock down the picture she had hung on that wall. *Verdammt!* She'd intended to remove it before he turned up. It was a large oil portrait of a young man.

The man in the painting possessed Kuznetsov's unmistakable ice-blue eyes and the same angular forehead, but the mouth was different, fuller and more self-indulgent. His hair was a striking white-blond, his lean limbs cleverly portrayed inside an old-fashioned linen jacket and jodhpurs. One hand lay on the neck of a beautiful pale horse and at his knee a creamy hunting dog gazed up at him in adoration. Ingrid was no judge of art but she liked this. A sunny happiness flowed out from the canvas and made her long to step into the picture. A fine artist, she thought. It must be wonderful to be able to capture the soul of someone in oils – instead of slapping gold paint on picture rails. Why it had been hidden away under an army blanket in a disused back bedroom, she couldn't imagine. So she'd brought the handsome young man out to be company for her while she worked, but now she regretted it.

'Your brother?' she asked.

'No.'

Kuznetsov wrenched his gaze from the painting and drew a long quivering breath, as though coming up for air. 'Finish up quickly and leave.'

Ingrid sensed this was her moment. Though it had arrived earlier than she expected. Some people run when they see trouble. They flee. They fail to seize the chance to walk through open doors, but not Ingrid. Kuznetsov was her open door.

She leapt from the plank to the floor with the grace of an acrobat, walked over to him and stood much closer than was comfortable for either of them. He towered over her, so she found herself addressing his nostrils and the tip of his broad chin.

'I am small,' she said bluntly. 'I am plain and I am colourless. Nobody notices me. When I am in a room, people forget I am there.' She gathered the next words on her tongue. 'I can help you.'

'What?' He was growing angry at her presumption.

'I don't mean decorating more apartments for you.'

'So what do you mean?'

'I mean I can be of use to you.'

'You?'

So much scorn in one word.

'Yes. I live in the west, in the British sector of the city, but I often find work here in the east. When I pass through the checkpoints I am barely seen. They wave me through.'

'Frau Keller, the only use you can be to me is as a painter of walls.'

But Ingrid was used to taking risks. She hadn't stepped out each night for much of her life on to a high-wire that was more than ten metres off the ground without knowing how to scrunch her fear into a secret ball in her chest.

'Herr Kuznetsov,' she said. She refused to call him *Tovarisch*. It was Russian for comrade and he was not her comrade. *Not yet*. 'You are making a serious mistake.'

'I do not make mistakes.'

'I think you do.'

She saw a dark flush rise up his neck, his eyes flinty and fully focused on her now. He no longer looked urbane.

'Get out,' he ordered.

She stared straight back at him, unblinking. 'Did you really think I wouldn't find the microphones in the walls?'

The silence stretched the fabric of the room till the newly painted walls felt ready to crack, but Kuznetsov kept his nerve and Ingrid admired that. He removed his hat, tossed it aside and shrugged off his cape. He gave her a long thoughtful stare before striding over to the cocktail cabinet, shapeless under its dust sheet. He returned with two fresh glasses and the bottle of vodka from the window sill, from which he poured them each a drink. He held one out to Ingrid.

'*Na Zdorovie!*' the Russian said, raising his glass.

'*Prost!*'

She knocked hers straight back. It burned in all the right places and she kept a wary eye on where he had propped his cane. Kuznetsov seated himself on the gilt chaise longue that stood in the centre of the room, without removing its protective white sheet.

'Come,' he said. 'Sit.'

Ingrid thought about it. Did she want to be that close? She slid her hand into her knife pocket and took a seat at the opposite end of the chaise longue. A smile appeared on his face but she wasn't fooled by the ease of it. He was watching her as intently as she was watching him. This close to him, she was very aware of his elegant white silk shirt and silver tie-pin, which made her feel even grubbier in her stained khaki overalls with a mess of paint under her fingernails.

'Now,' he said pleasantly enough, 'what is it you want, Frau Keller?'

'I want what I said. To be of use to you.'

Annoyance flickered in his eyes but he controlled it. 'Why would you want that?'

'Because in exchange you will pay me well.'

'Why would I do that?'

She sighed. To rattle him. 'Do I really need to spell it out? You planted hidden microphones in the walls of this apartment and then invited members of Stalin's Politburo to stay here, so that you could listen to their private conversations. You obviously gather intelligence. I don't know who you're working for – Russia's MGB or MVD, I assume. It may be to blackmail somebody or even to report back to Stalin himself for all I know ...'

He laughed, a chill sound that sent tremors through her, but his expression gave no clue to his thoughts.

'Are you threatening me, Frau Keller?'

'No. I want to help you.'

'How?'

'I told you. I can carry messages or packages or I can redecorate important officials' homes to snoop through their secrets or ...'

He laughed again, but this time she caught genuine amusement in it.

She smiled at him. 'People ignore me, Herr Kuznetsov, unless I am dressed in sequins. They don't see me, they don't know I exist. It can be useful.'

He leaned back and studied her. 'Perhaps I have underestimated you,' he said softly. 'Tell me about yourself.'

'There's nothing to tell.' Ingrid didn't like looking back, there were too many stumbles, she wanted to look forward, only forward. 'My father owned a small circus in Berlin, so I was swinging on a trapeze before I could walk. My mother was mauled to death by a tiger when I was child. I married Otto Keller who also worked in the ring, and later the circus was disbanded when my father was killed in the war and the money ran out.' She shrugged. 'That's it.'

'How do I know I can trust you? You live in the western sector. You could be a plant by the Americans.'

'No. I'm not. Believe me, I'm not.' She leaned forward, her eyes intent and fierce on his, one small paw gripping his sleeve. 'My country,' she said, 'has had its guts ripped out, first by Hitler and his scum Nazis, then by the western Allies and their never-ending bombs. Germany is rubble. Our only way forward through this hellfire is by harnessing the power of our workers. Germans are good workers, Herr Kuznetsov. Strong and disciplined workers. Give us the tools and we will rebuild our country. It is obvious to me that communism is the only answer to the greed and savagery that has brought us to this state and is still festering in our ruins. I believe it is the only way to set my country free.'

He studied her, narrow-eyed, assessing. 'What proof do I have?'

She laughed, a thin mousey sound. 'I could have reported the microphones to the police. But I didn't.' She shrugged her bony shoulders. 'The Americans and British destroyed my city and killed my father and my uncle, so believe me when I say I have no love for them.' She gave his sleeve a quick shake. 'Test me. Ask me to carry out a task that will show you I'm not a plant. You will see. I work only for myself, no one else.' Her breath came at him in a hot rush. 'I hate Americans. I hate the British. They destroyed my life.'

She saw his expression change, a subtle shift, a loosening of the tension that had been in his eyes ever since she'd mentioned the microphones. Something in her voice had got through to him, something raw and unguarded. Slowly he nodded his head. He sat up straight and became more formal. 'We might be able to do business.'

Somewhere in a street not far away a shot rang out and a woman screamed, a Russian bullet for sure and a German woman. It was not uncommon and always shocked the hell out of Ingrid. She shivered, but her companion didn't even blink. Oh yes, there was money to be made here, but it would come at a price.

'Could you shoot someone if necessary, Frau Keller?'

She didn't hesitate. 'Yes. If it was necessary.'

He paused, smiled with that thin mouth of his and spoke in a gentler tone. 'This job is not for people who are too soft by nature. Not for people who bruise easily.'

'I am not soft and I do not bruise.'

In the room a quietness settled between them, an understanding. They were both trying to find their own path of survival.

'Good,' Kuznetsov stated crisply. 'Because tomorrow I will send you to start a job at Tempelhof airport.' He lit himself a gold-tipped cigarette and exhaled with satisfaction, 'What happened to that tiger that killed your mother?' he asked.

'He was shot.'

CHAPTER TEN

✦ ✦ ✦

ANNA

I stepped out of my workshop into the Soviet sector, where the streets seemed to shift and swirl with dark shadows though it was still only mid-morning. A thick greasy fog hung low over the city. It was the kind of weather we dreaded. Zero visibility. How could planes possibly land in this murk? Yet day and night the sound of their engines overhead never ceased, steady and strong, Berlin's giant heartbeat in the sky.

All my life I'd believed in goodness. I'd seen it in my father's smile, felt it in Martha Dieleman's touch on my cheek, breathed it in with the turn of the seasons, with the green scent of new leaves each spring and with the first sparkle of ice glittering like glass in the winter skies. But the day I lost Felix, I lost my belief in goodness.

Goodness used to make Berlin shine, a brightness that was reflected in its inhabitants' eyes, in the rhythm of their heartbeats and in the flash of sunlight on the cathedral dome. But now the streets were gaunt and grey. The buildings of East Berlin cowered under heavy black stains. The stains of death. I saw them. Wherever I looked. The wind ripped the last dead leaves from the naked branches of the city's trees as easily as Soviet agents ripped people from their beds. As easily as my mother ripped my child from his crib.

If only I'd known the danger, I would never have allowed my child out of my arms. But my mind was feverish and soft-edged. Last night I dreamed I found Felix splayed on his back at the bottom of a zinc bath that was filled with ice water. The veins on his eyelids were like grey cobwebs, his skin the mottled white of the soulless marble statues in churches. I dreamed I touched him. It was not the first time, nor will it be the last.

✦ ✦ ✦

I stood in front of the Dielemans' apartment on Ku'damm in West Berlin and banged my knuckles on their grand oak door. There was no electricity in the city except for two hours at one o'clock in the morning, so no point ringing the bell. The door swung open half way and was then thrown wide. Two strong arms drew me tight to a well-corseted bosom that smelled fiercely of camphor, as Frau Martha Dieleman gathered me to her. She was a woman who didn't take no for an answer and dispensed affection as freely as Americans dispensed candies.

'Anna!' Martha kissed my chilly cheek.

She swept me and my bicycle, which I had hauled up their three flights of stairs, into their large apartment. I'd known the Dielemans all my life and happy memories crept out of the dark oak panelling the moment I set foot over the threshold. I smiled at Martha.

'How is Klaus?'

'He'll be much better for seeing you, my girl. Come, I will make us coffee.'

'I can't, Martha. I'm in a rush to get home. But you have real coffee?' I added in disbelief.

Martha rolled her eyes, warm and round as chestnuts. '*Dummkopf*,' she laughed. 'Who can find coffee in Berlin any more? Unless you are American.'

'What is it then?'

'Ground tree bark. Don't wrinkle your nose like that, *schatzi*.'

'It's so sharp.'

Martha slapped me heartily on the back. 'So am I when people don't drink my coffee.'

I succumbed. I always did to Martha.

The cold in the Dielemans' huge salon felt like something that lived there in the structure of the walls. But always the warmth of their greeting wrapped around me so that I didn't notice the smoky curl of my breath in the room and the nudge of damp against my skin. Martha and Klaus Dieleman were bundled up in thick coats, Martha's a stylish navy blue and her husband's a sombre black. They were both swaddled in woollen scarves which made them look bulky, but I wasn't fooled. Underneath they were skin and bone. This couple used to wear the most chic Parisian gowns and suave suits. Now look at them. They looked like sheep in winter fleeces too heavy for them.

'Come to me, young Anna, let me look at you.'

The man's voice boomed out at me from his seated position near one of the arched windows, the kind of voice that had no trouble filling a room, even one as large and imposing as this one. The salon was magnificent with its two crystal chandeliers – never used now corniced ceiling, oil paintings taller than I was and an array of antique Bohemian glass pieces as colourful as a peacock's tail. When I was a child the room used to shimmer with light and laughter, and I'd watched open-mouthed as men danced with lipsticked men and Marlene Dietrich, wreathed in a gold tuxedo and cigarette smoke, draped herself over the grand piano. Sleek furs and diamonds shimmered in a riot of glitz and glamour. Now the room was cold, the life sucked out of it.

'Klaus,' I said, drawing close to him, 'how are you?' I worried about this man who had been my father's closest friend.

Klaus Dieleman was seated in a basket-weave wheelchair with a wall of scarlet cushions behind him. A Russian mine had shattered his leg when he was leading a charge on the Eastern Front and he was forced to sit now with it raised on a stool, its bandages hidden by a bright patchwork blanket. Any mention of his leg, and his good humour would evaporate. He had been a banker with thick wavy hair that was as stubborn as he was. His dark eyes missed nothing and right now they were fixed on me. I lifted his hand and wrapped my fingers around it fondly.

'So, Anna, what news have you brought for me today?' he demanded.

'Have you heard about the searchlights? Marshal Sokolovsky is increasing the number of searchlights to be directed up into the air corridors to dazzle and confuse American and British pilots as they come in to land at night.'

Marshal Sokolovsky, a brilliant military brain, was the Commander-in-Chief of the Soviet Military Administration in Germany. At the end of the war in 1945 an agreement had been signed by the Soviet Union with America, Britain and France creating three air corridors from bases at Wiesbaden and Rhein-Main in the western zone of Germany to Berlin in the Soviet zone. It was along these air corridors, each one only twenty miles wide, that the airlift now operated, handling over 1,400 flights a day.

The transport planes conveyed more than 4,500 tons of cargo to be distributed throughout the western sector of the city. But America had just deployed an extra eight squadrons of C-54s – that's seventy-two aircraft – to reinforce the fifty-four already in operation. This had triggered an angry response from the much-decorated Marshal Sokolovsky. He was doing everything in his power to harass the Allied aircraft without actually shooting them down. If he shot them down, he knew that all hell would break loose. World War III was only one mistake away. Everyone was on edge.

'Marshal Vasily Sokolovsky may be head of Soviet Occupation Forces in Germany but he's also a vile barbarian,' Klaus growled. 'As well as sending up planes to buzz the incoming aircraft, to push them off course and tip them out of the sky, he has also got his men making obstructive parachute jumps inside the Allied air corridors. Grossly dangerous!' He thumped a fist down on the arm of his wheelchair. 'Lunacy!'

'So I heard.'

'*Mein Gott*, it's only by the magnificent flying skills of the young pilots that none of them has crashed yet.'

'I learned a piece of important news yesterday. Apparently US General Tunner flew in from Rhein-Main and is shaking up the whole system to make the planes' turn-around times much faster out at Tempelhof.'

'You're very well informed, Anna.'

'Oh, I just pick it up on the streets.'

As soon as I'd said it, I regretted my words. Klaus was caged here in the apartment, unable to stop off in bars for a beer and the latest gossip. With no warning he reached up and snatched off my woollen hat. My dark hair bounced, short and springy as grass.

'You look a mess,' he said bluntly. 'You've been at the scissors again, haven't you?'

'Yes.'

'It looks awful.'

'I know.'

'My little Anna, your hair used to be such a beautiful glossy black mane. Now look at it, no better than a bird's nest.'

Klaus could be infuriating, but I'd loved him for as long as I could remember. He'd been my father's dearest friend. I seized my hat from him and jammed it back on my head. It was yellow and matched my gloves. Together they battled the greyness.

'Coffee,' Martha announced, as she placed three fine Limoges bone-china cups on to a side table and gave her husband a smart smack on the top of his head. 'Leave the girl alone.'

I smiled at Klaus. 'You old grouch,' I laughed and sipped my coffee. It was disgusting.

'Good?' Martha asked.

'Yes.'

'You are even worse at lying than your dear father was,' she laughed. Her tone grew careful as she asked, 'How is your mother?'

'She's well.'

There was an awkward pause, a tiny pinprick in time, and I hurried out to the hallway, retrieved my bicycle and wheeled it into the Dielemans' salon.

'For heaven's sake, Anna,' Klaus grunted at me in disgust. 'Look at the state of that bicycle. It's a disgrace. It needs a damn good clean.'

'I know.'

We all stared at the bicycle. It was a Diamant 67, metallic blue and so lightweight that I'd carried it with ease up the three flights of stairs to the apartment. It was a fast machine, with a smooth Fichtel & Sachs three-speed derailleur gear system.

Papa and Klaus had been cycling fanatics. Before the war they used to spend weekends together racing each other up and down the rugged

Harz mountains. The dense greenness swallowed you into its heart and your legs ached till they burned. I know because I went there with them and pedalled like the wind to keep up. They had opened a new world to me, a wonderland of forested peaks and deep gorges that put pine-scented air in my lungs. I loved to sit and listen to their stories around a campfire without Mutti there to tut that they were unsuitable for my tender ears.

'Papa would be happy to see my bicycle carrying this,' I stated firmly and removed the tyre pump from its clips on the frame. Inside the cylinder, where the pump mechanism should have been, I had made a secret hiding place and from it I extracted a narrow roll of cotton wool. I placed it on Klaus's lap. His large hands folded back the white layers to reveal three delicate glass vials of amber liquid. Precious penicillin. He stroked one. I heard the air heave in and out of his lungs.

'Dear child,' was all he said.

'You still have your syringe?' I asked.

He nodded. 'You must have sold your soul for these, Anna. Where did you get them? From the Americans?'

'In a roundabout way, yes. Someone at Tempelhof airport is apparently stealing medical supplies from the shipments that come in from America. Some of it is making its way undercover into East Berlin which is where I found these.'

'Lying around on a street corner for the taking, I suppose.'

'Of course.'

He didn't ask what I'd bartered for them and I didn't tell him. Instead his big laugh boomed out with delight. 'Anna, come here, girl.'

I bent down and he nearly cracked my bones with his embrace.

'Thank you, Anna. *Dankeschön, mein Liebling.*'

Only then did I notice that Martha's brown eyes had filled with tears as she stared at the three vials of penicillin. None of us mentioned that handling them was illegal and could get me shot.

There was a loud knock at the front door.

◆ ◆ ◆

The man with the ebony curls set my teeth on edge. He entered the apartment the way a strange dog enters an unfamiliar room, nerves taut, his almost black eyes darting in every direction. He was a swarthy, stringy fellow and carried the smell of petroleum about him. I could imagine him syphoning it out of the petrol tanks of military vehicles at night. He wore a peaked cloth cap and a camel coat with an extraordinary number of capacious pockets. It wasn't hard to guess what they were for.

'Cigarette?' he greeted Klaus.

He crossed to Klaus, who had draped his rug over the glass vials, and dropped a carton of Lucky Strikes on his lap.

'I got more than expected for that last painting,' the newcomer said. 'So a small bonus for you.'

Not a stranger then. Belatedly I glanced at the artworks on the walls and noticed great pale gaps where once had hung beautiful oils. How had I not noticed earlier? The unknown man looked at me and then at my bicycle.

'Anna,' Martha said, 'this is Otto.' She paused. 'He helps us out.'

'Hello, Anna,' he said. 'Good to meet you.'

He smiled at me and the smile transformed his face. The sharp edges vanished, softened by a warmth that made me feel wrong-footed, and his handshake was as warm as his smile.

'Hello, Otto,' I replied.

'And how are you today, Frau Dieleman?' he asked Martha.

'Well enough,' she responded, sinking both her hands into her coat pockets. Clearly she had no intention of shaking hands with her visitor. 'Coffee,' she muttered and walked out of the room.

Otto turned to Klaus and shook his hand instead. 'Seen anything interesting today?' he asked, gesturing to the Busch binoculars at Klaus's side. There was a false heartiness in his way of speaking and I sensed that it was for my benefit.

Klaus opened the carton, lit one of the cigarettes and drew on it deeply. The first in a long while, I suspected.

'Good?' Otto said.

'Yes.'

I had the odd feeling that they were not talking about the cigarette, and it made me wonder about the connection between the two men. It wasn't hard to guess at Otto's activities. The black market had become a way of life for many in Berlin and we all knew which street corners to head for, which shady doorways to loiter in. How else had I acquired the penicillin? Otto had obviously been selling off the Dielemans' paintings for them, but what had he come to strip them of this time? Something about this man made me nervous.

My bicycle and I edged towards the door but I saw Otto lean close to Klaus and lower his voice. 'One of the C-54s hit down too hard,' he murmured. 'Its undercarriage collapsed.'

'Those damn tricycle undercarriages are far too flimsy for the weight they are transporting. Bad design.'

'The aircraft was bundled to one side, out of the way on to the concrete apron to await repair.'

'So who unloaded the crate?'

'That's the trouble.'

'Not our man's team?'

'No.'

'*Scheisse!*'

Klaus seemed to have assumed I'd joined Martha in the kitchen. Whatever was going on here was not my business, and in Berlin you learned to keep your nose out of other people's whispers. I grasped the door handle and silently edged the door open.

'The plane was bringing in sacks of coal,' Otto was saying. 'We like to use the coal transports because they are so filthy that nobody bothers to go rummaging inside them unless he absolutely has to.'

'So the plane lost its place in the unloading line.'

'Yes.'

'And our crate?'

The vertical contours of Otto's bony face lay in shadow but I could make out the downturn of his mouth.

'It's gone,' he said.

Klaus reached out and sent my coffee cup flying to the floor. I slid out the door, taking my Diamant with me.

In the kitchen I hugged Martha goodbye. Her amiable expression had vanished.

'Are you alright, Martha? What's going on with Otto?' I asked, lifting her hand in mine, my thumb softening the ridged veins on the back of it. 'And Klaus?'

'We are well. Even better with the penicillin you've brought for his leg. Thank you, little one. Can I give you something for it?'

'No, no, nothing.'

But she removed a pair of delicate porcelain lovebirds from a shelf and pushed them into my coat pockets. 'If you don't take them, Otto will.'

'Who is this Otto?'

'Not someone you want to know.'

'Is he doing shady deals with Klaus?'

She rolled her eyes. 'My Klaus can be an old fool at times, but I will keep him safe, I promise. Don't worry.' She gave me a sharp look. 'You don't look well.'

I dug up an easy smile for her. 'I'm tired, that's all.'

Neither of us mentioned hunger. It was as much a part of us as the colour of our eyes.

'I heard yesterday,' I said, 'about women in an East Berlin canning factory packing up yet more machine parts into crates to be transported to Russia. Stalin is stripping East Germany naked and will leave us with nothing. Despite the blockade, you are lucky to live in West Berlin, not East Berlin.'

Martha embraced me for a long moment. 'Give my love to your mother.'

'I will.'

I headed back into the hallway where I had propped my bicycle, and to my surprise Otto was standing next to it, hands on hips, inspecting its rusted frame, eyes narrowed. I nodded, gathered my blue Diamant to me and wheeled it out on to the landing. Otto held the apartment door open, bestowing his warm smile on me.

'If ever you want to sell your bicycle, Anna, I'll give you a good price.'

I shot down the stairs.

CHAPTER ELEVEN

◆ ◆ ◆

ANNA

If I cast my mind back, I could remember a time when I'd thought of my life as happy. When there was sunlight inside me. But not now. Certainly not now. I think that maybe happiness is not a noun, but a verb. You have to keep doing it, or you forget how. Just like you need to keep running or juggling or playing chess, if you don't want to forget how.

The closest I came to feeling that sunlight inside me now was when I was seated on my bicycle, but today, as I swung up on to the saddle, I was conscious of Otto looking out of the apartment window high up on the third floor and I didn't want him seeing me blasting off like a cat on fire, so I took it at an easy pace, a gentle second gear. I didn't want the swarthy intruder to give himself credit for making me flee. I wanted him to look at me, then turn away and forget that I exist.

It's safer. Not to exist.

I cycled down Friedenstrasse, past the park which lay naked and bleak on one side, remnants of old baroque buildings on the other, some still miraculously in one piece, and I pedalled slowly. Not just to avoid all the wretched potholes but because I needed time to look about me.

Don't mistake me, I love to cycle fast. The exhilaration of speed thrills me somewhere deep and visceral inside, the wind whipping my face, the drag of air into my lungs, the power in my legs, and the surging sense of freedom. These things send me hurtling off the face of the earth until freedom becomes something that I *am*, not something that I seek. But now freedom was no more than a faint shadow that I dimly remembered.

As I cycled I was inspecting each child I passed. My head swivelled from side to side, scouring each pavement, every pushchair, any corn-haired toddler clutching his mother's hand. I had to fight off the urge to snatch off their woollen hats and cradle their young cheeks in my hands.

I spotted a little boy about the right age, blond and boisterous, and as always he drew me to him the way pale moonlight draws moths. He was slashing a stick at the edges of the park, poking it into the auburn drifts of shrivelled leaves, and I braked quietly, dismounted and wheeled my bicycle along behind the child and his mother. I took a breath to steady my voice.

'*Guten Morgen*,' I said as I drew alongside them on the path.

A milky fog was swirling through the trees and hanging from the bare branches. It was a bad winter for fog. 'A good day for fighting dragons with your stick,' I said, smiling at the child.

He lifted his head and gazed up at me, wide eyes surprised. Blue eyes, yes, but the wrong shape. Cheekbones too Slavic. I nodded at the mother and stepped back on to the road, remounted and rode on as if my hopes hadn't just had their fingers burned.

'How much do you want in exchange for them?' the man asked.

'Ten potatoes, a bunch of carrots and the rye bread.' I inspected the market stall with its scant spread, aware of other hungry Berliners circling his wares. Just the sight of the grubby vegetables made my mouth water. 'And five onions,' I added, pushing my luck.

The stallholder laughed. 'Nice try, mädchen.'

He lacked both front teeth but wore a good thick fox-fur coat against the cold and I couldn't help wondering how many potatoes and onions he'd bartered for it. Too few, I was certain. My mother's mink went for a pittance long ago and I still hated to think of someone else strutting around in it.

'Plus twenty dollars,' I said firmly. I perched the pair of porcelain lovebirds on my palms to tempt him.

'Five potatoes, the carrots, half a loaf and one onion. That's your lot.'

'But look, the birds are beautiful Sèvres porcelain. Worth hundreds of dollars.'

'Hah! Berlin is drowning in the pretty objects you people thought were so important before the war but are now desperate to sell. You can't eat porcelain, can you? You can't fill your belly with diamonds. They're worthless these days.'

The man was right. Of course he was right, but I was in a hurry. I needed to take this food home to Mutti and then race back to the American pick-up point in time for my place in the truck at four o'clock. *Sixteen hundred hours*. I felt excited at the prospect of the night ahead.

'The food plus ten dollars,' I said.

'One dollar.'

'Five dollars.'

He shook his head, but lifted one of the birds from my hand, cradling it. I knew I had him then. The workmanship was exquisite.

'Four dollars,' I said. 'My final price.'

We shook hands.

I set off down the busy Holzmarktstrasse where the mounds of collapsed buildings were covered with teams of *Trümmerfrauen*, the women employed by the state for a pittance to do the backbreaking work of clearing up the rubble. They were crawling like beetles over the broken masonry, passing their buckets of bricks from hand to hand and I was grateful that I was not yet reduced to that. Not yet.

This time I cycled fast, head down, intent on getting home to Prenzlauer Berg, so intent that I didn't at first notice the large black car that slid alongside me. As its sleek bonnet with its three-pointed star came into view on my left, I glanced across at it. It was too close, far too close, a dangerous driver. He didn't even look at me but as he accelerated, the car's rear door swung open while still moving and slammed hard into my front wheel. The Mercedes raced away at high speed.

My bicycle shot into the air, spokes whirring manically. I opened my mouth. I wanted to scream my rage, but before any sound could emerge I crashed down on to the pavement in a tangle of limbs and wheels and I heard something break.

CHAPTER TWELVE

◆ ◆ ◆

ANNA

My eyes wouldn't open.

'*Mein Gott*, Anna,' my mother gasped as she opened our apartment door. 'You look d ...' but the word failed her.

Dead? Is that what she thought? Did I look dead? I was on my feet, so I couldn't be dead, but my mind wouldn't work right. I had leaned my head against the doorframe with relief after dragging myself up the four flights of stairs and jabbed at the wooden door panels with my foot.

'Let me in, Mutti.'

But the words stayed inside my head. My hands were hooked on to the mangled remains of my bicycle and couldn't let go.

'You look terrible, Anna. What happened? You're bleeding.'

She steered me inside and removed the handlebars from my grip. Her small hands were holding my shoulder, fretting at it. I could feel blood running down into my eyes and realised that's why they wouldn't open.

'I'm alright.'

She eased me down into my usual armchair next to the tall tiled stove, but of course there was no coal or wood in it to light a fire and the apartment was freezing cold. I began to shiver, my hands in shredded gloves dancing on my knees. She released her hold on me and I heard her small slippers on the parquet floor heading towards the kitchen. A moment later she was back with a bowl of cold water and started to bathe my face with soft little dabs. I didn't move a muscle because I didn't want her to stop. Right now, despite everything that had gone before, I needed her.

My mother's thin figure hunched over me. She was wearing her coat and her fair hair was hidden inside a rainbow-coloured woollen hat she'd knitted out of scrag ends of wool. It made her look cheerful but she wasn't. My mother was never cheerful. As I sat there, feeling her fingers tentatively picking grit out of the gash at my hairline, for one brief moment I recalled a time when my father was alive and her large blue eyes and long golden hair were full of shine and movement. But not any more, those days were gone. She was forty-three but looked fifty-three. I studied her face, the secretive eyes, the fine lines. Her beautiful mouth. Something churned inside me. She saw me looking and drew back, her face shutting down.

'For Christ's sake, Anna. It was your blasted bicycle, wasn't it?'

'Yes.'

'What happened?'

'A car happened.'

My head was pounding and I wasn't ready yet to think about the metal door that had chosen that exact moment to swing open and slam into my poor bicycle. A random act of violence? Or deliberate? First the explosion, now this.

'I've warned you so many times that bicycles are dangerous machines. Look at the state of your arm.'

My sleeve was hanging in bright scarlet shreds and I could feel pain pumping on every heartbeat. She whisked off my torn coat, then my bloodied jumper and blouse, right down to my petticoat. A deep tear in the flesh of my forearm ran from wrist almost to elbow, the flap of skin had peeled back, but my mother carefully unfurled it, bathed it, pressed it back into place and wrapped a towel around my arm to stem the bleeding.

'God, you're skinny,' she commented.

'So are you,' I managed.

Her expression was one of disgust. 'That's not the point right now. I'll get some bandages but this should be stitched.' Her tone was matter-of-fact now. 'You need a doctor.'

'We have no money for a doctor.'

Her eyes tightened at the corners, taut little crows' feet, but she didn't disagree, and fetched a fresh bowl of water, extra towels and a clean linen sheet which she proceeded to cut into long strips. She knelt in front of me, bathed and dressed all my cuts and grazes, plucking out grit and threads of fabric with a sharp pair of tweezers and sluicing it with a shot of cognac from a silver hip flask – where the hell had that come from? – and I uttered no sound and she made no noises of comfort. That's how it was between us now. As if there was a sheet of glass in the way.

'Tighter, Mutti. Bind it tighter.'

She did as I asked. When she'd finished I said softly, 'Thank you. I am grateful.'

She looked at me then, assessing me. 'It's going to hurt for a while.'

'I'll live.'

'You call this living?' Her voice was abruptly brittle. 'Look around you. We live in the Russian sector. Our once beautiful apartment has been vandalised. The communist housing authority decided in their wisdom that we do not deserve to have so much space to ourselves, so they hacked it into three miserable dwellings. How long do you think it will be before they vandalise our minds and hack them into three as well? It is only going to get worse, Anna. Not better.'

'No, I can help make it better. I have a new job,' I told her.

She jumped to her feet, astonished. 'You mean a proper job? With proper money?'

I let the insult to my lovingly restored bicycles pass. 'Yes.'

'That's excellent news.'

'But I have to start today.'

'What's the job?'

'Working out at Tempelhof.'

She frowned, suddenly uncertain. 'Doing what? There are thousands of men employed there, so …' She left the rest of the sentence unspoken. 'Will you be working in one of the offices?'

'I expect so,' I lied.

'With your arm like that?'

'Yes, I have to turn up today or they'll give the job to someone else.'

'You can't, Anna.'

I didn't have the strength to argue, but pushed myself to my feet and made my way on shaky legs to the bathroom where ice lay in white cobwebs across the inside of the window. My head and my arm throbbed but it was true what I'd said. *I'll live.* So I quickly splashed cold water over my hands and neck, wriggled into clean clothes and combed my short hair. My hair was dark, so the blood didn't show.

I practised a smile in the mirror and by the third time I'd got it almost right. My mother gave me one of her old coats to wear, a touch short but passable, and I knew it was time to go back out on to the streets. I didn't want to. I pulled my woolly hat down low over my forehead to hide the damage and tried not to lean for support against the wall.

'I'll take the U-Bahn,' I said. Berlin's underground train system was running in a half-hearted kind of way. On the trains travelling from the eastern sector into West Berlin, Soviet border guards conducted ruthless checks on passengers for smuggled goods.

'Here, have a swig of this before you go. You need it.' She held out the silver hip flask.

Such a small gesture, this offer of a sip of cognac. But to me it meant more, far more. I accepted the flask and wet my lips. The burn of the cognac was not exactly unpleasant. I passed it back to her and she held out her other hand. On it lay a diamond brooch in the shape of a leaping gazelle which I hadn't seen since the day at the Hauptbahnhof when we watched Papa board the military train in his grey uniform. The diamonds caught the light and flared like a pool of fire on her palm.

'Go buy yourself a doctor,' she ordered.

My fingers closed tight over the brooch and I could feel the stab of its sharp little horns. How many photographs of three-year-old boys could I buy with a gazelle?

CHAPTER THIRTEEN

◆ ◆ ◆

ANNA

'What the fuck happened to you?'
'I had an argument with my bicycle.'
Stefan, the metalworker in a thick felt hat with ear flaps, chuckled and put out a hand to hoist me up into the back of the truck. 'Looks like you lost. Nice bruise.'

I touched my chin. It was sore but that was the least of my worries. My arm was the problem. Fortunately it was my left arm, but I was pretty sure that for hauling sacks of coal I was going to need both.

'You okay?' asked Walther, his moustached friend. It turned out he was the eldest of ten brothers and sisters, so he was well accustomed to offering comfort.

'I'm fine, thanks.'

I squeezed in between two middle-aged women, alongside the sixteen men already in the truck. When I'd arrived, the khaki Chevrolet truck had been idling in the courtyard and the sight of the big white American star on its door, as well as the bulky form of Stefan standing in the rear, came as a relief. All I had to do now was do the job, arm or no arm.

We juddered into motion, rolled out on to Lindenstrasse and set off south in the direction of the airport. The rear canvas flap of the truck was raised and I watched the light begin to drain from the sky during the eight-kilometre journey. The fog was lifting at last, revealing streaks of scarlet and indigo hovering on the horizon. They gave me a sense of hope, these rainbow colours. Except my Noah was piloting a C-54 Skymaster instead of an ark.

◆ ◆ ◆

Tempelhof.

Weltflughafen. World Airport. That's what it was called.

An impressive name for one of the great wonders of the modern world. This is what Hitler had intended his grand airport to be, a wonder, designed by Ernst Sagebiel to resemble an eagle in flight with semi-circular hangars forming the bird's spread wings. Its vast five-storey blocks were faced with honey-toned limestone that in the summer caught the sun as if by right. It was declared to be the largest roofed building on the planet, extending in an elegant sweep to well over a kilometre from end to end.

I climbed out of the Chevy truck with my band of Berliners and stood in front of the airport building, awestruck. The scale was gigantic. It was a throwback to the time of Roman arenas, a testament to the glory of Monumentalism. Despite the desperate state of our country now and the unforgivable horrors that had gone before, it was impossible, totally impossible, to stand there and not feel a sense of German pride. It was beautiful.

But the noise. *Mein Gott*, the noise of the engines. How did they stand it? It made my ears ache. Relentlessly, aircraft after aircraft roared along the runway, churning the chill air. Runway lights spiked a path through the gloom for the Douglas Skymasters, Skytrains and Avro Yorks that poured out of the sky like locusts, a never-ending stream of them, but instead of stripping food, they were bringing what the Americans called *vittles* to West Berlin. Thousands and thousands of tons of it, enough to keep 2 million people from starving day after day, month after month, a plane landing or taking off every thirty seconds. Operation Vittles, the Berlin Airlift in action.

Why did they do it, these brave American and British fliers? What made their governments take such a risk and spend so many millions of dollars to save a country that had been their enemy only three short years ago? Freedom. That was why. To keep West Berlin free. Such a small word – *free* – a word that people only truly value when they have lost it.

An American soldier with a large bullet head under his USAF cap and a military swagger of command marched up to our group standing on the great forecourt in the twilight, gave us a nod of welcome and barked, 'Come on, let's put you lot to work.'

Fast, efficient and organised.

Welcome to the world of Tempelhof.

CHAPTER FOURTEEN

* * *

INGRID

T he street was dark and narrow as a mine shaft, no lamps working, no moon to light the way. Ingrid's hurrying footsteps were
soundless because she'd wrapped cloths around her shoes. She used
her torch sparingly to save the battery on the long cold trudge back
home to Blumenthalstrasse. It was up in the British sector, and the
U-Bahn subway had ceased running for the day, but she had to make
it home ahead of the evening curfew. Military patrols cruised the
streets to enforce it, but each time she heard the rattling approach of
a jeep's engine she shut off her torch and stepped into a doorway.
Behind a wall. Under an overhang. Any place where it was safer.

'Do you want me to call a car to drive you home?' Comrade
Kuznetsov had asked her politely at the apartment.

'No.'

Definitely no.

Their conversation had been strictly business, nothing more, and
at the end they'd shaken hands on a deal, sealed with a glass of
schnapps this time. She had hoisted her tool bag and stuffed into her
pocket the envelope he'd handed her. When she finally reached
home, her cheeks were stiff with cold and she was relieved to bundle
herself into the tiny apartment she shared with Otto. The kerosene
lamp was burning, fouling the air, and her husband was seated in its
yellow glow at the kitchen table, knife in hand, skinning a squirrel on
a sheet of newspaper. His dark head lifted, the curved blade pausing
its work, and he smiled a welcome that melted the ice within her. His
smile always warmed her deep inside where it mattered. He wasn't a

handsome man, too narrow in the face, but she loved the way his smile always lit up a room for her. It had always been that way.

'Been out on the town, have you?' Otto laughed, tapping the face of his wristwatch, a Smiths Mk VII that he had acquired from a British RAF navigator. He was good at acquiring things.

'I've been painting the town gold,' she said.

'Gold?'

She yanked off her gloves and displayed the smears of gold paint on her fingers. 'Literally,' she grinned at him. 'For Kuznetsov.'

Ingrid pulled the envelope from her pocket and tossed it on the table beside the squirrel. It landed with an impressive thud.

'What's this?'

'Take a look,' she urged.

Her husband wiped his hands on a blood-stained cloth and flicked open the envelope. It was stuffed with money. Not filthy old worthless Reichsmarks either, these were brand new Deutschmarks with the 'B' for Berlin stamped on them, printed in America, the ink scarcely dry.

His jaw dropped and he gazed up at her in astonishment. 'I'm impressed.'

She laughed, satisfied, and felt a crazy rush of excitement, alongside the thread of fear that had wound itself tight around her gut ever since Kuznetsov's blue eyes had first searched hers.

'How do I know I can trust you?' he'd asked.

More to the point, how did she know she could trust him? It was like the high-wire act all over again. That moment when you take your first step. Feeling for its mood. Finding its weakness. She moved close to Otto now, threw off his cloth cap and buried her hands in his magnificent black gypsy hair.

'Leave the squirrel, Otto.'

He grinned up at her and dropped the knife. It gave her a thrill to see in his dark luminous eyes how much he still desired her. Her, a mousy little nobody whom most men wouldn't look at twice. He wanted her.

'Tell me exactly how you earned that money.' Otto rose to his feet and pulled her towards him. 'Kuznetsov is a handsome bastard, even though he is a Russki.'

She pressed the length of her body hard against his, both arms curling around her husband's wiry neck and her lips seeking out the soft smoky taste of his mouth. Danger always did this to her. Made her bold. Made her greedy. It made her skin throb and her groin itch till she was desperate for frenzied sex with Otto, whom she'd adored since she was six and first saw him flying through the air on a trapeze. He'd been only eight years old and already had nerves of steel.

'I painted his apartment, that's all.'

'Did he offer you more work?'

'Yes.'

'Another apartment to paint?'

'Yes,' she lied.

She sank her teeth into his lip. 'Couldn't you get your lazy hands on anything better for dinner than a miserable squirrel?'

His fingers were unbuttoning her coat and sliding inside her overalls. 'Fuck, you're a scrawny little *Miststück* these days, aren't you?'

'So find me a chicken to eat.'

But their words were meaningless now, just sounds escaping between their hot breath, noises that accompanied the tearing off of overalls and sweater and shirt, the unbuckling of belts, and the forcing of skin against skin.

'Surprise me,' she whispered and, standing on tiptoe, she swept one knee up over his hip, gripping him to her.

'I got something for you today,' he said, breathing hard.

'What?'

Their kisses attached themselves to tongues and teeth, the taste of each other tearing moans from them, but Otto was suddenly holding something in his fist and streaks of light glinted between his fingers. She let her tongue trail over his knuckles. They smelled of blood and squirrel fur.

'What?'

Otto opened his fingers, stretching them out one by one, and when the object in his hand was fully revealed, all she could say was, 'Shit!'

'Pretty?' he asked.

'Very pretty.'

It was a triple-strand pearl necklace. Milky perfection. Shimmering with fiery flares that came and went as Otto rolled them between his fingers, the lamplight turning liquid as it flowed over them. But Ingrid felt a rush of panic and couldn't bear to touch them.

'No, Otto, damn you, when will you listen to me? One day you'll go too far with your "acquisitions". The authorities will catch you, lock you up and throw away the key. You'll rot in hell.'

'I didn't steal them, Ingrid, if that's what you think. I'm doing a deal with a seriously rich *Mensch*. Honestly. All above board, my little —'

'Yeah.' She tore her skin free from his. 'Like Stalin's *Arschloch* is above board.'

She remembered then. A sudden stab of sorrow twisted inside her and she bent to scoop up her khaki overalls abandoned on the floor. From the pocket she extracted the pearl cross she had 'acquired' yesterday and held it out on her palm.

'Otto, I found a dead body.'

CHAPTER FIFTEEN

◆ ◆ ◆

TIMUR VORONIN

The temperature had dropped below zero and the east wind on Prenzlauer Allee could rip the skin right off your face. Major Timur Voronin raised the collar of his greatcoat. The scars on his neck were a pain in the arse when they froze, so he'd learned to guard them when the wind blasted all the way from his home city of Omsk, located in south-west Siberia. Now there was a city that knew what cold was.

Here in Berlin, Russian soldiers were growing soft; he'd noticed that since he'd returned. They had it too easy. They chose to forget what the Red Army had been through to get here, and now they made the most of the German wine and the German *Fräuleins* and the thankless hours of standing around in the streets doing nothing except trying to look like victors with second-rate rifles slung on their shoulders. That was no bad thing though. It made his path simpler. Their senses were dulled, their eyes grew lazy. He smiled to himself.

The city was shrouded in darkness. It was a disgrace that the electricity was strictly rationed, but he'd seen in person why it was so. Everything was being looted and transported back to Russia. He was overseeing the transport trains himself, packing them full of machinery and electric cabling and cooking stoves and dismantled cranes and silver candlesticks and tin baths. The list was never ending. Looting everything. To the victor the spoils.

He moved easily through the blackness, seeing with the cat's eyes that had learned as a boy to cross the darkest of Siberian forests at night. This was child's play. The street had barely changed since he'd last seen it in 1945, except maybe some of the rubble cleared away.

Certainly none of the holes that peppered the road surface had been repaired.

He wondered if her bicycle still suffered with punctures.

She'd sworn at him mightily and cursed the whole of the Red Army for destroying her road. As if she owned it. He smiled again and kept moving, tight against the wall, but nothing shifted among the shadows in the street. Fifty metres ahead lay her apartment building, five storeys of ornate stonework and large ornamented doors. It had been a smart street with fine turn-of-the-century houses that had amazed him when he first saw it. Such housing for ordinary people. It had baffled him. And angered him. These German people packed so many things into their houses, it made no sense. Why did they want so much? In Russia you had what you needed and sometimes not even that.

She had told him he must think again.

There was no light in her window, but there was no light in any window, because kerosene was rationed and not to be wasted. He stepped into a doorway, a relief to be out of the wind, rubbed blood back into his neck and denied himself a cigarette. He waited, watched and froze.

After two hours of nothing but an occasional rat, he crossed the road. Using a tool from his pocket he jemmied open the lock to the main door of the building and stepped silently inside. It smelled different from how he remembered; the scent of luxury that used to pervade the very fabric of the house had gone. He took the wide steps that twisted up to the fourth floor at speed. The wrought-iron banister, yes, he remembered that too, the feel of its scrollwork under his palm. No apartment doors opened to challenge his presence, though he heard a raucous quarrel taking place behind one of them.

On the fourth floor he stopped, listened and felt his breathing accelerate. He lifted his hand, removed his leather glove and knocked on the door.

CHAPTER SIXTEEN

◆ ◆ ◆

ANNA

'Come on, *schnell, schnell*. Make it snappy, you lovely *Fräuleins*,' the flying officer chivvied. 'No time to waste. I need to get this old gooney bird back up in the sky.'

Gooney bird. I smiled. That's what the American pilots called this kind of transport plane, a term of affection for all its hard work. I liked these brave men for showing such affection. In reality it was a twin-engine Douglas C-47 Skytrain, the backbone of much of the Berlin Airlift, and right now this one had just had three and a half tons of coal and construction tools stripped out of its belly at breakneck speed on the floodlit airport apron. The pressure to work flat-out was unremitting and created a constant tension that crackled throughout the airbase. It was freezing cold. The night air inside the plane hung thick with coal dust, layers of black gold that shimmered in the lamplight and caught in my throat.

I felt as though I was standing inside an old wheezing whale whose khaki-green ribs arched around me, smelling strange, and I swivelled my broom even faster down the curved walls, along the trail of wires and over the reinforced floor-platform. I swept the coal dust into a mound on the floor where my companion was already crouched and waiting to scoop it up into a sack. Not a gram of precious coal was wasted in this operation.

My companion inside the belly of this old whale was Magdalene. She was a woman a couple of years older than myself, who liked to roll her eyes every time anyone ordered her to speed up, which was often, despite the fact it had no discernible effect on her steady rhythmic movements. She was as cumbersome and as broad as a Rhenish carthorse, with the same dense chestnut hair and huge hands and feet. Her face was shiny with sweat as she hefted her shovel. Coal leaking from the sacks was even worse than salt at corroding the planes and their cables, but Magdalene insisted on taking her time and scowled at any of the American pilots who dared to hurry her. Yet she smiled at me each time she slid big fist-fuls of coal dust into my coat pockets when heads were turned.

'We're done,' I yelled to the pilot.

'Okay, off you go. Hop to it.'

'I've got it,' I said. I hoisted the sack of coal dust on to my shoulder, making sure to use my undamaged arm.

I'd been lucky. A sergeant had taken one look at my physique, sighed and assigned me to sweeping duties inside the planes, instead of hauling sacks. 'Work hell for leather,' he ordered. Whatever that meant. 'We have no more than minutes to turn the plane around or it'll miss its flight slot.'

I nodded. '*Schnell*,' I'd assured him. But that was before I'd been paired with Magdalene.

I nipped down the steps positioned just behind the wing and Mag-dalene followed at her own leisurely pace. Outside it was even colder. Once on the concrete apron we stepped into a tumultuous world teeming with activity, saturated with sound and urgency. Male voices everywhere. Vital orders shouted. Men hurrying. Noises reverberat-ing in the darkness outside the reach of the floodlights. The whine of crates being winched. The low grind of truck engines ferrying be-tween planes and warehouses, and always there was the great roar of the ever-present aircraft and the unmistakable odour of aviation fuel.

They swooped down on to runways, these angels of mercy, mira-cles of metal and 100-octane fuel. Then before you could blink they were racing to claw a path up into the freezing night sky again, lights flashing, propellers slicing through the last shreds of fog. Pilots fighting the clock and exhaustion. I watched one of the gooney birds haul itself up into the endless blackness and I wondered if the young captain was gripping the controls with blind terror at what the Soviets might have waiting for him up there. The blackness swal-lowed him and he was gone.

◆ ◆ ◆

Magdalene and I trudged over to a huge metal container and emptied our sack of coal dust and small stray black chunks into it, along with dozens of other workers doing the same. In the dank night, mist soaked our hair and clung to our skin so that we all looked dangerous, with black smears like warpaint across our faces. Many were raw-boned 'displaced persons' from the post-war refugee camps whom Magdalene treated with even less respect than she did the Americans.

'They come from all over Europe and are taking the bread from our mouths and stealing jobs from our people,' she insisted.

'As long as they buy bicycles, I don't mind.'

'Bicycles?'

'Yes.'

'Was that your job before this?'

'Yes, I loved it.'

She laughed, a great snort of sound. 'I should have guessed. You're so thin and wiry and you move so fast. Just like a bicycle. I can hear the wheels turning inside your head all the time, everything well oiled.'

Really? Was that how she saw me?

She flattened the sack and folded it neatly before placing it on the tangled heap where everyone else was tossing theirs.

'Do you ever consider,' she asked, 'how much thought has gone into the making of each one of these sacks?'

'No,' I said, surprised. 'I can't say I do.' I was hungry now and my arm was sore.

'The Americans have worked their arses off to create exactly the right kind of burlap, one that is lightweight – because weight is everything in these planes – but woven tightly enough to cut down the loss of coal through the material.' She ran her fingers fondly over one of the filthy sacks. 'It has to be durable too. To be used over and over again.'

'You seem to like sacks more than you like Americans.'

'My father was a miller. I grew up with sacks. I used to knot them into dolls and sleep with them in my arms.' She slid her eyes across at me. 'Sacks are useful too. You can hide things in them.'

That came as a jolt. 'What kind of things?'

She turned away and started to lumber off towards the great curved terminal building lit up against the darkness of the night sky. Abruptly she clapped her large hands together. 'Come, Anna. Time to eat.'

We didn't speak, didn't waste words. We sat at a long metal table, four of us. Four women. We gazed at our plates, our hands tucked between our knees to stop us snatching up the food with our fingers like feral children.

'Dig in,' Magdalene grinned. 'What are you waiting for?'

'To make sure I'm not dreaming,' I said, inhaling the aroma of hot food as if it were the finest perfume from Paris.

We dug in. All around us in the great marble hall that had been put to use as a canteen, knives and forks were clattering. Men in uniform were taking their breaks, their voices heavy with fatigue, but I barely heard them because the taste of meat in my mouth became all that I was. When faced with this plate of US Army beef stew, this thick shiny gelatinous gravy that barely moved and the small iceberg of mashed potato floating within it, my desire for the food was so overwhelming, so all consuming, it swept away everything else, even my hot shame at filling my stomach while others starved.

'What are you doing out here among these aeroplanes,' Magdalene asked between mouthfuls, 'if you prefer working with bicycles?'

She was wiping up the last traces of her meal with a thick slice of white bread and sighed with intense pleasure each time she sank her horse-size teeth into it. *White* bread. Made with *white* unadulterated flour.

'I need the money,' I said.

'Don't we all,' commented the woman in her mid-forties who was seated opposite Magdalene.

Her name was Hilda. She wore her dark brown hair tucked under a velvet turban that had seen better days and she had features as hard and sharp as flint. Her movements were quick and precise and she was exactly the woman I'd have chosen if I needed someone to work twelve-hour shifts.

'Especially Ingeborg,' Magdalene added. 'Her apartment roof collapsed on her last week.'

I turned my attention to the fourth woman in our little group. Ingeborg was sitting opposite me, very still and saying little. She was around thirty, a shadow woman, clad in grey from head to toe. She kept her hands immobile in her lap when not eating and there was a gentleness to her face that struck me as rare these days. Most of the time her eyes were downcast, but when she did look up, her pearl-grey eyes shone as though an inner light burned behind them.

'I'm sorry,' I said softly.

She shrugged her grey shoulders and smiled at me. 'Don't look so concerned. God will provide. *Consider the ravens: for they neither sow nor reap; which neither have storehouse nor barn, and yet God feedeth them: how much more are ye better than the fowls!*'

Of course. I recognised that stillness. The downcast modesty. The greyness. And that shining light of conviction. I was educated at a convent school and all the novice nuns moved like shadows. I wondered why she had renounced her calling and I slid my undamaged hand across the table towards her.

'So where are you living now?' I asked.

'In a ruined church.' She said it with pleasure.

'It must be cold.'

'I come here to get warm. Hard labour is good for me.' She tilted her head wrapped in a grey scarf and fixed her gentle gaze on me. 'And you?' She lifted one hand and laid it light as a bird's wing on mine. 'What is it you seek here?'

I didn't see it coming. No warning. The sudden welling up of need within me, a squeezing, wrenching, clasping need that nearly choked me. How had she done that with just a touch of her hand?

'A child,' I said. 'I seek a child.'

All three women edged closer. I could feel their breath, smelling of onions and gravy, but I could also feel their concern, and the warmth of it was like a blowtorch on my steel barrier. It opened a path for the pain to eat into me all over again.

'Your own child?' Ingeborg murmured.

I hesitated. 'He was mine. Briefly. Then he was taken.'

'What happened?' Hilda asked, always direct and to the point.

But I had said too much. I lifted my hand, not the one still nestled under Ingeborg's, but the one throbbing on my knee. I pressed it over my mouth to lock the words inside. Magdalene uttered a moan. Hilda gave a gasp. Ingeborg whispered a soft Latin prayer. They were staring at my hand and I didn't understand why, until I tasted the coppery tang of blood on my lips.

I snatched the offending hand out of sight.

'*Mein Gott*, Anna, what have you done to your hand?' Magdalene jumped in at full volume.

'Hush,' I muttered. 'It's nothing. I came off my bicycle, that's all.'

'It's not nothing,' Hilda pointed out, this time with the sense to keep her voice low. 'You can't work like that.'

'I need this job.'

'Anna,' Ingeborg continued to curl her hand around mine on the table, 'tell me about the child.'

To her the blood was a fleeting distraction, nothing important. She possessed that kind of focus, she knew how to sweep away the smoke and mirrors to find the nugget of truth that lay behind them, but she was too late this time. I had my words back under lock and key.

'Perhaps you can help me,' I said. 'I've visited all the official orphanages in the east and west of the city, but had no success. He's not there. I'm trying to hunt out the unofficial ones now. You know the ones, where someone lets a bunch of kids live in their basement or sets up a soup kitchen for them. Somebody who offers them an occasional bed for the night now that it's winter.'

She'd know of somewhere or someone. I was certain she would.

'I know a woman. She used to be a headmistress,' she said. 'She has set up a dormitory in her basement and a makeshift school in her living room for children who live on the streets. Sometimes I help with the teaching.' She smiled shyly. 'My Latin and mathematics are good.'

'Latin and mathematics. For a three-year-old?'

A faint blush rose from her neck. 'Of course not. But the pupils sometimes have little brothers or sisters in tow, so maybe ...' Her voice trailed away.

'Maybe.'

'It's up in the British sector. I could take you there if you wish.'

'Yes, I'll try any chance of finding him. Thank you.'

'What's his name?'

I felt a prickle of pleasure as my lips formed his name. 'It's Felix. Felix Wolff. It means happy or fortunate.'

'The boy doesn't sound very fortunate to me, if he was taken away from his mother,' Hilda murmured.

'He probably has a different name now anyway,' I pointed out. But she was right and I hated that she was right.

I stood up abruptly. 'Time to get back to work.'

'What about your arm?'

'My arm is fine.'

We made our way out of the canteen. I was eager now to get the night over, but just before we reached the door that led outside to the runways, Magdalene whisked out a large white handkerchief. She started to bind it round my left wrist to soak up the blood.

'This will keep you going,' she said.

But the square of cotton failed miserably to stop the steady drip-drip-drip on to the marble flooring and just then, at the worst possible moment, the door swung open and a figure strode in.

'Well now, if it isn't Fräulein Wolff, the tank builder.'

I looked up. Before me in full flying gear stood Captain Noah Maynard, the American pilot from the recruitment centre, his dark hair scrubbed by the wind, USAF goggles dangling from one hand. The intense energy coming off him could have heated my apartment for a month. He took one sharp glance at the bruise on my chin and at what looked like scarlet coins scattered along the corridor and around my feet, then focused on my hand. He frowned.

'Get back to work,' he said in German to my companions. 'Fräulein Wolff, follow me.'

◆ ◆ ◆

I entered the infirmary and I finally understood. How poor we were. Dirt poor. To Americans we must look like trash from the gutter. In the Tempelhof infirmary I stepped into a world of plenty far beyond my expectations. I was dazzled by so much shiny metal equipment, so many machines, trays of apparatus and display cases of medical supplies. It put the state of our German hospitals to shame.

With military efficiency my arm was swabbed, stitched and dressed, all with attentive smiles. Before I knew it I was walking back down the corridor, my arm in a sling, pumped through with painkillers and Captain Maynard loping alongside me. Here, within sight and sound of his beloved aircraft, he was a different man, more at ease. This was where he felt at home, out here among his Skymasters, not recruiting needy Germans on the streets of Berlin.

'You don't need to chaperone me,' I said with a smile. 'Don't you have a plane to fly?'

'I'm on a break while the guys on the ground fix an oil leak.' His dark eyes inspected me, his flying jacket slung over his shoulder. 'Feeling better?'

'Much better. Thank you for helping me.'

'You're welcome. But you shouldn't be working with that arm, you know. You should rest it. Get yourself off home.'

'I'm fine now, good as new.' I pulled my bandaged arm out of the sling and waved it about to demonstrate. 'See?' I'd have tucked the cotton sling into one of my pockets but they were packed full of coal dust, so I left it hanging around my neck.

He gave me a sceptical look.

'I mean it, you know, Captain.'

'Mean what?'

'That I am grateful. Thank you. For your help.'

He laughed self-consciously. 'We're allies now, America and Germany. Look at us all.' We were passing a long low window and he swept an arm out towards the night's activity, the frantic unloading of cargo, the stacking and hoisting and hauling. The high-powered lights carved gaping holes in the darkness, outlining the figures hard at their labour. 'Germans and Americans working together, shoulder to shoulder. We're all trying to help each other.'

'You call it the airlift,' I said. 'We call it the *Luftbrücke* in German – the air bridge. I like our name better. A bridge between us, connecting our people with yours.'

He smiled. I could see he liked that thought.

'You speak excellent German,' I pointed out.

He nodded, but didn't explain.

'Do you know,' he said instead, 'that when the Soviet Red Army entered Berlin, before the US Army had reached the city, the German commander of this Tempelhof airbase received orders from his superior to blow up this magnificent structure, so that it wouldn't fall into Russian hands? But he loved it too much and he refused. Instead he committed suicide.'

'No, I didn't know that.'

'I respect the man. He understood the importance of keeping safe for future generations the great monuments to German achievement.'

'They used to assemble Stuka dive-bombers and Focke-Wulf fighter planes in the main hall here during the war.'

To my astonishment he laughed. 'I've heard that before. Wonderfully resourceful.'

This man baffled me. I wasn't sure whether or not he was making fun of us Germans. American humour, it seemed, was as foreign as their big showy cars and their big healthy teeth.

'I've heard,' I said without any show of annoyance, 'that when your American troops started bringing in your aircraft to this airport, you removed the spire of one of our local churches because it was in your way.' I stopped walking. We had reached the exit. I smiled up at him. 'Wonderfully resourceful.'

I pushed the door open with my shoulder and walked into the night.

I stepped out into a feathery drizzle just as a group of about ten US Army soldiers sprinted past me in formation, boots loud on the tarmac. I had no idea why they were running. Some emergency further down? A truck tipped over? A load broken loose?

It didn't matter.

The point was, I was suddenly among them, surrounded, jostled, bumped. Conscious of the stale sweat on their uniforms, the heavy mustiness of their damp coats. The smell of hair oil under their garrison caps. I was smothered by their maleness and in that brief moment of confusion I lost who I was.

I stood absolutely still and closed my eyes.

And in an instant, in a violent flicker of time, I am there. Back in the filthy stinking alleyway piled high with rubble and broken bricks. A light drizzle is falling on my face and I am fighting for my life.

'Blyad,' he hisses over and over in my ear. 'Blyad. Blyad.'

Whore.

'Ty grebanaya shlyukha.'

You fucking slut.

It is broad daylight. I am no more than five metres away from a busy street where people are going about their lives, seeking out bread and raising umbrellas. I can hear the metal-clad wheels of a cart rumbling down the road. A mother scolding her child. The wash of what passes for normality in our devastated city continues as if my existence is immaterial to its needs.

My screams are silenced. Jammed. Raw in my throat. A hand clamps hard over my mouth, crushing my jaw till I fear it will break, and the stench, dear God, the stench of his fingers is vile ... how many other women have they been inside? His harsh voice shouts words at me that I don't understand.

Rage grows savage within me. Fear hammers on my heart and I fight to rip out my attacker's eyes. I lash out with my feet but his leg pins them to the ground with ease and his strength appals me. Terrifies me. I feel myself descending down a deep dark hole of shame. For one fleeting second my arm manages to break loose – even now I feel how that small triumph shot a bolt of adrenaline charging through me – and my fingers curl around a jagged chunk of masonry.

◆ ◆ ◆

'Fräulein Wolff?'

A hand seized my wrist, yanking me from under the black landslide of images in my head, and I opened my eyes. The American pilot stood before me in the shifting shadows outside the Tempelhof terminal building, an expression of concern on his face.

'Are you alright?'

I jerked away. The soldiers had gone. I stared down the long line of Douglas Skytrains that looked like a roost of huge metal swallows with their pointed wingtips. I drew in a deep breath and turned back to my rescuer with a smile of sorts.

'You Americans have so much of everything,' I said. I shouldn't have said it, but I did. 'Absolutely everything. An abundance of the requirements for life. Including kindness. Thank you for your kindness tonight, Captain Maynard, but I'm alright now. I must get back to work or I'll lose my job.'

He didn't abandon me or walk away.

'It's true,' he admitted. 'We have many things, Fräulein Wolff, many advantages, but not everything. We still have so much to learn. We do not have a wealth of history behind us like you. Not a Mozart or a Beethoven. Not centuries of culture. These things shape who you are and ...'

'And look where these things have got us,' I said bitterly. 'Overrun by a violent Red Army in one half of our city and begging for work hauling filthy sacks for victorious American overlords in the other.'

We stood frozen in stillness, eyes locked on each other. What I'd said was unforgivable. Not so much the words, but the way I'd said them. I hung my head.

'I'm sorry,' I said softly.

I expected the pilot to stalk off through the spitting rain, determined to think twice before offering a helping hand to a thankless German *Fräulein* again.

'Shame and guilt do not make easy bedfellows for a nation,' he said bluntly. 'I understand that. Whatever it was that upset you just now, I hope I was not the cause.'

I shook my head, all out of words. We started to move quickly in the direction of the planes, the raindrops looking like an ice storm in the grip of the powerful lights, when a great howling scream gusted towards us. We broke into a run.

A hoist on the back of one of the trucks had broken loose from its moorings as it was swinging its load from one of the aircraft across to a flatbed truck. The result was a tangled mess that had come crashing down on to the wet ground. In the darkness I could make out twisted steel chains, an iron hook, great chunks of metal that might have been engine parts, and what looked like an arm. Chills shuddered through me, and when the crowd of men finally shifted the load off the figure lying under it, I saw the mangled form of a woman I could only just recognise. It was Hilda.

CHAPTER SEVENTEEN

◆ ◆ ◆

ANNA

M Y body ached. My icy feet seemed to belong to someone else as
I entered Prenzlauer Allee. It was dark and freezing cold, and at
the checkpoint they'd just waved me through with an impatient nod. I
walked quickly, but still it took me two hours in the dark and in the rain
at the end of a twelve-hour shift. Dawn was not even a glimmer on the
horizon and the U-Bahn not yet up and running, but the darkness gave
my thoughts somewhere to hide.

First Herr Schmidt's operative, the one working on my case. *Missing*. Then an explosion and a car sends me crashing off my bicycle.
Now Hilda. *Dead*. Had they been innocent accidents? Coincidences?
Maybe so.

Maybe not.

Was I being paranoid? Seeing things that were not there? Was I? I
stared out into the first flakes of snow, spiralling into each other as
recklessly as my thoughts. *Am I?* Poor Hilda, I barely knew her, not
even her last name. Hilda Braun, apparently. Unmarried and a teacher
in Hamlin before the war. There was no connection between us, no
link, except we ate one meal together in the canteen, that's all. So
where did that lead me? To the obvious conclusion that any connection
between these four events had to be purely fanciful.

And yet. Was someone targeting me?

'Got anything for me, mädchen?'

My pulse jumped. The bundle of rags that was tucked into the wide
doorway of my apartment building rose from the ground. Through the
snow-streaked darkness I could make out the familiar dirty-blond head
of a young boy and the gleam of a pair of permanently angry eyes.

'Yvo! You scared me.'

He didn't care. Why should he? He was too busy scavenging a life among the ruins to care. He claimed to be nine years old, but who knows? These days lies were common currency, we all used them.

'Any news?' I asked quickly.

In response the boy thrust out an upturned hand. I placed on it the slice of white bread that I'd hidden in my skirt pocket in the Yanks' canteen. It vanished whole into Yvo's mouth. I waited. A sour odour seeped from his ragged clothes and I unlocked the door to my building.

'Do you want to come in for a wash if we have any water?'

Yvo backed off a step, still chewing hard. It was as though I'd suggested a night indoors to a tundra wolf. That's what they were, these waifs. *Wolfskinder*. Wolf children. They ran in packs, defending each other, feeding their weakest, stealing whatever they could, huddling together at night in small filthy dens, warring for territory, and always hungry. I pictured my Felix among them. This Yvo was a pack leader. He would puff his puny chest out at me and demand more, always more. More money, more food, more anything. However much I gave him, it was never enough, but I understood. We all wanted more.

'Tell me what's new,' I said.

'There are two of them.'

'What ages?'

'A girl. She says she's eleven but she's lying.'

'A girl is no good to me.'

'There's a boy with her. Four years old, the girl says. She pretends he's her brother but she's a fucking liar and he don't look four to me.' He sniffed loudly and wiped his nose on his sleeve. 'She's as dark as a Jew and the boy's got eyes blue as a hedge sparrow's egg.'

Hope slipped its fingers into my hand.

'Where are they now?' I asked.

'In one of my homes. Safe.'

Homes? His use of the word wrenched something loose in me. They were primitive lairs hollowed out among the ruins and he had them scattered throughout the Friedrichshain district, shifting his wolfpack from one to another to avoid predators. It was only his acute survival instinct that kept them safe.

'I'll come,' I said.

'Tomorrow.'

'Why not today?'

'They have to learn to trust me first. The Russkies have been shooting at them for sport, so they're jumpy.'

'Where shall I meet you?'

'Same as last time.'

'Tomorrow morning.' There was little point pinning him down to a time because a clock had no meaning for him. 'I'll bring something.'

'Make it something good.'

I snatched off my woollen hat and stuck it on his dirty head because his own cap had been stolen by a member of a rival gang the previous week. Foolishly I wanted to wrap my arms around his stubborn skinny frame but I knew he'd floor me if I tried it. We both gazed up the unlit street at the swirling flakes and I felt needle-sharp specks of ice chiselling at my cheeks. The silence was too loud. I couldn't hear any planes.

'Fuck the snow,' he muttered fiercely, 'it shows every footprint.'

He stepped out into it. I blinked my eyes against a sudden squall and he was gone, swallowed by the darkness.

An orange?

Impossible. Yet there it sat. On the tiled floor at the top of the stairs, trapped in the beam of my torch as I approached the door to my apartment. As if anyone in this starving city would possess an orange, let alone drop one.

No. It had been placed there.

Impossibly orange. Glowing in the darkness. Gleaming. Gorgeous.

The heady scent of it overwhelmed my senses. I craved this impossible orange, scooped it up, cradled it on my palms, stripping off my gloves so that I could touch its thick reptilian skin and feel for the fingerprints of the person who had placed this gift at my feet. There was only one person in the world who would do such a thing.

I unlocked the door and crept to my bed, dropping my mother's coat on the floor, too bone weary to undress. Under the chill bedcovers I curled myself around my orange, I held it against my cheek and pressed it to my lips. I whispered a name.

'What's wrong?' I demanded, panicked.

It was a warm summer evening back in 1945 and the last rays of sun were gilding the windowpane. The intoxicating fragrance of the blossom of the city's abundant linden trees scented the air and I had baked a rabbit pie for Timur, the smell of its thick gravy making me ravenous.

Ravenous for him.

Timur arrived at our apartment as punctually as usual, but he looked anguished. I could see pain pulsing behind his eyes and dread slid into my veins.

'What is it, Timur?'

He stood oddly still, a stiffness in his limbs where there was usually such an easy flow of energy and I was terrified that he'd been wounded by some vengeful Berliner eaten up by hate. It was my constant fear for him. A knife in his back. A bullet in his arm. A blow to his head. I looked for blood. Saw none. I breathed.

'Look, Anna, look what I've brought you.'

He placed a large bulging sack in front of me, untied the string around its neck and I could see tins and tins of food, jars of sauerkraut and bags full of flour, potatoes and cabbage. It must have cost him his month's pay. A pot of caviar lay on top and two bottles of vodka.

'The caviar and vodka are for your mother,' he said. His voice was so flat it broke something in me.

'Timur, what's …?'

Realisation hit me then. I backed away from the sack as if it contained poison or could burst into flames and turn the room into an inferno.

'No,' I insisted. 'No, no,' and then again, 'No, Timur. Take it away. Take it all away, I don't want it.'

Instead I stepped around the sack, careful not to let my skirt brush against it, till I was close to Timur and I laid my face against his. I could feel the sinews of his cheeks as tense as wire under his skin and the dull rhythmic thudding of his heart.

'Listen to me, Timur. No, I don't want your sack of food.' I heard my voice rising but I couldn't make it stop. 'I know what it means.' I wrapped my arms around him and gripped his strong beautiful body tight against mine. 'I want you. Don't leave.'

Gently he shook his head, but he couldn't bring himself to say the words that we both knew were coming. We stood that way a long while, clasped together, breathing too fast, limbs entwined, and I willed time to stop and the world to cease turning.

I put my lips to his ear and whispered, 'I hate Stalin. I hate the fact that you belong to him.'

Very softly, so softly it was barely more than a sigh, too low for any hidden microphone, he murmured, 'So do I, my love, and all he stands for.'

I was greedy for him. His hands cradled my face and I cried out his name. We made love one last desperate time, skin craving skin and his heart hammering itself into the depths of mine, and then he was gone. Transferred to Warsaw. 'I'll write every day,' he promised. I vowed the same. 'I'll come back,' he swore.

I couldn't drag my eyes from his face.

I stood barefoot in the street watching him walk away, storing up the beauty of him, the smooth swing of his hips and the long stride of each leg. I hoarded somewhere secret within myself the bold strength of his back and of his fine mind, and the unexpected vulnerability of the valleys at the back of his naked neck under his officer's cap. When he vanished from sight with one final wave, I slammed my palm against the rough stone wall, tore my skin to shreds. I was shaking with rage at Stalin, as much as with raw fear for Timur. He took my whole heart with him and I felt love splinter inside me like glass.

That was more than three years ago, three long lonely years. Stalin stole Timur from me and I never heard from him again.

I could hear my mother moving around the apartment, shifting furniture. She kept the place fanatically clean, every surface free of blemish and scrubbed to within an inch of its life, which was a full-time job with the amount of masonry dust that blasted through the city each day. A long triangular slice of sunlight had slapped itself down on my quilt and my small sparse room was filled with golden motes that drifted as I breathed. I rolled out of bed, taking my orange with me, and pulled on my dressing gown over my grimy clothes. The orange was as warm as a beating heart in my hand and I slipped it into my pocket.

I opened my bedroom door.

My mother was on her hands and knees with a cloth and a knitting needle, scraping out grit from between the wooden blocks of the parquet floor, grit that only she could see.

'You didn't take your boots off,' she said sharply. 'There's black coal in here.'

'I was exhausted.'

'That's no excuse.'

She didn't look up from her task.

'Mutti, did someone call here last night while I was out?'

'No.'

'Are you sure?'

'Of course I'm sure.'

I couldn't tell. I wanted to believe it was a lie, to imagine a knock on the door, a smile, a greeting, an impossible orange on an outstretched hand. I wanted it so bad I could feel a rumbling inside me and I had to wrap my fingers around the fruit in my pocket to quieten it. Mutti finally turned her head. Her hair was tied up in a golden knot on top of her head and her eyes looked bloodshot and sore, a sure sign she hadn't slept well.

'How's your arm?' she asked.

'Much better. I had it stitched by a doctor ... thanks to the money from the brooch you gave me.' I pushed up my sleeve to display the bandage.

She studied it from her position on her knees and I held my breath. Finally she nodded, satisfied. 'Good,' she said. 'Was there any money left after you'd paid the doctor?'

'Some. Not much.'

She scowled at the floor, clearly thinking of the true value of the diamonds. 'Buy some proper food with it. I'm so sick of bread that's made from sawdust.'

'I will.'

'Were you working in one of the offices?' Her eyes strayed to the coat that I'd left smeared with coal.

'No,' I admitted. 'I was put on sweeping out aircraft after they'd been unloaded. I brought home some coal dust for us in my pockets.'

'I saw.'

She resumed her task. That was it.

I picked up the coat and found that it had been brushed and its pockets emptied. 'I'll try to bring home more tonight, so we can light a fire.'

She continued to pick out minute specks with her needle.

I washed in the bathroom in a ridiculous trickle of yellowish water, gave a token inspection to the plum-coloured bruise on my chin but turned quickly away from my reflection in the mirror. It was not a face I could bear to look at for long. At the door of the apartment I hesitated.

'Mutti, are you sure?'

'Sure of what?'

'That no one came.'

'I may be senile, Anna, but I am not deaf.'

'You're anything but senile.'

She raised her head and gave me a slow smile that made me uncomfortable. 'Exactly,' she said, and resumed her scrubbing.

I walked out. The peacock diamond brooch was burning a hole in my pocket.

I looked over my shoulder as I hurried to my workshop. Again and again I turned, spun round, suddenly, unexpectedly, I peered down a side street, scoured the ruins of a church I passed, stepped into a doorway and scanned the pavements. Always looking behind me.

I was acting like a hunted creature. Because that's what I felt like.

Was I really hunted? Or was I haunted? Was it the past I expected to see padding silently behind me? The past lining me up in its crosshairs. The past grinning at me with big bloodied teeth. The clouds of yesterday had been swept aside and the sky was a clear blinding blue, sharp as a knife, so that I ducked my head against its brilliance and watched my breath lead the way in the icy air.

I had to find Herr Schmidt. That's where I'd start.

CHAPTER EIGHTEEN

◆ ◆ ◆

ANNA

I stood in front of a large muscular-looking building, five storeys of heavy grey stonework. It was just off Möllendorffstrasse, round the corner from where the glorious gothic town hall lay in ruins, and despite the bright sunshine the cold chipped away at my bruised chin. We were in the Lichtenberg district in the east of the city, though in the last three years I'd tried to avoid this area. It housed the offices of the all-powerful Soviet Military Administration in Berlin, as well as its shadowy MGB security service, and together they created an atmosphere that hung like poison gas in the streets, unseen but always there on every corner, in every breath I drew into my lungs. You could vanish from these pavements with no trace left behind. Not even a footprint. You no longer existed.

The door of the apartment building was large and patched with planks of wood, its red paint peeling now like sunburnt skin. At my side Herr Schmidt raised his hand to knock, but paused to inspect me. This time he was wrapped in an enormous wolverine-fur cape and the damaged side of his face was bone white as if no blood reached it today. I wondered how much it pained him.

'Nervous?' he asked.

'No, not nervous. Hopeful.'

It was a lie. But it was easier that way.

'It's been more than two years of searching,' Herr Schmidt pointed out. 'You could give up, you know. It is an option.'

I gave him a quick sideways glance to check if he was serious, in which case I had the wrong man.

'Never,' I said and rapped on the door.

◆ ◆ ◆

The huge wolfhound growled at me, deep in its throat, and its lips lifted in a black wave above its teeth. I eased back a step from the child and saw the animal's hackles lower.

'No, Rolf!' the small child scolded the dog and clamped his stubby fingers around the hound's long grizzled muzzle.

Three years old, his neck ringed with dirt. This was the alert little boy from the photograph in my workshop. I wanted to snatch him away from the danger of having his hand bitten off but the dog took the rebuke without a murmur and lowered its long neck so that the child didn't have to stretch up. Their two pairs of eyes stared at me as if I were the danger.

'Hello, Bernd,' I said softly to the boy.

He curled a fist into the dog's shaggy grey fur, leaned against its rangy slab of a shoulder and tucked his chin to his chest. He made no sound.

I crouched down so that we were eye to eye, trying to ignore the nearness of the great wolfhound head that towered over us both. We were in a cobbled courtyard surrounded on all sides by tall stone buildings and an iron staircase, a streak of golden light slowly crawling down one wall as the low winter sun hauled itself up over the roof.

'Look what I've brought you,' I said.

I held out my hand. A green rubber ball nestled on my palm. It drew the gaze of both Bernd and Rolf like a magnet. I smiled. I wanted him to smile back at me. Like before. Long before.

'Take it,' I said softly. 'It's for you.'

I eased it towards him. No reaction, just wide blue eyes fixed on the ball. I waited, studying his stubborn little face, the way his temples had a slight concave spot, the curve of the elongated bottom lip, the springiness of his shaggy blond hair, and I tried to squeeze them to match the ones I remembered in the three-month-old baby I had lost.

'Here.' I offered the ball again.

'Take it, *Dummkopf!*' said the man in the leather apron behind me.

But Bernd pressed himself back against the huge dog, tightening his grip on its fur so the animal leaned its long bony neck forward and gently removed the ball from my hand with its teeth. Its thick gingery chin-whiskers tickled my palm. The child screeched with laughter, stuck his small hand deep into the creature's mouth and extracted the ball. The dog wagged its skinny tail. My smile widened and I longed for this kid in his hand-me-down shirt and his grimy trousers to be the boy I sought.

'Well,' the man said. 'Is it him?'

'No.'

'Are you sure?' He kicked the metal toecap of his boot against the cobbles in frustration. 'I could maybe lower my price.'

'No.'

He grunted. 'I could sell you the dog instead,' he muttered. 'He's a bastard to feed.'

'No.'

I reached into my pocket and pulled out the smallest of the precious banknotes I had been given in exchange for my mother's diamond brooch.

'There,' I said, handing it to him. 'Feed them both.'

He pocketed it fast before I changed my mind.

'*Auf Wiedersehen*, Bernd,' I said reluctantly to the child, who was already throwing the ball for the dog to chase. He didn't look round.

I walked out of the courtyard, Herr Schmidt's crisp footsteps echoing behind me. The air in my lungs felt hot and sore.

'Did your man turn up?' I asked. 'The operative who went missing while working my case.'

The pained look in Herr Schmidt's eyes, even in his glassy crooked one, was answer enough and I wanted to reach out to him, to offer some scrap of sympathy, but I didn't know how. He was a private man with private thoughts.

'I'm sorry,' I murmured and laid a light hand on his arm, the wolverine hide acting as a protective skin between us.

'So you should be, *Fräulein*,' he said, 'because his death puts a spotlight on you.'

A spotlight? I glanced behind me, just in case, but there was no one untoward in sight and no big yellow spotlight. We were back in

Friedrichshain, skirting the edge of the wooded park, and off to our right I spotted a boy high up on a stunted branch of one of the silhouetted trees, swaying at least fifteen metres off the ground, his shadow dancing on the frozen ground far beneath him. How he'd climbed so high, I couldn't begin to imagine. He was hacking at one of the tree's boughs with a small hand axe. I stopped breathing when I realised it was Yvo, my bread-eating companion from early this morning.

At the base of the tree stood two small waifs, both dark-haired, their necks craned back to watch his progress and with each swing it looked as if he would fall and plunge to his death. But he clung on tight with his spindly legs, defying gravity. All the trees in the park looked like desolate lollipops, their lower branches stripped away for firewood, their bark stolen, their trunks long, grey and obscenely naked.

'Are you listening, Fräulein Wolff?'

'I'm listening.' But my eyes remained fixed on the boy.

'I think you will only be satisfied,' Herr Schmidt continued, 'if I gather every single child in Berlin together, herd them into a giant room and let you inspect each one of them in turn.'

Was he mocking me? Showing me the impossibility of the task?

'Would that make you happy, Fräulein Wolff?'

I gave a little puff of laughter. 'Happy? I'm not asking for happy, Herr Schmidt. Just for one particular three-year-old boy.'

'Are you aware that the British are flying some of the sickest children out of Berlin to be treated in the British zone of Germany?'

An icy gust sliced its way across the parkland and I saw Yvo slip. His feet scrabbled frantically as he dangled from his fingertips but he managed to hook one leg up over the branch and save himself.

'I've heard about those air ambulance flights,' I said to Herr Schmidt. 'I am praying he is not sick.'

Neither of us mentioned the number of children whose small bodies froze to death on the streets each night.

'Herr Schmidt, please tell me about your man. Your operative.' I dragged my gaze away from Yvo as he slithered expertly down the trunk, scooped up the booty of the severed branch and raced off with the younger kids scampering after him. I turned to look at the man at my side in his showy cape. 'What happened?'

'He turned up dead outside a building in the British sector.' His words gave no hint of emotion or distress, but I could see on the undamaged side of his face the effort his calmness took. 'I thought Karl Becher could handle a job like that in his sleep, a straightforward search for a missing child.' He halted on the gravel path and looked me full in the face, so that I had nowhere to hide. 'But it's not just a missing-child case, is it, Fräulein Wolff? It's more than that.'

There are so many ways I lie to myself to keep myself going, we all do it here in Berlin, day after day, but this is not one of them.

'You are right, Herr Schmidt, it's not just about a missing child.'

'So? Tell me. What is it about? If you want my help, tell me.'

'It is about a murder.'

Russians had a way of marching. It wasn't the crisp, precise and well-oiled machine that the German Army had become under the Nazis, it was more like a family of bad-tempered brown bears lumbering along. I turned my head away as a unit of Soviet soldiers marched past, boots echoing up the street. The woman queuing in front of me outside the bakery hunched her shoulders and spat with venom on the ground. Our eyes met briefly as she checked behind her.

Neither of us spoke. East Berliners had learned the hard way that speaking is dangerous. You never know to whom your words will be passed or when you'll hear the smash of a rifle butt against your front door just before dawn, the brown bear lumbering into your living space. So we smiled and left it at that. The queue was quiet and orderly, each of us clutching our ration card and hoping that the baker had received a delivery of half-decent flour this morning, rather than bulking out the gritty dough with more sawdust. We were used to waiting, queuing and hoping, dreading the voice that called out 'All gone.'

We inched forward, ducking against the wind.

'Do you know anyone who is selling oranges?' I asked, dropping my voice low.

Her eyes widened, amused by the absurdity of the question. She had the kind of face that liked to laugh. 'Are you mad? No one has oranges in Berlin. Except the Yanks. I'd swap one of my kids for an orange any day of the week.'

I nodded, thinking about how the Americans dehydrated every-thing – absolutely everything – to make it lighter to transport. Potatoes, eggs, milk, baby food, pet food, vegetables, medicines and even meat, all dehydrated. American oranges would arrive as a sun-scented pulp.

'How much do you think a real orange is worth?' I asked.

'Why?' She peered at me closely, suddenly suspicious, as the queue shuffled forward a few paces, then stopped. 'You got one to sell?'

'No, of course not. I was just wondering.'

She laughed. 'Just fantasising, you mean. Yeah, we all do that.'

I didn't tell her it wasn't oranges I fantasised about.

After the bakery, I switched to the destitute streets in Mitte district, the ones where the drunks hung out, where whole blocks of buildings lay on the ground with their innards ripped wide open. But without my bicycle I felt exposed. I would have to fix it fast, but first, the *Brot Dame*. The bread lady.

That's what they called me. The kids, the *Wolfskinder*. I found myself a perch on top of one of the slabs of broken masonry and I looked down on a street of ruins, a grey jumble of lost hope, lost lives, jagged walls and collapsed ceilings, but no one paying the slightest attention to me and not a child in sight. I stuck two fingers between my lips and let rip with a shrill whistle that startled a pair of crows into the air, their black wings sending shadows scuttling through the ruins like cockroaches.

The whistle was my calling card.

They came from nowhere, as wary as foxes. Children approached slowly at first, but scrambling closer, offering me grubby stares, and I wanted to reach out and hold each small smelly body close. Some I'd seen before but others were new and they hung back, uncertain as I sat cross-legged on my slab, tearing chunks off the dense dark loaf of bread in my lap, and I held a piece out to every child in turn.

'Hello,' I said to each one. 'I'm glad you've come. Here, enjoy some bread.'

They nodded. One or two smiled.

I smiled back and, when they let me, I wrapped an arm around a skinny pair of shoulders or cradled a small soiled hand in mine. I counted eleven of them today, one tallish girl of around ten years old with timid features though she wasn't timid and an overlong greasy fringe that she treated like a shield. Her eyes were hard to look at. There was too much in them, far too much for one so young. She sat down beside me, not touching, but almost.

'How you doing, Resi?' I asked.

'I'm good.'

'Staying safe?' She wore an ugly black dress that was too long for her; it came almost to her ankles. I understood why.

'Yes. Me and my girls watch out for each other.'

Her *girls* were actually her three younger brothers. They were fierce dark-haired little creatures who hovered nearby, chewing in silence on their chunks of bread and ready to hurl themselves on me if I made one wrong move.

'Got any scissors?' Resi asked.

'Not with me. Why?'

'I want you to cut my hair.' She raked fingers through the tangles of her long tawny locks and tugged hard at them. 'Make it like yours. Like a boy's.'

Again I understood why. 'I'll bring scissors next time. Do you have somewhere dry to sleep tonight?'

'Yeah, we've found a really good cellar. It used to belong to a furniture store –' she sneaked a half-smile at me – 'so I'm sleeping on a velvet sofa now.'

I laughed. 'Sounds good.' I paused. I always had to tread with care around Resi. She could flare up at times. 'I have some gloves for you in my bag.' Her own were ragged. 'And a book. I wondered if you'd like something to read. There are pictures for your brothers in it too.'

She twisted away so I couldn't see her face.

'It's the story of *Heidi*,' I said softly.

Her shoulders were trembling. 'I miss ...' She stopped herself with a shake of her head and a hand over her mouth, but sneaked a glance back at me, her cheeks wet and glistening, ' I miss ... everything.'

I hugged her to me, whether she wanted it or not. Of course the child missed everything. At night in her dank cellar she must dream of pork schnitzel and the soft fur of her dog against her cheek and the sound of her mother's quiet voice with a story at bedtime. They all did.

She pulled away from me. 'I saw you coming,' she said, pointing in the direction of the long straight road beyond the mass of rubble. 'You were walking. Where's your bicycle?'

'It had an accident.'

She looked at my bruised chin and shrugged. 'Accidents happen,' she muttered. '*Brot Dame*, do you know you were being followed?'

'What?'

'I spotted him.'

'Who?' My pulse thumped in my throat.

'A man.'

'What did he look like?'

She let a long silence stretch between us, delicate as a cobweb. If I blew too hard it would break. I could see she wasn't sure whether to get involved or cut and run.

'He wore a cap and a duffle coat, a navy one,' she said. 'White hair. He was behind you, a long way behind. You suddenly crossed the road and started to run, so he rushed after you but on the opposite side.' She gave a snort of amusement. 'He panicked when you stopped dead and looked back.'

'I was checking for a tail. What did he do?'

'He leaned over a baby in a pram.' She laughed outright. 'The mother hit him and his cap flew off. That's how I saw his white hair.'

I felt sick. How had I missed that?

'Up on top of the ruins, I get to see a lot of things,' she explained. Life on the streets had sharpened all this girl's senses.

'And then?' I asked.

She pointed to a shabby block of shops still standing at a crossroads further up the street, where a queue of people waited outside in the cold. 'He's over there in that doorway.'

I don't think I've ever moved so fast. Down off my high perch in one leap, lucky not to turn an ankle, and flying over the mounds of broken masonry to the road. Cars blared. Blind to all else, I raced across to the shop doorway.

The queue was lined up outside a grocery shop and I scoured it for a dark duffle, but it wasn't there, so I pushed my way right inside the shop, despite angry objections, but still no duffle. I asked a middle-aged woman if she'd seen a man in a duffle coat but she shook her head, her faced etched with sympathy.

'Lost someone, have you, *Fräulein*?' she asked.

I could see in her eyes that she had lost someone too. Grief isn't neat or quiet. It is messy and uncontainable. It is dirty and drenched in blood. I was good at pretending to myself that I was in control of what rumbled around inside my head as I went about the daily grind of survival, but then, if I relaxed my grip for even one second, explosions of grief would blast through me. It was like carrying a bomb around in my chest. When I least expected it, when I was darning a hole in my jumper, when I was tying a shoelace in the street, the grief-bomb would detonate. And I was destroyed all over again.

I thanked the woman and set off down the nearest side street, searching for the sound of running footsteps and watching for a flash of navy. I raced up and down, dodging and turning, hackles raised as I scoured the few shops and bars that were scattered throughout the area, then back to the broad street I'd started from. I passed many men in caps and winter coats, but no duffle coats. No one running. No one trying to duck out of sight. No one leaning over prams. The man had vanished into thin air.

I stopped to catch my breath, which plumed out into the cold clear air in long trails of frustration. My left arm throbbed. My mind ached with questions. Who was this white-haired man? What did he want with me? Was he a danger?

Eventually I forced myself to abandon my hunt and set off at a run in the direction of my workshop. I needed new wheels under me.

'It's mine,' the youth objected.

He was no more than twelve or thirteen at most.

'*Nyet*. Is mine,' the ruddy-faced Russian soldier stated.

He slapped the boy's head, coiled his hefty fist around the twig that was the boy's wrist and snatched the chocolate bar from his hand.

'Fuck you,' the boy yelled, earning himself a harder slap.

'Leave him,' I said.

The sun was directly overhead now. It made my shadow squat and ugly at my feet, but the city streets had taken on that gilded look, a radiant sheen that made it easy to remember when Berlin had been one of the finest cities in Europe. It was while I was running back to my workshop that a deep throb-throb-throb of aircraft engines had grown louder overhead, sweeping low, and it seemed to mingle with the pounding of my feet on the pavements. At first I was too busy keeping a sharp eye out for duffle coats to notice the solitary plane, but then I heard excited cries behind me and I swung round.

Children of all ages were swarming towards me.

I glanced up. The single USAF aircraft was low, far too low, and for a sickening moment I thought it was about to crash. It was circling over East Berlin instead of West Berlin as though the American pilot had lost control or lost his way, but then I saw the air full of what looked like dandelion seeds, small white triangles floating down to earth from the plane, pale pockmarks in the thin blue expanse of the winter sky, and I understood. The candy bomber was here.

'Leave him,' I said again to the Russian soldier.

When you have plenty, you can afford to be generous. It's when you have nothing that it's hard, but even so, the generosity of one American pilot, Lieutenant Gail Halvorsen, took our breath away in Berlin that winter. In the dark bleak days, his generosity shone bright, a spark for us to warm our cold hands on.

One day in the summer of this year, Lieutenant Halvorsen got talking to a bunch of skinny German kids, about thirty of them, who were hanging around the Tempelhof airport perimeter fence, watching the never-ending flow of aircraft swooping down from the sky. Halvorsen was captivated by the children's spirit in the face of such privation and he handed them the few sticks of gum in his pocket, regretting that there was nowhere near enough for everyone. But he didn't shrug and walk away. He promised to drop more for them out of his C-54 the next day.

'How will we know which is your plane?' they'd asked.

'I'll wiggle my wings, so you'll know.'

That's how Uncle Wiggly Wings was born. He gathered as many sweet rations as he could beg, borrow or steal from others in his squadron and used string to tie packs of gum and chocolate and raisins to white handkerchiefs to act as parachutes. True to his promise, the next day Lieutenant Halvorsen wiggled his wings and tossed out his homemade miniature parachutes to the waiting children below. In that moment he became the Candy Bomber, or the *Rosinenbomber* in German, a national hero. Several times a week he scattered his generosity to the children of Berlin and word quickly reached the airlift commander, General Tunner, who gave it his official blessing. Operation Little Vittles was created and such a touching display of care for our children forged an extraordinary bond of friendship between our two countries. It healed old scars. Sweets of all kinds flooded in from America.

This is what I was witnessing now, America's generosity drifting down from heaven on white angel wings. A host of them. Isn't that what they're called – a host of angels? All around me children were laughing and leaping to snatch the miniature white parachutes out of the air or scooping them up off the ground. But when I saw a Red Army soldier seizing a Hershey bar from a boy who was made of nothing more than skin and bone, anger erupted inside me and I forgot to be cautious.

'Leave him.' I shouted it this time.

'*Otvali!*' the soldier swore at me.

'Give the boy back his chocolate bar.' I added, '*Po\zhaluysta*. Please.'

The Russian scowled at me. A distance of about five metres of road-way separated us and I had to fight against an urge to leap across it, to wrap both my hands around his thick neck, thumbs clamped on his Adam's apple, and squeeze hard, because I knew he'd do the same again. Steal from a child. Seize a parachute, take the candy. Even from a three-year-old.

What happened next unfolded so quickly that it ran out of control before I could stop it. At first there was only one Soviet soldier, but now suddenly there were two, then three of them, the other two drawn by the lure of the handkerchief-parachutes and their tiny cargoes. All three were battle-hardened Red Army men. They immediately pocketed more and more of the chocolate bars, gathering them up and stuffing them into their brown greatcoats. Their Tokarev rifles poked over their shoulders and their loud bullying voices roared at the kids.

'Bugger off!' they shouted. '*Verpiss dich.*'

But the children didn't give ground. About twenty of the grubby urchins circled us, making grabs for the descending handkerchiefs, leaping and running, dodging the slaps and the punches. The boy in the soldier's grip managed to twist free and barged into me before running off. Noise and shouts everywhere blunted my reaction but then I saw what the boy clutched in one hand as he ran, heels flying. A flash of colour between his fingers. A blur of orange in his hand.

I touched my pocket. It was gone.

'My orange!'

I took off, racing after the boy. No, no, no. *You. Do. Not. Steal. It.* He was fast but I was faster. And then I heard it. In all that confusion and fury and blind panic, I heard it as clearly as a fist smashing through glass. The unmistakable metallic click of a rifle bolt sliding into place.

'No!' I screamed.

The noise of the bullet shuddered off the walls of the buildings, quickly followed by a second, making my ears ring, and the boy in front of me fell. Flat on his face in the dirt. His arm flung wide, the sleeve of his coat turning scarlet, and the orange rolled into the gutter.

'Don't,' I begged.

I touched my fingers to the lifeless face of the boy on the ground. 'Don't go. Stay with me. Please stay, I ...'

But his eyelids didn't even flicker as I ran a finger under the bony corner of his jaw, seeking a pulse that wasn't there. My throat choked up as I bent over him, my eyes flooded with tears, and I swore to all the gods that were using Berlin as their plaything that I would give the boy a thousand oranges if they would bring him back to life.

I turned his limp body. Tried to pump air into his young lungs, but his shirt was soaked with crimson. One of the rifle bullets had punched its way right through his puny chest, the other ripped a hole in his arm, snapping the bone. Grief and guilt swamped me but I was dimly aware of noises around me. Raised voices. Vehicle engines. A laugh. A shouted order. All indistinct. Blurred. Brown uniforms out of focus. And then one single voice detached itself from the rest.

'You're covered in blood,' it said in a tone of quiet concern. 'Are you hurt, Fräulein Wolff?'

Russian faces divide into two types. A generalisation, I know, but it's true. There are those from the north – like the soldier who had seized the poor boy – who possess broad faces and blunt noses, with pads of fat on their cheeks and around their eyes to keep out the bitter northern cold. The second type couldn't be more different. The underlying structure of their faces is as precise as spun steel, finely shaped with long cheekbones and high sweeping foreheads. There is an inner strength to them that can be intimidating and the man standing in front of me with the look of concern on his face was one of the latter.

He bent over me. Did he think I couldn't hear his words, spoken in perfect German but with a Russian accent that made the sound of them soft and unfamiliar? Or did he think that I chose not to reply? Some strong emotion turned his pale grey eyes darker, to almost a brackish purple, and his nostrils flared so wide that I could feel the hot breath from them. Then I watched him force his features smooth again.

'Fräulein Wolff?'

I longed to taste again the salt on his skin, to feel once more the firm weight of his bones pressed against mine. To crave the flicker of fire across my lips as my mouth crushed his.

CHAPTER NINETEEN

◆ ◆ ◆

TIMUR

The sight of her sent a shockwave through Major Timur Voronin. She was crouched in the dirt and her thinness was like a physical pain to him, her lovely face all razor-sharp angles and deep hollows. Its cheekbones seemed ready to cut right through the taut layer of her skin, and yet in this miserable dusty street she shone brighter than his brightest memories of her, stronger than his own heartbeat.

Relief kicked in at the realisation that the blood on her coat was the boy's, not hers, but she was not the Anna Wolff he'd left behind. He could see that. Her mother had spoken the truth, she had changed. He could see it in her eyes. He shouted an order to one of his men, who immediately retrieved the orange from the gutter and placed it in his commanding officer's hand. Timur took hold of Anna's arm, raised her to her feet and wrapped her fingers around the orange. He gave no sign of what touching her again after nearly three and a half empty years did to him.

'Go home, Fräulein Wolff,' he ordered. 'We will deal with this.'

She snatched her hand away. 'And him?' She pointed directly at the soldier who had shot the boy and was now standing with slouched shoulders, staring down at his rifle as though it was the guilty party. 'Will you deal with that trigger-happy bastard?'

'Yes, he will be dealt with in the appropriate way. This is an army matter.'

Her gaze raked Timur's Red Army officer's uniform, its gold and scarlet epaulettes, its two silver stars. 'The appropriate way? And what is that?' she demanded. 'If I give you back your orange, can I take his rifle and shoot him in the back myself? The same way he shot the boy?'

'Go home, Fräulein Wolff.'

She dragged a gloved hand across her mouth, shutting down the words that threatened to pour out and leaving a smear of the dead boy's blood on her chin. She stepped back from him.

'That boy is somebody's child,' she said bitterly.

She set off down the street at a run, long desperate strides, as if she couldn't get away from him fast enough. As if he were contaminated.

She had changed.

CHAPTER TWENTY

◆ ◆ ◆

INGRID

Ingrid could smell it. The money. The stench of it made her positively dizzy.

She took a long look around Tempelhof airbase. Her pass had got her through its guarded gates and she inhaled the rich aroma of all those beautiful American dollars. The number of huge planes on the ground, unloading their cargo, was eye-popping, never mind the queue of them droning down from above, plus the battalion of trucks and the never-ending tankers of aviation fuel. The scale of it all was mind-blowing.

This Operation Vittles must be costing the United States a Fort-Knox-busting fortune, and Britain too, for that matter. The RAF was flying its Yorks and Handley Page Hastings transport planes, so Otto informed her, into Gatow airport in the south-west of the city, while France was flying into the newly built Tegel airport in the north-west. Bringing everything a city needed to survive, right down to the last galvanised nail and box of dried egg powder. So many flights every day and all through the night.

Dangerous, Otto had said. Already there had been fatal accidents. Mistakes made. Pilots too fatigued to think straight as they kept their cargoes coming. Thousands of tons of life-saving goods every twenty-four hours. Otto was right. Who would miss a box here, a crate there? A bag of sugar. A roll of bandages. A carton of light bulbs. Dried baby milk. A pack of Hershey chocolate bars. Was General Tunner counting each one? Like hell he was. So much to choose from, if you were brave enough to take a risk.

But Ingrid was after far more than chocolate bars.

◆ ◆ ◆

'Ketchup?' Ingrid offered.

'You bet your sweet brown eyes,' responded the American with a teasing smile.

She smiled back.

This was new, this attention. She'd never been noticed by men unless she was in one of her glitzy circus outfits. Until now. This airman had greasy overalls and black fingernails, a mechanic of some kind, but they were all the same, these Americans. Attentive. She squeezed a jet of blood-red sauce on to his hamburger, encased it in greaseproof paper and passed it over, through the open hatch of the catering truck.

'Thank you, honey.'

'Not so cold now,' she commented. Kuznetsov had taught her the right English phrases.

The serviceman brushed his fingers along her hand as he took the hamburger and she let him. No offence, Otto, my love, but these guys are lonesome for a woman, any woman.

She was under no illusion. Soldiers and airmen were only attentive because they were desperate, so many men and so few women, but that was fine by her. She'd take what she could get. Cocooned in the catering truck within sight of the main runway, she was safe from marauding hands and warmed by a sizzling grill behind her and the aroma of charred meat. How Kuznetsov had arranged this job for her at Tempelhof she had no idea, but he had, and she could see why. She had a ringside seat for everything going on.

All morning she had exchanged smiles and chatter with a stream of Yanks who'd come ostensibly in search of a hamburger or Coke or what they called a cookie. Word had got around that a new young *Fräulein* was in the truck, but Corporal Rocco, who used to be a pastry chef at Schrafft's in Manhattan, kept a sharp eye on her. He was the cook, if flipping a burger could be called cooking, which Ingrid doubted.

The catering truck was there to speed up the turnaround time of aircraft by keeping pilots and navigators and necessary ground crew outside in the cold with the Skymasters, instead of lingering inside a warm canteen. The whole place buzzed with a sense of urgency and everything was done at top speed. There were also jeeps that raced to the cockpits, supplying doughnuts and hot coffee. Their General Tunner's plan had worked, his obsession with precision was producing results. The time it took to unload one of the C-54s had been slashed from seventeen minutes to five, and where it once took sixty minutes to get a plane back up in the air, it now took thirty. But the airmen were under constant pressure and it showed on their faces. So here she was, an extra pair of hands in the truck at the beck and call of Rocco, who wielded his greasy spatula like a weapon if anyone hung around her too long.

'Don't take any nonsense from that bunch of bozos, Ingrid,' he told her.

'They're nice.' She smiled. 'And polite.'

Rocco snorted, 'Polite as rattlers.'

She laughed. She'd enjoyed her morning and learned that soldiers and airmen liked to complain. Like all men, in her experience. They complained about their long hours of work, about their officers, about the food and the fog, about constant oil leaks on the C-54 piston engines and faulty pitch control pumps – whatever they were – and most of all about the scab-assed Russkies. So far today she'd also discovered that a section of Tempelhof's main runway was in need of urgent repair and …

'Excuse me, ma'am, coffee, please. Black.'

This one was a flier. In full flying gear. He had Italian-brown eyes but set way back under dark bushy brows as if he had secrets to hide. No chat, no smiles, not from this one, but he studied her closely as she poured out his coffee.

'Not so cold now,' she recited for the twentieth time.

'It's colder where I come from.'

There was a pulse in the air between them. She felt it the way you feel a drumbeat.

'Where's that?' she asked in a casual tone.

'Fairbanks. In Alaska.'

She blinked. Glanced away. The winter air was so cold and bright it shimmered around her.

He'll come to you. Just remember the words I teach you, Kuznetsov had urged.

'Alaska is a long way from Berlin,' she parroted.

'I like Berlin.'

She nodded and kept nodding, unable to stop. 'My name is Ingrid.'

'I'm Noah.'

'Hello, Noah.'

He gave her a faint smile, sipped his scalding black coffee and let his gaze settle on Rocco's broad back behind her. The cook was busy oiling his grill and whistling 'I've Got a Girl in Kalamazoo'. He was a fine whistler. Noah placed the flat of his hand on the counter for no more than a half second and when he removed it, a small blue envelope lay there.

The forget-me-not blueness of it caught Ingrid off guard, a love-letter blue, a blue to make her blush, but without hesitation she slid it into the pocket of her coarse khaki apron. Her heart thumped hard at the back of her chest. This was it, the moment she stepped across the line. The blue envelope could see her hanged. Her stare pinned the American in place, and she could hear her own breath even above the roar of the planes, but Noah looked as if he had nothing on his mind except wrapping his fingers around his coffee for warmth and getting back to his cockpit.

'Thank you,' he said in that loose, easy way that Americans have, as if they've known you forever. 'Have a nice day.'

Flier and coffee walked away, but the forget-me-not blueness stayed. It seemed to burn its way right through to her skin.

CHAPTER TWENTY-ONE

◆ ◆ ◆

INGRID

It was true what she'd told Kuznetsov. Guards didn't bother with her, not even the nice polite American ones. At the end of her shift when daylight was sneaking away towards the darkness of the western horizon, Ingrid wasn't searched as she left Tempelhof airport. She was all ready to unbutton her coat but the GI guard made some remark she didn't understand and waved her through the gates. His manner wasn't rude, not like the Soviet guards. American and British soldiers were polite to women.

A group of cleaners was also finishing their shift, so she tucked in behind them and descended down into the underground bowels of Berlin at the U-Bahn station. You never knew which trains were running and which ones weren't these days, but she was lucky and hopped on one on the C Line that would take her back to the city centre. At least there were no gun-happy police stalking through the carriages here in the west, the way they did in the east, checking IDs and searching passengers for contraband.

But she couldn't relax. She focused her mind on keeping her breathing steady and placed her hands on her lap. Directly under them, pinned into the lining of her coat, lay the small blue envelope.

'*Gott*, that smells good, Ingrid. You been out hamstering?'

Hamstering was the term used by Berliners for scurrying around trying to find food.

'Not today,' she said.

The mood in the small apartment sprang to life with the burst of energy that Otto brought into it, half in and half out of his coat, sniffing the air. The greasy odour of meat frying on the cranky old gas stove had him licking his lips before he'd even hung his coat on its hook. He entered the tiny kitchen and immediately Ingrid felt his arms slide around her from behind.

'Had a good day?' she asked.

She flipped a hamburger with a flourish in imitation of Rocco, and the hiss and spit of hot fat made Otto moan in her ear. She expected the usual rush of pleasure at his touch on her skinny shapeless body. No arse and no breasts to speak of, straight up and down like a pencil, but this time the pleasure didn't come. How could it when she was carrying what felt like a bomb in her pocket? Instead it was excitement that spiked in her chest, sharp and painful, and she wanted Otto to back off in case the reason for her excitement came blurting out of her mouth.

Abruptly Otto detached his body from hers as if her thoughts had flowed straight into his head. 'Where did you get hold of that?'

'What? The hamburger?'

'You've been hanging around with Americans, haven't you? They're the only ones with hamburgers to spare. You've been out at Tempelhof airport?'

He was always quick.

'Yes, I was.'

'I know exactly what those flathead Yankee soldiers are like, Ingrid. I deal with them all the time. What did you do for them in exchange?'

'Nothing. Don't go all stupid on me.'

'You don't get slices of meat for nothing, we both know that.' He leaned over and sniffed her hair. 'You stink of fried onions, *Liebchen*.'

'You smell of whisky,' she countered.

Attack was always her first line of defence. She tossed the hamburger on to a plate with a slice of white bread that Rocco had slipped to her as she was leaving the catering truck. She dumped it all on the table with a clatter.

'If you must know,' she said, hands on hips, 'Herr Kuznetsov sent me over to Tempelhof airport with a message for one of their quartermasters who kindly gave me the hamburger as a thank you.'

Otto sat down at the table, tapping his fork on the edge of his plate, and regarded her with a frown. 'What message would a Russian be sending to Tempelhof?'

'I don't know. Didn't ask. Eat up.'

'Don't you want to have some of it?'

'No. I'm going out.'

His head jerked up. 'Why?'

'To meet Kuznetsov. I have to hand over the reply to his message. The American supplies officer hinted that he wants to get his hands on a truck of fresh vegetables from local farmers in East Germany. You know, turnips, swedes and potatoes, that kind of stuff, under the counter, of course, nothing official. Instead of the dehydrated muck they fly in.'

Otto pushed a forkful of fatty meat into his mouth and ran his tongue across his lips. It left a trail of grease. 'So?' He twisted his head to watch her. She loved the coolness in his eyes, a clever coolness that veiled the kick in his heart whenever he smelled a deal. 'Did they come to an arrangement?'

Ingrid shrugged. 'I have no idea.' She started to massage the tension out of the muscles at the back of his neck, relishing the wiry strength of them, and she felt him drop his guard. 'What was your day like?' she asked, wishing she had a beer to give him.

'Shitting awful. The old Dieleman guy in the posh apartment on Ku'damm is being a stubborn bastard.'

'The one with the messed-up leg and all the paintings?'

'That's the one. I went over there to arrange a new deal but he won't agree to it.'

'Then the man's a *Dummkopf*.'

Otto grunted and went on eating his meal in silence.

Gently Ingrid pressed her lips to the back of his head, inhaling the scent of him. 'Otto,' she whispered, 'if ever I don't come home, kill Kuznetsov for me, will you?

'Why am I here?' Ingrid asked.

She didn't pick up the glass of wine that the waiter had placed in front of her on the pristine white linen. Not yet. She knew she had to keep one step ahead of Kuznetsov at all times or he'd chew her into pieces and spit them out.

'Why do you think?' the Russian said smoothly. 'You have something to give me, I believe.'

'I could have passed it to you in some back alley, no one the wiser.'

'Would you have preferred that?'

Ingrid glanced around her as if considering the choice. She'd never been inside a place as fancy as this before. The Watzmann restaurant, named after one of Germany's highest mountains, was dimly lit and oozed discretion and opulence. Its sumptuous velvet drapes and silky carpets muted the murmurs, its clientele was well-heeled and powerful because only those in power could afford such luxury in the east. Ingrid knew Kuznetsov was granting her a privilege even to be in the same room as these people, breathing the same rarefied communist air. In the background a string quartet played soft music that made her skin feel as if it was melting and the low shimmer of candlelight flared on gold and diamonds like a lick of fire. So no, the choice wasn't hard.

She gave a shrug. 'I'm not here for this.' She kept her voice low.

They were seated opposite each other in one of the booths, isolated, private, shadowy. Lit only by a single candle behind an amber shade, so that Ingrid was forced to lean closer to see the whites of his eyes.

'So what *are* you here for?' he asked.

His sudden change of tone caught her by surprise. It was sharp and for the first time Ingrid felt a thin thread of fear. What was she to him? Another expendable information gatherer, nothing more. A workhorse. A donkey. She raised her wine to her lips to make herself forget that the soles of her feet felt as if they had walked over a bed of coals today and she studied him, to see how he did it, how he could scare the hell out of her with just a tightening of his unblinking blue eyes and a twist of his voice. The stillness of him was the stillness of a snake.

'I'm here because we both want the same,' she said.

'And what is that?'

'Money.'

The corners of his eyes relaxed and she let her breath out in a silent trickle.

'Money is not everything, Ingrid. You will learn that. There is more to life. What I want is to see Berlin as a united city once again.'

'So do I. It is my home.'

'I mean under communist rule and without the Allies. With Stalin's face plastered on a brand-new Reichstag, the hammer and sickle flying from the top of its dome.'

She said nothing.

He smiled. 'I like you, Ingrid. You are an opportunist.'

'Why have you brought me here?'

'Look around you,' he said softly. 'Learn.'

She turned to inspect the other diners and dancers, the women in their elegant beaded gowns, the men puffed up in their black dinner jackets or in Soviet officer uniforms, bristling with medals, each one soaked in German blood. She knew she was an object of curiosity to them in her tired navy dress with its white lace collar. Like a waitress. Out of place. She'd thought of donning her sequins to show off to the diners how a quick double flip over a chandelier is done, but no, behave yourself. Learn. So she did as she was told, she observed them, the way the women tilted their heads, how they held their knife and fork as if made of nothing but air, how they laughed and lit too many cigarettes and emptied too many glasses. How the men muttered to each other behind their cigars.

She wanted to leave. 'Now, Herr Kuznetsov, shall we get down to business?'

He knocked back his schnapps in one shot. 'Tell me, Ingrid Keller, what do you want money for so badly? What is it you are after?'

'That's my business.'

'I have work for you to do, and that makes your business my business.' He crafted a smile and arranged it on his face. 'Is it for that man of yours?' he added. 'Otto?'

'No.'

His eyes fixed on hers. 'So it is for you alone.'

'Yes.'

'To escape your humdrum sordid life?'

'Yes.'

'To have lovely things? Beautiful Paris dresses and jewels to flaunt in front of people like these.' He flicked a hand towards the other tables. 'In front of people like me?'

'Yes.'

He laughed, a short harsh bark of sound. 'You'll have to learn to lie better than that, Ingrid.'

She wanted to slap the bastard. Instead she pushed aside the silver salt and pepper set and slid her snowy napkin across the table to him. He drew it on to his lap before returning it to her without the blue envelope that had lain hidden beneath the linen folds. Instead a plump brown envelope lay in its place.

'Good,' he murmured. 'No problems up at Tempelhof?'

'None.'

For a long minute he continued to stare at her, assessing each little muscle movement of her face, but she didn't drop her gaze.

'You did well, Ingrid.'

'I can do better. Much better.'

'I'm sure you can. That's why I want you back at Tempelhof tomorrow.'

He lifted the blue envelope from his lap, examined it to make sure it was still sealed and then drew the candle from behind its shade to sit in front of him on the table. He held the corner of the envelope in the flame.

Ingrid gasped. 'No,' she whispered. 'I risked my life to bring you that.'

As the flames crackled and took hold, he rotated the envelope to protect his fingers and an agitated waiter appeared at his elbow with a jug of water, but Kuznetsov ignored him. Heads turned to stare. When the forget-me-not blueness was engulfed in fire, he dropped it on to the ashtray and the acrid smell of burning intensified. The waiter poured water on the blackened ashes which hissed and spat on to the white linen, speckling it like a bird's egg.

Kuznetsov brushed the waiter away and laughed, his amusement lifting the lines on his face and making him look younger.

'Look at you, Ingrid, with your eyes trying to be so fierce.' He leaned his elbows on the table, his handsome face scarcely a hand's width from hers. She could smell the schnapps on his breath. 'I like you, my little mouse, I like what I see inside you. But did you honestly think I would trust you so easily? The sheet of paper inside that envelope was blank.'

'Fuck you,' she said and left the restaurant.

Ingrid felt humiliated. Stupid. As dumb as she looked.

Because of course Kuznetsov would test her, he'd have been a fool not to and Kuznetsov was definitely no fool. Why had she not thought of that? Why hadn't she seen what was obvious?

This was a lesson.

He was teaching her. Never, never, never take anything or anyone at face value, not even him. Right. She had learned her lesson and would be a step ahead of him next time.

She threw open the door of her apartment, determined to leap on top of Otto because bone-grinding sex with him would scour away the bitter taste of fear that had dogged her every step home from Tempelhof today, rid her of the slime of disgust that lay in the Watzmann diners' every glance in her direction. Hot lustful blood hammering through her veins would smash to a pulp the ridicule in Kuznetsov's eyes when he said, 'Did you honestly think I would trust you?'

Some people use drink to forget. She used sex.

'Otto!'

He wasn't in the middle of the small room in his singlet and wide leather support belt performing his barbell lifts, as she'd expected. He went through a routine every evening without fail and she loved to watch. She could barely keep her hands off him. Instead he was hunched close to the brown-tiled stove, poking something into the flames, something dark and soft that looked like material. A cap of some sort?

'Otto,' she said again.

He swung round, his cheeks red from the flames.

'You're home early,' he said at once.

'It was boring as hell, so I left.' She came up to him and kissed his warm desirable mouth. 'Miss me?'

'Always, *schatzi*.'

'What are you burning?'

'Nothing much. Just rubbish to keep us warm.' He changed the subject abruptly. 'I was up at the circus barns today, *schatzi*. The animals were in high spirits but ...' he sighed, his face pinched. 'I still miss Leonardo.'

'So does Fridolf.'

Leonardo used to be the jewel in their circus. He was a magnificent smelly lion with a huge black mane and angry yellow teeth that split bones like biscuits. But her father had been desperate for funds for animal fodder the winter before the war, so Leonardo had to be sold to a Spanish zoo. Otto had cried for a month. He only ever cried over animals, never people.

She had been glad to see the lion go. It wasn't that Ingrid hadn't liked Leonardo, it was that Leonardo hadn't liked Ingrid. He'd only liked men. It was that simple. The stupid lion was putty in the hands of her father. He used to put his head inside the creature's great mouth as part of his act. Or Otto would get Leonardo to snarl and rage at him in the ring as he held up a flaming hoop for the big cat to jump through, but it was all a pretence. Otto insisted that Leonardo enjoyed the game but that didn't stop Ingrid from being convinced the lion would one day shred Otto to pieces just to spite her. Sometimes its claws used to flash up in her dreams at night, striking at her own throat. So yes, she was glad Leonardo was sold, but she never told Otto.

She took a firm hold of her husband and tore off his shirt so fast she heard a button shoot across the floor. 'One day,' she said, 'I'll save up enough for us to go to Spain to visit Leonardo.'

That pleased him.

CHAPTER TWENTY-TWO

◆ ◆ ◆

ANNA

My diamant's buckled wheel was a bastard. It wouldn't shift. I cursed it, rushing the job of replacement, and that was never a good idea.

'Swearing at it doesn't help,' Kristina laughed, as she slid into my workshop in her pea-green coat, a pair of grubby cycle pedals in her hand. It was good to hear my friend's voice. It drowned out the Russian voice, the *Go home, Fräulein Wolff,* that still echoed in my ears.

'It does help,' I insisted.

Was I swearing at the bicycle? At myself? Or at Timur?

Timur, Timur, Timur. His name was freewheeling through my head, the man I thought I'd never see again except when I lay in bed at night, eyes closed, my heart leaking into the darkness. My greasy fingers were shaking now as I worked. After shifting the rear brake out of the way, I lifted one tip of the spring clip on the chain link and turned it round to release the end. The outer side plate was then removable and the link slid out.

'Gerd found these for you among some rubble.' Kristina smiled with pride. Her son was always on the lookout for treasure in the ruins.

I stopped work and straightened up. 'Thank him for me. He has quick eyes. How is his arm?'

'A bit better today, but …' Kristina took one look at my face and dropped the scavenged pedals on to the work counter. 'Oh, Anna. What's wrong? What has happened?'

'He's back.'

'Who's back?'

'The Russian.' I couldn't say his name.

'Timur Voronin?'

'Yes.'

'Here in Berlin?'

'Yes.'

'Oh, Anna.'

She stepped close and wrapped her arms around me, holding me tight, holding me together, which was exactly what I needed right then and I loved her for it. There are times when someone else can spot where the cracks are better than you can yourself, times when a friend is able to see exactly when and where you need her arms.

'Have you spoken to him?' she asked.

'Yes.'

'And?'

'Nothing. Nothing at all. Our paths crossed in the street by accident. He wasn't looking for me, just doing his job. He must be stationed in Berlin again, but how long he's been here I have no idea, maybe months or even years, so ...'

'Don't, Anna.'

I detached myself without a mention of the boy, the one with a bullet in his lungs. 'I must get back to my bicycle because I need it in working order for tonight.'

Kristina inspected the damaged wheels. 'An accident?'

'Yes, it got into an argument with a car. Don't look like that, I'm fine, barely a scratch. Lucky that I have a pair of replacement wheels for it.'

'Luck has nothing to do with it.'

She was right. In the summer of 1939 any fool could see that war was coming. Germany had been heading down the tracks at full speed with no brakes, so I had scurried around preparing for what was to come. I had squirrelled away my stock of bicycle parts in various hiding places, in basements and attics and lock-ups, to last me through the lean times ahead. In fact the war years had turned into boom years for the bicycle shop because of the shortage of petrol. Now I was working my way through my stash of wheels, hub gears, derailleurs, sprockets and chains, and was able to get my Diamant back on the road fast.

'Have you arranged to meet him again?' Kristina asked in a carefully neutral tone, but disapproval twitched at the downturned corners of her mouth.

'No.'

'I won't leave you,' he'd vowed, holding my hand on his heart.

But then he had.

He'd gone and not a word since. Not one damn word. He'd left me in the dark and it is hard to be brave alone in the dark. Didn't he know that? Or didn't he care?

'You'd do better to stay away from him, Anna,' Kristina urged.

I didn't argue. I didn't want to admit she was right.

'Are you going back out to Tempelhof tonight?' she asked.

But there was something in her voice. I looked up from the wheel nut I was tightening. 'Yes. Why? What have you heard?'

She shrugged. 'This morning I was serving breakfast at the Feldberg Hotel here in the Soviet sector and there was one table full of military uniforms and smart suits all muttering to each other. An early meeting of some sort and I heard …'

My busy fingers paused. 'What did you serve them?'

'What? Oh, just the usual breakfast. That's not the point. One of the suits, a fat man with hedgehog hair said …'

'What did you serve them? Tell me.'

Kristina sighed but smiled. 'Warm white *Brötchen* …'

'The ones with poppy seeds?'

'Poppy seeds and sesame seeds.'

My mouth was watering.

'Westphalian ham,' Kristina continued patiently, 'glazed Bavarian ham, salami, bratwurst, jams and fruits, thinly sliced cheeses …'

'Which ones?'

'Limburger, Butterkäse, Emmental,' she was ticking them off on her fingers, 'Bergkäse, Tilsit and a couple of smoked ones.'

My stomach growled painfully.

'Honey?'

'Yes, honey too.'

'Real coffee?'

'Enough, Anna,' she said softly. 'That's not why I'm here.'

I dreamt about food, every night. We all did. If you've never gone hungry, day after day, night after night, if you've never known the hollowness of slow starvation, you won't understand.

'I thought you came here just for the pleasure of the smell of my oily bicycles,' I laughed. The sound of it didn't convince even me. 'So what did you overhear at breakfast?'

'The men weren't aware of me. I was invisible, a shadow, as I poured their coffee.'

'Berlin is a man's city, Kristina. You know it is. Run by men *for* men. With its male councils and its never-ending military uniforms. They don't even notice us women unless they feel the need to hunt for sex or food. If you'd been a male waiter serving them their breakfast, they'd have held their tongues.'

'I came to warn you.'

'Of what?'

'They were talking about your district of the city.'

'Prenzlauer Berg? What about it?'

She took a breath, her eyes fixed on mine, and I could feel sweat in my hair. It knew before I did that I should be frightened.

'They're doing a sweep,' she said.

A sweep. It's what we dreaded.

I burst into our apartment, out of breath from running up the flights of stairs while dragging my Diamant with me.

'Mutti!' I shouted.

But I was too late. They were here. Heavy dark uniforms crashing and banging through the rooms, the air so full of the stink of them that I couldn't breathe. Flat against one side-wall stood my mother, rigid and silent, her back pressed hard against the faded silk wallpaper. Had she been put there? The way you stand a doll? She was oddly clothed in a silvery satin evening gown and her threadbare woollen nightrobe. The skin of her delicate face was the same shade as her dress. Colourless. Lifeless. A waxy sheen on it, except for one blazing cheek. I wanted to snatch her away and run.

'What's going on?' I asked the thick-necked Soviet officer in charge who had the self-satisfied look of a man who enjoyed his work. I kept my words polite and respectful enough.

'Who are you?' he demanded.

'I live here.'

'Name?'

'Anna Wolff.'

'Papers?'

I produced my identity and ration cards. *Here, you bastard, look, they're genuine documents, all with official stamps.* But my throat constricted with fear when I handed them over because once in Soviet hands they could be torn to shreds on a whim and then I'd be no one.

I looked about me. Take your thieving hands off that ivory inlaid jewellery box on the table, I wanted to yell at one of the other soldiers, the one who couldn't stop himself smiling at his good fortune. It was the gift Papa had given to my mother on their ivory wedding anniversary to mark fourteen years spent loving each other beyond the rainbow, that's what Papa always used to say. He was that kind of man. The officer studied my papers. A frown twisted his heavy brow into hunched ridges under his cap, his top teeth hooked into his fleshy bottom lip while his eyes darted from the papers to me and back again, his shoulders twitching, like a cat judging a jump. I looked at my mother.

She didn't look at me. Her eyes stared unwaveringly at a spot on the floor, her mouth clenched in a hard line. Every couple of minutes she spat on the wooden flooring, and each time she did so, the raw-boned soldier who was tearing open her bureau and plundering her belongings responded by slapping her across her face. She uttered no sound, didn't even look at him, but her left cheek was the colour of a burst plum. It broke my heart. How long had this been going on, this sequence of spit and slap?

A crash came from inside my mother's bedroom and I darted in through its door before the officer could lay a restraining hand on me. This violent ransacking of our apartment, it felt like … the alleyway all over again.

Chills shook my chest when I saw the mess. Cupboards upended, dressing table drawers turned out on the floor, precious possessions thrown around, ornaments in pieces under the thick heavy boots, all on full view in the harsh light from the window.

'Leave my mother's belongings alone,' I said sharply. 'And these shutters are kept closed. Always. Day and night.'

Not for three years had the shutters in my mother's bedroom been thrown back like this.

The two uniforms in the room ignored me. It hit me then that there was an acid stench in the room. I looked around at the chaos and saw a yellow wetness soiling the pristine white surface of my mother's *Decke*, her bedcover. One of the bastards had pissed on it. For me it was the end.

Disgust robbed me of caution, of sense. I lashed out at these men who seemed to possess no shred of compassion in their souls. But even as I snatched up a wooden coat hanger that lay at my feet in order to bang it down on the pair of hands defiling the privacy of my mother's ebony writing slope, something snagged my eye, something small, something grey and fuzzy. I froze. My mother's wardrobe stood open, her elegant gowns strewn on the floor. That much I'd expected, but the fact that the doors of my father's dark mahogany armoire had been forced open did surprise me. It had remained locked since the day he died. But now its doors had been wrenched wide apart, hanging crookedly on their twisted hinges, the wood splintered and buckled. Oh, Papa.

I shook my head to clear it but the grey fuzzy thing was still there. Not conjured up by the chaos of my mind then. I blinked hard and stared at the small toy animal that had half tumbled out, clinging on with one cobwebbed limb. A moan slipped out from between my lips. I swooped down and scooped up the little toy wolf cub into my arms. Its sweet grinning face made me smile. I smiled and smiled back at it, tears rolling down my cheeks.

'Hello, Wolffi.'

Nothing reached me after that. I felt something unhitch inside my chest, something that had been fastened too tight, and I retreated from the room. I took up a position next to my mother, rigid against the wall, needing to be near her, but I didn't stare at the floor as she was doing. I gazed down at a pair of cornflower-blue glass eyes and for once I let my mind wander where it wanted.

I knew exactly where it would go. Of course I knew, but this time, with Wolffi's furry little body clutched in my hands, I was utterly powerless to stop it and the memories came, drowning me.

I was seated on my bicycle inside our apartment next to one of the tall windows, my shoulder comfortably tucked against the window frame, one foot propped on the cold floor. Wolffi was perched cheekily on the handlebars. Outside, dawn was throwing amethyst streamers across the sky and turning the roofs of Berlin into sheets of polished steel. I cradled my wakeful baby in my arms, humming softly, happily, hopelessly addicted to his skin, to the newness of it, the scent of it, the sweet intoxicating taste of it. I could feel my love for him thrumming in every pore and it warmed me deep within. Nothing else mattered any more because everything else had grown grey and out of focus. The world had stepped back. The sorrows, the pain, the loss, the devastation of war and the sheer bloody degradation of invasion, they all faded to a blur when I held this exquisite new life in my arms. He breathed so perfectly. I gently pecked at my bicycle bell and Felix's beautiful blue eyes widened with wonder when it bleated at him. He gurgled at me and butted his head with delight against my shoulder but from across the room I heard my mother's voice snap sharp as ice, 'Put the brat back to bed.'

A tangle of emotions rippled through me as I glanced at my mother now, still standing poker-straight against the wall beside me, her throat moving as if she was preparing to spit again. Her long corn-yellow hair was well hidden under an elegantly tied black scarf, not a single curl on show. A permanent tug-of-war between love and anger marred every word that had passed between us these last three years, but as I slipped my arm through hers, for once there was no need for words.

At that moment the Soviet lieutenant yanked out a drawer of what few scraps remained of our silver cutlery and clattered it out on to the floor, where the younger soldier gathered them up into a bulging sack.

I put my lips to my mother's ear. 'Mutti,' I murmured in a voice so weightless I could barely hear it myself, 'where have you hidden Papa's old gun?'

CHAPTER TWENTY-THREE

◆ ◆ ◆

TIMUR

Timur flew up the stairs in great strides that made the banister shake and the stairwell echo to the sound of his boots. Behind him he could hear laboured breaths, as if someone was attempting to keep up, yet he knew that it was only his memory of racing up these same stairs to wrap her in his arms and feel her pulse pounding in time with his. But memory is a strange beast. You can't always trust it.

The noise of a crash came from the floor above.

What the hell were they doing up there?

Sounds of slamming of doors and the splintering of wood reached down to him as he rounded the last turn of the stairs and readied himself for the confrontation ahead, acutely aware that he would be overstepping the mark. This was not his territory but he was past caring about such niceties. The thought of Anna in there made his foot falter on the final step.

The apartment building felt icy cold and there was a feral stink to the landing as if one of the city's wild cats had slunk in last night to escape the wind howling off the river. He entered the apartment, throwing the door back on its hinges to let whichever greedy bastard was leading the sweep know that a senior officer had arrived.

In front of him stood the kind of man he recognised only too well, the kind of soldier that the Red Army was breeding now that they were the victors and not the vanquished. A man with a naked lust for what was not his.

'What the hell do you think you're doing, Lieutenant?' Timur demanded and swept an arm around the devastation that was Anna's home.

The extent of the damage shocked even him and he felt sick for the two women pressed up against the wall as though awaiting execution. It looked as if a whirlwind had found itself trapped inside the apartment and had thrashed its way out, leaving behind a scene of carnage.

'Inspections are supposed to be neat, Lieutenant. They are meant to be organised. Where is your clipboard? Where is the inventory of every single item you are removing from this apartment?'

Looting. Pure and simple. Timur knew he was tarred with the same brush. Oh yes, he'd done plenty of it himself but on a much grander scale, denuding factories, stripping laboratories and ripping out machinery from textile mills. Ah, but he'd kept precise lists of everything for Moscow. Neat. Organised. As if that made it better.

'Name?' he demanded.

'Lieutenant Glinin, sir.'

'Get your men in here.'

The soldier managed a crisp enough salute but wasn't quick enough to hide his sulky eyes. He was thick-set and thick-headed, too slow-witted to realise his mistake. His heavy greatcoat stank of God-knows-what and his men were no better as they filed out of the bedroom with bulging pockets. Timur wondered: if he put a bullet between Lieutenant Glinin's eyes, would anyone care? Probably not. He was tempted. It wouldn't be the first time.

'Tidy this place up, *bystro*!' he ordered. 'At the double! And I want to see a list of everything being confiscated before you leave here.'

'But sir—'

'Just do it, Lieutenant. Or shall I have you arrested for insubordination?'

'Sir, my orders were to—'

Timur lifted the flap of the holster on his hip and the grooved metal grip of his Tokarev TT-33 pistol fitted snugly into his palm as he drew it out.

'Are you refusing to obey an order by a senior officer, Lieutenant Glinin?'

'*Nyet*.' The soldier's heavy top lip was bone white.

'Good.'

But the pistol remained in Timur's hand while the four Soviet soldiers inspected the ransacked belongings and started to sort through what could be salvaged. Only then did Timur allow himself to turn his gaze back to Anna. Her dark eyes were fixed on a small grey toy rocking in her thin arms, indifferent to the chaos in the apartment, to the Russian soldiers, to the items being recorded and placed into sacks.

Indifferent to him.

It was the flames that drew them. Like moths. Timur used the pages of one of the books that Glinin's men had shredded – though it pained him to do so – and the wood from one of the antique cabinets smashed to pieces by their rifle butts. He threw it all inside the big cold belly of the green-tiled stove and flicked open his lighter. The wood burned with a hungry roar and succeeded where his words had failed. The heat drew the two women away from their wall.

They stood with their backs to the warmth rising from the open doors of the stove, their faces towards Timur, their expressions as blank as dolls. They'd learned well, these women, these strong German women, how to survive when the enemy stood before them among the ruins of their home.

'No, Anna,' he said softly. 'Don't. I am not the enemy.'

Her eyes didn't even flicker, her lips didn't tighten. Such self-control was the result of … what? How many times had she stood mute against a wall? There was only a passing resemblance between the mother and daughter – one blonde and blue-eyed, the other so dark – but a similarity lay in the shape of their eyes, and the set of their chins betrayed the blood bond. They didn't touch each other now. A small gap existed between their shoulders and made Timur aware that there was a distance between them, a stiffness, that hadn't been there three years ago. What the hell had happened to drive them apart at a time when they needed to cling together?

'I'm sorry,' he said but it came out too brisk. In a gentler tone he added, 'Sorry for everything.'

Anna continued to stare at him blindly, as though for her he wasn't there. He didn't exist. His words had no sound, and that was worse, far worse, than if she had hurled abuse at him. The one who saw him as clear as day, the one who leapt at him with teeth bared and hands raised as though to throttle him, was the mother, Luisa Wolff. When he'd first known her she'd been a beautiful woman with a breathtaking smile, but now she was so pale and thin a breeze could have snapped her outstretched arms, though her eyes burned deep blue in their bony sockets.

'You can keep your *sorry*, Russian,' she spat at him. 'We have no use for it. You people have destroyed our lives, stolen from us everything we valued – not only our possessions.'

She slung a hand towards what remained of her furniture, the inlaid Italian cabinet that had been glass-fronted till an hour ago, the French bureau denuded of its drawers, the scroll-edged table with three legs now instead of four, the portrait of a strong-faced man in mountain walking gear that had hung on the wall but now sat lopsided on the floor. Its frame had been snapped into three pieces, its canvas slashed for no other reason than a pleasure in violence. Timur knew the man in the painting was Wilhelm Wolff, her dead husband.

The woman's face twisted as she slapped a hand through the air only a whisker in front of his face. She slapped it back and forth again and again. 'You have robbed us of our decency, Russian, of our self-respect. You've trampled on our hopes, you have made us hate and made us live in fear and turned us into animals. Survival is all we have left. Survival and crippling humiliation.'

Her voice didn't rise. She made no attempt to scream her rage at him and that made it all the worse. She spoke in a quiet voice that came out as tight as if it were tied up in chains and all the time her hand kept striking at the air right in front of his face. Slap, slap, slap.

'Frau Wolff,' Timur said in a formal manner, 'I apologise for what occurred here today. I will do everything I can to retrieve some of your possessions once they have been recorded and warehoused.'

He took a step back from her. He could have seized her flailing wrist and put a stop to the air-slapping but he didn't. *Chyort!* Had he been robbed as she'd been robbed, he'd have done a damn sight more than slap at the air.

For the first time Anna spoke. 'We have friendship, Mutti,' she murmured as she stepped forward and took hold of both her mother's wrists, wrapping each one gently in her own hands. 'We have love. They cannot steal that.'

But she was talking to her mother. Not to him.

To him she said quietly, 'Get out of our apartment. Get out, Russian, and take your sorry with you.'

She'd called him *Russian*.

Timur's hand was opening the heavy oak door that would take him back out on to the street. *Get out, Russian*. She'd said it to show that his presence was no less repugnant to her than Lieutenant Glinin's had been.

She'd called him *Russian*.

No name. As though he had no existence of his own. The coldness of her voice had wrenched something vital inside him.

His hand on the door paused. His ears had picked up the soft sound of feet flying down the staircase from above and he knew instinctively that they were her feet, setting the cold air swirling around him, bringing the acid stink of the feral cat with it. Within seconds she stood before him but this time he knew better than to expect anything other than venom from her.

Alone together.

How many nights had Timur lain awake dreaming of this? Sometimes he'd imagine he heard the sounds of her beside him in bed, her light breathing, the rustle of her long silky hair on the pillow, and it would take him hours to stop staring up at the black ceiling, remembering. The daylight in the hall was dim and speckled with despair, windows boarded up because glass was like gold dust throughout the city, but still he saw what the wretched hollows of starvation had done to her face. He saw the bruise on her chin and the cut high on her forehead. They both stood motionless and silent.

'Anna.' He forced out her name.

She winced and her head ducked away, as if he'd struck her, but she didn't utter his name in response. Her eyes were wide, her pupils huge with an emotion that could have been hatred or could have been desire, he couldn't tell. She darted forward, a movement so sudden it caught him by surprise and her mouth pressed hard against his. No soft brushing of lips, no gentle reminder of what they had lost, nothing as polite as that. No, this was a fierce claiming of what was hers.

Take it, he wanted to shout at her. *Take whatever it is that you want, because every part of me is yours.*

He reached forward with an arm to encircle her, to crush her to him and imprint her fragile form deep into his flesh where it belonged, but he embraced nothing but thin air. She was gone. Not even the scent of her remained. Just the faint shimmer of movement on the stairs and the whisper of her feet as she bounded away, abandoning him down in the shadows. He heard the door of her apartment slam shut.

Had he imagined it? Was the kiss another figment of his Anna-starved brain?

Yet when he ran his tongue over his lips he tasted her. She was there. With him. Threaded into the fabric of him whether she wanted it or not.

CHAPTER TWENTY-FOUR

◆ ◆ ◆

ANNA

'Sorry, ma'am, your entry pass has been cancelled.'

'What?'

'Your entry pass to work here at Tempelhof airport has been cancelled.'

It was the next day and when I arrived for work the American uniformed guard at the perimeter gate spoke the words slowly as if he thought I was too stupid to understand English. I wanted to remove his clipboard from his hand and smack him on top of his smart peaked cap with it.

'It's a mistake,' I insisted.

'No mistake.'

'But why was my pass cancelled?'

'Can't help you there, ma'am.' The young soldier picked at one of his pimples, shrugged his shoulders and waved me away as he turned to the impatient workman next in line behind me. No one wanted any hold-ups.

'Wait,' I said, puzzled and with a growing sense of unease. 'Please. There is someone here who will vouch for me.'

The guard hesitated. The last of the daylight was draining from the sky as the thick net of darkness rolled in from the east. It was the end of a day that I could hardly bear to part with because today I'd tasted again what I had lost.

'Thank you for coming.'

Captain Noah Maynard threw me a grin. 'You seem to like getting into fixes,' he said. 'Or is it that fixes like following you around?'

It was far too close to the truth for my liking but I smiled neverthe-less and made it look real. He deserved it. He had swept into the perimeter gatehouse with an energy and an officer's arrogance that had elicited a polished salute from the guard who without a murmur handed over his clipboard with its list of names. Mine was crossed out. Captain Maynard instantly scribbled it in again at the bottom of the list – Fräulein Anna Wolff – in a flurry of black ink and handed the list back to the poor browbeaten American soldier.

'She is reinstated,' Noah Maynard declared.

'Yessir.'

A hesitation. Maynard narrowed his dark-fringed eyes. 'Who crossed her name off the list?'

'I don't know, sir.'

'What do you mean, you don't know, man? Someone must have marched in here and removed Wolff's name.'

'The list had already been amended when I came on duty at twelve hundred hours today, sir.'

'Who was on duty before you?'

'Private Orville, sir.'

The soldier stood stiff as a rifle, arms clamped to his sides, his eyes fixed nervously on the clipboard in Maynard's hand. I'd have felt sorry for him if I hadn't been so mad at him.

'When is Private Orville next on duty?' Maynard demanded.

The guard switched his gaze to the door of the gatehouse, obviously hoping this Private Orville would miraculously materialise.

'I don't know, sir.'

Noah Maynard put a tick next to my name and initialled it to author-ise my presence on the airbase. He marched me smartly out of the gatehouse, the air so cold it made my eyeballs ache, and we entered the tumult of noise and urgency that a military airbase on constant alert throws at you.

'Thank you,' I said again.

'It's lucky I was still on the base this evening. That goddamn oil leak is still giving us trouble. Keeping all these crates up in the air for so many flying hours is a non-stop battle for our guys, so we're using a bunch of ex-Luftwaffe mechanics as well now to keep things moving. They do an amazing job.'

'I'm glad Germans are helping. But I don't understand why my name was removed from the list.'

He laughed, an easy rolling sound. 'The US Military is a law unto itself. Mistakes happen.'

He shrugged his broad American shoulders, implying it was of no matter, and we set off at a smart pace past the magnificent statue of the eagle on display. The statue had been cleverly redesigned from its original depiction of Germany's great imperial eagle to create the bald eagle of America, the symbol of US independence. Rub German noses in the dirt, why don't you? Once we reached the runways at the rear of the great sweep of the main building the roar of aircraft engines rattled my bones. We faced the newly extended 2,000-metre landing sheet of asphalt.

'Is there any news,' I asked, 'on who was behind the explosion at the recruitment centre?'

'No.' He grimaced. 'The police have pulled in the usual communist suspects but have no positive leads yet, I gather. A bad business.'

'Murdering communist bastards,' I murmured under my breath.

For a moment he inspected me with the close attention to detail that he'd give to one of his planes. 'You look tired.'

'I missed out on my sleep today but I'm okay. I'm strong.'

Again that laugh. 'I don't doubt it. But come with me.'

He led me to a catering wagon that was tucked off to one side of the runway. It was painted a military khaki colour that would have made it merge with the night if it hadn't been topped by a garishly painted sign shouting *Food Truck*. I sped up.

'Two coffees, Ingrid,' he said to the nondescript girl behind the spotlessly clean counter.

Her face was bony and small-featured, her eyebrows thin, her manner effortlessly self-effacing. But there was a tension at the corners of her mouth that I recognised, the effort of keeping things concealed. These days we all had something to conceal, we all had shadows.

Except Captain Maynard. He turned to me with a wide open grin. 'That should wake you up.'

Two coffees arrived. 'Milk and sugar?' the girl asked. As if it were normal.

I nodded.

I watched her add a spoonful of dried milk and stir in two spoonfuls of sugar. Actual white sugar. A snowy mound of the stuff. I didn't dare recall how long it was since I'd tasted any. Her quiet colourless eyes gave me a long stare, then she added a third spoonful. I wanted to wrap my arms around her and her teaspoon. Instead I picked up the coffee, inhaled its aroma as if it were the finest cognac and sipped the scalding sweet liquid.

'Thank you.' I drew a deep breath.

'Smell that?' Maynard asked. 'That's benzene. Sweet and heady. It's added to aviation fuel to give it a higher octane and make the aircraft fly faster. Right now, God knows, we need all the speed we can get.'

He came alive when he talked planes.

The girl behind the counter was pulling on a pair of woollen gloves and winding a brown woollen scarf around her head.

'Finished your shift?' Maynard asked her.

'Yes.'

'Good. Walk Anna over to the personnel office for her to re-register, will you?' After a moment's thought he added, 'Please.'

'Not necessary,' I said quickly, embarrassed. 'I can find it myself.'

'Of course you can.' He glanced around at the large number of men on the floodlit aprons, unloading and loading trucks, working on fixing aircraft under the sweep of the canopy or refuelling vehicles, all shadowy faceless figures coming and going through the darkness, some in uniform, some not, a mix of Americans and Germans. Not a woman in sight. 'But it's safer,' was all he said.

Ingrid and I paused to watch an aircraft's landing lights hurtle down like Martian outriders coming out of a boot-black sky.

'How well do you know the captain?' I asked.

The young woman's eyes moved like an animal's. Alert and wary. They regarded me now with blatant curiosity. 'Why? You interested in him?'

At close quarters I could see she was older than I'd first thought and wore a wedding band on her finger, but she was small and slight and her voice was soft, as if in hiding from the world.

'No,' I said.

'Why the question then?' she pressed.

'He's been kind to me a couple of times. I was wondering why.'

'Have you tried looking in a mirror, *meine Freundin*?'

'It's not like that,' I said.

'Isn't it?'

'No.'

'With men it's always like that.'

I looked down at the packet of Lucky Strike cigarettes she was drawing from her pocket and we only just avoided the massive shoulder of a flatbed truck packed to the gills with metalwork, pipes and poles hanging off the back. To my surprise a deep male voice bellowed at us from it as it ground its gears and rumbled past us.

'*Guten Abend*, mädchen. How you doing?'

A massive hand waved in my direction and I recognised the cannon-ball of a bald head and the jovial smile that went with it. It was Stefan, the metalworker from the queue outside the recruiting building. It was thanks to his lies that I had landed this job at all.

I waved wildly at him. 'Good, thanks. You?'

'Thirsty work.'

'I owe you a beer,' I yelled after the truck as it trundled away, its headlights punching a hole in the blackness, and he stuck an upturned thumb out the window.

'A friend?' my companion asked mildly.

'Sort of, yes.'

'You're from the east, aren't you?'

'What makes you say that?'

She smiled. 'You East Berliners are like cats padding over hot coals. All burnt feet and raw nerves. Ears twitching.'

I couldn't argue with that.

'Yes, I'm from Prenzlauer Berg. I'm guessing you live in the west of the city.' I'd noticed my companion's cheeks didn't drain of colour whenever a military uniform passed too close.

'You're right,' she admitted, but that was all.

She didn't strike me as the kind of person who would reveal much about herself, so I didn't probe. We continued to slip unnoticed through the semi-darkness, heading towards the office. Somewhere behind us a C-47 Douglas hit down too hard and there was a sickening screech of wheels. With every take-off and landing, danger lay in wait for these young men. Ingrid offered me a smoke and I took a cigarette, thanked her and tucked it out of sight behind my ear to trade later for a chunk of bread or a black-market potato. But I wondered why a person would offer a possession of such value – a cigarette is a form of currency in Berlin – to a total stranger. Berliners tried to be generous to each other whenever they could, but right now not many could afford the luxury of kindness. The struggle for survival did that to you. It made you less of a human being. More of an animal.

The personnel office for the airport's German employees existed in a tiny slice of space carved out of the grand sweep of the massive building. Its door opened straight on to the outside world via a concrete approach, so that we would not soil the neat inner corridors of officialdom with our dirty German boots. To my surprise when I pushed it open, Ingrid stepped inside with me and placed herself just inside the door like a guard dog. I felt a rush of gratitude. She must have been weary from standing up in the catering van all day in the cold, but I could think of worse jobs. Like shovelling coal dust till it coated your teeth and your eyeballs.

The American sergeant behind the desk raised his head, almost hidden behind the mountain range of buff files that extended across his desk. He had a well-fed face, but his eyes were bloodshot, as if he'd either been crying or drinking or both.

'Yes?'

'I am a worker here at Tempelhof,' I said in English. 'But today there is a mistake. My name was taken off the list. Captain Maynard spoke for me and put it back on, but I come here to make it official.'

The sergeant wasted few words on me.

'Name?'

'Fräulein Anna Wolff.'

'Work detail?'

'N-34.'

He rose briskly to his feet and went over to a bank of metal filing cabinets against one wall. He opened a drawer and started to rummage through its contents, making little snick-snick noises as he flicked through the files, his back turned to me for less than a minute. I felt a shift of air at my cheek and Ingrid drifted past me. The sergeant had probably barely noticed her by the door. She was that kind of person, sort of transparent, but now she peered closely at the files on his desk. She reached forward, slid one of them from its pile and stashed it under her coat, all without a sound. By the time the American turned back to his desk, she was next to the door once more, looking bored.

I was stunned.

The sergeant frowned and my mouth went dry, but all he said was, 'It says here that you were injured. Not fit for work.'

The medic. He's the one who removed my name, damn his smiling teeth.

'No, it was a scratch, nothing more.' I waved both arms around in the air like an idiot. 'See? I'm okay now.' Anything to keep his gaze off Ingrid and, more specifically, off what was hidden under her coat.

A quick scribble with his fountain pen. My name reinstated. He lost interest.

'You can go.'

'*Danke.*'

I was out of that door before he could blink.

◆ ◆ ◆

Ahead of me Ingrid vanished into the darkness, a ripple of shadows and she was gone. The words 'Stop, thief! Stop! These people are our friends,' thumped around somewhere inside my head, but the one that came screaming out of my mouth was, 'Run, girl!'

Americans, Brits and French. En masse they were all the same to us. Saviours or invaders? Both, that's the honest truth. They thought of us Germans as conquered scum, the lowest of the low, all tarred with the same Nazi brush, but they were helping us nonetheless. Unlike the Russians who were stripping us naked, America's Marshall Plan was providing more than 15 billion dollars to help finance rebuilding efforts. The brainchild of US Secretary of State George C. Marshall, it was a four-year plan to reconstruct German cities, industries and infrastructure that had been heavily damaged during the war.

And how did I repay them? By helping a complete stranger steal God-knows-what information from them. Why did I do it? Solidarity. Us against them.

How to track down a nun. Alright, an ex-nun. Sister Ingeborg. The one with the face of an angel in the canteen and no roof to her apartment.

I kept glancing over my shoulder but no one was pursuing me from the personnel office, no pounding boots or rifle butts between my shoulder blades, so it wasn't hard to persuade myself that the sergeant would assume the missing file was still lurking somewhere in the mess on his desk. That's what I kept telling myself. Whether or not it was true was another matter.

I found Ingeborg. She was bent over, dressed in her usual grey and scrubbing out the lavatories, scrubbing and singing. The sweet sound of her voice, raised to heaven in a hymn, rebounded off the tiled walls as if it were a whole choir of Ingeborgs and I could feel myself starting to smile. I didn't think I possessed any more smiles.

'Hello, Ingeborg. It looks like you've drawn the short straw tonight.' The place stank of disinfectant.

'I do the work willingly,' she laughed. 'For my Lord.'

Her pearl-grey eyes shone with contentment and I believed her. And envied her.

'What's the matter, Anna?'

'What do you mean?'

Carefully she laid down her brush and scouring cloth, walked over to one of the washbasins and soaped her hands, delicate hands that were unaccustomed to physical labour. She glided up close to me and took my cold hand in her warm one, an intimate gesture.

'What's wrong?' she asked with concern. 'What has happened?'

'Is it so obvious?' I grimaced.

'You look as if you've been swallowed by Jonah's whale.'

I couldn't tell her that the musky scent of a Russian Red Army officer's greatcoat had torn open my heart earlier today or that the taste of his lips against mine had broken me. Instead I said what I'd come to say.

'I need to meet the children you mentioned last night who are being sheltered in the school where you teach.'

Her hand squeezed mine. It was a tight determined squeeze that ground my bones together.

'We'll find your boy,' she promised.

CHAPTER TWENTY-FIVE

• • •

ANNA

I wouldn't cry. I swore to myself that I wouldn't cry.
I'd nailed my heart back together.

But when I saw the row of hopeful blue eyes staring up at me as if I'd been sent down to them by God, how could I not cry? Sister Ingeborg – for that's what they called her – introduced each one to me by name.

'This is Peter.'

'Hello, Peter.'

'This is Oskar.'

'Hello, Oskar.'

'This is Matthias.'

'Hello, Matthias.'

'This is Gunther.'

'Hello, Gunther.'

I smiled at each anxious little face and placed a thin strip of Tempelhof canteen cheese on the upturned palms. Spotlessly clean pink hands. The head of the establishment, Frau Bertha Neumann, looked on. I liked her. Straight-backed and plain-spoken, though weathered and faded somewhat, just like her school, as if she'd come through too many storms, but she had a solidity about her that was reassuring. These few *Wolfskinder* were the lucky ones.

Frau Neumann clearly believed that cleanliness was the path to godliness every waking hour of the day. Unfortunately, at the end of my Tempelhof shift I'd collapsed, filthy, on my bed for a few hours of what had felt more like a brain-dead coma than sleep, but when I woke, water had oozed from our tap only one gravy-brown drip at a time and the queue for the standpipe in the street snaked around the block. So I curled my own coal-rimmed fingernails out of sight in-side my gloves.

'And this,' Ingeborg added, 'is Poldi.' Her voice melted into a warm chuckle. 'He's our cheeky little monkey.'

That was it. I fell in love. That fast. My heart quickened and my fingertips ached to touch Poldi's smooth sinless skin. Corn-coloured hair mown short and feathery on his eggshell skull. A mouth too wide for his three-year old jaw that was constantly on the verge of breaking into a grin. Yes, Ingeborg was right, a cheeky grin, but it was the child's eyes that hooked me, the colour of a winter-blue sky, with a quickness to them and an awareness far beyond his tender years.

Were they Felix's eyes?

Almost. So close. So unbearably close.

A desire for this child, this precious Poldi, rocketed through me like a gunshot. My arms begged to hold him. I longed to kiss him and to teach new things to those bright blue eyes. To sing him to sleep at night and to prop him up on his first bicycle. I wasn't prepared for this unexpected torrent of love, this blossoming within me. Could this child become *my* child? *My* son? Could Poldi fill the gaping space within me that ached relentlessly day and night? Or would it be a betrayal of my own Felix?

My gloved fingers started to tremble and Ingeborg stepped forward, her face glowing with happiness, her grey arms outstretched to em-brace me. 'It's him, isn't it? Your son.'

'Yes.'

I imagined that I would take little Leopold – Poldi for short – by the hand and ride home with him on my bicycle. But it was not that simple, far from it. Frau Neumann was a stickler for the rules. There were forms to be filled out, names and addresses to be registered with the appropriate children's welfare department, rubber stamps to be inked, authorisation to be given, checks on me to be made.

After all, this was the British sector, the heart of law and order and paperwork. The British sector covered the finest six districts of Berlin, extending from Spandau in the west to Tiergarten in the centre of the city and contained not only the magnificent Charlottenburg Palace but also the Grunewald forest and Siemensstadt, an industrial complex of vast size. Its machinery had been looted and ransacked by the Russians of course, and the sector's streets were a mass of bombed rubble, but the British forces were working relentlessly to rebuild. Surely that would keep them far too busy to check on me.

'How long?' I asked Frau Neumann.

Three days, she promised. Maybe four. A week at most. I must wait. It would be proof of my commitment.

I couldn't bear to let go of Poldi's hand, as soft as butter in my own.

CHAPTER TWENTY-SIX

◆ ◆ ◆

INGRID

W hy here?

Ingrid stood in front of a run-down block of apartments, still on its feet but only just. It was an *Altbau* building from the 1890s, in the Mitte district of the Soviet sector.

Why here?

It wasn't Kuznetzov's style. Too dilapidated. Its once-elegant stone scrollwork was hanging off, its façade thick with soot and most of its windows boarded up. The kind of place where black-market deals went down and where rats gnawed through the wiring while you sat there.

Why here? What was his purpose? She couldn't work it out.

She felt sweat gathering in her hair and was tempted to take out the military file tucked into her knickers and retrace her steps.

Instead she banged on the door.

A Red Army soldier opened it. Unshaven and silent in an oversized greatcoat clearly intended for someone else, he marched her down a short corridor and into a complex of cobbled courtyards that stretched behind the building. These old tenements were always overcrowded and dingy places, but she could see no sign of life in the windows of the apartments that surrounded her.

There were four storeys of rusting balconies, each one occupied by a single Soviet soldier armed with a rifle. Each rifle aimed at her. The soldier at her side mumbled something in Russian and kicked open one of the doors on the ground floor. She walked into the lion's den. Just like old times.

This time she matched him. Her jacket was every bit as stylish as Kuznetzov's and her two-tone shoes were a beautiful buttery leather.

They made her taller. Less in his shadow. Of course they were second hand, you couldn't get anything new in the shops, but these were classy and barely worn. Otto had come home with them for her and she felt like someone else in them.

A lot of old-style Berlin apartments were L-shaped and renowned for their *Berliner Zimmer*. It was an awkward kind of room that connected the street-facing part of the apartment with the inner courtyard behind, and it was here to this haven of darkness with its heavily carved turn-of-the-century furniture that Ingrid was escorted. The whole place felt designed to break her nerve.

Didn't he understand yet? She could walk a twenty-metre high-wire with no safety net. She had no nerves.

'Ah, my little Ingrid.' Kuznetsov opened the conversation with a wide gesture of welcome, almost a bow.

'You are correct in saying I am little,' she said, 'but I am not yours.'

She noted the slow blink and the adjustment in the way he stood. His clothes and his pale hair looked soft and silky today and she had a strange urge to reach out and stroke him.

'You Germans are so …' he paused, smiled a small smile, 'precise.'

'I've brought you something. I know you will like it.'

He held out a hand as if doing her a favour. 'Let me see.'

Oh, he was good at hiding his eagerness, but she could smell it on him, sharper than his cologne. Her nose was finely trained to smell out an animal's fear, and equally its musky scent of pleasure. The buff file in her hand was the equivalent to the chunk of bloody flesh on the end of the stick that her father had used to train the big circus cats.

'Here.' She handed it over, the USAF stamp clearly visible on its front cover.

He skimmed through its pages and his lips grew loose with satisfaction. 'You're good. And you're right. This is interesting.'

'More than *interesting*,' she corrected.

He smiled again and nodded at her thoughtfully.

She did not mention that she had studied the file's contents with care. It contained a full list of the day's aircraft movements and cargoes. Minute by minute. The exact number of Skytrains and Sky-masters flying in and out of Tempelhof today, dozens of them every hour, their precise landing and take-off times and patterns, all adhering to General Tunner's strict schedule. No room for error. And in addition it listed the cargo manifest of each one, amounting to more than 4,000 tons a day. It itemised the food: 641 tons of flour, 150 tons of cereal, 106 tons of meat and fish, 900 tons of potatoes, 51 of sugar, 20 of milk, 32 tons of fats and 3 tons of yeast. And then there was the coal, hundreds of tons of it, the vital life-giving black gold.

'It beggars belief,' Kuznetsov said softly, 'that that they can do this.'

'Berliners all thought it was impossible.'

'It's a crazy idea that should never work. Supplying more than two million inhabitants by air is logistically impossible. Stalin told us that the Allies would quickly pull out their measly two battalions on the ground and that all of Berlin would then fall into our grasp. Conquest by siege and starvation, he called it. We'd wipe our Red Army boots all over West Berlin.' Kuznetsov started to prowl the edges of the room, restless and frustrated. 'But Britain's Foreign Minister, Ernest Bevin, and the US General Lucius Clay are men obsessed. They swear they'll never abandon the city.'

'Good,' she said.

He frowned. 'Why good?'

'Because it makes work for the likes of you and me.'

He halted mid-stride. She'd hooked him. He sucked in the damp air that hung heavy in the room and to Ingrid's horror he came over to her and wrapped an arm around her shoulders. She stood rigid, not sure what to do. No man ever bothered to touch her. Only Otto.

'You're learning,' he murmured in her ear.

He led her downstairs.

The basement was dank and smelled bad. It consisted of a cold dim corridor littered by mice droppings and illuminated by a single naked light bulb that cast a glow like a spill of honey on the floor. Five green-painted doors on each side of the corridor were all closed, all retreating into shadows, all with exterior iron bolts.

Ingrid told herself she wasn't afraid. No nerves, she reminded herself. She was too valuable to him, much too valuable. But she had no doubt about what went on behind those bolted doors.

'Choose a door,' Kuznetsov told her.

She gave him a blank stare. He was hatless but not cane-less. White shirt, crisp lavender tie, a soft cashmere coat. On the very tip of one of the points of his shirt collar lay the smallest dot of dried blood. On anyone else she might have thought it was a shaving nick.

'I don't wish to choose a door.'

'Go ahead,' he insisted, 'any door.' As if offering her candy.

'No.'

'Choose a door.'

'No.'

A patient half-smile. 'Choose a door, Ingrid, or I shall choose one for you.'

She gestured to the one furthest away from her on the left. 'That one.'

He strolled over, slid back the bolt and pushed open the door. She didn't move. The smell grew worse.

'Come, Ingrid. Look at this.'

Her feet worked. She didn't know how they worked. She looked inside the tiny room. It was over-bright. White walls, a glaring lamp, a table and two chairs. The table looked like it belonged in a blacksmith's workshop because on it lay a neat row of pointed metal tools. Some had teeth. Behind the table and looking directly at Ingrid stood a man not in uniform.

'Comrade Kuznetsov,' he said with respect.

A burst of Russian words followed that Ingrid didn't understand. She looked with distaste at the man. Everything about him was soft, his floppy hair, his loose belly, his cheeks. His plump pasty fingers. But not his eyes, no, not his eyes. They were like steel ball-bearings. Behind him on the white wall was a large smear of what was, unmistakably, blood and she wondered if it was there by design as a warning, or by accident.

In front of the table another man sat on the second chair. *Sat* was the wrong word. Huddled. Hunched. Buckled. Bent. Broken. Pick one, any one. They all applied. He hung forward, his head almost on his knees. He made no sound but flies hummed around the dark hole where his ear was missing. Violence simmered in the room and a cold sweat clung to Ingrid's clothes. She stepped back into the corridor and Kuznetsov closed the door with a gentle click.

'What is this place?' she demanded.

'It's a place of learning.' In the dim light Kuznetsov stood tall and still, regarding her intently.

'Was the Watzmann restaurant the carrot,' she asked, 'and now this is the stick?'

She didn't touch Kuznetsov but she wanted to. Not to stroke him, not this time. She had learned from Otto how to break a man's jaw with one punch on the right spot.

'Would you care to look behind another door?' He was so polite. So courteous.

'No.'

'Are you sure?'

'Yes.'

'Do you know why I brought you here?'

'To frighten me.'

He shrugged his elegant cashmere shoulders. 'No, no, Ingrid. On the contrary, I would never do anything so crass to you.'

'Why then?'

'To show you that you will be well protected. You are part of a network now and we take care of our own.'

'Who are *we*?'

'Who do you think we are?'

'A bunch of murdering bastards who snatch people off the street and hack off pieces of their body to get answers.'

His laughter filled the corridor. He was genuinely amused, although she couldn't imagine why.

'We are the MGB, the Ministerstvo gosudarstvennoy bezopasnosti. That's the Ministry of State Security to you. And yes, it's true,' he boasted, 'that we took another two scientists from under the British noses last week. Right outside the restaurant in Moabit in the British sector where General Herbert was eating his dinner. They were chemists from Kraftwerk West, the bombed power plant out at Spandau.'

'Where will you take them?'

'To Moscow of course. They will be invited to join our Soviet push towards a great technological future.'

'And if they refuse?'

The smile flickered again, the bared white teeth of a Siberian tiger. 'You ask too many questions, little Ingrid.' He started to stride in good humour back up the corridor. 'Come, you have done well today. I will take you for coffee at—'

'Wait.'

He turned. 'What?'

'I have something else.'

It felt like sliding one foot out on to the high-wire.

'What else?'

'Let the man go free first.'

Kuznetzov's eyes widened with surprise. He was the kind of person who did not like to be surprised, she imagined, as he took two slow steps towards her. The light bulb flickered but neither noticed.

'Are you telling me that you have more information that you will trade for that piece of scum's life?'

'Yes.'

He came closer, so close she could smell his cologne again. 'Do you know that man?' he asked with no attempt to hide his irritation at this unexpected twist.

'No.'

'What kind of information are you offering?'

Adrenaline was pumping as she slid her second foot smoothly on to the high-wire. 'Let him go free right now. Then I will tell you.'

They stood facing each other in the bleak corridor, a stand-off, no sound. The doors and walls must be soundproofed, she thought, as she watched the rise and fall of his chest. That's how you tell when an animal is about to attack.

'*Da*,' he said at last, 'you've got yourself a deal, Ingrid, but I didn't think you were such a sentimental fool. You disappoint me.'

He called out something in Russian and two guards came running. They entered the end room, emerged half carrying, half dragging the prisoner without an ear, frogmarched him up the stairs and across the courtyard and threw him out into the street. He fell on his knees, scrambled to his feet and fled, still hunched and huddled, still broken. But free. Ingrid and Kuznetsov both witnessed the release.

'Satisfied?'

She nodded. 'Yes.'

'Good. You are a little fool.'

He took hold of her upper arm and walked her smartly towards his black Mercedes parked at the kerb. 'Now the information, Ingrid Keller. Tell me.'

She jerked her arm out of his grip. 'I saw her,' she said.

She might as well have stabbed him with the knife strapped to her thigh. His face drained of colour and as he reached for the car door handle a tremor hit his hand.

'You saw her?'

'I did.'

'Where?'

'At Tempelhof.'

'You spoke to her?'

'Yes, I spoke to Anna Wolff. It's possible she has already been arrested by the Americans, for stealing the file.'

With a smile that showed only the pointy tips of her own tiger teeth, she climbed into the car.

CHAPTER TWENTY-SEVEN

♦ ♦ ♦

ANNA

'Hey, Yvo.'

The boy was waiting for me. In Tiergarten, as arranged, in the British sector. He was perched on top of the stump of a tree that had been felled for fuel and I felt a spike of relief at the sight of him. Still surviving. Another day, another night, though no more than a scarecrow in chopped-down US Army fatigues and an old patched Red Army padded jacket stripped of its badges that swallowed his skinny figure. I wondered where on earth he'd got his hands on that little lot but was glad he looked warm. I worried about this kid more than I cared to admit.

I almost didn't turn up, my mind so full of Poldi and how I would embrace him into my life. But I'd promised Yvo, the young ratbag, when he'd loitered in my doorway that I would come today, so he would be expecting me. Not me, as much as what I would bring for him and for his pack of *Wolfskinder*. And I was still keen to take a look at the blue-eyed child he'd told me about, the one hanging around his pack with a Jewish girl.

I'd cycled at full speed down Charlottenburger Chaussee ahead of a swelling wave of fog that was rolling its way through the city, and I'd arrived with no real expectation of success. How many hundreds of little blue-eyed boys had I chased after in the last two years and nine months – I'd lost count – and each time I'd seen my small bird of hope ripped out of my chest and its neck broken.

But here I was. Yet again. The Tiergarten had once been the grand hunting domain of the Kaisers, the home range of wild boar and deer, but the once-magnificent forest was now reduced to firewood due to the shortage of coal. It made me sad to come here to bear witness to the pitiful handful of trees that had survived out of over 200,000. But now, by order of the British authority, much of the stripped 500 acres of wasteland had been used to create 2,500 plots for the city's inhabitants to grow potatoes and vegetables. So a few lucky Berliners, wrapped in bulky layers of scarves and coats, pottered around the landscape with spades and garden forks over their shoulders, hunched like gnomes digging for treasure.

'Nice outfit,' I greeted Yvo.

He puffed out his bony ribcage to fill up the space inside the padded jacket that would easily have housed three of him.

'What you brought for me, mädchen?'

'Pork fat.'

He catapulted himself on to the patch of ground in front of me and snatched at the hessian bag I dumped at his feet. He was always hungry. Like he was always dirty. He'd once admitted to me that he had no idea how he'd come to be in Berlin and that inside his head he clung to fading memories of a large garden with sunflowers and cows on the other side of a fence. He was probably less than the nine years of age that he claimed but already was one of the city's rats, scratching to survive. He and his pack lived in small filthy child-shaped spaces, but he knew where to lead his wolf cubs to find clean water and taught them how to pad the inside of their shirts with old newspapers for warmth. And how to steal a crust of bread with an innocent face and quick hands. He was as infuriating as he was brave.

I waited. I'd learned patience. With Yvo food came first, talk came later. He squatted on the damp earth, plunged his hands into the bag and within seconds his sallow cheeks were bulging with fistfuls of coarse bread and cold mashed turnip, his lips glistening with pork fat. I'd never known anyone who ate as fast as Yvo, but I didn't tell him to slow or to take it easy. He knew the dangers out here far better than I did.

He stopped as suddenly as he'd started, saving the rest to share among his pack members. He licked his lips, then his fingers. I laughed and he scowled at me, warning me off. I waited some more, pulling my mother's coat tighter around me and shifting from one foot to the other as damp seeped up through the paper-thin soles of my shoes while Yvo rummaged through the remaining contents of the bag. Would it be enough?

Without a word he swung the bag's strap over one shoulder and set off at a fast pace across the expanse of grassless earth that had once boasted a forest.

'Come,' he called out.

I must be mad. My bandaged arm yelped. The children giggled.

I was squeezing myself through a ridiculously narrow grating at the foot of a brick wall, dangling half in and half out and likely to remain that way. With typical gusto, Yvo grabbed one ankle and yanked so hard I landed in an undignified heap inside a mouldy cellar. I glanced around. I was inside a building at the top of Parochialstrasse, the street that had gained a moment of fame when the communist leader Walter Ulbricht hosted the first meeting of Berlin's first post-Nazi town council there. That man had much to answer for.

They stood in a circle around me, Yvo's wolf pack, six of them, grinning down at me and for one brief second I imagined them tearing me to pieces, feasting on my limbs and my liver for days to come. But no, their small eager hands helped me to my feet instead and I dragged my mind back up from its black hole.

'Line up,' Yvo ordered.

To my surprise the six children rushed to line up in a row like miniature soldiers in strict order of height. All boys, between four and eight years of age, I'd guess, but starvation stunts growth, so maybe older. For certain these kids were starved. Bones like knife blades under their filthy skin and pinched scabby lips. Right in front of me the smallest child wet himself with excitement and nobody cared.

'Here, take it, Willy,' Yvo said to him with the kind of tender smile I had no idea his surly face was capable of. I loved him for it. He handed over a strip of pork fat from the greaseproof paper in my bag and it vanished at once.

The second child held out a hand that I'd swear had not seen water in weeks and he received a slightly larger strip.

'Eat slow,' Yvo ordered. 'Make it last.'

'Me next,' bleated a curly-haired lad next in line. His mouth was wide open, his baby-pink tongue dancing in anticipation.

And down the line Yvo went, first with the greasy strips of white fat for each one, then with a dollop of turnip mash on to each grimy palm and a final march past, handing out chunks of bread the colour and consistency of dried mud. God only knew what was in it but it was all I could get. With my first beautiful western Deutschmarks from my Tempelhof masters, each banknote stamped with a nice big B for Berlin, I'd raced down to the black marketeers hanging around under one of the bridges over the Spree and bargained hard for my haul. Now I peered into the dark corners of the dank cellar. I'd done my part. Time for Yvo to do his.

'Leah,' Yvo called out.

'Come forward for your share, Leah,' I murmured and the darkness in the far corner shifted, black against black.

I heard a rustle of material like the ripple of a bat's wing. Her feet made no sound but suddenly she was there in front of me.

'Hello, Leah.'

'Hello.' Her mouth faked a smile.

'I've brought you food.'

'*Dankeschön.*'

She was tall for her age, a sweep of long dark locks, neat and tidy, not in tatters like the boys. A strong young face, with jutting cheek-bones and a large nose, and there was a stillness to her that made me want to step forward and peel off the mask of politeness, to take a good look at what lay behind it.

I held out the bag. 'Help yourself,' I said. 'The boys haven't scoffed it all yet.'

She didn't hurry. With eyes fixed intently on mine, she reached for what remained of the bag of food with her free hand. Her other hand was already occupied. Only now did I see the small clean fingers clutched in hers. My pulse kicked when I realised a small figure had wrapped itself tight in her long black skirt, so that I could see nothing of it except a ruffled stalk of hair. It was pale. Ice blond.

'Who have we here?' I asked.

'My brother.'

'What's his name?'

'Lars.'

'How old is he?'

'Four.'

The little figure looked too small for four. I crouched down on the stinking cement floor in front of the child, close enough to stroke a strand of his hair if I'd chosen.

'Would you like a piece of bread, Lars?' I asked, each word a whisper. I was terrified he'd run and be out of that grating before I could tell my heart to stop hammering.

The boy burrowed deeper, but Leah murmured something to him in a language I took to be Yiddish and eased his clinging body further forward, though his face was still buried in her skirts.

'He's shy,' she said.

'I don't blame him.'

I slipped a harmonica out of my coat pocket, cupped my hands around it and ran my lips over its row of holes in a sweet ripple of sound. Gasps and giggles broke out around me as the music bewitched them and the boys pressed closer wanting more. One stroked the back of my neck.

'Would you like it, Lars, the harmonica? I brought it for you. It used to belong to my father.' I held it out to him, brushing its cold metal surface against his hand.

At last his fingers uncurled from his sister's and hooked around the harmonica, while at the same moment his face emerged from her skirts. Instantly I felt as if I'd been punched in the chest. The shy little boy's eyes were huge, but they were an opaque summer-sky blue, milky and sightless. His small face must once have been lovely but now it had a twist of scar tissue pulling it out of shape. Unerringly his lips found the holes on the harmonica but no sound came out.

'Blow,' I said. 'Blow hard, Lars.'

When a shriek blasted out from the instrument, we all jumped and hooted with laughter, no one louder than Lars himself at hearing the noise he had produced.

'Thank you,' his sister said through her brother's delighted giggles. I could see a thin layer of the mask had peeled away. 'Thank you. You've made Lars happy.'

For me, it changed everything.

I stood in the doorway of my basement workshop and inspected it objectively.

There are moments that alter your life. We all have them, the crossroads, and I recognised that this was one. I felt it as surely as I felt my own heartbeat.

For almost three years I'd been scrambling around trying to find one special child, one beautiful beloved boy and it had scraped me raw, but you can't bleed forever. Eventually you run out of blood.

My workshop was a good enough space, long and narrow with the skinny window with the grating up near the ceiling, and crucially, it was dry. Right now it was crowded with tools and cogs and oil-stained rags, bicycle wheels propped against the walls and skeletal metal frames awaiting repair, but I let my mind imagine it empty. I tried to calculate exactly how many child-size makeshift beds I could fit inside it if I stripped out everything else.

I reckoned twenty.

Twenty-five at a push.

I took down a screwdriver from my array of tools and started to unscrew the worktop from the wall.

CHAPTER TWENTY-EIGHT

◆ ◆ ◆

TIMUR

'That man Gniffke is making a fool of us, Kotikov –' Marshal Vasily Sokolovsky pointed an accusing finger squarely at his deputy – 'and you were supposed to put a stop to it.'

General Alexander Kotikov, to whom he was speaking, was the pugnacious military commandant of the Soviet Sector of Berlin. And he was acutely aware that his predecessor on the Berlin Kommandatura, Lieutenant-General Smirnov, had been summoned back to Moscow in a hurry. After only a few months in the job, Kotikov did not intend to make the same mistakes. He was quick to find words to defend himself but on this occasion failed to appease his senior officer.

Further down the oval conference table the air in Major Timur Voronin's lungs moved soundlessly in and out but his tongue lay stiff and heavy in the base of his mouth. He hoped it had enough sense to stay there though it itched to give voice. But he was no fool. In front of him prowled the almighty Sokolovsky, the Supreme Head of the Soviet Military Administration in Germany, an official Hero of the Soviet Union and the exact equivalent of God within the communist zone.

The marshal was not a man to cross, not if you were wise. A phalanx of medals was flaunted across his broad chest alongside the Order of Lenin, the Soviet Union's highest honour, so each of the seven other uniformed officers in the room breathed with care. Timur felt a darkness within himself whenever he was in this man's presence, and it sickened him. He studied the hard face with its straight-line mouth and handsome square jaw and kept his own mouth shut.

He had nothing but respect for Sokolovsky's exceptional prowess as a military leader of the Soviet Army, but you didn't step in his path any more than you stepped in front of a T-34 tank. It was Sokolovsky's job to spearhead the removal of all Allied forces from Berlin, and he jabbed his fingertip in the direction of the city map that hung on one wall, next to an absurdly huge portrait of Joseph Stalin. He glared at Kotikov.

'Did you inform the Americans that we have declared Erich Gniffke to be an enemy of the Soviet Union?' Sokolovsky demanded.

'Yes, Comrade Marshal.'

'Did you tell them he has been found guilty of corruption and fraudulent practices?'

'Yes, Comrade Marshal.'

'And still they welcomed him with open arms into the western zone?'

'Yes, Comrade Marshal, they did.'

'*Poydi k chertu!*'

The marshal's rage revealed itself in the florid colour that spiked into his cheeks and in the clenching of his strong peasant teeth, but no one spoke. No one met his eye. The silence in the well-appointed oak-panelled office fell over the seven men seated around the table, men accustomed to wielding power, until one with well-oiled hair parted in the centre gathered up his courage and declared, 'Erich Gniffke is a traitor to his country and to communism. He deserves execution.'

Timur listened to the chorus of agreement from around the table, but his own tongue stayed where it was. Erich Gniffke was one of the German leaders of the SED, the German Socialist Unity Party, which was known to be in Moscow's pocket. When Griffke had resigned as chairman of the secretariat of the German People's Council he'd declared that a totalitarian dictatorship was being imposed on Germany, denying all democratic rights to its citizens. From that moment his days had been numbered and he'd fled to the west.

'General Tunner will laugh in my face,' Sokolovsky growled. 'I prefer the sound of American tears to their laughter.' He scanned the men in the room. 'Which of you brings me news that will make Tunner weep instead?'

'We should implement our usual retaliation,' suggested the officer seated opposite, a burly figure with brandy on his breath. 'Take two of their filthy spies and throw them into Sachsenhausen, Special Camp Number One, then see whether the Americans are still laughing.'

'Or we could teach Tunner a lesson,' proposed the white-haired General Antonov who was seated on Timur's right, the oldest and calmest man in the room. 'Let's snatch one of their top scientists from the western sector of the city. That will get Tunner hot under the collar.'

Marshal Sokolovsky exhaled heavily. 'Not easy to achieve, Antonov. After our last abduction of the two chemists, their scientists are guarded like gold bars day and night.' His head dropped between his shoulders like a battle-scarred old lion as his eyes ranged over each man. 'Other tactics?'

Timur's tongue moved for the first time. 'Comrade Marshal.'

All eyes turned on him. He was the lowest-ranked officer in the room, only here to present a report. Sokolovsky took his time resuming his seat, jotted something on a pad in front of him and folded his hands over it.

'Proceed,' he said.

'I have recently been dismantling a factory in our Soviet sector.' Timur used the word *dismantling* advisedly. Not *looting*. Never *looting*. 'In the Kreuzberg district. During the process of doing so, I discovered listening devices embedded in the walls of the managing director's office and in the lavatories. Both had been recently redecorated.'

The silence in the room was pin sharp. Talk of secret microphones brought them out in a sweat, each one of them. Timur could smell the tang of fear mingling with the fug of cigarette smoke in the room.

'And how exactly does this affect General Tunner?' Marshal Sokolovsky demanded with impatience.

'The recordings are of one of the general's personal aides committing large sums of money to invest in the factory. An injection of American money to ensure it didn't collapse. A clear breach of Allied protocols. Western finance, as you are aware, is not permitted in any form in Soviet-controlled territory. General Tunner's aide made it plain that they are secretly offering investment to any East German company that will spread the word that capitalism and America's Marshall Aid are the only way forward for Germany. It is blatant use of bribery and subversion and a breaking of protocol.'

Sokolovsky drew a black line across his pad. 'Who made the recordings?'

'That is unknown at the moment.'

The creases around the marshal's eyes folded into deep shadows. 'I need the precise details, Major Voronin. Names and numbers with which to confront Tunner.'

'It's all here.'

Timur produced a crisp white folder, placed it on the table in front of him and slid it forward. The soft whisper of paper over polished wood was the only sound.

The marshal nodded approval.

'There's more.' Timur allowed himself a faint smile. 'The factory makes porcelain sanitaryware. I am currently loading its stock of baths, washbasins and toilets on to railway wagons at Friedrichstrasse station to be hauled to depots in Moscow. So within days Muscovites will have the pleasure of shitting on a product that is American-sponsored.'

Sokolovsky roared with laughter and thumped the flat of his hand on the table, making even the most hardened officers in the room jump. Kotikov pushed back his silver quiff and joined in the laughter.

'I applaud your work, Major. Keep it up. I want to see a full report on the transport trains by tomorrow.'

'Yes, Comrade Marshal. But there is one thing I require.'

'Spit it out. What is it?'

'I require access to the warehouses where acquisitions from recent household sweeps have been stored.'

'For what purpose?'

'To pack their contents into crates to transport to Moscow. That's in addition to the industrial equipment I've already requisitioned for the Motherland. Today I arranged a shipment of machinery from a factory that manufactures glass bottles and medical vials. These will of course be beneficial to the Soviet Union. But I feel the arrival of more personal items along with them will also be appreciated.' He paused. 'By our Great Leader.'

All eyes swivelled to the portrait of Joseph Stalin above their heads, his stare as formidable as his moustache. For a moment Timur pondered what it would be like to meet the 'Father of Nations' in person, this ruler of such a vast union that crossed continents and swallowed countries whole. It was whispered that he was a quiet and small man, unprepossessing and severely scarred by smallpox. But relentlessly ruthless. His chosen name, Stalin, meant 'man of steel'. He was a man who ruled through terror. That was the leader Timur was here to serve.

Sokolovsky studied Timur for a full nerve-grinding minute, but finally he nodded at the white-haired general. 'That's your department, Antonov. See to it. Give him access.'

'Understood, Comrade Marshal.'

Timur turned his head and met the resentful gaze of the Red Army general on his right, the man who only an hour ago had denied him access to the guarded warehouses along the banks of the Spree. He could almost hear the cracks opening in the ice under his feet.

CHAPTER TWENTY-NINE

♦ ♦ ♦

ANNA

A navy duffle coat stepped out on to the road, in full view, making no attempt to avoid my scrutiny. The overcast sky and the ragged walls of the buildings riddled with bullet holes had merged to form a leaden grey shroud that seemed to suck the life out of Berlin's pedestrians as I pedalled down Bauerstrasse. My head was churning over the question of where and how I could procure blankets and mattresses to cram into my workshop, and I almost didn't spot the duffle coat. He was moving swiftly and I swung my wheel right across the tram tracks.

Definitely a man, I could tell by the length of his stride and by his striped charcoal trousers as he crossed on to the pavement at the corner of Prenzlauer Allee, but his navy duffle coat was buttoned to his chin, hood right up so I couldn't see his hair. Was it white like Resi had said? Was this the man she said was shadowing me?

It was just beginning to drizzle as I skidded to a halt in front of the duffle coat, blocking the path.

'*Arschloch!*' the man swore at me. 'What the hell are you doing?'

'Are you following me?'

He threw both his gloved hands between us to ward me off. 'Are you crazy? You're the one who was behind me. You're on a bicycle and I'm on foot. Do I look as if I'm following you? Do I?'

I didn't have an answer.

'Would you mind pulling down your hood, please?' I asked.

'I most certainly would. Leave me alone.'

'I'm looking for someone with white hair,' I explained. 'I thought it might be you.' I kept it polite but I knew it was too late. I'd already alarmed him.

'I don't have white hair.'

'Show me.'

He stepped smartly around my bicycle, hurrying away as if I were foaming at the mouth.

Was I? Foaming at the mouth, seeing threats where there were none? People around me had died, there was no denying that, but it didn't necessarily mean it was connected to me. Did it? Or was there someone out there who had put a target on my back?

By the time I reached the apartment I was wet through and cold, but I barely noticed it because as I reached out to open the door my eyes snagged on the solitary nail hole in the door at eye level. The memory of how it came to be there flooded my mind and it hurt, like a bruise that I couldn't stop touching. Timur had arrived at our apartment with apples. It was in the early days of that summer of 1945 when my mother was still ill in bed and when Russian soldiers had been loosed like a pack of rabid hounds to rip apart what was left of Berlin and Berliners.

'You are pale,' Timur had commented. 'You don't go out enough.'

'It's too dangerous. Yesterday Russian troops even forced their way right up here to our floor and banged on our door. Next time they will kick it down.'

I saw something darken within him. He took a knife from his pocket, sliced off one of the *pogony*, the red-and-gold shoulder boards on his khaki uniform that indicated his rank of Soviet Army major. He asked me for a nail and hammer, and he hammered the elaborate piece of insignia on to the front of our door.

'There,' he'd said. 'For protection.'

It had worked. The Soviet soldiers never came again.

When I finally pushed the bruising memory aside and walked into the apartment, shaking the rain off my coat, my mother was down on her knees scrubbing the floor. Her knuckles were blue, not with cold, but with ink stains from where the bastard Russians had thrown down a glass inkwell on the oak floor when they did the sweep. It had exploded into a thousand glittering glass hailstones and the ink had seeped into the grain of the herringbone woodblocks. We'd mopped it up earlier but my mother wouldn't rest until she had scoured every trace of it out of the apartment, the same way she had scrubbed every trace of Felix out of the apartment.

Except for Wolffi. I'd hidden the toy away now. It didn't belong to her.

I dropped down to my knees in front of her so that we were on the same level and she looked up from her work, startled. She had a scarf wound around her head and wore a hideous heavy black dress to her ankles that looked like a priest's cassock. I wondered where on earth it had come from.

'You're wet,' she said.

'It's nothing.'

I yanked off my sodden woollen hat and ran a hand through the soaked spikes of my hair. It smelled of the city, that distinctive stink of wet cement and empty bellies that followed us around like shadows.

'It's been a bad day, Mutti. Are you alright?'

'Nobody in this godforsaken city is alright,' she declared.

'That's why we have to help the ones even worse off than we are,' I said in a quiet tone.

The scrubbing stopped. Instantly. Her blue eyes fixed on me. 'What have you done?'

'Done?'

'Tell me, Anna. Tell me straight.'

'I've invited a little boy to come and live with us.'

She sucked in a great wave of air that lifted her on to her feet, her scrubbing brush and bucket of water abandoned. She leaned over me, so that when I looked up I could see the slender tunnels of her nostrils and feel the hot breath being expelled from them.

'Not *him*,' she said.

'No. Not *him*. Not ...'

I was about to say his name – my sweet Felix – but she cut in before I could release it into the cold loveless room.

'Who then?'

'A little boy. He's about three or four years old and his name is Leopold but he's called Poldi for short. He's living in a kind of orphanage run by an ex-headmistress over in the British sector but they don't know where he came from or what happened to his parents. He just turned up one day, begging for soup. They say he was a shrivelled little scrag of a thing, he looked like a twig when he arrived and was covered in sores, but now he is much better. They've been good to him. But there is so much competition for their beds that ...'

'They throw them out on to the streets when they've got the children fattened up a bit, so they can take in new ones. I've heard of that practice. It's normal.'

'You'll like him, Mutti.' I smiled up at her.

'Of course I won't.'

'Mutti, you have no reason to dislike this one.'

'Is he another Russian bastard?'

I trod with care. 'No one knows for certain, but I don't think so. He looks Scandinavian to me. Danish or Swedish maybe, with a wide open face, feathery blond hair and sky-blue eyes. Paler skin and higher cheekbones than most kids. Definitely Swedish, I would say.'

'Of course you would say.'

'Please, Mutti,' I whispered.

She reached out one of her damp blue-stained hands and laid it flat on my head, and it felt exactly the way the local priest's hand used to in blessing on a Sunday when I was a child. The intimacy of the gesture startled both of us. There was a slip in time as our eyes held on to each other, me on my knees, my mother staring intently down at me, and I longed to know what it was she wanted of me. Because she wanted something. I could feel that. I could feel it through the light pressure of her hand on my head, but how could I give it to her when I didn't know what it was?

'I know it will complicate our lives,' I said softly, 'but we will manage.'

'And tell me, who will look after this Poldi child when you are out at Tempelhof airfield?'

I said nothing.

'Have you thought of that?' she persisted.

I rose to my feet and her hand fell away, parting us. 'Yes, Mutti, I have thought of that. Most of the time when I am working a night-shift he will be asleep, but yes, there may be a couple of hours when Poldi will need you.' I felt a flutter of something in my throat, something that told me to stop, but I didn't. 'I think you owe this child that much.'

'I owe this child nothing.' Her eyes grew bright. 'Nothing at all.'

'You do, Mutti, you owe him a life.'

'Why? I've never even met him.'

'You owe a life to Poldi to replace the one you stole from Felix.'

The words were out. And I could hear them crashing around the room, doing more damage than Lieutenant Glinin and his soldiers ever did.

'Anna,' she breathed. 'Don't.'

But words were forcing their way out now, burning through my tongue, and I couldn't have stopped them even if I'd wanted to.

'You got rid of little Felix when I was sick with fever.' I was fighting to keep my voice from bouncing off the walls. 'Yet you won't tell me how or where you got rid of him, what you did with him, whether you drowned him in a bucket like an unwanted kitten or threw him in the river. I don't know whether his helpless little body is hidden under ruins somewhere or lying at the bottom of a well or if he is living in one of the sewers along with the rats and the slime. I don't know because you won't tell me. But we can't go on like this forever.'

'Enough, Anna,' she said sternly.

'Please, Mutti, please. Just tell me.'

'Oh, Anna.'

Suddenly her hands were holding my face, stopping it from trembling and I could feel each one of her fingers cupped around the bones of my cheeks. Her hands were firm and steady.

'I've told you, Anna, I don't know what happened to the Russian bastard.' Her gaze was sad. Layers and layers of sadness. 'I left him outside the door on the street.'

'I don't believe you.'

She drew my face close to hers, her words a faint whisper. 'Anna, my daughter, you are damaged. You are broken into so many bits that I can't put the pieces together again.'

A loud knock sounded on the door and I jerked away.

CHAPTER THIRTY

◆ ◆ ◆

TIMUR

'Get out, Russian.'

The mother barred Timur's entrance, the door opened no more than the width of his foot, but this time he was prepared. He could see that her colour was high and she held herself rigidly in her long black gown. He was tempted to make soothing sounds, the way he used to with his horse when it got spooked back at his dacha in Russia, but he doubted that she would respond with anything other than bared teeth.

Instead he reached into one of the three sacks at his feet and produced an unopened bottle of good Russian vodka and one of her own cut-crystal shot glasses.

'*Za vashe zdarovje*,' Timur said. 'To your good health, Frau Wolff.'

She opened the door.

He showed them what he'd brought. Then he left them to it. While they emptied the sacks one by one, he found himself a chair by the stove which he lit with some smashed sticks of rosewood that had once been a bookcase. He watched the two women, both the mother and Anna, as they reclaimed some of their stolen belongings and removed each item with care from the sacks. A silver-backed hairbrush or a set of fine-quality copper pans, all greeted with respect and pleasure and replaced on whatever surface or in whatever cupboard they belonged.

He couldn't watch Anna enough. Never ever enough. Like a man starved of the sustenance that had kept him alive, he could feel it flowing back into his veins. The heat. The fire. The liquid primal awareness of being alive. It melted the ice that had gripped his gut when he opened his eyes each morning. He could feel himself finding the path back to living, to loving, instead of simply existing. Small things created little kicks of joy. The way she turned her slender neck, how she tipped her head, the curve of her little finger, the angle of her hip, the lift at the corner of her full lips when she found a silver photograph frame that contained a snap of her father seated on his bicycle and grinning at whoever was taking the picture. She stood it in pride of place and took a step back to smile at it. Timur could sit here and watch her for eternity.

He knocked back shots of vodka and took bites of pickled cucumber between each shot. He smoked cigarette after cigarette, lighting the next one from the butt of the old one, because that way only smoke came out of his mouth. Not words. Words made trouble. Words were no use to him. Only his eyes.

The one shock was Anna's hair. *Chyort!* Since being back in Berlin he'd only seen her wearing a woolly hat ugly as sin, but now he saw that she'd hacked off the gleaming mane that used to stream out behind her on her bicycle like the shimmering black wings of ravens. Once when cycling behind her he'd run smack into a lorry and broken his wristwatch because he'd been so mesmerised by her hair in flight.

'Russian.'

Her mother stood in front of his chair, her gaze narrowed on the vodka bottle and the two empty crystal glasses waiting at his elbow. He filled one for her. She drank it straight down and exhaled hard, expelling the heat of it.

'Now go,' she ordered.

He had been expecting it. He had served his purpose.

'Do not return,' she added.

He didn't ask why. They knew why. The daughter stood with her back to him.

'Frau Wolff, I have one more gift for you before I leave.'

He slid his hand into the side pocket of his Red Army jacket and withdrew a small jewellery box. Its brown leather was well scuffed and worn smooth as skin, betraying how much of a favourite it had been. He caught the faintest moan that rose from her, as though it ruptured something inside her to see the box in his Russian hand.

'Five minutes of time alone with your daughter, Frau Wolff.'

Anna spun around. 'I am not for sale,' she declared. 'Go buy yourself one of the whores down in the brothels on Ku'damm.'

'Five minutes, Anna, that's all I ask.'

He opened the box and let the white satin interior speak for him. Nestled inside was a gold locket and lying face to face like lovers inside the locket were small portraits of Luisa Wolff and her husband, Wilhelm. The mother snatched it from him and swept into her bedroom, slamming the door behind her.

Anna stared at the door. Timur didn't move, didn't speak, letting the room and her anger settle around them.

'Anna.' His voice was tender.

He didn't know how to reach her. Great loops of barbed wire seemed to encircle her, keeping him at a distance.

'How are you?' he asked quietly. 'Other than this.' He gestured at the ravaged room and grimaced. He remembered it as five times the size and so sublimely elegant that he had stood gaping in wonder like a stupid Russian *muzhik* the first time he'd entered it, carrying the injured figure of Anna's mother in his arms. 'I apologise for the actions of the lieutenant and—'

'Three years,' she said fiercely. The words were an accusation. 'More than three years. And not a word from you.'

'That's not true, Anna.'

'You gave me your oath.'

Timur remained in his seat, gripping its wooden arms to keep him there. If he stood, it would be over, she would order him to leave. He could see in her dark eyes how close she was to that point.

'Yes, I gave you my oath, Anna, and I was true to it. I wrote to you but not once did I receive a reply.'

'Don't lie to me. Don't. I'd rather hear the truth than have you lie to me.'

'I sent you more than a hundred letters, week after week, month after month, I swear it. I sent birthday gifts and Christmas presents because I wanted to put a smile on your face. Each time I was transferred to a new posting I sent you my new address, yet all I received in return was silence. A stone wall of silence. Yet I never gave up hoping that you had not found someone else.'

'Please, don't lie to me.' This time her voice was so soft he barely caught her words. 'I feared you'd been shot by one of your anti-communist partisans. A thousand times I lay in bed at night seeing you dead, sprawled on the ground in a pool of blood, a bullet in your skull. An axe smashed through your chest, ripping jagged holes in your heart. Sometimes I imagined you calling my name as you fell.'

Her eyes glittered but she refused to shed tears.

'But each morning,' she continued in the same low voice, 'when the cold light of dawn pushed the night and its shadows away, I faced the reality of what I knew must have really happened. You had found yourself another girl.' She tossed her head as though to throw that image out of her mind. 'Maybe many other girls, how do I know? And you'd be swearing an oath to them as easily as you did to me. Were they Russian girls? Pretty laughing Muscovites who could speak your language and share your bed.'

'Stop it, Anna. There has never been anyone else but you, not since the first day I laid eyes on you. I love you and I always will.'

Her whole shape changed, it blurred at the edges. Her anger softened, slowly melted to sorrow. She shook her head. 'It's too late.'

He rose to his feet, but she didn't order him to leave. Instead she took a step towards him.

'It is too late for us. Too late for me. Ask my mother, she will tell you – I am too damaged.'

'No. You're wrong. I know you've been through hell and I know you're only just surviving.' He reached out and slid his hand along her forearm. Her coat was wet. She stood totally still, staring at the spot he had touched as if she expected it to burst into flames. 'I know how you feel about Russian soldiers, but let me save you,' he murmured, 'from this misery.'

'I don't need you to save me. I can save myself. I am working at Tempelhof airfield and earning my own Deutschmarks.'

It was a dismissal. 'At least let me help you.' This time his tone was polite. 'As a friend,' he said. 'Nothing more.'

'Thank you.'

A polite response. Nothing more.

The room filled up with a hard-packed silence. Neither moved, neither spoke.

'Anna, do you have any idea how many Soviet troops are stationed in East Berlin?'

'Too many.'

'Let me tell you.'

'No.'

'You need to know, Anna. You need to be ready. Our Soviet sector contains a garrison of eighteen thousand troops. And stationed outside the city in the Soviet zone of eastern Germany, we have a further half a million.' He paused. 'Half a million.'

She was caught unawares by the grossness of the figure.

'Would you like to know how many Allied troops are stationed in the western sectors of the city?'

She shook her head.

'Scarcely seven thousand,' he informed her. 'And eighty-nine per cent of West Berlin's electricity is generated in the east. This week a Soviet barrier of steel pipe railing was erected across Potsdamer Platz and this is just the start, Anna. There are rumours. Constant whispers.'

'What?' One of her hands clutched at the patch of her coat that he had touched. 'What kind of rumours?'

'That it will be impossible for the Allies to keep the airlift going through the bitter German winter. That Berliners will starve to death in massive numbers, that they will freeze into corpses inside their own homes. That Red Army tanks will roll across and invade West Berlin, driving out your Americans and the British and French before the year is over.' He lowered his voice. 'Plans have been drawn up, commanding officers are being briefed.'

He was startled by her sudden burst of laughter, scornful and sting-
ing. 'They wouldn't dare. It would start another world war.'

'Stalin is convinced that President Truman and the people of
America have no stomach for a repeat performance. I only tell you this
because I want to warn you, to keep you safe. You need to be prepared.'

Abruptly she broke away and moved towards the door, her thin
shoulders slumped. 'Go now, please,' she said quietly.

But he remained where he was.

'Anna, it is possible that my letters to you were intercepted by Soviet
intelligence officers. They would want to sever any intimacy between
us, a Red Army officer and a German woman whose father had been an
active opponent of the Communist Party of Germany, working against
Walter Ulbricht on its Central Committee.'

She turned to face him, but now there was a gentleness etched into
the hollows of her face that set memories of the person she used to be
rustling through the apartment, and he felt keenly the connection between them, even while she denied its existence

'Of course you would say that,' she said. 'Even if there were no letters. How can I trust you? Tell me how.'

He didn't argue. Only she could decide whether to believe him. He
walked past her into the tiny hallway and opened the door on to the
landing where he paused to say a formal goodbye and found her right
on his heels, so close that his hand lingered on her damp shoulder.

She didn't leap away.

'So Major Timur Voronin, tell me this instead.' She looked up at him
with a sudden smile, totally unexpected, and he felt the past and the
present meet each other in this brief moment. 'What presents did you
send me?' she asked.

He laughed. She was always clever. Was this a test? To see if the
presents were real or another lie?

He matched his smile to hers and started to list them. 'A music box
in the shape of a heart that played Tchaikovsky's 'Dance of the Sugar
Plum Fairy'. A scarf from Pavlovo Posad with bright floral patterns.

A pair of stout black *valenki* because our Russian felt boots are the best in the world on snow. A bottle of the finest vodka and some Bashkir honey with *sushki* to eat on a cold winter night and a beautiful Zhostovo metal tray that I knew you'd love because it was painted with wild flowers that are supposed to bring peace to our tormented Russian souls and …'

'Enough, Timur, enough.'

Did she believe him? He couldn't tell. But she had laughed and licked her lips at the mention of the honey. And she had called him by his name, not *Russian* like before. She placed her hand on top of his where it still rested on her shoulder and that bonding of her skin to his skin brought him intense happiness. Then she stepped away.

'Goodbye, Timur,' she said, her expression grave again.

'*Auf Wiedersehen.*'

He left the apartment, dragging his heart out of there by brute force.

CHAPTER THIRTY-ONE

• • •

ANNA

I was glad of the noise, the relentless roar of the aircraft, so loud it blasted all thoughts out of my head. I was glad of the leaden ache in my limbs. It dulled the grief. Tempelhof swallowed me up and silenced me. I became a cog, unfeeling and unthinking, while the wind that scoured the wide expanse of the airfield was piercing and I welcomed the numbness it brought me.

I love you, he'd said.

And I'd handed his words right back to him. I'd discarded them like my mother discarded an unwanted child, when all I longed to do was hold on to them, to wrap myself tight around them.

But could I believe him? Could I trust him?

This was Berlin, a city of lies, a city of spies. I must never ignore the fact that he was a Red Army officer. Did Major Timur Voronin already know when he walked into our apartment today with his bribes that I worked at Tempelhof? Is that why he came? To find out information and learn what was going on out here?

The night sky was a mottled charcoal black, streaked with dirty grey fingers because the fog that had plagued the city all month was rolling back in now that the rain had stopped. It clogged my lungs worse than the droplets of aircraft fuel that swirled across the runways. Originally there was only one runway, little more than a ragged strip of grass that wallowed in mud in the winter, but the American commanders, General Tunner and General Howley, had transformed it. They'd had three new steel and asphalt runways constructed and to build them the bulldozers had had to be brought in by plane. They were too heavy to be transported in one piece, so they were sliced into segments, then welded back into functioning bulldozers once in Berlin. It was Captain Noah Maynard, the American pilot, who had passed on that little gem to me. He was so proud of his country.

I envied him that.

'You're quiet tonight, Anna,' my work companion grumbled.

The atmosphere on the base was even more tense than usual, everyone aware that the Russian MiG fighters were up in force, buzzing the incoming planes in the air corridors. No one wanted any more crashes. And the state radio station in the Soviet sector had been blasting out through loudspeakers in the streets that the Allies were preparing to withdraw from Berlin. It wasn't true but morale was low.

Nevertheless, Magdalene, my coal-sweeping companion, was in a cheerful mood. Her uncle had brought her a basket of crisp russet apples and that's all it took to make a Berliner happy these days. No one asked where he'd got them. She'd presented me with one and I'd tucked it under my hat which was tied on with a headscarf today to stop the wind ripping it off. While I laboured away sweeping out the planes, she chatted and rested her broad backside against the curved ribs of the aircraft whenever the urge took her. I had to work twice as fast to make up for it, but that suited me fine. No time to think, no time to remember.

But when we next emptied our sacks of coal dust into the giant bins, where the night's floodlights sent our shadows gyrating on to the concrete apron like black demons from the abyss, I slid deeper away under the overhang.

'Magdalene.'

She followed me, curious. 'What you up to?'

'Will you cover for me for a moment?'

'Why?' I could see the gleam of her big horse-teeth grin in the gloom. 'Where you going?'

'I need to slink away to speak to someone. I won't be long.'

'How long?'

'Fifteen minutes. Probably less.'

'You're meeting up with that American pilot, aren't you?' she chuckled. 'That Captain Maynard. I spotted him earlier, cussing at his plane for something or other. He's a *Mensch* I wouldn't mind dragging into my barn back home.'

'No, Magdalene, I'm running over to the food wagon. I promise I'll bring you back a hot coffee.'

'You got yourself a deal.'

I found Ingrid silhouetted in a pool of yellow light next to her snack wagon, restocking one of the supply jeeps with doughnuts and hot-dogs. Apparently that was what America's mighty fighting force lived on. The jeep was in the hands of a pretty young German girl who drove off into the darkness with a wide smile on her face at the prospect of feeding more of the handsome American pilots stuck in their cockpits, eager for take-off. Other jeeps flitted back and forth like mosquitoes in the thickening fog.

'Clearly a girl who enjoys her work,' I said. 'It beats shovelling coal dust, that's for sure.'

'They pick the prettiest girls they can find with driving licences,' Ingrid said. 'To stop the pilots leaving their planes and causing delays.' She nipped back inside the food truck, poured steaming coffee into a paper cup and pushed it towards me. 'You okay? You don't look so good.'

'Better for this, thanks.'

'You got problems?'

'Everyone in Berlin has problems.'

Ingrid laughed and even her laugh was self-effacing. 'Come see me some day in the city,' she said, 'and I'll show you something to cheer you up.'

'I'd like that.'

There was something about this soft-spoken thief that I liked, though I wasn't quite sure what.

'Where's your boss?'

There was no burly cook wielding his spatula behind her.

'Corporal Rocco? He's been roped in to be third-base umpire in to-night's game.' I looked blank. 'Baseball,' she added by way of explanation.

There were no customers in the vicinity, so we were alone. Nevertheless I kept my voice low and leaned close to the counter.

'Ingrid, I've been expecting a heavy hand to land on my shoulder at any moment because of that file you removed from the personnel officer's desk. But there's been nothing. No summons to his office. I don't understand it because he knows who I am. My name was on that list.' I took a sip of my scalding coffee to give us both time to consider the trouble I could be in. 'I'm surprised to hear nothing.'

'Don't be. You won't hear any more about it.'

'How can you be so sure?'

She poured herself a dash of hot milk into a cup and downed it in one. 'Don't worry. It's because either the stupid personnel officer's desk is such a mess that he hasn't realised it's missing, or he is keeping his mouth shut because he isn't willing to make himself look incompetent.'

'I hope you're right. What did you do with the file?'

For the first time her bony face with its jutting angles shut down on me. 'That's not your business.'

'Did you sell it to someone?'

'You're better off not knowing.'

Yes, I was willing to believe that. Sometimes it's safer not to know. I studied Ingrid. There was something of the fox about her, sharp-featured, quick-witted, keen-eyed, ready to take advantage of whatever crossed her path. She, like me, had been shaped by Berlin.

'Anna,' she said speculatively, 'do you talk much to the aircrew when you're cleaning out the planes?'

I looked at her, oddly. 'We never have much time, we're always rushing to finish up fast and get the plane turned around. But yes, sometimes the guys want to chat while I work. Why do you ask?'

'Oh, you know what military men are like, always on the lookout for pretty young women to listen to their tall stories and I bet they love to talk to you about back home.' She reached under the counter and came up with a bottle of bourbon. It was already half empty. She tipped a shot of the firewater into my coffee and into her empty cup and gave a soft laugh.' Rocco won't miss it.'

The roar of aircraft pistons passed overhead as we knocked back our drinks. Four Pratt & Whitney engines powering a C-54 Skymaster, even in tonight's shifting fog because they were landing by instruments, and I felt a tightening of my fear for those young men risking their lives for us. The memory of some of the fleeting conversations I'd had with them swirled through my mind.

'There was one airman this evening,' I said, feeling the heat of the bourbon kick in, 'a navigator, Lieutenant Lou Curtiss, who was telling me he's desperate to fix up his car back home in Alabama but he's got no money. He gambles.'

'Is that so?'

'And an eager young man from somewhere in New Jersey, ginger hair and gentle cinnamon eyes. His wife, Lucy, gave birth to their first baby yesterday and he didn't know whether to laugh with happiness or cry because he is so far away.'

'Congratulations to him.' She raised her cup. 'What's his name?'

'Chester. Why?'

'Oh, I'll look out for a Chester and offer him a shot to wet the baby's head. That's all.' She regarded me closely. 'You and I, we have to get by. You know that, don't you?'

She stood back to reveal a whole row of hotdogs beside the grill behind her, waiting to be heated, and I was counting them greedily in my head before I could stop myself. Ten, fifteen ... twenty. Twenty fox-red beauties, fat, ripe and luscious, just begging to be devoured.

'You know anyone who needs feeding?' Ingrid laughed, really laughed this time, then pulled out a small blue notebook from her apron pocket and a smart little pencil, scribbled something in it, shut the book and tucked it away.

Why did I feel I'd just let Chester and Lou down? But my gaze was glued to the row of twenty hotdogs and there was only one thought in my head – if I had twenty kids in my basement ...

'That's her! That's Anna Wolff.'

I spun around, heart drumming, expecting to find the US Army sergeant in pursuit of his missing file. But it was a woman's voice and a woman's figure advancing towards me, a grey wraith emerging from the grey fog, her arm stretched out like a signpost pointing straight at me. It was Sister Ingeborg, but there was nothing of the nun about her tonight. Her face, usually so calm, was contorted by anger.

Two men swept forward from behind her in a rush of dark uniforms and raised voices, and placed themselves right in front of me, blocking my exit. Dimly I registered that they were in West Berlin police uniforms, not US Army or Air Force.

'Fräulein Wolff?' said the taller of the uniforms.

'Yes.'

'I am arresting you on suspicion of the abduction of the child named Leopold Weber, otherwise known as Poldi.'

The air stank of vomit and bleach.

They didn't believe me. Why would they? Not even when I showed them the apple under my hat that I had planned to take over to Poldi at the orphanage on my way home. As if an apple was evidence.

'Where is he?' I asked again and again.

But if they knew the answer to that, I wouldn't be sitting here in a police interrogation rat-hole, would I? At least I had the sense to be thankful. Thankful it was the West Berlin police's rat-hole I was in and not one belonging to the Soviet sector's *VoPo*, the Volkspolizei, the East German People's Police, who strutted the streets of the eastern half of the city like tin-pot dictators in their green uniforms and peaked caps. Many were ex-Wehrmacht. I reminded myself to be grateful I didn't have one of them sitting opposite me.

The same questions, over and over.

'Where were you between two o'clock and four o'clock this afternoon?'

'In my bicycle workshop.'

'Doing what?'

I almost said repairing bicycles but they might check on it.

'I was moving things around, making a few changes in its layout.'

Mistake. Wrong answer.

'Why were you making changes?'

My interrogator's manner was quiet and surprisingly polite and I had the feeling he wasn't comfortable questioning women. But he had a policeman's eyes, observant and intelligent, and he watched every breath I took while he fingered a mottled green fountain pen that lay on a pad in front of him.

'To use the space more efficiently,' I answered. 'It's a narrow basement room and it can get too cluttered at times.'

He waited for more. I sat silent, my hands in my lap, and noticed a spider spinning a web in a corner of the room, building a new home for itself. Setting out its trap. Was I in a trap without even knowing it?

'Were you rearranging your workshop to make room for a child's bed?'

'No.'

Oh, but he'd hit the mark. The wrong mark, but still the mark. Did my face betray it? I kept every muscle still.

'The address of your workshop?'

I gave him the address and the key.

'Do you really suspect I have a child hidden there?'

'We'll soon find out.'

'What happened to Poldi? Please tell me. Was he seized from the orphanage or out on a walk or in a park or …?'

'You went to see him at the orphanage, didn't you?'

'Yes.'

'Why?'

'I was looking for a child who went missing years ago and while I was working at Tempelhof I met Ingeborg. She mentioned that there was this place that took in street orphans.'

'And is Poldi that child?'

I shook my head.

'Fräulein Wolff, I ask you again, is Leopold that child?'

'No. He isn't.'

Did this quiet policeman see what his questions were doing to me? Did he hear the cracks opening up inside me when I spoke of little Poldi and wondered what he was feeling right now? Lost. Alone.

Afraid. Hungry and robbed of his fragile world. In desperate need of loving arms to cradle him.

Or was that Felix? My Felix.

With their huge blue eyes and feathery blond hair, they were merging in my mind, blending and entwining, and I could no longer tell where one child ended and the other began. The same way the love and the ache I felt for each of their small souls could no longer find its own shape. The policeman leaned forward, shiny elbows on the scrubbed table between us, listening hard. 'So what made you choose to offer a home to this Poldi?'

'I'd given up hope of finding the child I was searching for.' If he wanted more, he'd have to dig a lot harder.

'So why Poldi?'

I shrugged. 'Why not Poldi?'

'You live alone?'

'No.'

'Who lives with you?'

'My mother.'

'Her name?'

'Luisa Wolff.'

He unscrewed the top of his fountain pen and wrote the name down on the pad in small neat lettering.

'Did anyone see who took Poldi?' I asked. 'Please tell me. Someone must have been with him, surely? Were there witnesses?'

He frowned, a deep crease picking its way across his forehead, and studied me for a long time in silence before starting all over again.

'Anna Wolff, where were you between two o'clock and four o'clock this afternoon?'

CHAPTER THIRTY-TWO

◆ ◆ ◆

INGRID

'Busy?'

'Yes.'

'The men in good spirits?'

'They are happy to come here. Because I give food, hot coffee and my smiles. They are not drunk.'

'In good spirits does not mean drunk, young lady.'

'I see.'

Ingrid's grasp of English was improving but obviously not fast enough. This US Army sergeant was not exactly the chattiest. Ingrid tried out one of her smiles on him but with no effect. He had rolled up out of the fog, informing her that he was here to inspect the food truck and take a look at its stock and its operating system. She had no idea what an *operating system* was, but to keep him and his clipboard happy she showed how they arranged the supplies to be ferried out to the planes by the jeeps.

'Who keeps track of how much food and drink is consumed? You?'

Where was Rocco when she needed him? Hadn't his stupid baseball game finished yet? Probably all knocking back beers in the bar and that's why the inspection was being carried out now while she was in charge. An easy target.

'Is there a problem, Sergeant?'

'Supplies are going missing. Supplies means food and drink. Understand?'

Her smile didn't slip. 'The men like their doughnuts. They are hungry after many many hours in the sky.'

He didn't look like a man who cared about hours in the sky. He looked like a man who cared about his catering supplies and making the numbers tally at the end of the week. He was heavily built with a large square head and a boxer's nose, and Ingrid liked to imagine Otto going a few rounds with him to teach him manners.

'Now, Sergeant, you have coffee?'

'No.'

Ingrid lounged in the doorway of the truck and tried to look unconcerned. A hotdog was tucked into the bottom of her deep apron pocket because her shift was almost over. With casual indifference she slid a hand inside the pocket. Maybe she could chuck it out on to the grass, unseen in the dark.

Her fingers squeezed past the clean cloth neatly folded in the pocket and found the greaseproof package. She hated hotdogs herself but Otto was like the street kids and would devour anything. The guards never bothered with her as she scuttled, almost invisible, through the airbase gates, so as long as this officious sergeant didn't take it into his head to search her, the stolen food would …

Her hand froze. A flutter of panic.

Her notebook. Where was the notebook she kept in her apron? Her hand rummaged again and found the pencil. No notebook. Think, think, where had she put it?

There, on the shelf under the counter, a blur of blue. A twist of fear caught her throat. She had tucked it away on the shelf when Charlie – a flight engineer who lived in Chicago and whose Pa was apparently in danger of losing his shaving brush factory because of unpaid taxes – popped up right in front of her counter just as she was jotting something down, catching her off guard. Then one of the jeeps had turned up to be restocked before she had time to retrieve the notebook, followed by this arse of a sergeant.

She edged into the narrow space inside the truck.

'You can remain outside,' the sergeant said in a brisk tone.

He was obviously one of those who believed Germans should not be trusted to work on an American airbase, despite the fact that it couldn't keep up this pace without the thousands of German mechanics and unloaders who contributed to Operation Vittles. Ingrid inched a step towards the book but again he was too quick for her and snatched it from the shelf.

'And what do we have here?'

'Just some notes I make.'

'Notes about what? The supplies?'

'No.'

'What then?'

'About the men. There are many men and we talk. I forget which ones tell me what things, so I write it. That's all.'

He flicked open the notebook. She managed not to snatch it from his hands.

He started to read. 'Clarence Forrester wants new red shoes for his wife's birthday.' To her surprise the sergeant translated her German into English as he read aloud. 'Amos needs a new tractor on his farm in Wichita, Kansas, Gus Tribble longs to become a professional actor on Broadway in New York.' He looked up at her. 'What is the point of this?'

'I told you.'

'To remind you of what they said?'

'Yes. Sergeant, you Americans are all so handsome –' she smiled at him but knew that men had never been snared by her smiles– 'I like to listen to you all.'

He snapped the notebook shut and tossed it back on to the shelf with disgust. 'Don't think I don't know what you're up to. You *Fräuleins* are all the same.' He jotted a note on his clipboard, his large frame suddenly restless within the confined space, and Ingrid could feel his desire to get out of there. 'You all,' he continued, 'want to get your claws into one of America's fine young bucks and marry him, so that you can get out of this shithole.'

He barged past her out into the night and though she was relieved to see the back of him, she couldn't argue with his assertion. It was true. That's exactly what many young German women wanted, a gum-chewing, nylons-touting, dollar-waving ticket to the good life. And who could blame them? Try starving for a living and see if it shifts your priorities.

Ingrid retrieved her notebook but the twist of fear was back because she knew another mistake like that one could get her killed. She pushed the notebook into her pocket and turned to find a tall figure in a flier's uniform standing in the shadowy doorway, watching her.

'Noah,' she gasped. 'You scared the hell out of me.'

But this time, instead of presenting her with a blue envelope, the airman had brought her a roll of microfilm.

Noah spoke good German.

Ingrid inspected him as she took the hit from a tongue-numbing schnapps and wondered which came first with him – the knowledge of the language or the spying. Most Americans didn't know any German, a smattering of useful words at most, but Otto had told her that some men had been especially chosen to serve over here in the US military because of their knowledge of the language. That made sense. She downed another schnapps and her eyelids felt heavy but the top of her head felt weirdly light, as if it were floating. She placed her hand on it to hold it down in case it escaped and she found her hair warm and damp with sweat.

'What are we doing here?' she asked.

'Hiding,' Noah whispered and grinned at her. He was wearing dark plum lipstick. 'Don't you like it here?'

Here was a cellar. Someone had tricked it out as a bar with a low vaulted ceiling and hefty oak barrels stacked along two walls. It was dark as a dungeon except for a few stubs of black candles propped in wall sconces or stuck in beer bottles on the small round tables that had been daubed black and painted with a pair of red eyes.

'It's ... different,' Ingrid conceded.

'Good different or bad different?'

She gazed at the beautiful young man dancing topless and alone on the tiny stage in the middle of the room. He seemed to be going for a Tarzan look, swaying rhythmically in his skimpy fur loincloth, with a necklace created from some poor creature's huge teeth adorning his well-oiled and hairless chest. He had a striking set of muscles on show, and after living in a circus most of her life, Ingrid was an expert on muscles. Blond hair to his shoulders, a sheath knife on his hip and a thick sleepy snake writhing across his shoulders. Its head was green and pointed like an arrow and it kept reaching out in Ingrid's direction as if it could smell with its flickering tongue that she didn't belong *here*.

'Interesting different,' she said.

'It's safe for us here. No American troops would dare set foot in a bar like this.'

It was full of men. Men with men. Some sleek, young and beautiful, others old and lonely, their gaze tracking every twitch of Tarzan's hips. But most were just seeking a safe place where they could drink with their beloved and kiss without vile insults being hurled, no violent police arrests for *illegal fornication*. These were exciting dens in which to hunt for love and happiness. One raffish man looked glamorous in a full green velvet evening gown and false eyelashes that almost swept the floor, while another sashayed up and down in a black leather leotard that emphasised every bulge. Ingrid stared. She tried not to, but her eyes had a will of their own. Of course she'd heard that such places existed, Sodom and Gomorrah alive and kicking in Berlin, that was what people whispered, but now she couldn't wait to entertain Otto with first-hand details of pierced nipples and purple-painted eyelids. Kissing couples. Men decked out in scarlet rouge and thick white powder. Tongues licking – yes, licking – other men's necks and …

'Enjoying it?'

Ingrid dragged her eyes away and back to her companion. Was his lipstick there for camouflage? Or did he want her to leave so that he could stroke some leather? He was wearing a plain black sweater and merged into the shadows of the cellar.

'Why are we here?'

'I told you. So that we can talk without fear. Fear warps the mind and I want your thoughts to be clear and precise. You are special to us. I want you to know that.'

The way he spoke raised goosebumps on her arms. Who was this man whose voice came at her as smooth as the snake, yet as alien as its hiss?

'Why do you do this?' she asked. 'The spying. The betrayal. It's not your fight, because you are American. Is it for the money, is that it? Kuznetsov got to you with his nice crisp envelopes of dollar bills, did he?'

Noah laughed, causing the struggling candle flame to falter in its pool of liquid wax, and she smiled back at him. It was the schnapps smiling.

'No, Ingrid, there are more important things in life than money.'

Ingrid snorted inelegantly. 'You should try doing without it, Mr Stars-and-Stripes, and you would soon change your merry gum-chewing tune.'

'That is why,' he said, the laughter drained from his face as fast as it came, 'communism is the answer for a better life for the people of Germany.' He jerked his head forward abruptly, the way the snake had done. 'It's only the beginning, Ingrid. Has Kuznetsov told you?'

'Kuznetsov tells me nothing.'

'Our goal is to establish a communist society throughout Europe. We will create a new social order structured on the idea of common ownership of the means of production and the removal of the crippling social-class system.' His eyes shone full of a dark fervour. 'At last we will bring about the end of the capitalist exploitation of labour and each person will contribute and receive according to their ability and needs.'

He slid a tiny fold of brown paper on to one of the red eyes painted on the table. Ingrid knew it contained the microfilm. She stared at it. She stared at him. It wasn't too late to stand up and leave.

He waved a hand at a pretty moustached waiter and another schnapps materialised in front of her. She knew her head wasn't clear, her thoughts tripping over each other and she wasn't absolutely sure her feet would do her bidding if she aimed them at the door. She watched her hand reach for the glass and raise it to her lips while the other one slid the microfilm into the pocket of her skirt without consulting her.

Captain Noah Maynard nodded his satisfaction. 'Good.'

Was it? Was it good?

He eased back in his chair and lit himself a cigarette, mission accomplished. He offered her one but she declined. Through the grey veil of smoke his gaze followed the raffish man in the green gown as he stepped up on to the tiny central stage and started to sing to piano-accordion accompaniment. It was Marlene Dietrich's 'Falling in Love Again' and to Ingrid's horror she felt her eyes fill with tears as the mournful notes twined around her heart.

'*Liebe.*' Love.

'*Denn das ist meine Welt.*' For that is my world.

She let her gaze roam the room, seeing a hand caress a cheek as if it were the most precious thing on earth. *Love.* It would appear to be the most precious thing in everyone's world. Except maybe Kuznetsov's.

'Do you know –' Noah's voice was solemn – 'that instead of charging US servicemen with sodomy, which is a court-martial offence, the military have started to label them psychopaths?'

Ingrid could not take her eyes off the singer's eyelashes, ginger-tipped and nearly as long as a lion's.

'These servicemen,' his voice seemed to slide into her ear uninvited, 'are now given a Section 8 blue discharge. That means they are deemed mentally unfit to serve in the military. So they are being purged from bases and units and sent to horrific mental institutions. Can you imagine that? Stripped of your rights and dignity. Not allowed veterans' benefits.' He exhaled heavily and she felt his breath on her cheek. 'So relax, Ingrid, you won't see any American troops hanging around in here.'

She forced her neck to swivel round. 'What about you? Aren't you at risk yourself if you're spotted here?'

His deep-set eyes softened. 'There's no one here to report me.' He placed a hand over hers on the table and she felt the throb of heat in his palm. Captain Noah Maynard wasn't nearly as calm as he liked to pretend. 'Except you.'

His words blurred in her ears. He signalled to the pretty moustached waiter again who seemed to float over to their table.

'A black coffee for the *Fräulein*, please. She has somewhere to be.'

Ingrid stood on the riverbank. She was in the Soviet sector, shivering as the fog slunk up from the water on its belly like an invading army, grey and secretive. Across the River Spree in the British sector the bombed-out ruins of the Reichstag lay only metres away, its scars concealed under cover of night. The fog hid a multitude of sins, a legion of lies and spies, and Ingrid was happy for it to stay that way.

Kronprinzenbrücke used to be a lovely cast-iron bridge over the river and it held a special place in Ingrid's heart. Otto had given her her first kiss under one of its massive clinker-brick piers. She'd been yearning for that kiss for ten love-choked years, since she was six.

They'd been sheltering from a sudden summer cloudburst and she recalled the noise of the pattering rain that sounded like applause. Otto had worn a dark red shirt with an embroidered pocket, its sleeves rolled up to show off his beautiful muscles. She still remembered the taste of his lips that day and the intense aroma of his wet hair, jet black and wild with untamed curls, but the war had rolled in and taken its toll. On the bridge and on them. The bridge's timber frame and its three grand sweeping arches had been badly damaged, severing the link between Mitte and Tiergarten, but Ingrid still liked to linger here in its looming black shadow, walking along the river, nursing her memories.

'Good evening, Ingrid.'

She'd blinked, that's all, and he was there in front of her, dark hat, dark coat, dark cane in his hand. A part of the night.

'Good evening, Herr Kuznetsov.'

'I believe you have something for me.'

'I do.'

But she made no move to dig it out for him. Let him beg.

'You don't look so good. A bit unsteady.'

'I'm fine. No need to worry about me.'

'But I do worry, Ingrid. I do worry about you.'

'Don't.'

He raised his cane and rested its tip lightly on her shoulder. He seemed to be holding her still. She must have been swaying. She could feel the schnapps swilling around her mind, setting fire to her thoughts, and she cursed Captain Noah Maynard. She blinked hard, better to focus on Kuznetsov's features, but the edges of his face remained blurred. Was it the fog? Or was it her? She needed her wits to sharpen up, hell yes. The stakes were too high.

'You're no use to me like this,' he said with distaste and turned his head away to stare out at the impenetrable black void that was the river.

'I spoke with Anna Wolff.'

That got his attention. He swung back.

'And?' he demanded.

She took her time, measuring each word for size on her tongue. 'She didn't look good.'

'In what way? Be precise.'

'She looked sad. Dreadfully sad.'

'Did she say why?'

'No. But she looked tired. She was concerned about the file, the one I took from the base. Really jumpy. And she fears arrest as they know her name. Not mine.' She kept her sentences short and manageable. 'I told her to forget it. Said she was safe.'

That made Kuznetsov smile.

'What else?' he asked.

'She wanted to know what I'd done with the file. I told her ignorance …' Ingrid wasn't sure that word came out right, '… was better.'

He nodded approval and removed his cane from her shoulder. Somewhere in the darkness an animal called, a fox or a dog among the ruins.

'The package?' he said in an abrupt switch. He held out his gloved hand.

She made him wait. She rummaged first in one pocket of her coat, then the other, dug around for her skirt pocket and finally withdrew it from inside her brassiere. Some creature plunged unseen into the river, making her jump, but Kuznetsov didn't even twitch an eyelid. His hand was still waiting and she could feel his patience wearing thin.

She passed him the microfilm she'd received from the American pilot and in exchange a nice plump envelope materialised in her hand. It was then that she showed him her notebook, the one pawed over by the food-truck sergeant, the one with the list of American names and the reasons why each one might find a windfall of cash into their back pockets desirable. A new baby, the desire for a car, a father's business on the rocks, an acting ambition, a gambling debt, a wife's operation. And so it went on. All vulnerable despite their heroics in the air.

Kuznetsov turned the pages in silence. He must have had tiger's eyes as well as tiger's teeth to be able to make out the words in the dark. Ingrid was concentrating on staying upright and trying to prevent her eyelids rolling down, when an attack came out of the night.

A screech. A shout. Two men hurled themselves on Kuznetsov in a blur of punches and blows and kicks and thumps. A blade flashed in someone's hand and the night air was split by a scream that scraped Ingrid's ears raw. She threw herself at the dim shape of one of the attackers, seizing a fist that was wielding a knife, delaying its downward strike, only to be swatted to the ground like a fly by a third man. This one was a vast brick wall who wrapped his elephant-arm in a death grip around the throat of one of the attackers, his boot slamming on the chest of the second man on the ground. She heard ribs crack.

Five seconds and it was over.

Ingrid's chest was heaving as a hand yanked her to her feet. It was Kuznetsov.

'Thank you, Ingrid,' he said politely. As if she'd handed him a slice of cherry tart.

In his hand he carried a long thin sword, the one she'd always suspected was hidden in his cane, and even in the gloom Ingrid could see blood slithering down the steel. He bent, wiped its blade clean on the jacket of the attacker who lay unmoving on the gravel path in a black pool of glistening liquid. The other attacker was howling for air.

'Release him.'

The elephant-arm withdrew and the man collapsed to his knees, clutching at his throat and dragging in thin rattling breaths.

'Who sent you?' Kuznetsov demanded.

'No one,' the man sobbed. 'I'm just a thief who …'

'Was it Sokolovsky?'

'I swear, nobody sent me, I am only a …'

'No matter.'

Kuznetsov thrust the clean blade through the man's throat and stepped neatly aside to avoid the gush of blood. Ingrid screamed and vomited schnapps over her own boots. The silent elephantine stranger stepped forward, hooked his hands under the arms of one of the dead men and dragged the corpse down the slope to the black water's edge where a wave swelled in anticipation. One splash, then another and both bodies were gone. That easy. Ingrid could imagine her own body being tipped into the same greedy waters, the swirling currents reaching up to suck her down.

'Well, Ingrid, a baptism of blood for you.' Kuznetsov's lips moved into a line that was meant to be a smile but the rest of his face remained rigid. 'No bad thing,' he said quietly. 'You have much to learn but you are doing well. I thank you again for saving me from that piece of trash's knife.'

Ingrid scraped the back of her hand across her mouth to rid it of bile, stepped forward to stand face to face with him and held out a hand.

'So how much is your life worth?'

CHAPTER THIRTY-THREE

◆ ◆ ◆

ANNA

They left me there alone in the room like a dog in a kennel. Hours passed while I stalked the floor, six paces one way, five paces the other. I listened for sounds beyond the door but there were none. I watched the spider knitting its gossamer death trap and I counted the beats of my pulse, loud as a drum in my ear. I tried to unpick the tangled threads of how I got here, but there was no fraying end for me to grasp, for me to pull into a clear unbroken line of cause and effect.

I wanted Poldi. A deep gut-wrenching want. Wherever he was now, whatever tears were streaming down his pale cheeks, they were all down to me. I knew it to be true but I didn't know why. I kept telling myself that they had no proof, nothing to convict me of abduction. I was innocent. They would have to let me go, but there was no sign of it yet. More hours passed. I had no idea how many and there was no window to signify day or night, just four blank walls and the inside of my own head for company.

I want to warn you. To keep you safe. You need to be prepared.

My head snapped round, I was so sure Timur was in the room, his words comforting in my ear.

Let me help you.

Oh, Timur. I am beyond help.

But I was wrong. Or so it seemed.

When the door finally swung open, it wasn't the sharp-eyed policeman who strode in, but a totally unexpected uniform. A familiar battered seal-brown sheepskin flying jacket and long legs in olive drab trousers advanced on me and strong arms gripped me in a hug. Relief made me sway against him.

'Captain Maynard!'

'Sorry it took me so long.'

The American pilot smelled of cigarettes and clinging damp fog and unending night skies. And kindness. He smelled of kindness.

I detached myself. 'Thank you for coming. How on earth did you know I was here?'

His face looked dog tired. Exhausted. How many hours had he gone without sleep? I felt a wave of gratitude towards him and towards all the other pilots adrift from their homes and cast up in this foreign land. People said that the airlift flying crews were being pushed to their absolute limit to keep Berliners alive and I could see the truth of it in the way the lines of his face sagged with fatigue.

'Ingrid Keller sent me,' he smiled. 'Blame her.'

The daylight came as a shock, bright and dazzling. I was expecting a heavy night-time sky to be still hanging over Berlin, but brilliant sunshine greeted me as I hurried down the front steps of the police station. A brisk easterly breeze had ousted last night's fog and swept the morning sky clear of clouds, which gave the city a look of happiness that was a bare-faced lie.

'Where to?' Captain Noah Maynard asked.

'I need to pick up my bicycle from Tempelhof.'

'Perfect. I'm heading back there myself. Hop in.'

I climbed into his bone-rattling jeep, thankful for the ride, though it was all cold khaki metal inside and hard edges that caught my elbow, a tin can on wheels. But I was glad to return to the airfield as fast as the rough roads would allow and glad of Noah Maynard's company en route because his easy conversation kept at bay the question thumping holes in my head – who took Poldi?

Why?

I liked that Captain Noah Maynard kept it simple. 'Did you abduct the child?' he asked straight out as he swung the wheel far too fast round the corner into Diehlstrasse. This guy was hooked on speed.

'No, I didn't.'

His eyes swept over me, quick and appraising. 'Okay. That's good enough for me.'

'Thank you. The polizei are clutching at straws in there. They have no proof, no witnesses.'

He skirted round a dray horse hauling a cart piled high with oak barrels. 'There are far too many kids running wild in this goddamn city for them to fuss over one more that goes missing, you can bet your sweet life on that.'

'I suspect you're right.'

I could imagine this tall American striding into the police station, stirring things up, sturdy and strong and well fed, filling the place with his commands. Ordering my release, despite the fact he had no juris-diction here. But he was an American officer, and Germans – even German police – had learned the hard way not to gainsay an American officer's order. I stared blindly through the grubby windscreen as we tore south through the sun-bleached city.

I turned to him. 'Shouldn't you be flying a plane?'

He flipped me a grin. 'Darned hydraulic system went AWOL on me. I was lucky to limp in last night without causing an almighty pile-up.'

'Sounds like you need a new plane.'

'Yeah, landing is done on instruments, but I had minimal control of flaps and landing gear –' he exhaled a whoosh of air in a long whistle, 'so we hit the deck like a dead elephant. Thought for a mo-ment there it was time to sprout angel wings.' He gave a laugh, but I could see the muscle at the hinge of his jaw bunched with tension. 'So the mechanics are all over it today.' He glanced at me. 'Otherwise I'd have been back at Rhein-Main airbase this morning, not picking my teeth at Tempelhof.'

'Lucky for me then, Captain.'

'Call me Noah,' he said as we shot past the entrance to Schöneberg train station where a gaunt young man with a handcart was selling his books as kindling. It was only as we approached the airbase's well-guarded gates that my companion seemed to remember that he had a brake pedal and the jeep finally slowed.

Noah swivelled to face me. 'Have you given any more thought to what made you run from the explosion at the recruitment centre?'

It took me by surprise. 'Yes, I've gone over and over it and all I have is a vague sense of a man running, a man in a dark cap. But it's all a blur in my head, nothing clear.'

'Keep trying,' he urged.

'I will. Take care, Noah,' I said, concerned for the number of hours he was flying.

'You take care too.' He brushed my sleeve, as if to underline his statement. 'You got knocked about in the explosion. And that woman's death at Tempelhof and your accident were bad enough, but now a stolen kid and police arresting you? You seem to attract mayhem like a pot of jelly attracts wasps.'

A flutter of panic gripped my stomach. This American was making the same connections I had made. So I was not imagining it.

CHAPTER THIRTY-FOUR

◆ ◆ ◆

ANNA

*I*t was winter. Felix was strapped to my back in a papoose. I felt the heat of his little body tight against mine, waves of it seeping right through my coat and wrapping around my spine. My feet pedalled faster, lungs pumping, because he wasn't just hot, he was too hot. Far too hot. What do you do with a sick child and no doctor? No medicine. No help. No idea how to save my son.

It was less than a year after the war was over and the city was still in a state of chaos, uniforms of all colours crawling over it like flies.

'Where are you going?' the Soviet checkpoint guard demanded as I joined a queue to enter the western sectors of the city.

'To Ku'damm.'

'What have you got there on your back?'

He wandered around me so that he could take a look inside the papoose.

'It's a baby!' he exclaimed.

'A sick baby,' I said.

His face softened into the kind of smile reserved only for children and animals. 'A boy? How old?'

'Yes. Three months old.'

'I've got a daughter back home in Smolensk. That's on the Dnieper river, west of Moscow. I miss her.' He patted Felix's hot little hat. 'Milyy mal'chik. He shouldn't be out in this cold wind.'

He pushed aside those ahead of me in the queue and waved me through, but first he reached into his greatcoat and slipped a couple of hand-rolled cigarettes into my pocket.

'To sell for food. For you.' He glanced awkwardly at my breasts, well hidden under my coat. 'For your milk, you understand.'

'Spasibo,' I said and accepted the gift. I didn't tell him I had no milk.

Martha Dieleman knew what to do. Her gentle hands had whisked Felix off my back and into a bowl of tepid water. Then she lay him naked on her bed, his skin blotchy, and draped washcloths soaked in apple cider vinegar on his forehead and skinny little stomach.

'The acid draws the heat out and lowers the temperature,' she explained as I crooned softly to my whimpering son.

For his feet she made a garlic concoction and spread it on his little wrinkled soles. 'It will flush out the toxins and he will start to feel better.'

I spooned small drops of water laced with honey into his mouth and sang 'Der Kuckuck und der Esel' because the silly song always made him chuckle and right then I'd have given my right arm to hear my baby's chuckle.

It worked. After another hour of glassy-eyed grizzling his temperature started to fall, his forehead was no longer a furnace and he slid quietly into a deep soothing sleep. Only the crackling of each breath, like a wood fire spitting, kept me believing he was still alive. When he woke, his blue eyes were clear as mountain skies and I wept in Martha's arms.

I took him home, singing to him all the way as I cycled through the streets and the next morning he was his usual chirruping sweet self. Two days later I woke in the night with a raging fever and couldn't get out of bed. Days blurred. Nights melted away.

I never saw Felix again.

'Go away.'

The door started to close in my face but I slid a foot into the gap.

'Please, just a few words.'

'Haven't you caused enough harm here?'

'I did nothing to harm Poldi, I swear.'

But was that true? Was just my interest in the boy enough to do him harm? The tall woman in front of me was Frau Bertha Neumann, the guardian of her little band of homeless children, and I couldn't blame her for wanting to be rid of me.

'Leave,' she said sternly. 'Don't come near these children again.'

'I give you my solemn oath that I didn't take Poldi. Or arrange for anyone else to snatch him.'

'You claimed to be his mother, yet the police informed me that you admitted it was untrue. Lies come easy to those who are hand in hand with the devil.'

'Please, Frau Neumann, will you just tell me what happened? Maybe Poldi wandered off by himself or ...'

Her face was set in stone. 'I believed you would bring love to this place – our Lord alone knows how much these young children are in desperate need of love in their lives – but I was wrong about you, I see that now.' Her gaze settled just above my head as if she could see something there that I was unaware of. 'You are cursed, Anna Wolff. Do not bring the evil footstep of the devil to my door again.'

She slammed the door in my face and this time I didn't resist. Guilt tasted cold and metallic in my mouth. I'd thought my love would protect Poldi, but it was the exact opposite. The only way I could discover who'd taken Poldi was to find the person who was determined to inflict harm on *me*.

Who? Why? And how?

I swung up on my bicycle.

'Anna! Anna Wolff!'

I glanced over my shoulder and saw Ingeborg, the ex-nun, running up the road behind me, her pale grey shawl flapping about her like wings. She came up beside me, still panting.

'Ingeborg, I'm so glad to see you. I wanted to tell you myself that I had nothing to do with Poldi's disappearance.'

She levelled her gaze at me without a word, but her face slowly softened, muscle by muscle in her cheeks and around her pearl-grey eyes. 'I know, Anna. I'm sorry I accused you of abduction to the police. It's just that I was so upset and you were the obvious suspect but –' she shook her head, a delicate flick from side to side, impatient with herself — 'I was wrong. I should have had more faith in you.' She gripped my wrist on the handlebar. 'Forgive me.'

I shrugged, my shoulders stiff from a night in a hard police chair. 'There's nothing to forgive, Ingeborg. Just tell me what happened.'

'I took a group of the children out to Tiergarten for some fresh air and an open space for them to run around, six of them. Poldi was one of them.' Ingeborg's eyes filled with tears and her hold on me tightened. 'Poldi loved to play football and was fast for one so young. I didn't take my eyes off them, in God's blessed name, I tell you I didn't. Not until Bettina started shouting and pointing up towards the stretch of grassland nearer the road. A man had collapsed. He was lying on the ground and a younger man was bent over him and calling for assistance, so I did what anyone would have done, Anna.'

'Of course you did,' I said. 'You ran over to help.'

'I told Bettina — she's one of the older girls and very sensible — to watch the children while I …' Her voice broke.

'What happened with the man?'

'The one who had collapsed was old with a white bushy beard and steel spectacles that had cut his nose. Blood was dripping down into his beard. I helped the younger man get him into their car which was parked nearby.' She was shaking her head, back and forth, her fingers twisting around my wrist as if she could turn back time. 'When I ran back … to the children … I was too late … Poldi was missing.'

'What did Bettina say?'

'That she was playing chase with them and they were racing away in all directions. By the time she thought to look for him, he had vanished.'

'Did any of the others see what happened to him?'

'No.' She released my wrist, took out a white handkerchief and wiped her face, taking her time, hunched in on herself. 'We questioned them closely. So did the police. None of them saw anything. Children are very centred on the moment when they're playing, not on what's happening around them, dear God bless them.'

'Tell me about the men and the car.'

'Oh no, you don't think they were involved, do you?'

'Tell me about the second man, the younger one.'

'He was polite and well dressed. Dark hair, mid-thirties or maybe forties. I'm not good at men's ages.' She looked at me bemused. 'What else can I say?'

'What kind of car was it?'

'Black. Quite old. Dirty.'

That described just about every car in Berlin.

'So you helped the old man into the car?'

'Yes.'

'Front or rear seat?'

'Rear. And the younger man scooted in beside him, very solicitous. I think he might have been the son.'

'So who was driving?'

'I don't know. There was a man sitting in the driver's seat but I didn't see him properly because he had his hood up.'

I stopped breathing. 'His hood up? What kind of coat was he wearing?'

'A navy duffle coat.'

Let me make this clear. There are duffle coats in Berlin. I am aware of that. More than one, far more than one. Military surplus duffles at the end of the war spilled out into civilian use, so of course the likelihood of there being any connection at all between this duffle coat and the one that young Resi claimed had been following me was slim.

Ridiculously slim. Of course it was.

But not for one moment did it shake my conviction that there *was* a connection. I had no idea what it was yet, but I would find it. I would.

And I'd start with Otto.

While caged in the police interrogation room overnight, I'd traced my steps backward, one footprint at a time, like tracking an animal except the animal was myself. I followed them back through everything that had happened and yet I could find no point at which I'd ignored something vital.

But time and again one thing did snag. That thing was a person and that person was Otto, the shifty young black marketeer I'd crossed paths with at the Dielemans' apartment, sniffing around their artworks. He'd shown an interest in me that I didn't like. It made me uneasy. I don't mean a sexual interest, no, not that. It was in the way he looked at me with his quick dark eyes and even in the way he appraised my scruffy old Diamant bicycle and watched me from the window as I cycled away. Too intense. Too engaged. As though his interest went far deeper than a polite hello between strangers.

There was something not quite right there.

I needed to speak with the Dielemans about him and I very nearly swung my front wheel in the direction of Ku'damm to do so, but as I cycled, swerving around the worst of the potholes, I knew I was in no state for it. My mind was foggy and I was in need of sleep.

I headed east instead, towards a checkpoint.

It was late morning by the time I pushed open the big oak door to my apartment building and the sun was making an effort to show its face between the silver sheets of cloud. I wheeled my bicycle into the dim interior of the entrance hallway. Although the prospect of dragging it up four flights of stairs didn't exactly thrill me right now, it was too risky to leave it down here, even with a safety chain attached. I'd kept a sharp lookout as I pedalled home but had spotted nothing suspicious and no duffle coats running behind, so I drew a deep breath of relief, closed the door behind me with a heavy clunk and made for the stairs.

A shadow detached itself from the wall.

'Timur,' I whispered. My eyes feasted on him.

'I've been waiting for you to return. I heard you'd been arrested.'

'How on earth did you hear that?'

Instead of replying he put out a hand and rested it lightly on the handlebar of my bicycle. Not on me. My Diamant was the lucky one. But still it connected us.

'Are you alright?' he asked. 'Did they hurt you?'

Oh, Timur, such caring, such tenderness. My weariness slithered to the floor along with my resistance, and it took all my willpower to stop myself abandoning my bicycle and twining both my arms tight around this man. In the dim hallway where the cold was as thick as the ice on the Havel, I wanted him, and I hated myself for the burning need for him that clenched my innards beyond bearing. I turned my head away. I didn't want him to see me overwhelmed so easily.

'Anna,' he murmured, 'I didn't abandon you. I couldn't ever abandon you, because you are my heartbeat.'

I felt him remove the bicycle from my grasp and heard the scrape as he propped it against a wall, and then he held me. *He held me.* Just stood there and held me. His arms wrapped around me, I could feel the strength within them, and my head nestled into his neck, the rough surface of his Red Army overcoat burrowing into my cheek. It struck me that he smelled very male. I was used to a world of women and to my starved senses his skin smelled wonderful.

He nudged off my hat with his chin and gently rubbed his cheek back and forth against my spiky hair as if he could stroke all the pain away. I felt the shudders that ran through his body, like quakes deep underground. For one strange moment, I believed this must be another of my cruel night-time dreams and only the strong beat of his heart against mine told me otherwise. I don't know how long we stood there, fused together in the gloomy hallway. It felt like a lifetime.

When our breathing stilled to a rhythm that soothed us both, I lifted my chin. 'Timur, I almost died of grief.'

'I know. I know. I was stationed in Poland and in Moscow and on the border with China – it was hard up there in the Altai mountains – and still never a word. But I've come back. I was always coming back to you one day, my love.'

'We can't return to the way we were, Timur. I am not that person any more.'

He pulled his head back to examine my face. 'Anna, we'll find a new way forward. We'll work it out together.'

Then he did something I'll never forget. He chose a spot directly between my eyes and kissed me on that spot, firm and forceful, as if he knew that was where the real me was hiding. He whispered against my skin, 'I'll never leave you again.' And a great wave of happiness hit me. Drowned me. I wanted that moment of my life to last forever.

I drew him closer, so close I didn't know where he ended and I began, our thoughts and limbs entangled, and I pressed my mouth hard on his. My fingers wove themselves contentedly in his hair, dislodging his hard peaked cap to the floor. Just then the street door was flung open and a woman who lived in the apartment beneath ours breezed into the hall-way, funnelling a gust of chill city air with her. Timur and I stepped apart, but two of my fingers refused to relinquish his cuff.

'Hello, Anna.' My neighbour regarded Timur with interest.

'Good morning, Frau Meyer,' I said.

The woman's pleasant face was cocooned in a heavily embroidered shawl and she had a good-sized branch propped on her shoulder like a rifle.

'Let me carry your tree up the stairs,' Timur offered at once.

I thought she might refuse because her brother had been killed by the Russians, but she wasn't that kind of woman.

'Thank you, Major. How thoughtful.'

She relinquished the weight of the wood with relief, her many bracelets jingling, and Timur followed her up the stairs. I trailed be-hind with my bicycle.

'Anna,' Frau Meyer said over her shoulder, 'there was a woman here looking for you earlier.'

But I was too busy watching the way Timur's feet ate up each stair, how his heels hovered, politely adjusting to the pace of the woman in front of him.

'An older woman. Big-busted and in a sable coat,' Frau Meyer elab-orated. 'She went in to talk to your mother, I think, but not for long.

She came rushing back down and was all of a tremble when she passed me on the stairs.'

But her words could barely squeeze past the sound of happiness that was buzzing in my ears.

'It was Martha,' my mother said when I asked, but her interest was fixed on the pavement far beneath our window. 'Martha Dieleman.'

Timur had chosen to remain outside in the street. I'd opened the door to our apartment and found my mother standing right behind it. Her arms had pounced on me and pressed my body to hers in a ferocious grip that had shocked me, but she released me and pushed me away as fast as she'd seized me.

'What's going on?' I had asked, bewildered.

She had backed off and retreated into what was left of our drawing room. For once there was a faint ripple of warmth in the air, so she must be burning something in the stove, and I'd noticed there was a glass of vodka on the table.

'It was Martha Dieleman,' my mother said. 'She turned up here in a dreadful state.'

'Why was she upset?'

'It seems that Klaus has gone missing.'

'What?'

A shadow crossed my vision. I blinked but it remained and I felt flecks of sweat form on my forehead. I brushed them aside.

'When did he go missing?'

'This morning. While she was out.'

'But that's impossible. Klaus can't leave the apartment on his own in his wheelchair because the lift doesn't work.'

My mother turned from the window and focused her full attention on me. 'Exactly. She came here because she thought you might know something about it.'

'Me? Why me?'

'Because Klaus had told her that you were stirring up trouble.'

'What did he mean by that?'

'How should I know?'

My mother walked over to the glass of vodka on the little table and drank the last of it straight down. She shuddered, then looked at me and I could see now that her usually pale blue eyes were dark and glassy and I had no understanding of why.

'What trouble are you stirring up, Anna?'

'I've been searching for a child, that's all.'

A long silence stretched through the room and I stood very still. I was frightened that something was about to break.

'Anna, don't lie to me. Martha said she heard you'd been arrested.'

'Who told her that?'

'Someone called Otto.'

'Martha, tell me what happened.'

Martha Dieleman had swept me to her camphor-scented bosom when she opened the door of her apartment and sobbed on my shoulder. She felt fragile as I embraced her, so little left of the big-hearted and buoyant woman who used to fill the rooms with her laughter. She was still wearing her sable coat because the apartment was icy. I sat her down on their velvet chesterfield sofa and I wrapped her hands in both of mine before saying again, 'Martha, tell me quickly what happened.'

'He's gone. He's gone. Oh, Anna, my Klaus has gone.'

'Gone where?'

Her eyes filled with tears. 'I don't know. I went out to queue for bread as usual. When I came back, he'd disappeared and his chair with him. Dear God, Anna, help me find him, please help me.'

'We'll find him, Martha. The first thing is to discover how he got downstairs. Is his leg any better?'

Her hand rose and touched my cheek, soft as one of her feathers. 'Thanks to your penicillin he's been in a lot less pain. Anna, it grieves me so much to see him suffer. But yes, his leg has been better, definitely better, though still there's no possibility of him managing the stairs without help.'

'So it seems that someone came here, helped Klaus downstairs and then carried his wheelchair down. Did any of the people in the other apartments hear shouts or a struggle?'

'No.'

'What made you think I might have been involved?'

'Klaus was worried that you were in some kind of trouble,' she said uncomfortably, 'and Otto claimed you'd been arrested.'

'Who told Klaus I was in trouble?'

'Otto.'

'Where can I find Otto?'

'I have no idea. That man is always so secretive.'

'You don't know his address?'

'No. Only that it's somewhere in the west.'

'What's his last name?'

She shook her head, helpless. 'He's just Otto.'

Otto.

I rose abruptly to my feet.

'I'll do a quick search on my bicycle in case it's just a friend who has come to walk him to the park.'

Martha released a deep breath. 'Hurry, Anna,' was all she said. 'Hurry.'

Two beefy American soldiers sauntered along the pavement, olive drab caps at a sharp angle, grins as ripe as summer hayseeds. They were some distance in front of me, heading in my direction, but their laughter was louder than it had a right to be. I'd scoured the area, the side streets and the main roads, and was cycling along the eastern end of Ku'damm, the broad thoroughfare, once such a favourite route for classy carriages and ornate apartment blocks but which was only just managing to cling to life now, the famous lime trees felled for firewood. The Sunday parade of society's elite was nothing but a distant memory.

One of the beefy soldiers on the pavement turned his head and let rip with an admiring whistle when I shot past, but my eyes remained fixed straight ahead on the road. You whistle at dogs, not women.

I paid no more attention to them than I would to a dead rat in the gutter. All the girls knew how generous the GIs were in exchange for a smile but I pedalled faster. I was all out of smiles.

This was when everything turned bad. I can trace it to this exact moment, just after the GI's whistle. If the GI hadn't whistled, would I have carried on cycling straight down Ku'damm?

I think I would.

If that GI hadn't whistled at me as though I were a dog, I wouldn't have cut down the narrow *Allee* to get away from the sound of it. I wouldn't have. I know it.

CHAPTER THIRTY-FIVE

◆ ◆ ◆

ANNA

I popped out of the far end of the allee and despite all my good intentions, temptation proved too much for me. I was intent on searching for Klaus, but still there was no sight of him or of an abandoned wheelchair, and it took no more than a heartbeat to make the wrong decision. Instead of continuing straight on, as I'd intended, my front wheel swung right. There was always a chance that Klaus had headed this way too.

The roads were narrower at first. The buildings leaned against each other as though in need of a helping hand to stay upright, and the cobbled streets were busy. I rode on quickly to the grand Wagner Platz, still undergoing reconstruction, with piledrivers making the air shudder. I could feel sweat between my shoulder blades under my coat when I cycled past what had once been a parade of shops that I'd loved. Now most of them were dust.

I braked in front of a bombed-out building that had previously been a shop where, before the war, a grand sign had sat on proud display above the doorway. *Wolff Bicycles*.

My father's shop.

The two words had been picked out in gold-lettered script on an enamelled rich maroon background and I'd thought it the grandest shop sign in the whole world. The finest bicycle shop in all Berlin, Papa used to declare with a vigorous sweep of his arms.

He was killed at the Battle of Arnhem in the Netherlands in September 1944 and my mother and I were grief-stricken. We had thought him immortal. How could his laughter ever die? Seven months later the war ended and now we call Americans and Englishmen our friends. My father's shop had been blown apart by an American bomb, so there was no roof now to keep the sleet and snow at bay, and it distressed me to see it and yet I couldn't stay away. I came time and time again to catch his voice on the wind and to listen to the memories that always smacked into me with the force of a freight train.

'You can open your eyes now.' Papa is grinning down at me. 'Look!'

'Wow!'

We are standing on the pavement in a golden ray of spring sunshine, Papa and me. I press close to him.

'It's a Schwinn Aerocycle,' he announces.

Such pride in his voice. Such a smile on his handsome face. In front of us on display in the window of Papa's shop stands a gleaming bicycle, bright scarlet and silver. I want to rush inside and wrap my arms around it, it is so beautiful. Bright scarlet forks. Scarlet saddle. Scarlet tyres. I've never seen scarlet tyres before. I gaze at it with awe.

'Where is it manufactured, Papa?'

'It's American,' he says. 'A German immigrant set up the Schwinn company in Chicago.'

'American,' I whisper, as if he'd said it was Martian.

I don't breathe. I close my eyes. I picture myself riding it down Unter den Linden where heads would turn, and it leaves me breathless, the sight of that gleaming bicycle. That night I stayed awake, seeing that bicycle shine in the darkness.

The next day while I am at school, the Brownshirts, Hitler's bully boys, come with their truncheons and smash the window of Papa's shop, smash the bicycle, smash Papa's face. No American bicycles allowed. Just German bicycles. Understand? Smash.

I don't understand.

Instead of jumping back on my bicycle as I should have done to return to Martha, I walked along the remains of the wall and round the end of it to the ruined interior. The skimpy winter sun had found a break in the cloud cover and was casting cold shadows into the roofless shop, so that at first I had to look down and concentrate on where I placed my feet on the piles of broken masonry.

When I looked up, I froze. A man's body hung from a rope. By the neck.

No. It *couldn't* be true. My eyes were … no … my eyes were lying.

I looked away quickly, and then shot another glance back at it fast, as if I could catch it off guard, but the body still hung there with its back to me. It was the loneliest thing I'd ever seen. One end of the rope was slung over a broken beam high in the remaining structure, the other end tight around his neck. I didn't breathe. Didn't utter a sound. All I heard was the soft scrape of my shoe as it brushed over a stone, then I was scrambling as fast as I could towards the man.

'I'm coming,' I shouted, 'I'm here, I'm here.'

But I knew he was not hearing me. I could see he was dead even from here, even with his back towards me. A long black coat, his head slumped forward, his body limp. The ugly knot like a thick coiled snake sleeping at the back of his neck.

'I'm coming, I'm coming,' I kept yelling.

I clambered. I fell. I scrabbled to my feet.

As I came closer I registered that his hair was iron grey, his hands blue and motionless at his sides, but worse was that he was hanging too high above my head for me to get him down. If I raised an arm above my head I could just about touch his feet.

I had to climb around another large outcrop of fallen masonry to reach a spot where I could look up at the poor man's face. When I finally stood in front of him, I stopped breathing all over again. His face was colourless. Not even grey, just empty of everything. His large sunken eyes were closed and a network of creases was scored deep into his skin, etching out what he had endured.

It was Klaus Dieleman.

I reached up to Klaus's feet. I stretched up on tiptoe, grasped his shoe just to make contact and tipped my head backwards.

Tell me who did this to you, Klaus.

The rope creaked. It didn't make sense, this needless death.

I was unaware of the tears streaming backwards into my ears as I stared upwards or of the strange whooping noise coming from inside my lungs. I forced myself to inspect the rope above his head. It was black and greasy. How did whoever did this throw it up so high? A sudden swirl of wind snatched at the hem of Klaus's black coat, the same one he'd been wearing when I last saw him in his apartment, and wrapped it around his shin. I clung to him tighter, fearing that the wind would wrench him from me, and as I stretched my arms almost out of their sockets, one of his shoes slipped off his heel into my hand.

I studied it through tears of grief. Inside lay a short length of white string and attached to one end of it was a brooch in the shape of a small pearl cross.

CHAPTER THIRTY-SIX

* * *

ANNA

So I was back inside a police station. This one was again in West Berlin, so no Volkspolizei. It smelled of men, of uniforms that needed a clean, of tobacco and of long hours of work.

What did it look like?

I have no idea. It had rooms and corridors; that's the best I can offer. My eyes saw nothing but a thick rope around a neck and a dead man's closed eyes and naked hands. His fingernails blue. His black shoe gripped in my hand.

I remember a bald policeman. He'd ushered me down a corridor in the police station into a small room. A new smell. Was it fear? Or sorrow? Was it mine? Or had it permeated the walls year after year? I recall the soothing sound of his voice, though not the words he said. He brought me a glass of water and a clean white cotton handkerchief.

Was I crying?

Did I thank him?

He abandoned me alone in that room but this time there was a circular clock on the wall and I watched its black hand tick away every single minute. I suppose the police were checking on my story, searching for Klaus's body in the ruins, speaking to Martha, poor *poor* Martha. They'd be cutting Klaus down and taking him ... where? To a morgue.

Where was Berlin's morgue? On a cold slab where scalpels would do terrible things to him.

I didn't want to leave this room. I didn't want to go home to tell Mutti.

'You are certain the man you found hanging is Klaus Dieleman?'

How many times was the police captain intending to ask this same question?

'Yes.'

'You recognised him?'

'Yes.'

'How long have you known him?'

'All my life.'

'You say you were searching for him because Frau Dieleman asked you to. Is that correct?'

'Yes.'

'Why did you go to that exact spot today?'

'I told you. It used to be my father's shop. Ruined now but I still go there sometimes.'

'Why?'

'To remember him.'

'Why do you think Herr Dieleman went there?'

'I don't know. I presume he was taken there by someone.'

'Did that happen often?'

I shook my head. My mouth didn't seem to be working properly.

He studied the page of notes in front of him. 'You say he was a friend of your father's and needed a wheelchair to get around because of a war wound to his leg. Is that correct?'

'Yes.'

'In which case how do you think he got to your father's shop?'

'I don't know.'

'Do you think his wife took him there?'

'No. She was queuing for bread.'

'Might a friend have taken him?'

'Maybe.'

'Did you see anything at the site to indicate who the other person might be?'

I looked him straight in the eye. 'No.'

There was a long pause. The police captain ran a hand over his bald head in frustration. 'You do realise, don't you, Fräulein Wolff, that this is a murder case?'

'Yes.'

'I assume you do want to find out who murdered your father's friend and why.'

'Yes, of course.'

'So you will do all in your power to give us information that could help us find the murderer.'

'Yes.'

'Is there anything you're not telling me?'

'No.'

'Was he involved with any criminals here in Berlin?'

'Not that I know of.'

He had patient eyes. He nodded. 'I would like you and Frau Diele-man to identify the body tomorrow.'

My stomach curdled.

Again he glanced down at the papers in front of him on the table between us. 'Did Klaus Dieleman have any enemies that you know of?'

'No, none. Everyone liked him.' I slid one hand into my coat pocket and curled a finger around the pearl brooch that lay at the bottom. 'He didn't have any enemies. Unless you count Stalin.'

The patient eyes flicked up to my face, surprised.

CHAPTER THIRTY-SEVEN

◆ ◆ ◆

TIMUR

Timur watched her arrive at Potsdamer Platz, just as she'd promised. Her feet were heavy and her head was down and Timur
knew something in her had been wrenched apart in the hours that
she'd been gone. But the moment her dark eyes found his, they lit up.
Her stride lengthened, eager to eat up the distance between them,
and his arm reached out to her, but just in time it dropped to his side.
He smiled politely.

'Hello, Anna.'

She didn't respond, not at first. She stood in front of him on the pavement with her blazing eyes and her smile that wasn't remotely polite.

'Walk with me,' she said.

She set off in the direction of the river, wheeling her grubby bicycle,
and he fell into step beside her, not touching her. He had no desire to
bring the communist authorities down on her head, but now and again
when the street was clear he just trailed a finger along her saddle. And
it made her smile.

The rain came hissing down, bouncing off the pavements, and they
found a church in which to take refuge. It wasn't in great shape. Damage to its vaulted ceiling had been patched with more enthusiasm than
skill and it was leaking into a dozen white enamel buckets with a watery musical chorus. A handful of its arched windows had been boarded
up, blocking out the light as well as the rain, but the dim interior gave
an illusion of safety and they were both willing to settle for that.

There were no pews. Had they been burned? Instead they perched on
the stone footrest of a sleeping statue of some long-dead knight behind a

pillar and they sat in silence, content to be together. Their shoulders touched and their hipbones nudged close, and that was enough.

'Tell me, Anna, did you find your friend?'

'Yes.'

'Not good?'

'No. As bad as it gets.'

'I'm sorry.'

She leaned her head on his shoulder, her hat giving off a strong whiff of wet wool, and she told him about her friend Klaus Dieleman, about his friendship with her father, about his strange relationship with a man called Otto and about the thick greasy rope around Klaus's neck.

Timur listened. To her words and to the gaps between her words, to the quick intakes of air as if she were drowning and to the tears that she didn't shed. He listened to her teeth chatter and knew it was shock. He took off his greatcoat and wrapped it around her so that she looked like a giant mushroom and he gave her a swig of vodka from his hip flask which made her hiss through her teeth.

'Klaus is not the only one around me to die,' she said.

'What do you mean?'

She raised her head and fixed a solemn gaze on his face. 'Timur, I am giving you a warning. Stay away from me. People around me are dying.'

'Which people?'

'Anyone who gets involved with me in some way. An investigator I hired to search for a child was killed recently. An explosion blew up an American recruitment centre where I was queuing. A woman I barely knew died in an accident after we shared a meal at Tempelhof. One of your men shot a boy who stole my orange. A child I was trying to help was abducted. And now Klaus. Hanged like a common criminal. I tell you, Timur, I am a dangerous friend to have.'

'No, Anna, you are imagining connections that aren't there. These must be coincidences.'

'Must they?' She shook her wet head. 'I don't think so. I was also knocked off my bicycle by a car that drove too close to me.'

That sent a shiver through him. He took her hand in his.

'Listen to me.' He spoke lightly, nothing to alarm her. 'The driver was probably just not paying sufficient attention and the explosion was part of the city's general political unrest. As for the investigator, he must have been handling numerous cases, not just yours.'

She nodded reluctantly. 'Probably.'

'So any of them could have retaliated when he caught up with them. And at Tempelhof where there are thousands of people dealing with heavy goods and lifting gear every day of the week, accidents must occur regularly. And then the boy. The one with your orange.' He tasted bile in his throat and everything around them seemed to grow still, the rain on the boarded windows, the fretting of the damaged beams, the drip into the buckets. 'He was a trigger-happy comrade who wanted to show off his target skills on the poor kid, nothing more.'

For a moment her head hung down and she closed her eyes.

'And you say,' he continued, 'you believe Klaus Dieleman was in-volved in some kind of illegal deals with black marketeers, so he was a man inviting trouble. If he crossed the wrong person, any of the gangs could have put an end to him as a warning to others. It happens all over Berlin if you mix with dangerous characters. And I assure you that there are plenty of dangerous characters in this city right now. Nothing to do with you.'

She opened her eyes and raised them to his with a sad smile. 'Thank you, Timur.'

'For what?'

'For lying so well.'

He pulled her closer and kissed the side of her head. 'I'm not lying,' he lied into the sodden hat. 'It's common sense. You are imagining a connection to yourself.'

A clatter of the ancient iron latch on the church door startled them. An old woman entered with an ancient marmalade-coloured dog on a lead and the two of them shook off the raindrops in unison before set-ting off with enthusiasm for the altar. They radiated an energy and a happiness that warmed the cold bones of the church.

'Anna,' Timur said, keeping his voice low, 'does your mother still go to church every Sunday?'

Anna turned her face away. 'My mother hasn't left our apartment in three years.'

That shocked him. 'Anna, I'm so sorry. That must be hard to live with. For both of you.'

He didn't need to ask why. He remembered carrying Luisa Wolff, light as a bird in his arms, into her apartment and gently laying her down on her bed, her blood pooling on the white quilt cover beneath.

'What does she do all day?'

'I don't know really. She knits whenever I can scrounge wool from anywhere for her, even scraps of crinkly old used wool. She reads our stock of books again and again, dwindling because I keep burning them. She used to listen to classical music on our wind-up gramophone but your friend Lieutenant Glinin put an end to that when he smashed all her records. She must read the Bible because she seems to know it off by heart now. Not that she believes it any more.' Anna shrugged and pulled his greatcoat tighter around herself. 'And friends visit, but less and less.' She stared at her hand where he'd kissed it as if she could see the imprint of his lips. 'I don't know what to do with her.'

There was an ache in her words and he drew her to her feet. 'Let's go and find a record for your mother. Which composer does she like?'

'Chopin.'

'Alright. Chopin here we come.'

The smile was back. '*Spasibo*. Thank you.'

They glanced over to where the old woman was on her knees at the altar, the dog leaning against her, snoozing quietly, and Timur led Anna back down the side aisle to the oak door. The rain had stopped, the roofs glistened like glass and as she handed him his greatcoat he said, 'You mentioned that you were searching for a child.'

She nodded.

He studied her. 'What child?'

◆ ◆ ◆

It had come as a shock to Timur to learn that the mother didn't go outdoors any more. He hadn't seen that coming. No wonder Frau Wolff lived on a razor's edge. Mental isolation can do that to you; he'd seen it many times with men in the trenches on the front line, that expression in the eyes, that half a step away from self-obliteration.

And then there was the child.

He stood at the far end of Anna's street as darkness fell and watched her walk away from him. It was always hard, letting her go. She walked the way she lived, intent on finding her own path and with her awful bicycle at her side. He was jealous of that bicycle. It was absurd, but she loved that piece of junk metal so fiercely, touched it so lovingly and gave it small secret smiles that he would have happily died for.

Accompanying her right to her door wasn't an option. Anyone keeping watch on her apartment building and seeing a Russian officer in her orbit could flare up. Too much of a risk. So when he'd seen her step safely inside and her door close firmly against the night, his footsteps had carried him away from her street and back to the alleyway where it had all started. A hundred paces from her door.

It was an alleyway like any other, no worse, no better. Unlit and stinking, about four metres wide. One of the walls had collapsed, scattering broken masonry in the path of unwary pedestrians which made it dangerous in the dark for those foolish enough to venture in without a flashlight. But by day a thin slat of sky turned it into an accessible rat-run from Prenzlauer to the less affluent apartment blocks behind. It had become the place of nightmares for Anna and her mother, but for Timur this filthy scream-soaked passageway had transformed his life beyond anything he had ever dreamed of. Yet if he could, he would wipe out that chill April afternoon in 1945. Timur would erase it from the calendar. Eradicate it from history. For Anna, he would do that.

He stepped into it now in the pitch dark, flashlight in hand but not switched on. Instantly he could smell blood. He could hear screams, he could taste rage. It had been daylight on that April afternoon and a pencil-thin slice of sunshine had squeezed into the gap, a cool wind stirring the masonry dust, so that he had to squint when he heard the shouts in the alley. He had entered and immediately drawn his Tokarev TT-33 pistol from his hip holster.

He could still feel it, the twist of his heart at the sight of Anna on her back, sprawled on the ground. She was kicking and punching and screaming her fury like a wild cat at the two men lying on top of her but the weight of them was too much. Both wore the uniform of Red Army officers, tank regiment captains, though their peaked caps had been taken off and set aside on a chunk of masonry that had once been a chimney breast. To one side lay her mother, Luisa Wolff, clothes torn and her face and hair covered in blood. One leg was bent under her at a horrible angle and she wasn't moving.

'Get off the girl!' Timur had roared at the men.

'What? You wan' her?' slurred one of the officers.

Timur bent down, hooked an arm around the man's thick neck from behind and yanked him off the girl with all his strength. Only then did he get a look at the second officer. The back of his skull was caved in. Anna was kicking the body off her and leapt to her feet but didn't run. She dodged round Timur and crouched by her mother, ready to defend her immobile form from further attack, roaring her hatred at the drunken officer who was now on his feet. Blood flowed from her nose.

The officer lunged for her, seized her long black hair, twisted it round his fist and yelled, 'This one's mine. You can have the dead one.'

'Let her go.' Timur pointed his pistol straight at the officer's chest.

'What the fuck you doing?'

'Let her go, I said.'

'Don't be an arsehole. She's a bitch. Worth nothing. Look what she did to my friend there. She's a killer and deserves everything she …'

Timur pulled the trigger.

CHAPTER THIRTY-EIGHT

◆ ◆ ◆

ANNA

I slid my key into the lock of our apartment. I opened the door and found the interior dim. The evening had shut us in together, my mother and I, and slammed the lid on us. A single candle struggled to throw its flickering light in my direction but failed.

Across the room my mother was seated in her usual armchair next to the tall stove in the corner, though the stove was now cold. Her body was hunched over, harbouring what little warmth she could muster, lit by a muted halo from the candle. She was knitting, her fingers busy, flashing back and forth in a neat practised rhythm that required no thought. I tried to think where the wool had come from. It was old wool, I could tell by the crinkly strand of some garment unravelled. At the sight of me my mother rose to her feet, dropping needles and wool to the floor.

'Anna?'

Nothing more. One word was enough.

'I found Klaus,' I said.

'Thank God.'

That was my cue to explain, to mention the thick rope hanging from the broken wooden beam and the patient police eyes. To coax the words out from their hiding place, to tell my mother that her husband's dearest friend had been murdered.

'Where was he?'

'At the ruins of Papa's shop.'

A quick intake of breath. 'At Wolff Bicycles?'

I nodded.

'Why there?' she asked.

'I don't know. Someone must have helped him.'

Her eyes narrowed, a small sign of suspicion. 'Why are you home so late? What about going to Tempelhof?'

'It's my day off today. I was at the Dielemans' apartment and forgot the time.'

'Don't lie to me. Martha would never let you stay there till it was dark outside. This city is heaving with thousands of troops and she is well aware of the dangers.'

I distracted her by fetching the sack draped over my bicycle saddle. 'Look,' I said, 'look, Mutti, I have some coal.' I reached in and pulled out one of the glittering black lumps. 'There's not much, but enough for a couple of fires.'

'It's real coal too.' She smiled her approval. 'Not those foul stinking briquettes made of oil and sawdust.'

'And this as well,' I added, drawing from inside my coat a chunk of bread and *wurst* wrapped in greaseproof paper.

But my mother showed little interest in the food. She removed the sack from my grasp, for once heedless of the coal dust. 'Where on earth did you find such good coal?'

'I mended someone's bicycle for him. He gave me this in exchange.' One lie was as good as another.

'You did well, Anna.'

Did she believe me? I don't know. She set about laying a fire in the *Kachelöfen*, our tiled stove, and I couldn't help but notice the skittery way she moved. The mention of Papa's shop had shaken her.

That evening we played cards.

I craved a pause. A small hole in time that I could crawl into, where no man in uniform would try to shake answers out of me. I hungered for some quiet. I needed a moment to grieve for poor Klaus before I began spilling it all out on my mother. So we played cards. But tonight I couldn't keep the card numbers straight in my head. I lit another candle stub and we sat opposite each other at the small baize card table, drawn up close to the stove.

'Do you know why we play cards so often?' my mother asked me.

I placed a king of clubs on the table and glanced at her, surprised. She had her poker face on, its features set hard, and I had no way of knowing what was in her mind. We were playing *Sechsundsechzig*, a fast and furious game in which the aim is to take as many tricks as possible. I was losing.

'Because we both like to play cards,' I answered with a shrug.

'No. Because we both like to win,' she pointed out. 'So what is the matter with you tonight? You are all over the place.'

'I'm tired, that's all.' My throat was tight.

She placed a ten on top of my king and took the trick, pleased with herself, and added it neatly to her pile, then sat back in her chair. She abandoned her cards face down on the green baize. 'Well, Anna, what is it that is making you look like a whipped dog tonight?'

'I told you. I'm tired.'

'Anna, we're all tired. Tired of living.'

'No, not that. I'm not tired of living. There is too much I need to do.'

'Don't be foolish, Anna. Look around you. In this city it's the nearness of death each day that reminds us that what we do is meaningless.'

'Mutti,' I regarded her minutely, 'did Klaus have enemies?'

'Of course not. You know how popular he was. Everyone loved him.'

'Are you sure?'

Her arched brows drew tight together. 'What on earth are you talking about?'

I sat back, away from her. 'I just wondered.'

For fifteen minutes we played *Sechsundsechzig* in silence. The room grew warmer and I continued to lose.

'This,' my mother said while inspecting her new hand, 'is why we play cards so often, Anna. So that we don't have to talk to each other.'

The hurt caught me right between the eyes, a sharp needlepoint of pain. It made me blink.

CHAPTER THIRTY-NINE

◆ ◆ ◆

ANNA

I stood unmoving, listening to the wind trying to rip off one of our rat-tling roof tiles, and I stared out across the city. Night covered Berlin like a heavy blanket that allowed no light to creep in, except for the pinprick beams of the aircraft. Brave flashes of light. They poured down into the city the way a waterfall pours over stones, with never a break in its flow.

The relentless darkness stretched away from my open bedroom window, winding through the streets all the way to the Soviet Military Administration headquarters at Karlshorst in the Lichtenberg district in the east of the city. Here in a modest building graced with pillars, on 8 May 1945, the unconditional surrender of our German forces was presented to the almighty Marshal Zhukov, Russian commander of the 1st and 2nd Belorussian Fronts. With a stroke of a pen the war in Europe ended. And the GSOFG – the Group of Soviet Occupation Forces in Germany – became our official lord and master here in East Germany. That was where Timur was stationed now, at Karlshorst. I breathed out a great gust of air like the frustrated roar of a lioness.

I pictured that breath, warm and white, tasting of me. I pictured it sweeping along that dark path. Skimming the blackened ruins of fine buildings, slipping past the Volkspark with its crippled stumps of trees and weaving its way across the river and out through the bombed factories of Treptow. Finally reaching Timur in Lichtenberg, where he sits, lean legs stretched out in front of him, maybe reading … what? What are you reading? Or are you prowling? Or standing at an open window, as I am? I pictured him inhaling, so that my breath nestled deep in his lungs. He would know it was mine.

◆ ◆ ◆

I entered my mother's bedroom just before dawn and placed my candle on her bedside table, but the room felt claustrophobic with its boxes stacked on top of boxes. What was left of her possessions were all huddled together, fearful, like us.

When the Soviet Housing Committee had come strutting into our apartment, they had drawn chalk lines across the parquet floor to show where the new partition walls would be built, stealing our rooms from us. They gave some of our living space to a family with four children and some to an old couple with defeated faces. The old man was deaf and the partition walls were thin. They argued all hours of the day and night, but then made up by singing softly together. Sweet harmonies. I don't think they ever slept.

The shutters were closed, as always, though the clouds had drifted south overnight and the moonlight felt fresh and clean in my own small room.

'Mutti,' I whispered.

She shot upright in bed, hair tangled, eyes huge, and a moan slid past her lips.

'Mutti, it's me.'

She blinked and shook herself. 'Anna, I thought you were a ghost,' she gasped.

I looked down at myself, swaddled in my bed quilt, its cover pure white and ghostly. My mother's and father's initials were embroidered in one corner of the cover, forever entwined, part of her dowry linen.

'Whose ghost, Mutti?'

'Your father's.'

'I'm sorry I frightened you but there's something you have to know.'

So I told her. About Klaus hanging from the broken beam. About the black coat, the colourless skin, the new lines on his face. The depth of those lines. His legs dangling like a ragdoll's, the touch of my fingers on his feet and his patent leather shoe dusty in my hand. I described them all once and then all a second time when she asked me to. I described each detail.

'Now look at this,' I said finally. 'Look what I found in Klaus's shoe.'

I held out my palm. On it lay the exquisite brooch, the cross of pearls luminous in the candlelight, glowing with an inner fire. We both recognised the piece. We both knew who had bought it and to whom it had been given as a Christmas gift when I was fourteen and there was snow on the ground. From my father to my mother. And we both knew that it had disappeared three and a half years ago.

She took the pearl brooch and clamped her fingers tightly over it. She held her fist to her lips. With a soft sigh she collapsed against me where I sat on the edge of her bed. I held her tight and there was the scent of sleep on her skin. Sitting there within the circle of her darkness I was forced to face the fact that I was feeling something that was hard and cold and angry melt inside me. I could not go on being angry forever.

My mother shut herself away for hours while I sat on the floor outside her bedroom door like a dog, listening to her weep. When she emerged in the morning, she was red-eyed but controlled and calm, and the brooch was pinned to the collar of her dress where it belonged. Her fair hair was pulled severely off her face, a black ribbon tying it back behind her head. She was always pale but now her skin looked unlived in and it was a relief when she seated herself on her usual chair, picked up her knitting and let her fingers fly. When I walked over to the door, my coat on, woollen hat in hand, I was reluctant to leave.

'I have to go to Martha,' I said. 'But she's your friend too. Come with us to the mortuary to identify the body.'

'No.' She turned away. 'You go alone.'

'If you insist.'

'I do.'

Still I didn't leave. She wouldn't look in my direction and her eyes landed on everything except me. She rose, walked over to the window and for five minutes stood there staring out into the street without moving and without saying a word while her fingertips caressed the creamy surface of the pearls on her collar. I watched her.

'How do you think your brooch ended up in Klaus's shoe?' I asked.

She shrugged and shook her head. The morning light was thin and slate grey, her figure a slender silhouette etched against the dark clouds.

'Mutti, I am grieving too. And it will be hard on Martha. Please come.'

'I know, Anna, but the answer is still no.' I thought she was done, but a moment later she added, 'I'm sorry.'

The police captain's eyes were not so patient today, as though he had no more liking for this place than I. He stood behind us in the sterile room, accustomed to its discreet lighting and harsh chemical smell, but even so, I could feel his desire for Martha to enter the required signature on the form and leave.

Martha was not sobbing, not wailing or wiping away tears. She stood dry-eyed and dressed in black at my side, her spine straight and her arm through mine, holding on as she gazed down at her dead husband's face on the slab in front of us. I heard an odd sound and realised it was my own breath, a thin thread of effort. Inside my head I was hearing a voice that sounded like mine screaming *I will kill you*, and seeing a hand that looked like my hand snatching up a broken brick and crashing it down on a skull. A dull wet sound.

I jerked my thoughts away from it and focused them on the pearl brooch. How did it get into your shoe, Klaus? Did you put it there or did someone else? And was it put there for me to find? Or for the police to find? To trace it back to my mother.

'Frau Dieleman?' A respectful prompt from the police captain.

She nodded. 'He is my husband, Klaus Dieleman.'

A tear rolled down my cheek.

'Don't cry, Anna,' Martha murmured. 'Klaus is long gone.'

CHAPTER FORTY

◆ ◆ ◆

INGRID

'Stupid knucklehead, that one.'

Ingrid looked up. 'Why, what happened, Rocco?'

Tempelhof's runways buzzed with noise and activity, but she was pouring coffee into a cup and had missed whatever it was that had got her boss all riled up.

'Some pilot with meatballs for brains has burst yet another set of tyres by dropping his crate down like a sack of coals on the runway. That's the second one in the last hour. Goddammit, don't they know how to fly by now?'

'It's not flying, Rocco. It's the landing. They say it's very tight here, very steep. All the houses too close.'

'Yeah, but one mistake like that can screw up the whole system and delay other aircraft. They've got to keep moving. They're all links in a chain.'

Was that chain being broken because of Kuznetsov? Because of the airmen's names she'd given him in her notebook? Names that only needed a nice fat envelop slid into their back pocket despite the dangers. She didn't know for sure but she wondered.

Ingrid handed the coffee to the flier standing in front of her. Behind him two mechanics in stained overalls were approaching across the grass. Grease monkeys, Rocco called them, which always made her laugh.

'Here you go, Noah,' she said. She was learning the lingo.

He looked different without the lipstick and that thought made her laugh again.

'Thanks, Ingrid.' He picked up the coffee and smiled, dark eyebrows raised with amusement as if he knew exactly what was passing through her mind. 'Have a nice day.'

'You too.'

'Enjoy the magazine. It will help you to learn more English.'

Between them on the counter lay a copy of something called *Collier's*, a glossy American magazine with a rosy-cheeked cowgirl on the cover, wearing a white Stetson and looking as if she ate Ma's tasty apple pie every day of the week. Beside her a beautifully groomed Lassie dog stared straight out at Ingrid and almost brought tears to her eyes. Its faithful brown eyes reminded her of Greta at the circus. Greta had been a snow-white poodle and no dog in the world could ride a horse bareback the way Greta used to. Ingrid picked up the magazine and slid it smoothly into the front flap of her apron, curious as to what documents Noah Maynard had tucked inside it this time.

She watched the American hurry away, long and lanky inside his flying jacket, the pilots always in a rush. It was no wonder that mistakes were made. She felt the burn of excitement in her gut.

CHAPTER FORTY-ONE

◆ ◆ ◆

ANNA

'Is that the lot?'

The big voice boomed off the bare walls. It belonged to Stefan, my sheet-metal-worker companion from the queue for jobs at Tempelhof airport, and his bald dome of a head materialised around the door.

'And this,' piped up a young boy at his side. 'I'll carry this one.'

It was Gerd, my godson, his face alight with hero-worship for the mountainous metalworker, and the boy's golden wind-tossed curls were streaked with black grease where Stefan had ruffled them. Over Gerd's good shoulder hung a tyreless bicycle wheel, his other arm still in a sling, 'Don't worry, Tante Anna, I've got it.'

Kristina paused in her work at the top of a ladder and beamed down at her son. 'You mind your arm, Gerd.'

The six-year-old boy rolled his eyes at Stefan in a 'what men have to put up with' kind of way and swaggered to the door. These generous friends of mine had turned up to help with the final clear-out of my workshop, its transformation to a dormitory almost complete, and I had roped in Stefan and his sturdy handcart to do the heavy grunt work. Already two double mattresses leaned against one of the scrubbed walls, courtesy of Martha. I knew she could have sold them, but no, she insisted I take them for my shelter. It is such a fine line between the survival of self and the survival of humanity. The line is not set in stone. It sways. It blurs. And sometimes it breaks.

'Thank you, Stefan.'

I abandoned my scrubbing brush and the stubborn oil stain to give my man mountain a hug. He turned a dainty shade of pink and galloped out to his handcart with its final load piled to the sky and destined for Prenzlauer Allee. He and Gerd trundled off down the road, watched with a smile by Kristina on top of her ladder. She was perched up at ceiling height cleaning the workroom's long thin window.

'Gerd needs a Stefan in his life,' she said.

'They all do, these kids.'

She swivelled round to study me. 'You're taking on a lot, Anna.'

'I know.'

'Are you hoping that they'll come tumbling down these steps one day, Felix and Poldi, straight into your arms?'

'They're out there somewhere, Kristina, somewhere in the ruins of Berlin. I am certain of it. Some days I can feel their breath in the wind. They're here somewhere.'

'Oh, Anna.'

I resumed my scrubbing as if I could scrub away the doubt in her words, but almost immediately the door opened behind me and a man's voice declared, 'So this is where you hide yourself away.'

My head whipped round. Timur was standing in the doorway, filling it with his broad shoulders. I smiled at him, smiled as if I would never stop smiling, and asked, 'How did you find me?'

'I just followed the trail of bicycle parts and knew you'd be at the end of it.'

He swept off his cap as he advanced further into the room and his thick locks sprang back to life. He brought a wave of warmth and energy into the soulless basement, but before he could take another step Kristina shot down her ladder and placed herself between him and me. Hands on her hips, bristling with the hostility of a Red Army border guard.

'Go away, Major Voronin,' she said coldly. 'Get out and don't come back.'

I leapt to my feet. 'No, Kristina.'

But she hadn't finished. 'You hurt Anna more than enough last time, so don't imagine you can march in here in your big victor's boots and wave a Chopin record under her nose and do it all over again.'

'I'll not leave her again,' Timur declared, his solemn gaze fixed on me, not on her. 'I promise you that.'

I believed him. Instantly. Irrevocably. Insatiably. But Kristina was not so easily bought.

'What's to stop your lord and master in the Kremlin ordering you back to Moscow again for another three years? Another ten years?' she demanded. 'What then?'

He took one step towards me. 'I'll not go.'

'Has he been?' I asked.

Martha nodded. Her apartment was as cold as ever. 'Oh yes, Otto has been here alright, Anna, sniffing around what Klaus has left behind like a hyena on a buffalo carcass. Sneaking in for an extra mouthful.'

The loss of her husband had aged Martha almost instantly and it saddened me beyond words to see the new lines of sorrow carved on her face. Yet she had discarded the black widow's weeds in disgust and was wearing a bright red woollen dress that Klaus had always adored, though it hung loose on her now. A white silk turban on her head and lustrous pearls at her throat gave her a luminous glow that failed totally to disguise the blood-shot eyes and the ashen sheen to her skin, as though a veil had descended between her and the world.

'A hyena has strong jaws, Martha. Be careful.'

'You're the one who should be careful, *schatzi*. You'd do better to steer well clear of that man. What is it you want with him?'

'I want Otto to get hold of some blankets for me. For the children.'

But Martha shook her head at me. 'You believe he was involved in my Klaus's death, don't you?' she stated. 'The police are saying the murder was probably committed by one of the black-market gangs that Otto introduced him to. Hanging is one of their trademarks apparently, to warn others not to double-cross them.'

'But Klaus would never double-cross anyone, Martha,' I said impatiently. 'You know that as well as I do. Have the police questioned Otto?'

She collapsed down on to the button-back chaise longue and I felt the effort she was putting into staying upright. 'Yes, but the fools let him go,' she muttered, head bowed. 'There was no proof, no evidence. What exactly was he doing with Klaus? Other than selling our paintings and antiques, I mean.'

'Shall I tell you what I think?'

'You always were a clever one. Tell me.'

'I overheard snippets of their conversation that time I was here, and they were talking about private shipments of goods at the airport. Smuggled in especially for them. So I'm guessing they were selling your valuables in America because they are worth very little here and buying saleable goods like food and tools and medications instead, which were flown into the airport illegally and which they could sell here for much greater profit.'

'Oh, my foolish husband.'

'Have you looked to see if there is any money hidden away?'

'Have I looked for it? Oh, Anna, I've turned this apartment upside down and inside out searching for it. I smashed the lock on his bureau with a hammer but still found nothing.'

'So why do you think,' I asked, 'Klaus was so desperate to build up a stash of cash? What was it he wanted so badly?'

Martha slumped against the backrest. 'That's easy. He wanted to go and live in England.'

'England?' I was stunned.

'Yes, he wanted a thatched cottage by the sea with roses round the door like you see in pictures. He feared that the Soviets would soon be marching over all of Germany, and America would have no stomach for another war.'

'So where is the money hidden away for this dream cottage with its pretty roses?'

Martha stood up and walked over to an ugly French console table, full of carvings of writhing ivy leaves and gilt cherubs. On top of it stood a tall and utterly beautiful Sèvres vase. Its porcelain was the shimmering green of Berlin's linden trees in spring, when they seem to glow from within, and it had two gilded swans' necks as handles. Martha picked it up and carried it to one of the window sills in the drawing room, placed it in the middle where it was visible from down in the street and then she backed off, step by step, regarding the vase as if it might bite her.

'Is that what Klaus used to get you to do?' I whispered.

She nodded her white turban. 'Whenever he wanted to tempt Otto to come visit us, the vase was placed here. It was a sign.'

'You think Otto knows where Klaus's money is hidden?'

'Let's find out, shall we?'

I pedalled swiftly, no stopping to inspect random children or unknown men on the street, not this time. No duffle coats. Just ice glittering in the air, so that I was glad to arrive home and be met by a trickle of warmth from the green tiles of the stove.

My mother was in the centre of the room waltzing to the aching cadences of Chopin's Nocturne in E Flat which was playing on the gramophone. She was wearing the silvery evening gown again and her thin body drifted around the space in small circles, a dreamy smile softening her pin-sharp face. It wasn't hard to imagine who the invisible figure was who held her in his arms.

Without breaking her step, she turned her smile on me and said, 'Dance with me, Anna.'

I threw off my coat and hat and removed my gloves before stepping into her circle and sliding an arm around her waist, my body swaying in time with hers. Her hand sat in mine, small and lonely. I held it lightly and danced her around the small patch of parquet flooring that she had cleared and I wondered how long she had been dancing like this. They used to waltz all around the room, the two of them, Papa and Mutti, locked in their own private world, and I would watch, entranced.

We didn't talk but our bodies did. Our hips touching, our limbs gliding together as the music slid into the gaps between us. The gentle sadness of the notes flushed the tension away from our muscles and from our minds, and we were able to smile at each other while we waltzed. Three times we danced through the beautiful music of Chopin's nocturne, winding the gramophone handle between each playing of the record, until finally my mother spoke.

'Enough, Anna.' She withdrew from my hold and with it she withdrew the smile. 'Now go to your room.'

Go to my room?

My room was dire. No other word fits. Every corner was piled almost to the ceiling with bicycle parts or stacks of tools and wooden planking from my workbench and spare wheels propped against the walls like giant eyes. Stefan and Gerd had done the best they could and had crammed the contents of each cart-load from my workshop into as small a space as possible, but I had to stand on tiptoes to catch sight of my bed. I assumed my mother had ordered me to my room because she wanted me to do something about the chaos.

But I was wrong. I squeezed a path between a couple of metal racks and a repair stand to reach my bed and I saw one small cardboard box and one larger one dumped on top of my white quilt, shedding grubby cobwebs. I reached for the smaller one to remove it but I didn't recognise the box. It wasn't one of mine.

It was about twice the size of a shoebox and its cardboard flaps were closed. Gingerly I lifted one. Nothing exploded, so I sat down on the bed and opened the box. A fierce pain, so intense it brought tears to my eyes, blinded me when I saw what lay inside the box. Letters. Dozens and dozens of brown envelopes.

My love, you are my beating heart, and without you here, this is no life.
The words mesmerised me.
Are you well? I picture you pedalling through Tiergarten, your dark hair flowing like a gleaming wave behind you in the dappled sunlight and I miss your laughter. I miss your laughter like I miss my heart.
I folded the sheet of paper with great care back into its envelope and took out another from a different envelope.

It is cold here. The kind of cold that cracks your bones. Can you hear me cracking?

The paper was dry and soft. It felt old. How old? I looked at the date and it was dated two years ago. I took another.

Today I saw a deer in the forest. We were on night manoeuvres. And do you know what I thought? Not how beautiful the animal was, nor how velvety soft its muzzle must be, nor how proud its neck, nor how its legs looked like the most delicate silver filigree in the moonlight. What I thought was how many good meals it would provide for you and your mother, its tender flesh roasted. I worry. Are you finding enough to eat?

So many letters. A whole banquet of them. No, Timur, I don't need food when I have these.

I opened the second box. Inside were stacked the gifts he'd sworn he'd sent, all shapes and sizes, and I lifted them out, caressing each one in its brown paper wrapping. I gathered them around me like children, the tray painted with flowers, the musical box, the jar of glorious golden honey. One of the gifts, when I peeled back its wrapping, turned out to be a necklace, a pendant of beaten gold on a gold snake chain. Exquisite workmanship. I lay down on the bed, held the necklace to my lips and listened over and over to Tchaikovsky's 'Sugar Plum Fairy' on the musical box.

'Anna! Wake up!'

I retreated deeper into sleep.

'Anna!'

I closed my ears.

Somehow I was walking on a beach. I think it was the Wannsee but the details were blurred. It seemed to be just after dawn, the sky a drunken splash of pink and crimson and Timur was at my side, though he and I had never walked on a beach. Our feet were bare on the cool sand and our hands entwined, fingers laced together as if our limbs and our blood vessels grew out of each other. The feeling of happiness was so heavy on my chest that I could barely breathe.

'Anna! For God's sake!' This time my cheek was prodded.

I forced my eyes open a slit, no more. I was lying on my back. My mother was leaning over me on the bed, gripping the cartons that were lying on top of my chest, trying to remove them but my arms were locked around the boxes with grim determination.

'Let go,' she said.

'I'll never let it go,' I muttered in my sleep. Meaning Timur's hand.

'Anna, the day is passing. It's time for Tempelhof.'

Tempelhof. The word sucked the sleep from my brain and I sat up, arms still attached to the cardboard boxes.

'Why did you hide Timur's letters from me? And his presents? Oh, Mutti, that was cruel.'

'He was Russian.'

'But you knew I loved him.'

She shook her head, exasperated. 'I was trying to protect you.'

'From whom?'

'From you, you stubborn fool. And from him.'

'How can you say that when we both know he saved our lives in that alleyway?'

We never ever mentioned the alleyway, it was an unspoken rule.

She stepped away as if I were suddenly unclean, stumbled over a stack of bicycle parts and left with no further word. And I'd not had time to ask why she had given me the letters and the box of his gifts now. Why now?

In exchange for Chopin?

CHAPTER FORTY-TWO

◆ ◆ ◆

INGRID

'Otto!'

Otto raised a hand to return Ingrid's greeting. He was seated astride Vulcan, the fine Arab stallion, riding bareback with an easy natural rhythm. She ducked between the crosspieces of the fence and entered the field. At the sound of her voice the horse gave a kick of excitement and came over at speed, tossing his fine-boned head in welcome.

At full canter, with one fist gripping the thick white mane, Otto swept alongside Ingrid, grasped her outstretched hand and swung her on to the horse's back behind him without breaking stride. They had done it a thousand times in the circus ring and their timing had lost none of its edge. She wrapped her arms around her husband, merging their bodies into one, then just for the thrill of it she tucked her feet around Otto's waist and performed a plank, lying flat as a board and hanging out beyond the horse's rear quarters. Abruptly she flipped forward and into a handstand on its powerful rump, which made Otto chuckle and whip Vulcan round into a tight pirouette to try to dislodge her. He failed but she leapt off with a twist, landing on both feet in the mud.

Otto spun the horse, laughing, and came back to her at a walk, while Vulcan blew through his flared nostrils, enjoying the fun. When Ingrid ran a hand down the sleek arch of his Arabian neck, he whickered softly.

'Old times,' she whispered and nuzzled her face against the horse, breathing in the warm oaty smell of him. 'You're looking good, my friend.'

The horse did look good, with eyes bright, his tail carried high and proud. An ice-white sheen to his winter coat, well groomed, and a nicely rounded belly. This time last year it had been a different story. This time last year they had all been starving and Vulcan's bony ribs had stuck out like the bars of a cage. But his ancestors had originally been bred in the scorching Arabian deserts and this had given them the power of endurance and the ability to cling to life against the odds. Vulcan was a survivor. Like her.

Then the airlift had come to Berlin and brought its beautiful American dollars with it.

'How's Fridolf?' Ingrid asked Otto.

'Not good. But he doesn't complain.'

'You got him medicine?'

Otto nodded but grimaced. 'Our usual doctor at the Tempelhof infirmary is running scared, too many rumours going round, so I had to twist the arm of one of the new medics.'

Rumours constantly leaked through Berlin like rainwater leaked through the barn's cracked roof shingle.

Ingrid hated it when Otto took extra risks. 'Where is Fridolf now?'

'He wants to speak to you. He's over with the girls.' The 'girls' were two flirtatious sea lions.

She headed over to their enclosure and caught the knife thrower just emerging with an empty bucket.

'How are you doing, Fridolf?' she asked.

'Good.'

He didn't look good. He was quiet and wiry, all sinew and tendons, his fingers constantly on the move as though feeling for his knives. Fridolf Grossheim had been her father's right-hand man and was a master impalement artist. To the audience gasping in the stalls, that's a knife thrower. But right now he was looking hunched and sore.

'I'm glad you're here, Ingrid. I wanted to thank you.' His eyes were brimming with tears. Circus men did not cry.

'No need.'

'Thank you,' he whispered. 'Thank you.'

Affectionately she placed a hand on his arm. 'How's the ear? Let me see.'

He whisked off his heavy cloth cap, complete with its ear flaps. On the left side of his head where an ear should have been there was only a darkly scabbed hole. Ingrid had rescued him from Kuznetsov's interrogation basement, seen him stumble away, broken and earless on one side, into the street in exchange for her information about Anna Wolff, but she cursed herself for not arriving sooner. She tightened her grip on his arm.

'What did they want, Fridolf?'

'They wanted Otto.'

She bit right through the inside of her lip.

He added, 'They wanted to know what deals he is making and who with.' Fridolf stepped closer and he smelled of the fish he'd been feeding to the sea lions. The front of his jacket was dripping wet from their splashing in the dive tank. 'Don't tell Otto that I said so. I've only told him they wanted to know where our circus is hidden.'

'Did you tell them anything?'

He straightened his damaged body and gave her a withering look without deigning to answer the insult.

'But why Otto?' Ingrid said.

'Ask Otto.'

CHAPTER FORTY-THREE

◆ ◆ ◆

ANNA

'Let's ask Otto.' That's what Martha said.

Easier said than done. He had become elusive. I called in on her every day on my way out to Tempelhof but Otto was resistant to the siren call of the Sèvres vase, it seemed. I pondered on why, as I shovelled the corrosive coal dust out of the planes. Was he too busy with other shady activities or had he grown wary? Wary of Martha? Of the police sniffing around her husband's dealings? Or wary of me?

Otto scared me and I didn't know why. I could smell trouble on him that day in the Dielemans' apartment and now Klaus was dead and I was dogged by disasters. I loved Timur for pretending they could all be coincidences, but I was no fool. Yet it made no sense. Why on earth would Otto want to torment me?

I barely knew him, yet there had to be a link somewhere. Something. A hook that hitched us together. But what?

My mother's pearl brooch in Klaus's shoe seemed to be a message. But what did it mean?

I lay awake at night, my mind worrying at it, the same way it was worrying at little Poldi's abduction. But all I saw in the darkness was more darkness.

Timur's eyes missed nothing.

I hadn't even slipped off my coat when I saw his gaze fix on the slender gold chain at my throat. His beautiful slate-grey eyes popped wide with surprise and a massive grin spread across his face. There were specks of sawdust sprinkled through his dark hair like salt and my workroom – by which I mean the kids' refuge – smelled of the forest. He was cutting wood he had scrounged from somewhere for bed bases, but abandoned his saw and stared straight at me as if I'd turned into a gaudy peacock.

'Pretty?' I laughed.

'Very pretty.'

'Thank you.'

The space between us seemed to shrink though we didn't move.

'The gifts arrived at last then, I see,' he said.

'Yes. Thank you,' was all I managed.

'And the letters too?'

I nodded. 'My mother.'

'I did wonder.'

'I'm sorry.'

'No need to be sorry. The necklace looks lovely on you.'

'I'll never take it off.'

'It's from the Natalka gold mine. That's in the Magadan region of Siberia in Russia.'

'Were you there?'

'Yes.'

'Cold?'

'Cold enough to crack your teeth.'

I laughed, until I realised he was serious. I opened my mouth to say how much I loved the letters and the beautiful gifts and that I was sorry my mother had hidden them and how bitterly disappointed I was that I had failed to believe in him and that I would never let him down again because I loved him and intended to spend the rest of my life showing him exactly what that meant. I drew in a deep breath to say all those things, but instead I let out a wordless shriek and leapt on him.

I landed in his arms with a force that knocked the breath out of him and I swept my strong calves up tight around his waist.

'Anna, I ...'

My lips pressed down hard on his, fierce and unrelenting, to claim all the kisses I had been denied in the last three years, but a sudden knock on the door made us freeze.

'Ignore it,' he whispered in my ear and nuzzled my ear lobe with his teeth.

I was tempted. How could I tear my skin from his? But a second rap on the door followed quickly by a third made me narrow my eyes in frustration and jump down, straightening my skirt and slowing my breathing. Timur watched me go to the door as if I were a deer in one of his Russian forests that he intended to have for dinner.

I opened the door of the basement refuge.

'Yvo!'

In front of me stood the skinny young kid in the patched Red Army jacket with his gang of six *Wolfskinder* wide-eyed behind him. In his hand he was brandishing a fine-looking walking cane that I knew at once.

I hated to make Martha cry.

'It belonged to Klaus, didn't it?' I asked softly.

She was crooning over the walking cane, holding it to her cheek, loving it the way she loved Klaus. The handle was a depiction of a wolf's head formed from heavy silver on a stick of richly polished linden wood. It was one of a pair.

'Yes,' she murmured. 'It's his.'

'Do you have the other one?'

'No, they both vanished the day that Klaus ...'

A handkerchief appeared in her hand and she painstakingly wiped her tears off the wolf's head and off her cheeks before placing the cane neatly across her knees. She sat up, back straight, face composed.

'Tell me where you found it,' she said.

'I'd asked one of the city's urchins to let me know if he heard anything on the streets about the man who was found hanging in the ruins of my father's old bicycle shop. The kid's name is Yvo. He's the one who found Klaus's stick.'

'Where?'

'That's the odd part. It was stuck down a drain.'

'What?'

272

'A drain outside my father's shop.'

'But the police didn't find it. Or its pair.'

'Yvo has eyes sharper than a hawk.'

She reached for a beautiful Venetian silver candlestick that stood on the cedar-wood chiffonier beside her and handed it to me. 'Give this to your Yvo with my thanks.'

'He'll be very pleased.'

'Tell him that he can have the candlestick's pair if he finds the other cane.' She caressed the one on her knees.

'I'll tell him.'

'Klaus needed both to enable him to take a few steps, you know.'

'The big question is, who put the cane down the drain? And why? Was it to hide it or was it intended to be found?'

'The police will have to know about it,' Martha said but gripped the cane possessively and shook her head. 'They probably won't care. They have written it off as a gang crime and don't seem interested.'

'But *I* am interested, Martha. *I* want to know why on earth Klaus would have my mother's pearl brooch in his shoe.'

'I have no idea. Klaus always said pearls were the tears of the gods and brought sorrow to their wearer.'

'It seems Klaus was right. My mother was wearing that brooch the day of the attack in the alleyway. She stabbed her attacker with its pin and it got lost in the struggle. But now it's come back. And my mother is wearing it again.'

CHAPTER FORTY-FOUR

+ + +

INGRID

'Are you working late again, *schatzi*?'

'I have to, Otto.'

'I don't like it. You're always working late these days.'

'I'm earning good money for us.' She kissed the line of his swarthy cheek. 'Just think of that.'

Otto moved away from her, irritated. 'What work are you doing for him now?'

'Oh, a bit of this and a bit of that. Anything and everything. It varies all the time but he seems pleased.'

'Dangerous work?'

She laughed. 'Of course not. Dreary painting of dreary old apartments and things like delivering messages to people.'

'Which people?'

'I don't know. Just names, nothing much. Certainly not dangerous.'

Without warning he seized both her upper arms and held her rigid. 'Ingrid, everything Kuznetsov is involved in is dangerous, we both know that. I want you to stop.'

'No, Otto.' She wrenched free and smacked his chest. 'You're the one who put me forward to work for Kuznetsov in the first place and this is the result. Good work and good pay. So don't grumble now. I never grumble when you're working late, do I?'

As fast as his anger came, it went, and he rumpled her hair fondly. She hated it when he did that. She wasn't one of the circus dogs.

'Take care, Ingrid. I worry.'

'No need. I can look after myself.'

'That's what Klaus Dieleman thought.'

+ + +

Ingrid had altered her shifts at Tempelhof airport so that her time there overlapped more with Anna Wolff's. She'd taken to wandering over from the food wagon in her breaks, a spare coffee in each hand, to the place where the coal sacks were emptied. The air there was thick and unbreathable, black with grit and dust that coated her lungs. But still she hung around there, coughing in the cold and the dark, and sometimes she struck lucky.

'Thanks, Ingrid,' Anna said when she spotted her, accepting the coffee that Ingrid held out.

Anna's face was changing, as if the bones of it had realigned somehow. Ingrid wondered what the hell had happened. What had changed her? It was when she met Ingeborg – *Sister* Ingeborg as Anna introduced her, though she was no longer a nun – that for the first time there was talk of a missing child. Ingrid murmured sympathetic sounds, spoke in tones of hushed regret. She'd provided comforting hot coffee and asked the child's name.

'Poldi,' Ingeborg told her.

'A stray?' Ingrid asked. Not the right word. He wasn't a cat.

'An orphan, I'm sorry to say. Anna was going to adopt him but the poor child was abducted and we don't know where he is now. A terrible occurrence. But Anna is setting up a refuge for children in the east.'

'How wonderful of you, Anna,' Ingrid said. 'Especially when we are all having a hard time staying alive ourselves. Berlin's children need more people like you.' She gave a concerned smile. 'Can I help?'

'Yes. You must come to the shelter.'

'I'd like that.'

It was that easy.

Ingrid approached the ruined building the way she used to approach her father's lion: with extreme caution. Up on her toes and ready to dodge back if it so much as looked at her the wrong way. This was the eastern sector of Berlin. The street was soulless. Half of it was flattened into weed-strewn rubble and the other half was struggling to rebuild itself but failing, except for a few heaps of old bricks piled into shelters and sheets of tarpaulin stretched to keep the worst of the rain off. In the wind the loose edges of the tarpaulins flapped and crackled just like her father's long-tailed whip in the circus ring. It should have made her feel right at home, but it didn't. It felt like a warning.

Take care, Ingrid. I worry.

She slipped past the skeletons of what had once been houses, but which now had bedrooms laid wide open to the street and bathroom piping hanging down like snakes. It felt indecent. Yet somewhere among the ruins a woman was singing an operatic aria. Ingrid moved unobtrusively, checking doorways and keeping to the shadows. The day was blue-skied and there was the smell of cooking on open fires that drifted through the air, but few people were around. She found the basement she was looking for, descended the stone steps and knocked.

The door opened and a skinny kid stood there in a patched Red Army padded jacket, his cheeks gaunt, his amber eyes exactly like the lion's, arrogant and watchful. Only pretending to be tame. A wave of noise hit her from inside the room behind him.

He half turned his head, keeping one eye firmly on her. 'Quiet, everyone,' he said without raising his young voice.

The noise stopped.

'Who are you?' he asked. Rude. Offhand.

She swung the sack she was carrying in front of his nose. 'Mother bloody Christmas,' she said, but when he reached for the sack she jerked it away. 'Now let me in.'

There was a brief stand-off between them until Anna appeared behind the boy with a warm smile of welcome. 'This is a friend of mine, Yvo. Her name is Ingrid and she's here to help.'

The kid continued to glare at Ingrid. He didn't trust her. She didn't know whether it was because he didn't trust anyone or because he saw something in her that Anna had missed.

'Hello, Yvo,' she said but didn't bother with a smile. It would have been wasted.

The basement room was long, gloomy, low-ceilinged and bursting at the seams with children. All ages, all shapes and sizes, all states of raggedness and emaciation, most of them piled on top of the two big mattresses on the floor and chattering like starlings. Ingrid was struck by the sound of it, a free and cheerful flow of young voices. What on earth did these kids have to be cheerful about?

'Here,' she said and tossed her sack into their midst.

They descended on it as starlings would, but yielded immediately to Yvo and a tall girl called Resi of about ten or eleven years old with dark hair hacked off short like Anna's. They seemed to be in charge and started to divide up the spoils between the children.

'Thank you, Ingrid,' Anna said beside her.

They watched the girl extract from the sack a slightly squashed pack of hotdogs and a box of American Graham crackers that Ingrid had snaffled from the snack wagon. Rocco was an expert at turning a blind eye. Her fear was always the guards on the gate but, as usual, they hadn't bothered with her. The crackers were followed by a pack of Otto's baseball playing cards, a cushion from her own home and, surprising them all, a wooden jigsaw depicting a circus ring that Fridolf had made for her last winter. But best of all was a royal-blue clown's outfit from the circus costumes. The noise level escalated with each item.

Anna laughed and gave Ingrid a quick hug which embarrassed her but pleased her too. Anna had a nice laugh. She should use it more often.

'Come and meet Timur,' Anna said.

Timur?

For the first time Ingrid took her eyes from the children and glanced down to the far end of the narrow room. A male figure in black sweater and loose work trousers was bent over, engrossed in measuring a length of timber. By his foot lay a stack of long nails. Timber was scarce and nails were worth their weight in diamonds in Berlin. Who was this man who possessed both? Why was he here?

'Timur, this is Ingrid.'

The stranger straightened up and held out his hand. A good-looking man with a handshake that was firm and steady, his smile polite, but it was his steel-grey eyes that set off alarm bells in Ingrid. They were the kind that cut you open like a buzz saw. Right now they flicked from her across to Anna, and Ingrid immediately realised there was a connection between them.

'Look, Ingrid, at what Timur has built for the children,' Anna urged. 'Isn't it wonderful?'

She gestured at the row of four simple wooden cubicles constructed at the end of the room. The first two had chopped-down doors which Anna swept open to reveal a lavatory – just a wooden seat structure over a large bucket – and a washroom with a bucket already full of water for washing hands and faces and a large zinc tub to act as a bath for small bodies. The second two cubicles were empty and had old sheets pinned over their entrances.

'Changing rooms,' Anna announced. 'For if the older children feel the need for privacy.' In her hand she was clutching a tin cup of white powder. 'For head lice,' she said with a grimace.

Ingrid chuckled. 'You've done well. Those head lice won't stand a chance against you.'

'Nor the cockroaches,' Timur smiled. 'She was chasing them with a hammer like a great white hunter earlier.'

Anna again laughed easily and tapped his wrist in teasing reprimand, so focused on him that she failed to see Ingrid's jaw drop open when she heard Timur speak. But Timur saw.

He's Russian.

Scheisse! The man is Russian.

Clouds had come charging across the clear blue sky, bellies dark and heavy, putting Ingrid in mind of the circus tent that time it collapsed on them in a storm. Ingrid was walking down Friedrichstrasse alongside Anna Wolff who carried two tablets of soap in her pocket. They had spent an hour scouring the black-market huddles for bars of soap that felt less like pieces of cardboard and more like some concoction that would clean the grime from behind young ears.

'Have you got blood on your hands, Ingrid?'

Ingrid stopped dead. Anna had asked it casually, the way you ask if someone has tried oatcakes.

'Why do you ask that?'

'You seem the type.'

Ingrid inspected her friend closely and gave her a slow secretive smile. 'It takes one to know one.'

Anna laughed, but not her nice laugh.

'Was it a soldier?'

'A Nazi piece of shit,' Ingrid replied. 'I was working in some deserted barns with my husband and this *SS-Oberscharführer* rolled up, hunting down gypsies. He'd heard rumours there was one hanging around the barns.'

'Your husband is a gypsy?'

'Yes, he is, and it was dangerous back then. He changed his surname from the Romany one of Hanstein to hide the fact from Nazi gypsy-hunters. The piece of SS shit waved his rifle in my husband's face and was all ready to put a bullet through his brain. He hadn't noticed me. People don't. I'd been cleaning out the stable, so I stepped up behind the *Arschloch* and whacked his head in with my shovel and fed his body to our lion.' She shrugged.

'Your husband is a lucky man, Ingrid.'

'And you?' She glanced down at Anna's gloves. 'You've got blood on your hands too. I can smell it on you.'

'A Russian. A brick. An alleyway. The usual story.'

'What did you do with the body.'

'I left it lying there in the filth where it belonged.'

'But Timur is Russian.'

'He's different.'

They stared at each other with no words, then Anna stepped forward and wrapped her arms around Ingrid, there on the pavement in the middle of Friedrichstrasse. They stood like that until the rain started to fall.

CHAPTER FORTY-FIVE

◆ ◆ ◆

ANNA

Perspective is everything. I was looking down from Martha's third-storey window at Otto crossing the road. He looked small. Tiny as a kitten. Easily squashed. So when the knock came, I was ready for him. Martha opened the door and he walked into the apartment as if he belonged there, but he came to a halt, surprised, when he saw me standing in the salon. His narrow face grew narrower and I saw his hand slide into the pocket of his bulky coat and stay there. It wasn't hard to guess what lay in it. Did he see me as a threat then?

'Hello, Fräulein Wolff, what an unexpected pleasure.'

The wary expression vanished behind a warm smile that did indeed look like genuine pleasure. He had the art of smiling down to perfection.

'Thank you for coming, Otto.' I matched his smile tooth for tooth. 'I hope you'll be able to help me.'

'What can I do for you?'

'I need some blankets. Quite a few of them actually. You see, Otto, I …' I paused. 'Oh, it occurs to me that I don't know your surname. You are Otto …?' I left a gap for him to fill in the blank.

Smooth as silk he said, 'You don't need my surname. Otto is sufficient.'

'Very well. As I was saying, I need blankets because I've set up a refuge for street urchins. To give some of them a place to sleep where it's dry and safe. And I thought of you.'

'As a street urchin?'

I laughed politely at his joke.

Martha said, 'I'll make tea.' She disappeared.

The moment she was gone Otto said, 'A sad business. Klaus, I mean.'

'Yes, very sad. A savage death.'

'You're the one who found him, I hear.'

'How do you know that?'

'Word gets around. Klaus Dieleman was well known.'

'And well liked.'

'True. He was a good friend.'

'I thought you were just business associates.'

'Well, you thought wrong.'

The abruptness of his response caught me by surprise. I hadn't expected the sudden switch from smooth to razor-edged. We were still standing face to face in the middle of the large cold room and the moment of awkwardness lingered.

'What kind of business did you do together?' I asked.

'Just buying and selling.' The smile was back. 'The usual under-the-counter stuff.'

'Did you see him the day he died?'

'No, what makes you think that?' His black brows met in a deep frown. 'You think I was involved?'

'Of course not. Would I be here wanting to do a deal with you if I thought that?'

'I guess not.' But he was watching my every blink, every breath.

'The police seem to suspect the murder was committed by a black-market gang that he crossed in some way,' I said. 'What do you think of that idea?'

He shrugged his bulky coat, one hand still in his pocket. 'It's possible, I suppose.'

'The reason I'm asking you, Otto, is because you must have introduced Klaus to these gang members, so you must know who they are.'

He didn't take offence, or if he did, he didn't let it show. 'That's the line the police took at first when they brought me in for questioning because someone – was it you? – had told them that I was the link between Klaus and any black-market *Miststück*. But I tell you, Fräulein

Wolff, I steer clear of the gangs. They each run their patch of Berlin's underworld like it's their own personal kingdom and anyone who stands in their way or rats on them gets wiped out. I swear to you I don't go near them. Too dangerous.' He shrugged again and I almost believed him. 'Anyway, the police could find no evidence of a connection, so didn't waste more time on me.' He turned his head as he heard the rattle of cups on a tray and said quickly under his breath, 'I'm not a killer, Anna.'

I let that pass.

'Back to blankets,' I said.

Martha placed three cups of mint tea on a low table and said, 'Sit down.'

I noticed two things as I picked up my cup. First, the liquid was lukewarm because there'd been no electricity to heat water since three o'clock this morning, so this was out of a thermos. Second, the china was Martha's third best set. Either she'd sold the better two sets already or she regarded Otto as too much of a weasel to allow his lips anywhere near her best French porcelain. My money was on the second.

He didn't touch the tea. He leaned forward, elbows on his knees, and pushed his jaw out as though tempting me to overstep the mark and take a swing at it.

'Why exactly are you so interested in Klaus Dieleman's death?'

'He was my father's closest friend and I've known him all my life. He was my friend too. That's why.'

'Not because of his money?'

Martha jumped to her feet, her face crimson. 'How dare you insult Anna like that? Get out of here.'

He moved quickly, out of his chair and heading out of the room. I let him get as far as the door. 'Wait, Otto. Do you know what Klaus did with all the money your deals made for him?'

The coal-black eyes shifted from me to Martha and back again. 'No, I don't. And if I did, do you think I'd tell you?'

'Blankets,' I said. 'Bring me blankets.'

'And how will you pay for them?'

Martha marched over to the wall and removed an exquisite miniature oil painting of a child. 'With this,' she said.

My heart knew something was wrong before I did. It thudded a warning
the moment I saw Yvo sitting on the stone steps that descended to the
basement, just his head visible as I approached. I leapt off my bicycle.

'What is it, Yvo?'

'Trouble.'

'What kind of trouble? Is anyone hurt?'

'Someone asking questions.'

'Who?'

'A man.'

Yvo used words the way I used firewood. Sparingly. I hurried my
bicycle down the steps and rushed into the basement, my gaze sweeping the chilly space for danger. It felt subdued. Nothing worse. Three
of the older kids were playing cards on one of the mattresses, a girl was
reading to the little blind boy Lars from a fairy-tale book that had been
mine as a child and six of the *Wolfskinder* were lined up in a row. They
stood in front of a man in his forties who was seated on the long plank
that Timur had fixed to the wall as a bench and beside him perched
Resi, watching him and the other children like a hawk. I allowed myself a sigh of relief. One wrong move from whoever this man was and
Resi would claw his eyes out.

'Who are you?' I asked with no preamble.

'My name is Yuri Volkov. I am an inspector.'

'An inspector of what?'

'Of children's schools and welfare in East Berlin.'

'A Soviet inspector of German schools. I didn't know they existed.
But this isn't a school.'

He didn't stand up but removed an official-looking card from his
inner pocket and held it out to me. His name was on it and his photograph. A lean, confident face with fair hair swept back off his high
forehead. All with an official stamp and Russian words of verification
that I didn't understand. It meant nothing.

'I'm here to help,' he stated pleasantly.

'In what way?'

'By offering supplies of books and paper and pencils.'

'And food?'

'I'm afraid that's not my department.' He smiled apologetically. His eyes were a striking pale blue and studied me with care, too much care for my liking. He was probably wondering what I was doing here with these children just as much as I was wondering about him, but there was something cold at the heart of him, cold and sad.

'So, Inspector Volkov, what exactly are you here to inspect? As you see we are only just setting up.' I waved a hand around the room. 'I am working on getting hold of blankets at the moment.'

'And heating of some sort?'

'Yes.'

'I have been making a note of every child's name and probable age. We require you to do the same for every child that comes here. You understand?'

'Yes.'

'You have a lavatory facility?'

'Yes.' He didn't need to ask. We could both smell it. 'It is emptied several times a day on a strict rota.'

'Good. Your name, please?'

'Anna Wolff.'

He wrote it down in his notebook, smiling to himself. 'Anna Wolff. Good,' he murmured again.

'How did you hear of this refuge, Herr Inspector?'

'Here in the Soviet sector we keep a close watch on everything that goes on.'

'Are you intending to close us down? Is that why you're here?'

Resi, who had been tuned into every word, jumped off the bench. 'No, Herr Volkov,' she burst out, 'you mustn't close this refuge down, you mustn't. We all need it and Fräulein Anna is wonderful to—'

Volkov uncoiled from the bench fast, his pungent cologne rising with him. He was much taller than I'd realised and loomed over Resi.

'Little girl, don't ever tell me what I must and must not do.' His voice was cold and hard.

I stepped in front of him and pushed Resi behind my skirts. 'She meant no harm. It's just that she feels safe here and ...' I saw that he gripped a cane, an ebony walking cane with a heavy silver knob, and for a moment I thought he was going to use it. But a lot of men in Berlin walked with canes, the aftermath of wartime injuries. I was too jumpy. 'And none of the children wants to be out on the streets at night this winter.'

Volkov looked around the room, at each of the children and finally at me. 'You care about them, don't you, Fräulein Wolff?'

'I do.'

Where was this going?

'I'm sure you wouldn't want anything to happen to them.'

'Of course not. Why would it?'

'And the children must care about you.' His ice-blue eyes didn't waver from mine. 'They wouldn't want anything to happen to you, would they?' A meaningless smile stretched the corners of his mouth.

'Herr Volkov, is that a threat?'

'Of course not.' He tucked his notebook away in his pocket, pulled on skin-tight leather gloves, buttoned up his beautiful black overcoat and walked to the door. 'You'll be hearing from me.'

He didn't say goodbye. Didn't look round. Just that.

I'd be hearing from him.

Fear is a thief who steals who you are. It robs you of self and stands a stranger in your shoes. I am afraid.

I sat with Timur and I told him of Inspector Volkov's visit to my basement and mentioned that I strongly suspected Volkov was not his real name, though he was definitely Russian. The man was nosing around but I didn't know why. I asked if Timur had heard of this so-called Soviet Inspector of Schools but he had not. We were taking a break in the shadow of the giant concrete flak tower in what had been the beautiful Humboldthain Park, a green oasis in the middle of

Berlin's Gesundbrunnen district before the war. It was less a park now than a hideous dumping ground for the unending tons of the city's rubble as streets were slowly cleared. Timur had requisitioned a bicycle from somewhere and we had cycled here together along Brunnenstrasse up in the north of East Berlin, well away from my usual haunts.

Seated side by side on the edge of an old bomb crater that had a muddy sludge of rainwater down at the bottom, I felt safe with Timur and convinced myself that I had imagined the threat from Inspector Volkov. It was an innocent comment by the inspector, nothing malicious in it. I was being absurd. I rested my head against Timur's shoulder and shut out everything except the sensation of being with him.

'Anna, tell me about the child,' Timur said as we watched two crows fighting over ownership of a cabbage leaf.

'You mean Poldi? He was abducted from a park while in Sister Ingeborg's care but—'

'No, I don't mean Poldi.'

'Who then?'

'You know who.'

I rubbed my cheek back and forth across the thick material of his greatcoat. 'Felix has gone,' I whispered. 'I can't talk about him.'

He turned so that he could see my face. 'I understand it's hard,' he said. 'But I need to know. I need the truth. You said you had a child and that your mother gave him away when you were sick, but what I have to know is am I the child's father? In the three months that we were together in 1945, did we create a son?'

'No.' The word was flat. It carried the weight of truth in it.

'How can you be sure?'

'Because I can count. The attack in the alleyway by the two Russian soldiers was in April 1945. Felix was born eight months later. But you and I didn't …'

He wrapped an arm around me, as though to pull the memory of that time deeper inside him. 'Thank you, Anna. I needed to know.'

But I could hear the disappointment in his voice. For a while we sat there in silence but I knew there was more he wanted to say.

'I'm asking you to stay away from Otto.' Timur spoke wretchedly. 'It could be dangerous.'

'I can handle Otto, don't worry.'

'I'll find some blankets for the children. You don't need Otto.'

'Thank you, my love.'

'Do you believe Otto is connected with your School Inspector Volkov, or whatever the real name is of the Russian who came to your basement?'

'No. I get the impression that Otto is very much a rogue dealer who works on his own.'

An awkwardness slid into the slimmest of gaps between us.

'What is it?' I asked.

'Anna, do you know what the name Volkov means in Russian?'

'No.'

'It means wolf. The same surname as yours.'

Now I was even more afraid.

CHAPTER FORTY-SIX

◆ ◆ ◆

ANNA

I don't know why it took me so long to work it out. My only excuse is that I was running on lack of sleep, my days crammed with children, with my mother and with finding food, my nights jammed with the sounds of aircraft and sweeping of coal. And every second of every day Timur was there in my mind, a part of me, the way blood is in my veins and air in my lungs. I had no control over it.

So it was only now that I realised. My bicycle was the problem.

I'd been thinking of my Diamant as my saviour, the thing that was keeping me safe in the city by giving me enough speed to keep out of danger, but I was wrong. It was propelling me ever deeper into trouble. As long as I continued to stay out of harm's way by racing away from it at speed on my two wheels, harm would keep stalking me. Damaging those around me. It was time to dismount and to stop fleeing. I needed to turn and face whoever was behind me.

So I abandoned it. I left my bicycle propped behind the door of the apartment, while my mother settled into her chair with her knitting and Chopin for company, and I went out into the streets without my wheels. I felt naked, but I'd worked out that the only time I'd come near to chasing down the person tracking me was when I ran through the streets to find the white-haired man in the duffle coat. *Ran*. That's my point. I was on foot, my bicycle too damaged to ride. That's why he could get so close to me.

I set off down the street, knowing that the big target on my back had just got bigger.

My mistake came the day the rain swept in, lashing the city to within an inch of its life. Little rivers of dirt pooled around my feet as I stood in line in a queue outside the butcher's shop where I was wrestling with an umbrella that was determined to turn inside out. I was too wet and miserable to think of anything but holding my umbrella together. I stopped squinting through the rain. Stopped scanning the doorways opposite, stopped looking for a tall man with a walking cane and a black overcoat. Stopped expecting a pair of ice-blue eyes to appear at my shoulder.

'Anna.'

I jumped. Out of nowhere a small woman stood at my side in a vast maroon raincoat that went right down to her ankles and up over her head in an enveloping hood. I had to peer under it to see who had spoken.

'Ingrid, is that you?'

'I was passing and saw you.'

'I thought you said you live in the west?'

'I do, but I come over to the east sometimes on errands.'

Rain was running down my nose. I shook it off and envied Ingrid her cover-all. 'Perfect day for a swim.' I grimaced and her smile, a rare occurrence, distracted me from my sodden shoes.

'How is the children's refuge going?' she asked.

'It's good, the kids seem happy to be there, but I'm still waiting for more blankets. It gets very cold.'

'Do you have an oil stove yet?'

'Yes, it helps but we don't have enough oil to burn it for long each day.'

'Where on earth did you get hold of an oil stove in …?' She halted. 'Ah yes, of course, your Russian major.'

A truck rumbled past and its huge wheels threw a backwash of dirty rainwater over the queue, provoking shouts of protest and making us all shuffle closer to the wall.

'Anna.' Ingrid dropped her voice low and I had to lean close to hear her over the machine-gun rattle of rain on my umbrella. 'You can leave the children to look after themselves now, you know.'

'What?'

'You've given them somewhere dry to live in. You've done enough. You don't need to be there – they're used to watching out for themselves. You can stop now.'

I pulled back from her. 'Why on earth would you say such a thing?'

'Because you look exhausted. I'm worried about you.'

'I'm fine.'

'You don't look fine.'

I didn't know what to say. I was touched by her concern.

Still in that same low voice she continued, 'You should stay away from that basement for a while, I'm telling you. Give yourself a chance to rest.'

I stared at her earnest face, her lips thin and her skin white and slippery with rain. Something was going on here but I couldn't make out what it was.

'Thanks for your ...' I started, but that was when I saw him.

Across the road, a figure was turning off down a side street, little more than a dark blur in this watery world. Not tall. Not carrying a cane. Not striding with an arrogant step. But even so, all else vanished from my mind because he was wearing a navy duffle coat, hunched over, hood up. I dropped my umbrella and ran.

He moved fast for an old man, nimble as a cat.

I hurtled down the side street towards him, but he dodged into the next street on the left and then a quick right, weaving around pedestrians, in and out of traffic like a man who knew he was being chased. He must have had bat ears to hear the pad of my footsteps over the torrents of the downpour, yet I didn't see him look round. He had the acute instincts of someone who was accustomed to being prey, used to being hunted, and who knew how to flee.

We charged down the street, oblivious to shouts and stares as we bumped and barged into people. I didn't see them, I only saw him, a watery smudge of darkness. My heart was thudding wildly but my legs were strong from cycling, so I was gaining on him.

He sensed it. He ducked into a shop in response to an animal instinct to go to ground. I raced in after him but jerked to a halt. A row of men were staring at me, sitting in chairs, eyes hostile. It took a beat for me to realise I was in a men's barber shop.

'What do you want, *Fräulein*?' asked a soft-faced young man wielding scissors in his hand.

'I'm looking for the man who just ran into here.'

'Nobody came in here just now.'

'But I saw him.'

'Sorry, mädchen, you are mistaken.' He turned to his customers. 'Did you see anyone come in?'

'No.' It was unanimous.

'There you are,' confirmed the barber.

'He was wearing a dark duffle coat,' I insisted.

More head shaking. More lying.

And all the time he was getting away. I made a dash through the shop before anyone thought to stop me, swept aside the colourful bead-curtain at the rear of the shop and found myself in a small and smoky backroom where four men sat hunched over a roulette wheel. They looked up, even more surprised than I was, and one leapt to his feet but too late. I'd spotted the back door. Shouts and swearing snapped at my heels as I threw it open and landed in a narrow alleyway.

No one in sight.

Left? Or right? I chose left.

Good choice.

The moment I hit the main road I squinted both ways and spotted him, two blocks ahead, his hood ducked against the driving rain, but the rain was my friend. It had emptied the pavements of pedestrians, otherwise I might have missed the duffle coat. I took off fast and he must have thought he was safe because he had slowed, or maybe his legs were tiring or his lungs hurting. I wanted him to hurt.

I closed the gap between us. The more he slowed, the faster I flew over the flooded pavements until just ahead of us lay a bomb site. The duffle coat swerved. He took off across the ruins and I couldn't believe how expertly he leapt from one piece of jagged masonry to the next, as assured as a goat on a mountain face, while I slipped and slithered on the wet concrete, raking my hands and skinning my knees. He was leaving me behind.

I yelled rain-soaked curses at him and that was the moment he made an error. He vaulted off a final chunk of shattered wall into the street beyond, blinded by a sudden squall of hail, and smacked right into a burly man pulling a cart of laundry. The duffle coat went down. I tore across the distance between us until I was within half a dozen steps, just as he disentangled himself from the cart's pile of soiled sheets. For the first time I caught a glimpse of threads of white hair sticking out from under the hood. But as I grabbed at him, he lashed out with a foot, cracking it against my shin so hard it momentarily halted me.

He raced off down the narrow street, but I had no intention of losing him now. I dredged up a final spurt of speed and lunged for that hated duffle hood. My fingers sank into the wet material. I yanked at it but felt its owner swivel to one side as I did so, and suddenly I was being hauled by the hood through an open oak door on my right. I stumbled. Lost my grip. Lunged again and this time caught a fistful of white hair. I was standing in a dim cobbled yard and dragging in breath when I realised with shock that the hair I was clutching had come away in my hand. It was a wig. I looked up into a pair of furious black eyes.

It was Otto.

This was my mistake, the one they'd been waiting for. Behind me I sensed movement and a coal sack descended over my head, turning my world black.

CHAPTER FORTY-SEVEN

◆ ◆ ◆

TIMUR

Music can open doors. It can move hearts. Timur looked at Luisa Wolff and saw how her sharp edges were softening as she held the vinyl record in its brown paper sleeve close to her heart.

'You can't buy entry so easily,' she had declared at the door of her apartment.

He had smiled as he held out the gramophone record of Brahms's Piano Sonata no. 3 and a bottle of Russian vodka. When she narrowed her eyes to slits to reduce the size of the temptation, he waved under her nose a bulky bag of knitting wool the same forget-me-not blue as her eyes and a jar of potted veal.

'Damn you, Russian,' she said and stood back for him to enter.

'Thank you, Frau Wolff.'

She didn't invite him to sit down, but nevertheless he sat in one of the armchairs because he didn't want to tower over her slight figure in its grey wool dress.

'What do you want?' she demanded.

No preamble. Like her daughter, she could be very direct. That's what a fight for survival did to you. It stripped away all but the fundamentals.

He started gently. 'I want to thank you for giving my letters and gifts to Anna. I understand why you kept them from her so long.' He smiled. 'Thank you for not burning them all in the *Kachelöfen*.'

'It's not too late for that. We could do with the heat.'

He opened the vodka bottle and she fetched two glasses.

'I'll try to bring you some coal next time,' he said as he poured.

'I don't want you here and I don't want you sneaking round Berlin with my daughter.'

'I know that. I don't blame you but, Frau Wolff, it's too late. Anna and I love each other, we always have and we always will. We just lost our way for a while.'

'Because of me.'

'Yes, because of you. If you hadn't intercepted the letters, things would have been different, but that is behind us now and we move into the future together.'

'One day you Russians will be behind us too. Gone forever from our soil and from our government chambers. Then Germany can live again. I want my daughter to live again.'

Timur understood. He didn't want to, but he did. They both drained their glasses.

'Frau Wolff, I want to talk about your brooch.'

Her thin hand shot up to encircle it protectively. 'What?'

'Anna told me it went missing the day of the attack. Is that true?'

The day of the attack. The resonance of it spilled into the room. She nodded, her jaw tight.

Timur continued, 'May I see it, please?'

'No.'

'Alright, but Anna told me that on the reverse it has the name of the maker engraved.'

'Anna told you too much, Russian.'

'Frau Wolff, I believe your daughter's life is in danger and that brooch is important. It reappeared in Klaus Dieleman's shoe the day he died. How do you think that happened?'

She didn't answer but walked over to where the midnight-blue wind-up gramophone sat on the table and placed the record on top of it. Timur was passionate about Russian music but was willing to admit that Germany was no slouch when it came to composers.

'Play it if you wish,' he murmured.

'No. Your presence would only ruin it for me. I will play it when you are gone.' She glanced at the door hopefully but he remained where he was.

'The brooch,' Timur prompted her.

She lowered herself into the armchair near the cold stove, head high, back straight, and after one more lingering glance at the record she turned her focus on him. Her eyes were scathing.

'In the alleyway,' she stated in a flat tone, 'when I was struggling on the ground, your countryman tried to rip off this brooch that my husband had given me, because he recognised it was of value. His fumbling loosened it but he didn't get it out. So I wrenched it off and jabbed the pin into his throat. He screamed like a pig. I still hear that scream at night and I laugh.'

He poured her another drink. Her clenched fist on her lap was shaking.

'That was when the bastard wrenched himself off me, still screaming, and rolled over on to my daughter with his filthy comrade. Anna had the sense to lift a brick and slam it down on his skull. She made a good job of it.' Her eyes bored into Timur's. 'One less Russian on this earth.'

Timur refused to take offence.

'Did you go back to search for the brooch afterwards?'

'Never. My leg was broken in two places, remember, and I didn't walk for months.'

'Did Anna go in search of it?'

'No. She loathes the place as much as I do.'

There was a long silence.

'So someone found it and connected it with you by following up the inscription and presumably using the jeweller's records. Have you any idea who that someone might be?'

'None at all.'

'We are talking about your daughter's life, Frau Wolff.'

'I thought we were talking about the child. About Felix.'

'Do you know where he is?' Timur asked.

'No. I gave him away.'

'To whom?'

'I don't know. Whoever happened to be passing the door, I suppose.'

'Don't you care how cruel that was to your daughter? And to the child?'

'I promise you, he was a lucky child.'

'Why lucky?'

'Because he was allowed to live. Do you know how many thousands of your Russian soldiers raped our women? Do you realise how many of those women threw themselves out of fifth-storey windows or under trains? And how many of the poor unwanted bastards were born into hate?' She rose from her chair, releasing her hands, and stepped right up close, pushing her face into his, with her arms wrapped tight around herself, cradling the pain inside. 'Do you know how many of those bastard babies were quietly suffocated and their corpses hidden among the ruins? I tell you, Russian, that child was one of the lucky ones.'

She threw the last of her vodka down her throat, unpinned the pearl brooch and placed it in his hand.

CHAPTER FORTY-EIGHT

◆ ◆ ◆

ANNA

I am here. Though I don't know where *here* is. I touch the tip of my tongue to my finger to make certain it is real, this place. My tongue is warm, my finger cold. That is my only reality because I can see nothing. I am in a world of darkness. I hold my breath and can taste my fear like something alive in my mouth.

I was dumped here by rough hands with no more care than you'd dump a bag of coal, but when I dragged off the filthy sack over my head I was no better off. I was still surrounded by an impenetrable sheet of blackness. I punched a fist into it but it didn't split open. With hands outstretched, taking tiny tentative steps, I found a locked door and I explored with meticulous care four walls and a dusty boarded floor, so with confidence I can claim to be alone in a bare windowless square room, five paces in each direction. Empty except for a bucket. For toilet purposes, I realised. The bucket both frightened and confused me. Frightened me because it meant I was here to stay for some time and confused me because why would they want to keep me alive?

Who are *they*? How much is Otto involved and what does he want? Why am I here?

Why not kill me outright like they did with Klaus? Or beat me? Or break my legs? Or worse. The thought of worse made me vomit in the bucket and the stench of it seeped into the floorboards.

It's cold. I walk. Wall to wall, wall to wall, but my teeth still chatter. I don't think it's the cold that makes them chatter.

I hear voices. Not words, but the murmur of voices.

◆　◆　◆

They rise from beneath me, so I know I am upstairs. I race to the door, crashing into it, smacking my face, and I hammer on it with my fists till they are raw. I scream till my voice is hoarse and I stamp my feet on the floorboards till my soles are on fire.

No one comes.

I pause and listen. Silence.

I hammer. I scream. I stamp. Again and again. I listen, but the silence is as absolute and as suffocating as the darkness.

Either they have gone or they are sitting beneath me, staring up at the ceiling, waiting for me to stop. I don't stop.

Time becomes meaningless. It is a dimension that has no relevance any more. What does it matter if it is a minute, an hour or a day that has passed when each minute or hour or day are the same?

I need water.

I need light. But right now I need water more. I can sense the organs of my body shrivelling with need and my skin crawling with thirst. For the first time I am glad the room is cold. If it were hot, I would … what? What would I do? Slit a vein to drink my blood? The fact that the thought even entered my head terrifies me. I hear myself sob and the sound is that of an animal.

Finally I come to my senses, finally I am too exhausted for fear. I sit down in one corner, my back to the rough plaster of the wall, my knees up under my chin, arms wrapped around my shins for warmth and my face towards where I know the door to be though I cannot see it. I start to think.

CHAPTER FORTY-NINE

◆ ◆ ◆

TIMUR

'Hello, Ingrid.'

The young woman in the maroon raincoat nearly jumped out of her skin.

Timur fell into step beside her. 'Remember me?'

He watched her glance at him and look away quickly. 'Of course.'

'We met in Anna Wolff's basement refuge.'

'I am aware of that, Major.'

She was walking along one of the few smart streets left in the Friedrichshain district in the east of the city where clusters of handsome buildings remained untouched. The rain had stopped and the wet roads glistened like gold leaf in the sudden brilliant sunshine. It was an area where many of the Soviet overlords had ousted the owners of apartments and taken over the most luxurious ones for themselves, appropriating grand pianos and French impressionist artworks to adorn their walls. Timur wondered what Ingrid was doing here.

'I'm looking for Anna,' he said.

'I haven't seen her today.'

'She didn't come home yesterday. Did you see her up at Tempelhof?'

'No.'

'It seems she has disappeared.'

The small young woman at his side kept walking, eyes fixed straight ahead. 'She's a grown woman. She can come and go as she pleases.'

'Of course. But I'm concerned.'

'Maybe she has found herself a new lover, a German one this time.'

'Ingrid, your friend has disappeared. Don't you care?'

'Of course I do.' But she wouldn't look at him.

'Do you know someone called Otto?' he asked. 'He lives in West Berlin.'

'There are thousands of Ottos in Berlin.' She shrugged and walked faster. 'Of course I know an Otto.'

He lengthened his stride. 'This one was doing a deal with Anna to supply blankets for the children. He is the same Otto who was doing deals with Klaus Dieleman before he was murdered.'

Ingrid halted, evoking a grumble from the pedestrians behind who had to swerve. 'Major,' she said, turning to confront him, 'how did you find me?'

'A coincidence. I was passing and spotted you in the street.'

'There's no such thing as coincidence in East Berlin.'

Timur nodded grimly. 'That's true. That's why I question that you come to visit Anna at the refuge and she then disappears.' He moved closer. 'Tell me where she is?'

She should have slapped him for his assumption. But she didn't. Instead her voice grew soft as the winter sunshine. 'I don't know where Anna is, but don't worry about her. She is a strong woman, that one. She can look after herself. Goodbye, Major.'

She walked away. He didn't follow. He had trailed her all the way from the basement refuge, where she had been asking Resi if she could manage alright without Anna.

Without Anna.

He stepped into the doorway of a corner fishmonger on the opposite side of the street. Invisible behind the etched fish on the glass side window, he watched Ingrid hurry away, glancing back over her shoulder twice to see if he was following. She came to a halt in front of one of the smartest of the apartment buildings, all ornate stonework and fine symmetry, and used a key to enter. A quick blink and she was gone. He continued to stand there for a long time, memorising the faces that came and went.

'Ingrid,' he whispered, 'you are living on borrowed time if Anna dies.'

CHAPTER FIFTY

◆ ◆ ◆

INGRID

'Where is she?'

'You don't need to know, little Ingrid.'

Ingrid threw a folder on the table. She knew it contained detailed technical aviation drawings of the new Douglas C-74 Globemaster and, even more importantly, the top-secret rocket plane, the Douglas Skyrocket. Noah had delivered them to her at the snack wagon with a wide grin, not his usual style, so she knew the information must be good.

'Herr Kuznetsov,' Ingrid said with no sign of the turmoil churning her gut, 'let me go to Anna.'

'No.'

They were standing in the apartment where they had made their first deal, the one she had painted and then fancified with gold curlicues and picture rail. The apartment with the microphones. She must watch her tongue. Without the dust sheets it looked beautiful now, as serene and elegant as Kuznetsov himself, and she wondered how many of the Soviet politburo had knocked back their vodka and caviar here, plotting their plots, scheming their schemes, all unaware of who was listening. Kuznetsov poured them both a schnapps and she drank it down without a flicker of animosity, but she knew him well now. He could see right into her soul. Or so he thought.

She dropped the subject of Anna. She waited for him to light one of his black Russian Sobranie cigarettes; they always calmed him. 'I am worried about my husband's involvement in your activities,' she said without appearing remotely worried. 'The Russian major was asking me about him. He is sniffing too close.'

'Leave Major Voronin to me.'

He examined her with a long stare. He liked to study her. She had grown used to it. As if he were inspecting each minute change in her, the way a scientist studies a particularly interesting insect on a slide under his microscope. She stared back.

'I also am worried about Otto's involvement,' he said with careful consideration. 'He is a complication to your life.'

'He isn't a complication to my life. He *is* my life.'

'That's what worries me, Ingrid. I need you to be disconnected.'

'Disconnected? What on earth does that mean?'

'It means I want you in a position where you cannot be persuaded into a course of action by somebody posing threats to someone to whom you are connected. That someone being your husband, Otto.'

'What?'

'Don't look so anxious, Ingrid. I thought I'd taught you better. Never let anyone see you wrong-footed.' He smiled the smile he kept just for her, the smile she had wanted to tear off his face more than once.

'Let's forget about Otto,' she said.

'I hope you mean that.'

She turned her head and looked out towards the blackened bulk of the ruined cathedral. 'Have you been to Anna's basement?' she murmured.

'I have. As School Inspector Volkov.' He uttered a soft chuckle.

'So you've seen the children there.'

'Yes.'

'Then you've seen that they are only young. They've been through enough already, they don't deserve …'

'You are too sentimental.'

'They're just innocent kids.'

'Oh, Ingrid, no one is innocent. We are all born in sin, don't you know that?'

'Speak for yourself, Herr Kuznetsov,' she said acidly.

He laughed and a trail of ash from his cigarette floated gracefully down on to his coat, his dove-grey one this time. She'd never known a man possess so many clothes, so many beautiful clothes.

'The children don't deserve to be hurt just because of her,' Ingrid insisted.

He shook his head indulgently. 'Ingrid, my dear mädchen, you know perfectly well that's the whole point. Blame her, not me.'

CHAPTER FIFTY-ONE

◆ ◆ ◆

ANNA

Water has become my clock. It marks the passing of time in my finite black world. The first time it caught me by surprise but now I am ready. The first time I was far from ready. I was crouched on the floor in my usual corner, knees under my chin, my mind living a nomadic existence of its own, wandering back to the day in 1945 when Timur and I went swimming in one of the lakes that surround Berlin, the water like silk on our skin as our limbs entwined and ...

A key turned in the lock. The door opened.

A narrow sliver of light sliced through the leaden blackness for no more than three seconds and then vanished. The door closed. I hurled myself at it and hammered with fists and feet.

'Come back! Let me out!' I screamed at the retreating footsteps. Then I made myself swallow my rage and I begged. 'Come back, please. Please, come back.'

But no one came and eventually I conserved my strength. I knelt down on the floorboards and felt about blindly in the dark, fingertips exploring the dusty terrain till I found whatever had been pushed into the room. It was a bottle, a bottle of precious water. I pulled out the cork and gulped down a mouthful. My innards hissed and spat as if I had thrown water on a red-hot fire but I took only two more mouthfuls before replacing the cork. I had to make it last.

That was the first time.

The second time I was almost ready.

I worked out that if they wanted to keep me alive – and it seemed they did, though I couldn't work out why – they were going to bring me more water at some point. They weren't bothering with food, maybe because they wanted me to be weak, but they knew I'd die without water, so I remained close to the door at all times. I marched on the spot to keep myself awake but I could feel my limbs becoming more uncoordinated. I used one of my stockings, tying one end to my wrist and the other to the door handle, so that if it turned I'd feel it immediately, but when the next bottle arrived I had crashed into a deep sleep behind the door. Its opening startled me awake but too late. It was the only time I lay face down on the floor and howled.

So now I am ready.

I crave light.

Now that I have water, it is light that my eyes and my mind cry out for. Time and again, to escape the loneliness that I hide away inside my head, I go to a place where I am cycling along a towpath drenched in sunlight. Timur is beside me and the sunbeams bounce off the canal's glistening surface to burnish his skin and gild his cheeks. As if they cannot keep their fingers off him. He is laughing because I swerve to avoid a fat waddling duck on the sandy path and a weeping willow branch steals my hat. It hurts beyond all saying when I drag myself back down into the dark.

I am guessing that the water bottle arrives once a day. As the hours pass and my throat grows dry, I prepare myself. I sit or stand against the door crack at all times and I visualise again and again in my mind exactly what I will do when I hear the key in the lock.

My little Felix visits me too. All the time. And I am grateful. The weight of his head lies on my shoulder, the scent of his sweet milky breath is in my nostrils, I see his tiny toes flashing like silverfish in the bath.

At other times Timur visits me in my darkness.

He again scoops up my mother's broken body from the alleyway, leaving two dead Russian soldiers behind us, and we walk out into the street. It is the month of April, so we walk into a thin watery daylight but no one takes a blind bit of notice, no one would dream of questioning a

Red Army officer, not even one cradling a woman covered in blood and with a leg dangling like a broken branch. He carries her the short distance to our apartment, up the four flights of stairs, and lays her on her bed with such tenderness, murmuring gentle reassurances.

From nowhere he magics up a medic to set her leg and provides ointments for our wounds. From nowhere he puts food on our table and fire in our stove, and then he kneels down in front of me, a smear of my mother's blood still on his cheek and crusted in his thick dark hair and he says, 'I'm sorry.' And he weeps. For us. For Germany. And for Russia.

Each time he comes to me in my darkness, I fall in love all over again.

The third time. The key turns in the lock.

My pulse thumps in my ears and my breath hitches, as I stand poised. I once saw a lynx in the Harz mountains on a rocky outcrop on the far side of a forested valley. I couldn't see what its unblinking gaze was fixed on, but I have never forgotten the intensity of it or the tension in every muscle of its beautiful body as it tracked its prey. That is me now, as I unsheathe my claws.

The door opens no more than the width of a bottle, but it is all I need. I hear someone's breath, quick and nervous on the other side, and I smell tobacco. I strike. My hand shoots through the gap at waist height and there is a scream that tears at my eardrums after so many blank hours of silence. Gripped in my fist is a bottle, its base smashed against a wall earlier, so that its edges are razor sharp and savage. I feel them rake through garments into flesh. The man won't stop screaming.

I haul the door open. It gives, he buckles, and I step out on to a dim landing that is rapidly turning scarlet where my jailor is bent double, arms wrapped around his middle.

'*Suka blyat!*' he bellows at me.

I run.

CHAPTER FIFTY-TWO

◆ ◆ ◆

TIMUR

She sped into the apartment like a bat out of hell. Eyes huge, one of her grubby yellow woollen gloves covered in blood. Timur forced himself to stand back while her mother leapt on her. She clasped her daughter to her, uttering a long keening note that cut through the tears, but finally when all grew quiet, Anna detached herself from her mother and came to him.

She walked into his embrace and he wrapped his arms around every inch of her. He gripped her hard, welding her body to his own till there was no end to her or beginning of him. He felt her ribs convulse against his and she began to shake violently, rattling her teeth in her head, and he held her. Kissed her hair. Warmed her skin with his own while a flood of tender Russian words streamed out of him in an unbroken flow of comfort.

'I thought you'd left us, Anna,' her mother whispered from across the room. 'I thought you'd whisked away one of the children and run off to God-knows-where to start a new life.' She wiped a lace handkerchief across her face. 'I wouldn't have blamed you. We can never be free of them.'

'Free of the Russians?'

'No, free of the children. They will drag us to our grave.'

'Now we go back,' Anna said, eyes on Timur.

She had been washed, fed and watered but refused to rest. She'd told them in a few clipped sentences all that had happened but she remained shut down, out of reach.

'Stay here,' her mother begged, 'where you are safe.'

'Don't you understand, Mutti, that there is nowhere *safe* for me now until I find who the *Scheisse* is who is tormenting my life.'

Anna was wearing clean clothes and Timur noticed the pocket of her coat was dragged down by the weight of a weapon of some kind but he made no comment. As he was about to walk out of the door with her, the mother reached up and her small hand seized his throat. 'Protect her with your life, Russian, or I will come and rip your throat out.'

He nodded. No need for words. These Wolff women were wolves.

The wind was up, raking any bare flesh it could find and stirring up the crows that drifted like burnt paper from roof to roof. Timur hammered on the door of the building but received no response, so stepped back and inspected the upstairs windows. All were shuttered, loose slats rattling and paint flayed off, no sign of habitation.

'Are you certain this is the house you escaped from?'

Beside him Anna had narrowed her eyes to slits, unwilling to give the place a full stare. 'Yes.'

'Then I'll knock on a few doors.'

It was a typical rundown backstreet in the Mitte district, some bomb damage but a number of the buildings were still inhabited. At the knock of a uniformed Red Army officer, doors opened with no delay and frightened faces peered out at him, eager to answer any questions he had a mind to ask. Yes sir, sorry sir, I wish I could help, sir. Timur was used to the instant cowering submission and it turned his stomach. No one knew anything. The occupants of the house were never seen. A dead end.

'I'll take you home, Anna, and I'll come back here with a fucking great T-34 tank to take the door out.'

She looked at him, startled, and saw the anger cold and stark inside him before he had time to hide it. 'Oh, my Timur,' she breathed and leaned her slight body against his.

It was the *my* that did for him.

The crack and screech of wood panels as the door buckled satisfied Timur. He intended this house to suffer for what it had done to her. He had hijacked a sweeper unit of Red Army battle-hardened soldiers who were well accustomed to forced entry and the solid oak street-door was brushed away as carelessly as the cobwebs that hung on the other side.

Timur entered, the dark muzzle of his gun leading the way, alert for the slightest movement, but instinctively he sensed that the place was empty and the only sound was their army boots echoing on the grubby hallway tiles. It was a narrow four-storey building that smelled bad. No furniture downstairs, just a handful of cockroaches scurrying in corners and a stained mattress and wooden chair on the third floor. He mounted the final staircase and found what he was looking for on the fourth.

It was as Anna had described. Grim. A windowless hell of a room with walls painted black and the stench of urine rising from the floorboards, though the bucket in the corner stood empty. The thought of her alone here in the pitch dark brought bile to his throat and he raged through the rest of the house, slamming the butt end of his gun against window panes. He tore doors off cupboards and ripped up floorboards. But he found nothing to give any sign as to who had done this to her until he went down on his knees and dragged something out from under the bath.

It was a walking cane. A beautiful piece of workmanship, carved from gleaming amber wood and with a fine silver hand-grip fashioned in the shape of a snake's head. Timur examined it. The stick was broken into three pieces and streaked with dried blood.

Whose stick? Whose blood?

And why the hell was it lying here, designed to be found?

He left the door lying like a dead thing on its back, so that the homeless could take refuge in the house because it had started snowing outside, big puffball flakes straight out of a child's drawing. He returned to the Wolff apartment and it was the mother who drew him in. She stood with her hands on her hips directly between him and her daughter like a skinny guard dog.

'Well?' she demanded. 'Did you find him?'

'No, the place was empty, stripped bare. Except for this.'

He tossed the broken cane down on a table and both women stared at it, one bemused, one with eyes wide in an expression that gave

Timur chills. He removed the wooden remains of the cane, walked over to the stove that was releasing a thin trickle of heat and threw it into the meagre flames.

'Thank you,' Anna murmured.

She moved close, close enough for him to feel her breath and see purple flares in her dark eyes that hadn't been there before.

'It's the Inspector of Schools who came to my basement,' she said. 'Inspector Volkov, he called himself. He wanted me to know that. But why didn't he just kill me when he had the chance?'

'It's terror tactics,' Timur explained gently. 'A recognised tool of war. You terrify the victim.' He put out a hand and soothed a tremor ticking at the corner of her jaw. 'The threat of violence becomes as effective a weapon as actual violence, creating perpetual fear in the mind of the enemy. Don't let him launch his attacks inside your head, Anna.'

You think you know people. But does anyone really know what goes on inside someone else? Of course not. He saw her eyes suddenly spark and she threw back her head with laughter, so that the room lost its chill and her mother sat down in her chair, loosening the knots in her limbs.

'Timur,' Anna smiled, 'if that man comes anywhere near the inside of my head, he'll find he's stepped on one of your land mines. Then he really will need that cane of his.'

The warmth of her smile astounded Timur. Where on earth had she found it? Despite her mother looking on, he put his arms around Anna and she tucked her cheek tight against his neck.

'Timur, why is he trying to terrify me?'

Her mother jumped out of her chair, her manner brisk. 'Don't be foolish, Anna, we all know the answer to that. It's because he's Russian and Russians enjoy terrifying people for fun.' She turned to Timur and he realised that the scarf on her head was one he had sent Anna from Orenburg near Kazakhstan. 'Russian, you got more vodka?'

He reached into his pocket and pulled out a half-bottle which he held just out of Luisa Wolff's reach. 'Not all Russians enjoy terrifying people. Just like not all Germans like running concentration camps. Now, Frau Wolff, I'll trade this for that scarf you're wearing.'

She whipped off the scarf, draped it over his arm and snatched the bottle from him. 'Done.'

'Anna,' he said as he tied the scarf around her neck with a gentle touch, 'don't go out to Tempelhof today. Stay home. We don't know what this man will try next once you're out in the open and I have to leave, so—'

'But isn't that letting him win inside my head?'

'Please, Anna.'

He didn't want to leave. He couldn't bear to step away, and the only way to keep her safe until his return was to lock her up tight in the apartment, but she wasn't his prisoner. She had her own mind.

'Promise me, Anna.'

She nodded and he kissed her forehead.

'I'll find out whose name is on that house,' he said. 'Stay here.'

She smiled. But he didn't trust her.

CHAPTER FIFTY-THREE

◆ ◆ ◆

ANNA

'It's about the brooch,' I told my mother.

Mutti was seated in her chair by the stove, drinking vodka straight from the bottle. I'd never seen her do that before. Whatever was going on under her cool exterior wasn't good, but she sat upright, head un-bowed, and if the so-called School Inspector Volkov was ever foolish enough to kick down our door, I would bet on my mother.

'I know,' she said.

'Did you see the blood on the cane?' I asked.

We both stared at the stove.

'Yes.'

'I keep wondering how the cane came to break and whose blood is on it.'

My mother put down the vodka bottle in a gesture of annoyance. 'You heard your Russian. Your Inspector Volkov is trying to scare you. He probably smacked it against a wall and dipped it in pig's blood.'

'Or he beat little Poldi till he bled.'

'*Mein Gott*, no, Anna. You think so?'

'I don't know. I wouldn't put it past him.' I leaned forward and picked up the bottle, took a swig of the fiery liquid and shook my head. 'Do you ever wonder what kind of child Felix has become? What thoughts he thinks and what words he says? What he is doing right this minute?'

'No. Do you?'

'Every day. What if Poldi really *is* Felix?'

'He isn't.'

'How do you know? You haven't even seen poor little Poldi.'

'Anna, do you think I'm that stupid? To let even a bastard Russian child vanish without some identifying mark.'

I froze, the bottle almost at my lips again. The room shifted out of focus for a moment. 'A mark?' I edged forward, afraid she would bolt to her room. 'What kind of mark?'

'Do you remember the people who used to live upstairs?'

'Yes. The man had a huge moustache.'

'Exactly. Arnold was his name.' Her voice sank to a whisper though there was no one to hear. 'Do you recall his job?'

'No, but I remember he used to have horrible ink-stained hands.'

'He was a tattooist.'

My jaw dropped open. 'A tattooist? You had Felix tattooed?'

'Yes, I did.'

'Where? What part of his body?'

'His ankle.'

I imagined the pain of it. His high-pitched cries.

'What was the tattoo?'

'The letter A for Anna. So you would always be with him, as you were so keen on the brat.'

I should hate her, I knew I should, but I hugged her close, my tears streaming on to her cheeks. Then I grabbed my coat and hat and Papa's old sock with the Deutschmarks in it and left the apartment.

I am connected to my child by a steel thread. I can't help it, it is the way it is. Nothing can snap it, nothing, this steel thread of love. My mother would have nothing to do with him as a baby. Until the moment my guard was down because I was sick with fever when he was three months old, and then she put him out on the doorstep as if he were trash. *Trash*. Yet she marked him.

For me to find him. She knew that one day it would come to this.

The only telephone that still worked in our neighbourhood was inside the Hotel Wilhelm, a stylish old baroque building that had escaped the bombs unscathed and with its telephone wires intact. There was always a queue for the three telephone kiosks in the foyer but I was lucky today and managed to squeeze into one after only a twenty-minute wait. I dialled and inserted coins, breathing hard into the Bakelite mouthpiece that smelled of tobacco.

'Hello?' The voice in my ear was as always polite.

'Herr Schmidt, it's Anna Wolff. I need to see you.'

We met in the same street as before but this time there was no violin player and no watching man with polished shoes. There was just Herr Schmidt and me and the snow.

'An A on his ankle, you say?'

'Yes.'

He smiled at me, a full-on smile that twisted the private investigator's shiny scarred face out of shape. 'Now we're talking,' he said with easy confidence. 'If the child is alive and if he's in Berlin, we'll find him, I promise.'

If he's alive. If he's in Berlin.

'Thank you, Herr Schmidt.'

'Do you have enough money?'

'Yes, of course.'

His good eye centred on me and we both knew I was lying but he didn't challenge my statement.

'You're jumpy today,' he commented.

I peered up the road through the lace curtain of snow. 'I have reason to be,' I said.

He seemed in no hurry to leave despite the cold. His wide-brimmed black hat kept the snow from his face as he lit himself a smoke. 'Anna.' Herr Schmidt never called me Anna. He took a long drag on his cigarette. 'After our last meeting a man – a Russian – came to see me. He stopped me in the street and invited me into a bar to hear a proposition he wanted to put to me. Concerning you.'

A chill hit me. 'Did you have a drink with him?'

'Yes, I did.'

'What did he look like?'

'A tall imposing figure, long face, striking pale blue eyes, a mole by his left ear, fair hair swept back, stylishly dressed, highly polished two-tone shoes and a gold ring engraved with the initials P.K. Plus he carried an ebony walking stick.'

An investigator's description. But he added after a moment, 'The eyes of a man who would murder his mother in her sleep.'

'What did he want?'

'He wanted me to hand him a duplicate of every photograph of the children that I supplied to you and to inform him which boys you followed up on.' The cigarette was steady in his hand but his next words less so. 'He offered me a great deal of money.'

I had to look away. I stared down at his shoes, black brogues, highly polished. Snowflakes slid off them.

'Did you take the offer?'

A pause while he exhaled a white twist of smoke. 'No.'

'Thank you, Herr Schmidt.' I placed my hand on the sleeve of his black woollen coat and held it there as the snow sparkled on the dark material like a sprinkle of stars. 'Thank you.'

A roar of two Pratt & Whitney aircraft engines directly above our heads drew our gaze upwards through the falling flakes to the cargo plane, a C-47 Skytrain, circling slowly in the sky. Its tapering wings were banking and beneath them fluttered what seemed to be a rippling trail of miniature snow angels descending, hundreds of them. The Candy Bomber, Lieutenant Gail Halvorsen, was here again. The sweets and chocolate bars were floating down to earth on their tiny white handkerchief-parachutes and, before we could even blink the snow out of our eyes, into the street the children came tumbling. Running and laughing, shouting and snatching, jostling and yearning, shrill and excited, so many of them appearing from nowhere, short and tall, lean and wiry, girls and boys, like the rats in Hamelin.

Wherever you find sweets, you'll find children.

An idea burst into my mind and I squeezed the investigator's arm with an urgency that took us both by surprise. 'Herr Schmidt, do you know where there is a printing shop?'

◆ ◆ ◆

Why am I here? Because I cannot stay away.

I know I promised Timur I would remain at home, I know, I know, but I wanted him to have peace of mind while he was at work, dismantling another of our factories. We have talked about what he is forced to do each day and I know he regards it as barbaric pillaging, but he is trapped, a prisoner of the system he lives under. He has talked of his shame and of his anger, but we have not talked of how to put a stop to them. Not yet. But we both know the time must come.

Where is *here*? This time it's in my basement refuge with the children who had flocked in out of the snow. I'd filled my pockets with Mr Candy Bomber's sweets for them and they clustered around me like chicks as I handed out Hershey bars and tiny packets of raisins. I sat on one of the mattresses reading aloud the fairy-tale book with Lars, the blind child, snuggled on my lap and a cluster of young faces hungry for attention leaning against my shoulders or draped across my legs. A couple of the older girls were reading quietly to themselves on the other mattress. Here they could shut out the world and make their squares of chocolate last as long as humanly possible, while the boys played cards or fought over the handful of British Dinky toy cars that Timur had acquired for them.

I wanted more for these children, much more.

But first, School Inspector Volkov. I viewed him as a threat not just to me but to the children as well. So I sit here like a turkey on a plate waiting to be carved. He will come. I'm sure he will come for me, and my pulse ticks in my ear like a time bomb counting down the seconds. I glanced across at Yvo who was sprawled in front of the door in his padded jacket, our gatekeeper. He was watching over the children, a silverback, helping the younger ones learn how to pick pockets with an innocent smile and knocking the heads of the older ones together when they got too rowdy. I didn't interfere. I was teaching him to read and his mind was like quicksilver, shiny and fluid.

In a hidden pocket inside my coat lay my father's gun.

Yvo's ears were sharp. He was the first to catch the soft footfall on the outside steps and he leapt to his feet, a quick nod to me. I had eased myself out from under my blanket of children's bodies and was heading for the door when the knock sounded. I edged Yvo to one side, earning a fierce scowl from him in return, and opened the door a crack.

'Otto!'

I almost slammed it shut in his face, but I saw what lay in his arms so I widened the opening enough for him to dump it inside the door.

'Blankets,' he said. 'Twelve of them.'

'We agreed twenty.'

'Twelve was all I could get.'

They were a brownish sludge colour with a US Army tag on them. I signalled to Yvo to distribute them among the kids who were squealing with delight.

'We need to talk,' I said curtly.

He regarded me as warily as if I'd said we needed to fight and stepped into the room.

Resi shooed the children out of the top corner near the door to give us privacy and spread out one of the folded blankets for us to sit on. Otto extracted a pack of chewing gum from his top pocket and pushed it into her hand, which surprised me as much as it did her.

'What happened to you?' I asked as an opener.

'I had an argument with the metal handle of a walking stick.'

He looked awful. A black eye, a crooked nose and a swollen cracked lip.

'Because of you,' he added.

'What's going on, Otto? Who is that man? What's his name and what does he want with me?'

'His name is Spawn of the Devil,' Otto said with a savage twist of his swollen lip. 'And he wants you to join him in the hell he is living in. That's what he told me. He intends to drag you down into his own hell.'

'But why?'

'Fuck why! I don't know. Look, I need that painting off the old woman right away, the one in exchange for the blankets. Tell Martha Dieleman that I've got to have the money today. I'm getting out of here, out of Berlin before ...'

'Before what, Otto?'

'Before he finishes me off, like he's going to finish you. You escaped his grasp once; he won't let it happen again, I'm warning you. I'm taking my wife and whatever money I can get together and making a run for it.'

'A wife? I didn't think you had a wife.'

'Why not?'

'Because you seem so ... light-footed. I took you for the rootless kind who doesn't tie himself down.'

'My wife doesn't tie me down. She lets me be the Otto Keller I am. She's special. I'd never leave her behind.'

There was something so sincere in the way he said it. I stood and stared down at Otto Keller who had caused me such fear on the streets. 'You can have the painting when I get my other eight blankets, not before,' I told him. 'That was our deal.'

He leapt to his feet. 'Wait here,' he said. 'I'll be back within an hour.'

He was out the door and up the steps before I could argue, but I followed him on to the street and watched him run like one of the whippet dogs through the snow. The outside world was a muted white shadow of its former self, softer on the eye, and I almost missed the black car that was parked at the kerbside further up the road.

As Otto shot past it, three large figures lumbered out of the car and I heard a shout of anguish from Otto. A sack was thrown over his head and he was bundled into the back of the car. It drove off at speed, its rear wheels slithering sideways in the snow as I watched open-mouthed.

Welcome to my world of darkness, Otto Keller.

CHAPTER FIFTY-FOUR

✦ ✦ ✦

INGRID

Up at Tempelhof the snow had barely settled. The wind was so strong that it was causing all manner of problems for the pilots coming in to land. Visibility was dismal and the airmen were fighting exhaustion. Ingrid saw one aircraft lose grip as its tyres touched down, so that it skidded off the tarmac on to the grass, but still they kept coming, the great metal birds in the sky, kept setting down with their precious life-giving cargo shuttled in from the Rhein-Main airbase in the American zone of Germany.

Ingrid handed over a piping coffee and two large doughnuts to the smiling American at her wagon's hatch.

'Right kind of ya, miss.'

Dougie Halifax was his name, his details neatly jotted in her notebook. He was a mechanic from down south in Alabama with a soft rolling accent that she loved to listen to and beautiful brown skin that made her own white fingers look bloodless. She'd noticed that quite a number of the ground crew were brown-skinned, but not the pilots. Americans often scoffed at the British class system but they had one of their own, embedded within their military hierarchy. She didn't like it any more than she liked the way gypsies were ill regarded in Germany.

The minute that Dougie hurried away, Captain Noah Maynard was there. He must have been waiting in the snow flurries for a moment alone with her.

'Coffee, please, Frau Keller.' He was always scrupulously polite.

She poured two cups, one for each of them. 'Any news?' she asked, sipping hers.

He glanced behind her. 'No Rocco today?'

'No, he's decided I'm perfectly capable of running the snack wagon on my own, so he's working in the canteen instead.'

'Yeah, I heard he was fixing to move into the warm, now that the weather has taken a turn for the worse.'

'It makes it easier for us.'

'The guys reckon I'm sweet on you, I'm here fetching coffee so often.'

She smiled, amused at the idea of this fancy American officer being sweet on someone like her, but he remained serious. With casual ease he placed a package beside his coffee and with equal ease it slid into her apron pocket. 'We have to be careful,' he said.

'I'm always careful, Noah.'

'I know. It's one of the things I like about you.' He nodded, his dark eyes really seeing her. Not many people did that. 'Careful and reliable.'

She thought he'd finished, but after a long moment during which snow speckled his leather flying helmet like white feathers and an empty Skytrain roared off the runway to head back to Rhein-Main to be loaded up again for a return trip, he added, 'And ruthless too, I imagine.'

She leaned forward, surprised but pleased, elbows on the counter. 'What makes you say that?'

'It's there in your eyes, Ingrid. I see it. Kuznetsov does too and that's why he wants you working for him.' He took a step closer and for one startled second she thought he was going to kiss her. But no, he just smiled. 'I mean it as a compliment.'

'Good. I'll take it as one.'

'I told Kuznetsov never to turn his back on you.'

Ingrid burst out laughing and another plane, a Skymaster this time, slid down smooth as silk, its image fragmented by the swirling snowfall. Dusk was creeping in from the west under the snow's skirts and everyone seemed ready to knuckle down to a night of hard work, a night with the usual banter in the cold and the dark, the usual grumbles, a perfectly normal tag end of a frantic day. Yet something felt off to Ingrid. She couldn't work out what.

Unlike her father, Ingrid's mother was born a gypsy, a lot of circus folk were, and from an early age she realised she had the Sight. Her mother saw things before they happened, a gift that had always frightened the hell out of Ingrid, especially when her mother had foreseen her own death by the hand of her drunken son. Ingrid had always been glad it was a gift she hadn't inherited. It had passed her by. Mostly. Just sometimes a feeling would hit. Like the night she begged Otto not to swing the trapeze and he listened to her because he respected the Sight. He had cavorted on the sawdust below with the clowns instead, much to her father's fury. A rope had snapped. Giz was killed. It was after that that Otto swore to marry her because their souls were entwined. Today the feeling was strong.

'Captain Noah Maynard!'

Noah spun round. A figure had emerged from the gloom behind him and Ingrid instantly recognised Anna Wolff, swathed in a scarf and with her woollen hat pulled down low. Anna's face was barely visible, just her unmistakable eyes. Black and voracious. Craving something. Ingrid knew that tonight they were the eyes of death.

'Good evening, Fräulein Wolff,' Noah said in welcome. 'How's the coal business going? Keeping you busy enough?'

Anna gave a small laugh. 'I've been waiting for you to fly in this evening, Noah. I was told I'd find you here.'

'Okay, Anna, what is it that I can I do for you this time?'

They laughed together, warm and connected, sharing an unspoken amusement that Ingrid didn't understand. She stood quietly behind her counter, making herself invisible and trying to get used to this different Captain Noah Maynard. This stranger who chatted with such easy charm and produced such effortless laughter. Where was Noah Maynard, the stiff and solemn one whose guts were eating him up because he believed the capitalist West had got it all wrong, while the communists had got it all right? Where was he hiding?

'Hello, Ingrid,' Anna said.

Ingrid poured her a coffee.

'Thanks.' Anna focused her death eyes on the airman. 'Noah, I have a favour to ask.'

'Well now, that comes as no surprise.'

Again the laugh, the smile, the easy connection.

'How well do you know Gail Halvorsen?' Anna asked. 'The Candy Bomber. The pilot who drops the sweets for Berlin's kids.'

'Well enough. His unit is the 17th Military Air Transport Squadron and he's a fine flier.'

'Good.'

'What do you want with him?'

'I'd like you to give him these, please.'

She placed on the counter a large package tied up with brown paper and string and proceeded to untie the knot, peel off the paper and open it. It contained hundreds – maybe thousands – of single-sheet leaflets. Captain Noah Maynard stared at them in astonishment.

'Well now, what have we here?' He picked one up and held it out to Ingrid. 'What do you think of that, Frau Keller?'

Anna's head snapped round. 'Keller?' she said. Her eyes fixed on Ingrid. 'Is your surname Keller?'

'Yes.'

'Any relation to Otto Keller?'

'His wife.'

'Ingrid, why didn't you tell me before? I didn't know you two were connected. Otto Keller came to my basement today and when he left I saw him bundled into a car with a sack forced over his head and driven away at speed.'

The death eyes. They were boring right into her.

Ingrid raced out of the snack wagon and was swallowed by the snow. Above her the engines roared while inside her chest her heart screamed and screamed.

'Halt!'

Ingrid halted.

'What the hell is that?' the checkpoint guard demanded, squinting against the fluttering snow. Darkness had fallen and the wind had dropped.

'A pole.'

He exclaimed something in Russian. She stood passively, no resistance of any kind, not moving a muscle, eyes on the white road.

'It's very long,' he said, pointing out the obvious. He tipped his head back to gaze up at the wooden pole's end way above her head but ducked down again when snowflakes settled on his eyeballs. 'Four metres?'

She nodded. It was five metres exactly.

'What's it for?' he asked.

He put out a gloved hand and ran it over the pole's silky smooth surface. She resisted the urge to snatch it away. He could easily confiscate it.

'A friend has a dead crow blocking the downpipe from her apartment roof. I hope to dislodge it with this.'

He rubbed his hand in a suggestive manner up and down a section of the pole. 'I'm good at unblocking holes,' he said, grining at her, pleased with himself as he waved her through.

'Go fuck yourself,' she murmured quietly, pole tight in her grasp.

The easy part was getting on the roof.

The apartment building was four storeys high with two attic gable windows in the roof and a ridiculously simple lock on the front door into the central courtyard. Perfect. Ingrid broke in and took the wide inner stairs in great leaps, two at a time, torch in hand and her pole charging ahead of her, pointing the way.

The place was old, run-down and seemed semi-deserted. People here were careful not to enquire too closely into other people's business. Again, perfect. When she reached the top landing she kicked off her boots, put her shoulder to the rotten wood of the casement window and popped it open, letting in the night. She squeezed herself through it on to the snowy ledge outside and drew the pole after her, controlling its wild swaying. It felt good to be holding it once more, growing accustomed to the weight of it and finding its point of balance. She hadn't used it for years but it was like riding a bike. Your body remembers.

She handled it with ease, despite its ridiculous length of more than three times her own height, and gripping a small torch between her teeth, she swung out on to the roof.

Breathe. Keep calm. Reset your mind.

Focus.

How do you focus your mind on not skidding off a roof? When every part of you knows that if you fail, your husband will die.

Focus.

The tiles. Slippery. Sharp. A frosting of snow. Her soft-soled suede slippers had little grip. Lie flat, face down. Embrace the darkness. Inhale. The moment she attempted to move she felt her body weight dragging her down the roof incline, slipping and slithering on the ice. She jabbed her toes and fingertips harder into the roof tiles, skinning them, but it was the far end of the pole that caught on the guttering and halted her descent.

She breathed. Waited. Her heartbeat climbed back down and the small explosions behind her eyelids ceased. Edge crabwise to the side, then ease down the roof slope, toe by toe, to the metal guttering and the twenty-metre drop. She kept her movements flowing, no stops and starts, her progress as fluid as the snow itself, and at the very edge she slowly, carefully, rolled over and sat up, both feet wedged against the guttering. The wind. Stronger up this high.

She switched on the torch. No more than a quick check on her position, then off. She'd judged it right. Immediately below her lay the telephone wire that ran off into the darkness to the apartment block opposite. It had been attached to the stone wall by gigantic bolts designed to keep the wire secure, even in the face of the ice storms that rolled in from Siberia in the winter. She reached down with one hand and let her fingers examine the bolts on which her life would depend. They felt solid.

The wind worried her.

She dangled her feet over the edge of the snowy rooftop, wrapped up in the thick dark night of the city, and they found the telephone cable, just centimetres wide and no longer in use. She felt a ripple of excitement jolt through the soles of her feet. Coming alive. She shifted her body forward, hands gripped tight around the balancing pole. Right, that was the simple bit. Now for the part that she'd never expected to do again, the part that made the rest of the world fade into a grey dreary blur, a world of stay-at-home emotions and stunted vision. This part was the true pulsing point of life. The softness of her shoes, similar to ballet pumps, enabled her feet to curve themselves around the cable and she stood, suspended over a gut-wrenching void. The wire held.

Posture is everything in funambulism. That's the official name for it but Ingrid thought of it as plain old wire-walking. Tight-rope or slack-rope, it didn't matter to her, both were addictive. She felt it in her feet, the thrill. After Giz's fall in the circus ring she'd lost her nerve and that's when she had to stop. Stop or die. But here she was on a wire again.

Fear came at her, teeth bared, and she knew she had to tame the bastard thing or it would be her own lifeblood on the pavement below. She lifted her head, assessed the bite of the wind in her face, but it was steady, not gusting and not strong. She slid one foot forward and felt it immediately, the twist. Each step along a cable makes it spin underfoot and to keep from falling she knew she had to position her body so that it fought against the wire's innate desire to rotate. To throw her off. Bent knees. Back straight. Body directly over feet. Lower your centre of gravity. She adjusted automatically and took another step, seeking out the feel of the wire, starting to know its mood, adapting to its sway and its sag. Using the pole for balance.

One foot. The other. Sliding in front of each other, smooth, keep it smooth. Visibility was almost zero, just a flicker of white as the snow-flakes gathered on her eyelashes, but she didn't need her eyes, she needed her feet. She had often crossed a tightrope in the circus wearing a blindfold and walking backwards, stopping for a quick juggle in the middle. It's the feet that do the work, caressing the wire, embracing it.

A sudden gust of wind snatched at her. The slack wire started swaying and undulating under her feet like a live serpent. *Otto!* Adrenaline raced through her veins but the pole saved her. She adjusted it expertly in her hands, sought the sweet spot of balance. The pole not only spread out her mass and lowered her centre of gravity, it gave her a crucial moment of recovery time to correct the unwanted motion whenever she started to slip. The pole became a vital part of her, an extension of her arms as she moved forward and saw the bulk of the building on the opposite side of the street lumber into view.

'Otto!' she whispered aloud this time.

And then, very slowly, as she wire-walked through the darkness and across the street far below, she was overwhelmed by a sense of ease, a sense of simplicity that swamped the fear, stifling its constant chatter in her ear. Otto had always said she moved on the wire like a dancer. This was what she was born for. In the face of death she came alive.

'Otto,' she bellowed into the wind as snow fluttered down on to her tongue, 'Otto, I'm coming.'

CHAPTER FIFTY-FIVE

* * *

INGRID

Ingrid used her knife to unlatch the window and she was in. The question was, in where? It was the right street, the right house, but was Ingrid's guess the right guess?

She stood immobile, alert and listening. No sound. A fleeting flick of her torch revealed a bedroom of some sort but no occupant, so she crossed on silent feet to the door which she opened a slit, but the only sound was her pulse clamouring in her ears. A faint glimmer of light reached up to the landing from downstairs and her heart thumped because it meant someone was down there. She descended, a faint shadow on the dark staircase, her soft shoes voiceless, one flight of stairs, then another.

A door opened somewhere below. Ingrid froze, flat against the wall. A voice, not one she recognised but speaking Russian, then footsteps on a tiled hallway. A gust of icy air swept up the stairs as the front door was opened and closed. Silence.

Down another flight of stairs. On the first floor now, she crouched and peered through the banister rails. A dim lamp revealed the hall she remembered from when she was last here, a shabby, neglected, sad space with the dank smell of mouse droppings seeping from the skirting boards. Three doors led off it, and though she couldn't see it from here, she knew there was a narrow staircase at the back that led to a basement. From under one of the doors a pencil-thin line of light escaped and her heart grew sick. Damn the man. At this ungodly hour why wasn't the bastard in bed?

She wasted no time. Down into the hallway she scuttled in her soft shoes and on to the basement stairs without a sound. She descended to the basement, where the corridor was pitch dark and the doors invisible. But she remembered it, oh yes, she remembered it well, pin-sharp in her mind. The five doors on each side and Fridolf's cell at the far end on the left. The image of her circus friend slumped and silent as the grave, with his ear sliced off, sent a shudder through her.

It was her guess that Kuznetsov would bring Otto here for interrogation before he put a bullet through his brain and tossed him into the River Spree. It was a guess, no more than that, but it was all she had. She refused to believe that the bullet had already been fired, because she would know, surely she would, if Otto had gone over into perpetual darkness. She would feel it. The violent snapping of the golden thread that joined him to her.

She edged forward in the blackness, not risking her torch, and as she passed each door she laid a finger on it, felt nothing, and moved on to the next. It was when her hand brushed over the door at the end on the right that the heat came, a burning in her fingertips.

'Otto,' she breathed.

She reached for the lock with one hand and for the knife at her thigh with the other. She eased back the bolt, flinching at its murmurs, but it was well oiled, well used and ran smoothly. She opened the door.

Blackness. That was all that greeted her, blackness and the stink of faeces and blood. She risked a flash of the torch beam.

'Otto,' she breathed again.

He was there; what was left of his broken body was there. The yellow pinch of light revealed that the cell was empty except for a table and two chairs, and lashed to one of the chairs by a leather belt was Otto. Ingrid flew to him, wrapped her arms around the bloodied figure of her husband and held him tight. One single sob escaped her, nothing more.

She pressed her lips to his battered forehead, tasting gore, and soothed a hand over his black curls. They were wet and sticky. A sound rose from him, an inhuman sound that opened up a depth of dread inside her that no high-wire had ever come close to.

'Otto,' she whispered in his ear, 'we're leaving here. Can you walk?'

She unbuckled the belt that trapped him in the chair, but she had to hold him upright or he'd have collapsed flat on his face on the stone floor.

'Stand,' she ordered. 'I'll help you.'

She thrust her arms under his armpits. His legs started to shake and he couldn't rise. Using her own weight as a counterbalance, she levered him on to his feet and clamped an arm around his waist to keep him there, then draped his arm across her shoulders so that she could take his weight on herself. She didn't let herself think about how much agony she was putting him through, but she could hear his tortured snatches of breath in her ear. Like a wild animal in a trap. His head lolled against her cheek, his blood skating slick over her skin, and she let him stand there for a moment, rigid with pain, his whole body tremoring while he fought his way back up to consciousness.

'Come, Otto. Time to go. Before he finds us.'

A faint noise came from him. It possessed no words but she knew what it meant, the way she knew the grip of his hand when she used to fly through the sawdust-drenched air to him or the bite of his strong teeth on her throat when he could hold himself back no longer between the sheets.

'No, Otto, I'm not leaving you here. Come on, move your feet. Hurry, Otto.'

She took three steps towards the door, dragging her husband with her, and felt him start to slide down towards the floor.

'No, Otto, no. Hold on.'

She jerked him back to his feet and forced him to take a step and then another. Together they reached the door and she raked her shin on its edge in the dark as she manoeuvred him out into the corridor.

'I've got you, my Otto,' she whispered into his blood-matted hair and felt his swollen lips rasp against her skin.

Time is not a finite measurement. One minute. Five minutes. An hour. They are all the same, yet they are all different. Did it take a minute or an hour to walk the length of that cold basement corridor? Ingrid had no idea. But she could feel every beat of Otto's heart and every breath that crawled in and out of his broken lungs. At the stairs she hoisted him on to her back like a sack of coal and hauled him up, step by step, feeling her way with her shoulder pressed against the wall. At the top she lowered his feet to the floor and let him rest in the hallway just for a second, but his breathing was so ragged she was tempted to pour air from her own lungs into his.

That was when the overhead light flooded on, blinding them.

'As sure as night follows day, I knew you would come for him, little Ingrid.'

Kuznetsov stood in the grimy hallway flanked by two bull-necked thugs who looked as if they couldn't wait to tear Otto limb from limb. They grinned, like hyenas grin before they bite a leg off. Ingrid gripped Otto tighter and felt him stir to life. One of his grossly swollen eyes prised itself open a slit.

'If you don't get out of my way, Kuznetsov,' Ingrid snarled at the Russian, 'I will slit your fucking throat open.' In one hand she brandished the knife.

Kuznetsov laughed softly, insultingly. 'Don't be foolish. You know he's going to die here anyway, so why put yourself in danger to no purpose?' He stepped closer, wreathed in black: black coat, black hat, black heart. The black shadow of the devil.

Ingrid was tempted to plunge her blade into the pulsing veins of the Russian's throat, but she knew that if she twitched even a muscle the bull-necks would be on her and, more to the point, on Otto. Kuznetsov stood with a neatly gloved hand resting on his cane, a thin smile pulling his lips taut, waiting for her to make her move. He was in no hurry.

But it was Otto who made the first move. Somehow – Ingrid had no idea how – he threw himself at Kuznetsov with an agonised scream, spitting a wild spray of blood and mucus at his tormentor, but the Russian stepped back with a flash of annoyance to ward it off. Yet a droplet of blood-spattered phlegm found the high point of his cheek just under his eye and he swept it off as if it burned.

Ingrid seized her husband, gripped him tight to her because she knew what was coming. Kuznetsov's blood lust lay naked in his ice-blue eyes. They flared with intense pleasure, exactly as they had when he ran the man through with his swordstick on the riverbank. She wrapped her arms like a shield around Otto.

'A deal,' she said. Quick and clear.

'What deal?'

'I'll give you Anna.'

'I already have her. Lined up in my sights.' He nodded his sleek head. 'Thanks to you.'

'I'll bring you the missing son.'

She had him then. A pulse in those eyes, a pulse of weakness, of need.

'You have him?' he demanded.

'I know where the child is.'

'You're lying, little Ingrid.'

'No.'

She could hear Otto's breath growing fainter.

'It's not Poldi,' she stated, controlling her panic, 'you've got the wrong one.'

Kuznetsov drew a pistol from under his coat and aimed it straight at her head. So no games with the swordstick tonight. A bullet in the brain would suffice.

'Don't take me for a fool, Ingrid.'

He pulled the trigger. The explosion was deafening in the enclosed hallway, ricocheting off the tiles, and Ingrid flinched, braced for pain, but it didn't come. Instead Otto's body bucked in her arms and slithered to the floor, hitting it with a grunt as the air was knocked from his lungs. In the centre of his swarthy forehead a dark crimson hole bored deep into his brain.

Ingrid died. Her body remained standing, her hand still gripped the knife, her fingers bone white, but inside her everything died. Everything. She felt it. A tidal wave of blackness that wiped out every speck of light and life within her. She fell to her knees and seized Otto's hand in hers, but she was too late. It was already limp, muscles soft and his trapeze calluses collapsing at her touch.

'No, no, no, no, no, no, no …' she howled, howled, howled. 'No, no, no, no, no, no, no, no …' She couldn't stop.

A blow to her head silenced her.

'Ingrid, cease being a fool. Now's your chance to make something of yourself. He's gone and you can focus fully on—'

A roar rose inside her and she hurled herself at him with the knife outstretched, but a boa-constrictor arm hooked around her throat before the blade found its target as one of the thugs swung her off her feet, through the front door and tossed her on to the street like a bag of spare bones for the feral dogs. The other thug kicked Otto's body out on to the pavement after her. The door slammed. The night descended.

Ingrid sat on the cobbles with the snow falling and rocked her dead husband in her arms.

CHAPTER FIFTY-SIX

◆ ◆ ◆

TIMUR

T imur had disobeyed orders.

Sokolovsky would chew his arse off and put him under close arrest with a severe reprimand. *Svoloch*, he might even line him up against a wall and have him shot as an example to others, but Timur didn't give a shit right now. He'd reached his breaking point. There was no going back.

The laboratory he'd been ordered to dismantle was a small one, tucked away in the south of the city in the Köpenick district and it had done well to keep its head down till now. Yes, it had popped up on his deconstruction lists at intervals, but when he'd studied more closely what they were achieving there he'd slid it to the bottom of his mountain of paperwork and permitted them to continue to function undisturbed. What they produced in their laboratory was penicillin. Admittedly not in great quantities like the Americans and the British, but enough to save hundreds of German lives in Berlin and East Germany. Timur had seen too much of death to shut these miracle workers down.

Timur had watched over them. The scientists had researched and developed their penicillin using a mould culture – *P. baculatum* – from the Dutch company NG&SF and were now expanding their own production methods. He'd facilitated the acquisition of equipment for them and set a Soviet guard on their door to keep other inspectors out, a guard who had an insatiable liking for gin. Timur had kept him well supplied and the guard slept in his chair most afternoons.

'Don't.'

Timur had spelled it out loud and clear to the scientists.

'Don't, Herr Direktor, don't produce too much. If necessary, shut down the lab for a couple of months. Cut back on output.'

Word was circulating. Too many people were talking of the wonder drug coming out of there and Timur feared the whispers would reach the wrong ears, which is exactly what had happened. The summons came and Timur stood in front of the vast overbearing desk in Marshal Sokolovsky's grand panelled office with its ridiculous portrait of Stalin, taller than Timur himself.

'Major Voronin, you have served Soviet Russia well here in Berlin.'

Sokolovsky's face was grim. On his muscular chest his gold star medal, signifying a Hero of the Soviet Union, served to remind all those who stood before him that he held total power over life and death in East Germany. His heavy jaw and large proud nose were thrust forward as he stood, hands flat on his desk, his anger vibrating the desk lamp at his elbow.

'Now you disappoint me, Major,' he stated warningly.

'Comrade Marshal, I am preparing the looms from a carpet factory for shipment,' Timur informed him. 'I think Comrade Stalin will be well pleased with these. They are single rapier flatweave machines, ideal for very thick and rugged raw wefts.' Pile on the details. Distract the marshal from any thoughts of laboratories. 'They have high loomspeed and low yarn-breakage. Already I have transported the shedding devices, shafts, beams, bobbin creels and quantities of heddles to the railway depot. The looms themselves will be removed today and tomorrow everything should be in place for immediate shipment.'

The desk lamp ceased its tremble. Sokolovsky jerked his chin down in a nod of satisfaction, yet still the order came, as Timur had known it would.

'Dismantle the Köpenick laboratory first, the one producing penicillin, and transport it along with the scientists responsible for it to Russia. Remove them from the facility and throw them all on a plane to Moscow. *Nemedlenno*. Immediately.'

Timur was used to shipping equipment. He did not ship men like mice in a cage.

◆ ◆ ◆

He gave them one hour. No more. He used the public telephone in the foyer of the Feldberg Hotel and his eyes scanned each person idling in the well-upholstered armchairs as he dialled.

'Herr Direktor?'

'Speaking.'

'Pack up your laboratory and flee. Go into hiding unless you fancy a trip to Moscow this evening. You have one hour before I arrive with trucks and a unit of men to do the job for you. You've been warned.'

'No, no … Please no … I …'

'One hour.'

'No.' The professor's voice was hoarse, barely audible. Fear does that to a man. 'I need longer than—'

Timur hung up.

A thin crust of snow sparkled on the ground and lay heaped in the gutters where passing wheels had thrown it. The doorman was sweeping the pavement clear in front of the hotel's entrance with a slow lazy rhythm, but when Timur strode down the front steps he saw before him not the grubby ridges of snow but the edge of a cliff. He was about to step off it. He knew what the consequences of that phone call would be and he felt his pulse racing, but he would not ship men to become the slaves of Stalin. He would not.

'Major Timur!'

He spun round at the sound of his name. A young woman was hurrying behind him, a beautiful fragile face that he recognised but for a moment couldn't place. She wore an emerald green coat and unsuitable shoes.

'Kristina,' he said as his mind kicked into gear. It was Anna's friend, the one who wanted him out of Anna's life. 'I'm surprised to see you here.'

'I work here.'

'Of course.' He had known she worked in a hotel in the east but not which one and he felt a slight stir of alarm. Had she been eavesdropping on his telephone call?

'Major, I am glad to have the chance of a word with you alone.'

'What can I do for you?'

'It's not what you can do for me, it's what you can do for Anna.'

'Kristina, I am trying to do all I can to help her with—'

'No, that's my point. She doesn't need your help.' Kristina took a step back, unwilling to stand anywhere near him. 'Anna survived perfectly well without you after you deserted her and she can survive perfectly well without you now. All you'll do is hurt her all over again. If you really love her, leave her alone and let her find someone else.'

The thought was not new to him, but it tasted like bile in his mouth. 'I didn't desert Anna. I was posted elsewhere and wrote to her constantly, I promise you. My letters and parcels were intercepted and stopped.'

She exhaled her annoyance. 'So what's to stop the same thing happening all over again?'

'It won't.'

'How can you be sure?'

'I'm sure.'

Suddenly her face crumpled in distress. 'Oh no! You're planning on taking her back to Moscow with you, aren't you, and making her live there?'

'It has occurred to me, yes.' He softened his voice. 'But I decided against it.'

The approach of aircraft engines low over their heads caused them both to look up and a sprinkling of tiny white parachutes floating down to earth brought a smile rushing to Kristina's face.

'The Candy Bomber!' She started to hurry away. 'I must try to get one of them for Gerd.' But at the last moment she paused and said fiercely, 'If you love her, leave her. She has enough trouble without you.'

Oh, Kristina, you make it hard, Timur thought. He stood on the pavement with a feeling of deep sadness, watching her run towards the drop area, and he took note of all the children, as well as adults, racing each other to catch a mouthful of chocolate. That's what they were reduced to. That's what Soviet Russia had reduced them to and it made him ashamed of his own country.

He strode away, turning his mind to the immediate problem of the Köpenick laboratory he was about to steal, when he became aware of a fluttering, like dove's wings, above his head. Except it wasn't doves, it was paper. Another small sheet of printed paper brushed against his cheek and one landed briefly on the toecap of his boot before dancing in the wind and whisking away again. Timur glanced up. Hundreds of pieces of paper were drifting down from the sky alongside the parachutes.

Out of curiosity Timur snatched one out of the air and straightened it in his hand. It was a single-page leaflet, a printed flyer. The word 'HELP' in bold capitals leapt out at him.

HELP!
Seeking lost child.
3 years old, blond, blue-eyed boy, missing for years.
He has an old tattoo.
If you know such a child, bring him to basement at 48 Hinterstrasse.
Reward offered.

Oh, Anna, what are you doing? Timur screwed the sheet of paper into a tight ball in his fist and cursed under his breath. She was setting herself up, making herself a target, enticing a killer to come and play games with her. Dancing with death.

He thought about the laboratory and the specific orders he'd been given by Sokolovsky, then he made his decision, turned and walked away from the hotel. He headed for Gruberstrasse.

CHAPTER FIFTY-SEVEN

◆ ◆ ◆

ANNA

Every time the basement door opened, hope rose in my chest. Every single time. I couldn't make it stop. I studied the face of each new child who entered with my mouth as dry as a border guard's soul and my fingers itching to tear the sock off their right ankle.

I asked them to push up their sleeves first, right up to the elbow, and I inspected their forearms, wrists and hands. Such little hands, soft sweet starfish, grimy and clinging. It hurt me to let some of them go, but that inspection was just camouflage for the real thing. I then knelt in front of them, rolled up their trousers, both legs up as high as their pointy little knees, and most times there was nothing to them, nothing but scuffed skin and bone, miniature scarecrow sticks without a scrap of flesh on them. I smiled and gave each child – whatever age – who came through the door a chunk of bread and dripping. Some cried while they chewed on it, silent snotty tears that broke my heart.

I had hated selling the gifts from Timur. Loathed letting them go, the ones that my mother had hidden from me and which now meant so much, but they were all we had left to barter in the markets after the ravages of the sweep. I cursed again the bastard Lieutenant Glinin and his thieving pack of hyenas. But I have Timur himself now, I told myself, and felt the familiar kick of heat in my gut at the thought of him, so I can live without his gifts. These children can't.

Self-delusion is a strange thing. I fed on it hour after hour while no tattooed 'A' appeared on any of the small-boned ankles I was handling, but I kept telling myself it would be on the next. Or the next. Or the one after that. I lied to myself and swallowed the lies as eagerly as the kids swallowed their bread. The air in the cold basement grew warmer because of all the young bodies and there was an odd atmosphere of celebration, though we had nothing to celebrate. Except the bread and dripping. And hope. We all fed on hope.

The words *Reward offered* on the printed flyer I'd sent out had been a mistake, a costly one, I saw that now and I kicked myself, but it was too late to change. The damage was done. I flicked one of the sheets of printed paper under the nose of a young man with thick glasses who had set a snivelling blond child in front of me with a flourish and a jaunty, 'Here's your kid, *Fräulein.*'

The child's thin arm was tattooed with the image of a snake.

'I specified on the flyer that it was *an old tattoo,*' I yelled at him. 'This tattoo is brand new. Look at it. It's red and swollen and suppurating. How could you do this to a child?'

But I knew how. It was the word *Reward*.

He wasn't the only one. Others had had the same idea and my hope started to feel like a rickety thing that threatened to collapse. Kristina had joined me, helping to herd the children, so in a quiet moment I ripped off a small chunk of bread, wiped a smear of the beef fat across it and headed over to the far corner of the room where a solitary figure lay immobile. She was wrapped in my coat on the floor and staring dead-eyed into a hell-hole only she could see. It was Ingrid.

'Please eat, Ingrid.' I crouched down beside her and stroked her tangled hair. 'You need food to keep yourself warm.'

I broke off a tiny piece of the bread and held it to her bloodless lips, the way you would to a fledgling, but they remained closed. She looked terrible, her skin the same colour as the cement floor, and she hadn't moved for twenty-four hours.

'Please,' I whispered again.

Nothing, not even a blink of her wide-open eyes. She didn't even seem to know I was there. She had come stumbling down the basement steps yesterday in the early hours of the morning, while I was caring for one of the girls who was restless with a fever, and thrown herself into the darkened room, screaming. Howling.

'He killed Otto! He killed my Otto!'

Over and over. Weeping and wailing. Tearing at her hair and shredding her blood-soaked clothes, gouging her nails through her skin. Her grief was biblical in its intensity and scared the children rigid. I wrapped my arms around her tiny frame, murmuring wordless sounds, because what can you say when someone is caught in one of the circles of hell.

She stopped as abruptly as she'd started and became totally silent except for wrenching breaths. I drew her to the floor where we lay on a musty old curtain and I draped my coat over her freezing form, holding her tight to give her my warmth and to stem the uncontrollable tremors that shook her.

'Hush,' I murmured, 'hush,' though she was making no sound.

We lay there till dawn slipped a crimson finger through the long narrow window and then she told me who had murdered her husband. Pavel Kuznetsov. The same monster, she hissed, who had murdered Klaus Dieleman and stolen Poldi. I made a vow there and then in the form of a solemn whisper into her ear that I would kill that man.

Kuznetsov. I know your name now. I am coming for you.

CHAPTER FIFTY-EIGHT

◆ ◆ ◆

TIMUR

Timur was a tall man. His shoulder blades were broad slabs, his limbs were long, his hands were muscular. They looked able to wrestle a tank on to its back. He knew this was what people saw when they looked at him, and on top of that he wore a uniform that could make eyes go blank with fear. Yet he possessed the ability to make himself invisible.

When he was a boy growing up in the arse-end of Siberia, he would spend days tracking a musk deer or a sure-footed goral and he'd learned how to become part of the background, a blur, unnoticed and unseen by his prey. He taught himself the patience and persistence of a wolf, which is why he spotted the watcher at an upstairs window. The street outside Anna's basement refuge wasn't quiet, not today, her leaflets descending from the sky had seen to that. There was a steady stream of children scampering over the snow heaps and down the basement steps with the crumpled sheets of paper clutched in their hands, sometimes alongside a mother or father, more often in feral packs. And all the time the watcher was there at a window diagonally opposite the building, binoculars in his hand, observing and retreating into the dim interior, half hidden by cracked shutters.

He didn't see Timur because Timur had made himself invisible. Hour after hour ticked past and still the watcher was unaware of being watched. Timur became part of the stone doorways. He was no more than a scrape of shadow, a dimness in the brickwork. So that when the building's front door opened and a big-bellied man emerged with binoculars looped around his neck, twitching on his gut as he walked, Timur slid into step behind him.

It was the ice that alerted the man, the crunch underfoot. He didn't stop to look round at who might be following, but took off down the first side street. A man with a gut cannot run. Timur bided his time until they drew level with the deep shaded doorway of what had once been a toy shop, closed down now. Slam, a fist under the ribs. A cry. That's all it took. One arm across the throat and the man was pinned against the back wall, sweating and wheezing for air, shaking.

'Who are you?' Timur demanded in Russian.

'Sergei Kozlov.'

'Why were you watching the basement?'

'What basement?'

Timur sighed. 'Let's not play games. We'll try again. Who are you working for?'

'No one.'

Timur gave no second warning. He leaned in harder, jamming his arm like an iron bar against the man's voice box. Kozlov yelped and stood on tiptoe in an attempt to escape the pressure on his throat but he was trapped. He had the doughy flesh and the veined nose of a drinker and the teeth of a heavy smoker, and he knew he didn't stand a chance.

'Third time lucky, Sergei.' Timur gave an icy smile. 'We'll start from the beginning again. Why were you watching the basement?'

'To see who came and went.' Kozlov's voice was a thin whistle.

'Who wants to know?'

'I don't know his name.' Sweat was slithering into his spiky black eyebrows.

'Try harder.'

Timur increased the pressure on the delicate structure under his broad forearm and saw Kozlov's eyes pop open as threads of scarlet flared all over their shiny yellowish-white surface. They looked like scarlet spiders hatching out of his eyes.

'Sergei, fractures to the cartilage structures of the larynx or trachea will cause air to escape into your neck and chest. With a crushed trachea, breathing is impossible. So I'm asking for the final time, who are you working for?'

He eased the pressure, a fraction. Enough to let the man drag in a squall of air.

'I've never seen him. I know him only as Comrade Omega. He telephones me.' His voice was a croak, squeezing out sound over rocks in his throat. 'He gives orders. He sends me payment.'

'To watch people?'

'Sometimes.'

Timur studied the size of the man, the overweight ungainliness of him. The visibility of him. Something was not right.

'You've been watching the basement that's used by the children.'

The smallest of nods.

'How long?'

A gasp for air. 'Just today.'

Timur stepped back from Kozlov, releasing him, and the man bent over as far as his belly would allow, cradling his throat, dragging in great whoops of air and expelling them in violent curses.

'So what else is it you do for him?' Timur pressed. 'What is your expertise that he needs? What specialist skill?'

Kozlov struggled upright, wiped his damp face with the sleeve of his coat and shrugged. 'Nothing. I just watch and report to—'

Timur's hand seized the fleshy throat and twisted it. The man screeched. His fingers scrabbled at Timur's wrist but too late.

'Comrade Omega will kill me,' the man screamed, 'if I tell.'

'And I will kill you if you don't. You choose.'

Tears of panic were streaming from the man's bloodshot eyes.

'Tell me,' Timur spat. They both heard something crunch inside the man's throat.

Kozlov choked. 'I'm an explosives expert.'

CHAPTER FIFTY-NINE

◆ ◆ ◆

ANNA

'Anna Wolff, I know where you are. I am coming for you!'
A new child's voice rang out through the basement room, sharp
and piercing, silencing the chatter. I dropped Ingrid's limp hand and
spun round to see who had entered, but before my eyes could find the
small boy in the doorway, I knew exactly who had put those words in
his mouth.

Kuznetsov. He was here. Not in person, no, but in the sense of men-
ace that had entered the room with his words in a child's mouth. In the
doorway I spotted a cheeky young face with a grin too big for him and
huge pale blue eyes that were whizzing back and forth, searching the
occupants of the room, looking for me.

'Fräulein Anna!'

'Poldi!' I shouted with a rush of relief.

I ran to him, clambering over kids sprawled on the mattresses, and
he leapt into my arms, squealing with delight. He buried his small icy
face in my neck and I felt a sob power its way up through his small
body. I squeezed him hard.

'He made me say it,' Poldi whispered.

I stroked the back of his fragile neck. 'Who?' I asked softly. 'Who
made you say, *I am coming for you*?'

'The man.'

'Which man?'

'The one with the stick.'

'Was he kind to you?'

'Yes. He gave me a car.' He wriggled himself free from my embrace
and pulled out a metal toy car from his coat pocket. It was a good thick

344

coat. 'It's a GAZ Pobeda.' He grinned up at me. '*Pobeda* means "victory",' he announced proudly.

I dutifully admired it, but at the same time a chill crawled over my skin. This man, this Kuznetsov, had abducted Poldi because he believed he was the child I was searching for. But the flyers that I'd had released from the sky made it clear that my child possessed a tattoo somewhere on his body. Kuznetsov must have realised his mistake and thrown Poldi out to bring me a message.

I am coming for you.

That makes two of us, Comrade.

'Poldi, do you have any idea where you were in the city when you were with the Russian?'

The boy twirled the wheels of his car with his finger and shook his corn-coloured head. 'He said I must tell you.'

'Tell me what?'

'Something.'

I smiled encouragement and for the first time saw that Ingrid was on her feet, staring across the room at Poldi leaning against me. I bent down and spoke low in his ear. His hair smelled clean and fresh, unlike the other children. 'What something must you tell me?'

His fingers twirled the wheels faster and faster.

'What else, Poldi?' I urged softly.

His face screwed up into a tight little knot. 'I must tell you,' he whispered, 'that you must go home immediately.' But one of his needy little hands clamped on to my sleeve to hold me at his side.

You must go home.

I fled out the door, breathing ice into my lungs.

Pain is always relative. The loss of a finger is child's play when lined up against a knife in the gut or a limb hacked to pieces. I'd believed the pain was bad when Lieutenant Glinin's sweepers had swarmed into our apartment, destroyed and stolen our belongings and humiliated my mother with repeated slaps to her face.

I'd been blind. Stone blind. I'd failed to see how flimsy the pain had been back then. They'd left us a roof over our head and a bed to sleep on, hadn't they? Such luxury. How could I not recognise it? Most important of all, my mother and I had still had each other to cling to.

Now this.

I skidded to a halt, leapt from my bicycle and forced a frantic path through the throng of people who were crowded on to the pavement outside my apartment building in Prenzlauer Berg. Beneath a brazen blue sky, voices were raised and hands were pointing upward so that my gaze fixed on the fourth floor. Every window of our apartment was blown out. The woodwork shattered, curtains fluttered in tatters and the air was thick with cement dust. Only then did I become aware of the snapping and cracking of broken glass under my feet and that the hand pushing me back from the entrance belonged to the uniformed arm of a VoPo policeman.

'Stand back, *Fräulein*. There's been an explosion. No one is allowed in.'

'My mother is in there,' I screamed at him, as though my screams could sweep aside his arm and let me race up the stairs.

'No one is allowed in.' The VoPo was a brick wall. 'We have evacuated the building and are inspecting the damage.'

'Please, please,' I begged. 'I have to find my mother. She was up on the fourth floor. Let me through. I need to—'

A hand fell on my shoulder from behind but I was oblivious to everything except trying to reach the stairs.

'Fräulein Anna,' the thin reedy voice was insistent. 'Fräulein Anna,' the hand tweaked at my coat, plucking at my collar. 'We saw her.'

I spun around. Before me stood the Zimmermanns, the elderly couple who lived in the tiny apartment that had been carved out of our original floorspace, the ones who quarrelled constantly but then made up by singing together. They were covered in a fine skin of white plaster dust.

I gripped the lapel of Herr Zimmermann's coat and pulled him close. 'You saw my mother?'

'Yes.'

'When?' He tried to back away but I didn't let go.

'Just before the explosion in your apartment.' Tears seeped into his faded grey eyes. 'It blew our wall down, the one between your apartment and ours.'

He meant the paper-thin plasterboard that the Housing Committee had thrown up through the middle of our drawing room to create another set of rooms. I could imagine the devastation.

'Where did you see her?'

He dragged a handkerchief across his face, too tearful to speak. I shook him, I couldn't stop myself. 'Where? Where was she? Tell me. Where did you see her?'

It was his wife who spoke, clear and precise above the hubbub of noise around us. 'She was outside.'

'Outside?' My head jerked in disbelief. 'No, no. She never goes outside. Never.'

'It's true, Anna. We saw her. Through our bedroom window we watched her being marched out of the building by two men, one on each side of her. Like great bulls they were, gripping her arms and dragging her along.'

'Soviet men?'

'They weren't in uniform but they were Soviets alright.' She pulled her headscarf tighter, glanced around to check no one was watching, then spat with pinpoint accuracy on to a small mound of grubby snow that bore the imprint of a large boot.

'Where did they take her?'

'They chucked her into the back of a black car and drove off that way.' Frau Zimmermann pointed east.

I pictured my mother, alone, in a car with men who could snap her in two with a flick of their fingers. A bolt of fear inside her chest as she sat upright on the leather seat, blue eyes scathing, showing no sign of weakness. I thought of her outside.

Outside.

Mutti, I am coming. Believe me.

My mother was taken because of me. There. I have said it. *Because of me.* However fast I pedalled, I couldn't outpace that guilt as I raced down the road, my bicycle flying as if my life depended on it, except this time it wasn't my life, it was my mother's. I was hurrying towards my basement steps, only fifty metres away now, and already in my mind I was grilling Ingrid on the places where Kuznetsov usually hung out. The bars and restaurants, the nightclubs and even the brothels. She would know, surely she'd know some of his haunts, even though she said she didn't know where he lived. But would she be willing to share that knowledge with me? I recalled the look on her face across the room when I was talking to Poldi, her eyes wide. Why such shock?

At least I had a name to give Timur now. Pavel Kuznetsov. A Russian name for him to track down in East Berlin. Kuznetsov, you cannot hide, so start counting your breaths. They are numbered.

There was no fog today. The buildings were sprinkled with ice crystals that sparkled in the sunlight, little stabs of silver that made the street look alert instead of its usual sleepy drab self. On the right-hand side of the road the apartment blocks leaned against each other, tired, patched and ramshackle, ready to expire in the next gust of wind, but just about upright. The layout on the left, where my basement refuge was tucked away, was a different story. Buildings totally missing, like teeth kicked out, while bomb-damaged roofs had given up the ghost and staircases climbed up to nowhere. Above my basement rose a tangle of rusting girders and masonry rubble, populated by rats and by an occasional fugitive who knew where to lie low to avoid the VoPos.

So it struck me as odd when I saw someone shoot up from the basement steps at high speed. A short moustached man in a baggy overcoat and greasy black cap, no one I recognised, and in a huge hurry. But something clicked in my mind. A memory. Blurred at first but suddenly snapping into focus like a camera. A memory back at the recruitment centre. A figure running. Black flat cap, loose brown coat flapping. A Stalin moustache, head ducked low, a hessian bass carried in one hand. That's the traditional tool bag of plumbers and carpenters, a bit like a baby's woven cradle. Heavy-looking. A length of lead piping over his shoulder. A workman, just an ordinary workman, not worth remembering. But he'd been running away from the building as if his life depended on it and that was why I ran.

Now that same man leapt into a car that was parked opposite my basement with its engine running and roared off down the road.

I felt a stab of panic and pedalled faster but even so, I didn't see it coming. I had no warning. An explosion thundered through the street, crashing all around me, booming into my ears. Numbing my mind and sending me and my bicycle flying through the air as the blast wave hit me head on. A ripping raging ringing shrieked in my ears and felt like hot needles, and for a moment as I lay flat on my back on the road, staring up at a blue sky that had somehow retreated behind a thick gritty veil, I couldn't comprehend what had happened. I tried to drag air into my lungs. But it felt compressed, too thick to breathe, and I rolled on to my side, coughing and spluttering a slurry of grey muck on to the road surface. Even my teeth hurt.

Helping hands fussed over me. Voices and shouts, faces came in and out of focus. I clung to a man who had the build of a heavyweight boxer and hauled myself to my feet, and suddenly the whole street was swaying. I blinked hard. The remains of a door lay at my feet. I recognised it. It belonged to my basement. I gazed at it, lights flashing like fireballs across my line of vision, and I tried to work out how it got there. Only when I managed to drag a deep breath into my body did the cogs in my brain begin to turn.

I started to scream. 'No, no, no, no, no!'

The basement had vanished. Where the basement steps had been, there were now towering slabs of shattered walls, piled high with tortured blocks of rubble. The wreckage of the building's skeleton that had stood above what had once been my workshop had come crashing down. The basement – and everyone in it – had been pulverised.

I threw myself at the ruins in a frenzy and began to scrabble at the chunks of stone and brick, tearing them away, trying to rake a pathway, an airway, hurling them into the road. Hating them. Cursing them, because somewhere deep under them all lay the ravaged remains of more than twenty children. And I was the one who'd enticed them there.

'Poldi!' I howled.

'Yvo!'

'Resi!'

'Kristina!'

'Ingrid!'

The names poured out of me, along with the tears and the grief.

'Leah!'

'Lars!'

'Anneli!'

'Fredrick!'

'Greta!'

Dimly I was aware of others heaving at the slabs with bare hands. A fog of cement and voices and shouts and sobs swirled around me but it didn't touch me. It existed a world away. I could see nothing but the images in my head of fragmented bones and small crushed skulls and—

A strong pair of hands seized my shoulders from behind. They started to pull me away from the devastation, words drumming at my ears but they wouldn't slot together to make any sense. I lashed out in an attempt to break free but my wrist was caught in a fierce grip and I was spun around. Before me stood Timur. Relief swamped me.

'Help me, Timur, quickly. Help me. Help me get them out of there. Please, Timur, please ...' My words were crashing into each other.

My free hand scrabbled at his chest in its greatcoat but Timur took my face between his hands and forced me to look at him. To see him. To hold on to the steadfastness of him.

'They're alive.'

'What?'

'I've come back for you.' He soothed my cheek with his thumb.

'You don't understand,' I cried. 'They're all down there under—'

'Hush, Anna, my love, hush. Calm down. Stop trying to speak.'

When he removed his hand to place a finger on my lips, his palm was covered in blood. 'It's alright, Anna. Believe me. The children and In-grid and Kristina are safe. I got them all out of the basement before the bomber attacked. I led them away from here, made certain they were out of danger, and raced straight back in case you returned. Do you hear me?' He kissed my forehead and his lips turned red. 'They are safe.'

I leaned against him. I loved this man more than my life.

The factory felt like a cathedral. A vast empty space that smelled of smoke. The vaulted ceiling and intricate brickwork rose high above tall arched windows that held no glass. It had been removed by the Soviets along with everything else, and I was acutely aware that Timur had most probably done the removing. It used to house a shoe factory, a busy, noisy, bustling hub with the deafening clatter of hundreds of short-arm and long-arm sewing machines, all gone. As well as the tools, the pliers and punches, the thousands of lasts and dies and tack hammers. All sto-len from Germany. Jobs destroyed. How can we ever recover while the Soviet Union is leeching our economic lifeblood like this?

But the sight of the children safe within the abandoned factory kicked some life back into me and I hugged each one of them in turn. Timur had worked a miracle. More children were pouring in every moment like a flock of starlings, chittering and chattering, fluttering everywhere. The woody smell of smoke permeated the place where little fires of twigs were blooming across the concrete flooring to keep the children warm.

'You look like you've been in a brawl,' Yvo scoffed, squirming out of my embrace with a grin.

I touched my face. 'You're right. But the fight isn't finished yet.' I gestured towards the huddles of young figures. 'Where did all these extra children come from so suddenly?'

'I put word out about our new base here,' he muttered and added quickly, 'I promised them some scraps to eat.'

'I'll do my best to get hold of some.' Everything came down to food.

I drew Timur to one side, out of earshot of the kids. 'How did you know to get all the children out of the basement before the explosion?' I asked, baffled.

Timur told me about the explosives specialist who had been staked out in the house across the road from my basement. He told me about it while he bathed my face and stemmed the blood, his touch firm and unemotional, for which I was grateful.

'The explosives expert had made the bomb,' he explained in a matter-of-fact tone, 'and was there to study the impact of the amount of explosive he had supplied to his assistant, who was the man employed to actually plant the bomb. He said he found it informative, as well as pleasurable, to watch his explosions. But infuriatingly he only knew his employer as Comrade Omega.'

He cupped my jaw in his hand as he dabbed at my chin. I didn't ask how he extracted this information or what had happened to the specialist.

'Timur,' I said, 'this Comrade Omega has taken my mother.'

'His name is Pavel Kuznetsov,' I said. 'Heard of him?'

Timur shook his head, grim and watchful. 'No, it's not a name I know. But if he's an MGB man, that's not surprising. They have an army of agents here in Berlin and they keep their heads down.'

'Thanks to Ingrid, I now have his name. Kuznetsov. Surely it must now be possible to track down this bastard who likes to abduct people.'

'And to torture people.' Ingrid's harsh voice startled me as she stepped outside to join us.

Timur and I were in the factory yard. We were up against a wall, sheltering out of the wind, and he was holding both my hands in his because the damn things wouldn't stop shaking. Whether it was rage or shock or just plain white terror for my mother, I had no idea, but the touch of his skin on mine stilled my world and gave me time to think.

'Torture?' I asked Ingrid.

'Yes. Kuznetsov tortured my Otto before he shot him.'

My mother is in a madman's hands.

'I'm so sorry, Ingrid,' I said. 'This man Kuznetsov is utterly ruthless. He tried to blow up a basement full of children. Now he has snatched my mother and destroyed my home. This is never going to end unless I end it.'

'No, Anna.' Timur's voice was sharp. 'Kuznetsov is too dangerous. Let me handle it. Remain here and keep the children safe.' Timur had transformed into the military man he was trained to be. 'Stay here while I go and hunt down the murdering bastard.' He studied my face. 'I will find her, Anna. I will find your mother, I swear.'

'Timur.' Ingrid stepped forward. There was a flush to her cheeks instead of their recent ashen pallor. 'Take a unit of your soldiers to Schleiferstrasse. Number 59.'

'What's there?' Timur asked.

'It's a building that Kuznetsov uses sometimes. There are cells in the basement where he …' her mouth spasmed and for a moment she couldn't speak, '… where he has people interrogated.'

'You think he could be holding Frau Wolff there?'

'It's possible. It's where he held Otto, so it's worth a try.'

Timur drew me back inside the factory entrance, Ingrid one step behind. I knew what was coming.

'Do not leave here, Anna, while I'm gone. Promise me. I will return as quickly as I can. It won't help either of us if you put yourself in danger alongside your mother.'

I slid my fingers around his. 'And you, Timur. Stay clear of danger.'

I was asking the impossible.

'Here, take this.' He placed a large iron key in my hand. 'It locks the factory door here.' He banged the flat of his hand against the heavy oak boards at least three metres high, testing the door's strength. He seemed satisfied. 'After I leave, lock the door behind me and don't open it till I return. You understand?' His gaze was fixed on my mouth and I knew he would spot a lie on it as easily as a bloodstain.

I laid my cheek against his. Both were cold now. 'I understand,' I said softly.

He took my other hand in his, turned it over and placed his TT-33 pistol on my palm. The gun was chill and heavy, its grip ridged, a menacing chunk of black metal.

'Listen to me, Anna. If anyone tries to force their way in here, shoot them. Don't wait to ask questions.'

Stark words. We stared at the lethal barrel of the gun.

'You understand?' he asked again.

'I understand.'

'I'll be back,' he said. 'Lock the door. Trust no one.'

I locked the door and listened to the sound of his boots as he crossed the yard. I turned to Ingrid and gripped her arm. 'Tell me –' I shook her fiercely – 'where will I find Kuznetsov?'

I must leave.

I jammed Timur's gun into my coat pocket and asked my friend Kristina, who was playing a hand of cards with Resi and her brothers, to watch over the children for me. I took a long look around at my noisy flock of starlings, imprinting them on my mind and on my heart, aware that this could be the last time. I may not be back.

'Most of them have come out of the ruins,' Kristina murmured.

I nodded. We've all come out of the ruins. It's where we're going that counts.

I wanted to stop and check a few ankles for tattoos, but right now my desperate fear for my mother was driving me back out into the city. As I cut a path through the groups of children with their scabbed young faces and blackened knees, my gaze snagged unexpectedly on the sweetest curve of a small ear. It brought me to an abrupt halt. I blinked and looked again. Focusing properly. For I'd been fooled too often before to fall for the wishful thinking of my own eyes again. My gaze shifted to the rise of the forehead, the curve of the skull, the set of the eye sockets, the slope of the hairline. The dazzling blue of the wide eyes.

I hurried over and crouched beside the child, skinny as a weasel. He was crouched in front of a few smouldering sticks, poking a twig at wisps of flame, so that the smoke swirled and the flame spat and the child laughed.

Did you know a laugh can change your life? I didn't, not till that moment. Or that between one heartbeat and the next a door can burst open inside you, letting sunlight pour into dark desperate places. I knew that laugh like I knew my own fingernails. I smiled at the boy though he was too entranced by the fire to notice, but that was fine by me because I could squat there and study him.

My Felix. He was small for his age but I suspected that years of underfeeding had taken its toll. His hair was fine as thistledown and not just blond, it was white blond, white white blond. But filthy. His face was all bones, no pads of flesh, but I'd kissed that pointed little chin and stroked those cheeks years before and it was hard to keep my fingers off them now. I could feel happiness surging through me. It struck me dumb.

Opposite us on the other side of the fire hunched two older boys, street kids of about nine and ten, I'd guess. Sharp-eyed with sharp faces and sharp tongues.

'We brought him in,' the older one announced.

'We found the message,' the other one added, thrusting a scuffed copy of my flyer at me.

I accepted it. 'Thank you. Tell me a bit about him. What's his name?'

'Maus,' Felix piped up.

'*Maus?* What kind of name is that? Why a mouse?'

'Because he's small and squeaks a lot.'

The older boys fell about laughing, not a pleasant sound, a mean sound. Felix turned bright red, including his little ears, and he wouldn't look at any of us. I wanted to rip out their spiteful tongues.

'Where did you find him?' I asked.

'On a doorstep.' Another bout of sniggering. 'Chucked out with the rubbish when he was a baby, weren't you, Maus? No one wanted the stupid brat.'

I wanted you. God knows how much I wanted you.

Felix jutted his chin forward in defiance, but he kept his mouth shut and he didn't cry. Had he been taught that the hard way?

'So he's been on the streets with you ever since he was a baby, has he?'

The older boy shrugged. 'Yeah. We reckoned he'd get us more money when we're out begging. What with him having those big baby-blue eyes and all, and he did. Everyone feels sorry for him and gives us a few extra pfennigs or an extra chunk of bread when he's around, but he's getting in our way now that we're grown up.'

'And it's another mouth to feed,' the other, sullen-mouthed kid grumbled.

'It doesn't look to me as if you've been doing much of that,' I said sharply.

All three looked at me, surprised.

I turned to Felix and asked in a gentler tone, 'Do you have a tattoo?' He nodded.

'Yeah,' the older boy interrupted, 'that's why we brought him here. Show her, Maus, show the lady your foot, go on.'

Felix tucked his feet firmly under himself and sat on them.

The older boy made a grab for Felix's hair but he ducked.

'You little *Scheisse*, I'll knock your—'

'No!' I said. 'Leave the boy alone.'

'Look, lady. We want the reward. It says on that paper there's a reward.'

'If he's the right child with the right tattoo, you will receive a reward, I promise you that. So there's no need to be rough with him.' I brushed the older boy away, back to his side of the fire. I turned again to Felix. He was jumpy now and I feared he'd run.

'Listen to me, little one.' I refused to call him Maus. 'I am looking for a boy whom I lost almost three years ago. I love him very much and I want to care for him again and have him come to live with me. Do you understand?'

He nodded, eyes huge and solemn.

'He had a tattoo on his ankle and I would like to see yours, if you have one. To see if it's the same.'

Without hesitation he whisked off his tattered shoe and bared his ankle.

CHAPTER SIXTY

* * *

INGRID

I t wasn't yet dark. Ingrid would have preferred the cover of night but sunset was still a couple of hours off, which meant she felt exposed, perched here on the doorstep in Kirchestrasse in broad daylight. It was one of the smart avenues where the buildings flaunted freshly painted iron balconies and fancy stonework and any bomb damage had been fixed long ago. It didn't smell of decay like most of Berlin. It smelled clean.

That's because the Soviet elite had chosen to sink their hooks into this area, requisitioning the luxury apartments for themselves, the Soviet generals with their gold stars and red piping on their uniforms, the commanders and commissars, and the council ministers. They all purred along this street in their sleek black ZIS limousines. They were frequently joined by Germany's own communist SED officials, Walther Ulbricht's cronies with their glamorous glossy-lipped escorts on their arms. Ingrid had seen them come and go, gliding up the steps in their mink coats, and she knew she looked as out of place as a mangy cat with its ribs sticking out.

She scanned the windows in the apartments opposite. No furtive shadows lingering behind shutters. Beside her, Anna Wolff stood silent, strung tight. In the time since they'd left the factory and headed here by crowded tram, Anna had been wrapped deep in her own thoughts and said only one sentence. 'If we find my mother and she is being tortured and he kills me first, shoot her for me.'

Ingrid had nodded. She didn't argue. How much love does it take to kill someone you love?

Ingrid slid the key into the lock of the house towards the far end. The showy black door with its shiny brasswork opened without a murmur and she stepped inside the downstairs entrance foyer, ready to brazen it out if challenged. But there was no one there to challenge them, the hall was empty and on the back wall hung a vast hammer-and-sickle banner flaunting its blood-red scarlet. Beside her, Anna took a good look round at the white Italian marble tiles on the floor and the wide walnut staircase with its newel finial carved in the shape of a gigantic pineapple.

'Impressive,' Anna said. 'Of course. It goes with his cashmere coats and silk shirts.'

Her voice was scornful and it surprised Ingrid. She expected to hear anger and hatred, but not scorn. How could you scorn someone who was so good at his job? Because Kuznetsov *was* very good, it seemed to Ingrid. However much she loathed him, Ingrid wanted to be that good herself. He had earned his silk shirts.

'What floor?' Anna asked.

'Fourth.'

They made for the sweeping staircase, giving the central lift a wide berth. It would be too easy to get trapped in there. They were lucky, passing no one on the stairs.

Ingrid stopped abruptly in front of one of the doors.

'This is it. Ready?' she whispered.

'Yes.'

The key in Ingrid's hand was a copy of the one Kuznetsov had given her when he commissioned her to paint the apartment, the one with the piano and the portrait and the awful gilded picture rail, plus the vodka and the covert listening devices. She took a deep breath and slid the key in the lock.

Nothing. Silence greeted them. The hallway was neat and clean, and the elegant satinwood bureau emitted the sweet honeyed scent of recent beeswax polish. No other sign of habitation. Ingrid nodded at the closed door that led into the high-ceilinged salon and they crossed the hall. The moment Ingrid opened the door she heard the piano music coming from the far end of the room, something slow and soft and sad.

'Chopin,' Anna murmured at her side.

Ingrid ignored the music. She saw only the man seated at the piano, his head turned towards her, and she noted that he was wearing a riding outfit. Had he been out galloping through the forest around the Müggelsee? Yes, she could picture him, confident and athletic, keeping a tight rein on a handsome horse. A close-fitted navy riding jacket showed off his well-shaped shoulders, pale jodhpurs and a cream stock at his throat, but to her surprise the stock was held in place by the pearl brooch she'd taken from the dead man she'd found on her apartment building's front steps. It struck her as gruesome. The pianist's silvery blond hair was swept back and his smile was approving.

Pavel Kuznetsov.

'My little Ingrid, I knew you would work out correctly where I'd be.' His blue eyes swivelled to Anna and hardened. 'And you brought your tattoo-loving friend, I see.'

It was as if he'd hit a switch in Anna. Her shell of stillness cracked wide open. She went striding across the room towards Kuznetsov and his piano, but he continued to play with a light touch that flowed over the ivories, his back turned to her. A show of bravado. Ingrid watched as Anna whisked Timur's pistol out from her waistband and pushed the business end of the barrel tight against the back of the Russian's gently swaying head.

He didn't miss a note. The lilting music continued to flow effortlessly, the only sound in the large room.

'Where is she?' Anna demanded.

'And if I refuse to tell you?'

'You get a bullet in your skull.'

He laughed softly as the fingers of his right hand performed an intricate arpeggio run up the keyboard. 'If you wish to see your mother ever again, I suggest you remove that gun, sit down and we talk.'

'I don't talk to killers.'

'Is that so?' He paused. 'I hear that Major Voronin is a killer. You talk to him.'

Anna raised the gun and slammed its butt down on the back of Kuznetsov's head. Hard, but not too hard. A scarlet spurt of blood from a ragged split in his scalp marred the perfection of his hair and the music staggered to a halt. Ingrid blinked with shock and gave the Russian respect for the fact he didn't cry out. He raised both hands from the keys to protect his skull from further blows but Anna reached round and wrenched the pearl cross from his neckwear, tearing a gash in the silk.

'Where is my mother?' she demanded.

So fierce. Kuznetsov had misjudged her, Ingrid realised. He'd presumed Anna was no real danger to him, but this was a new Anna, eyes black with hatred and intent. An Anna whom Ingrid liked. She began to think she'd actually chosen the right partner in crime, because that's what this was going to be. A crime. She didn't kid herself. Not just stealing papers or smuggling documents through checkpoints or pocketing an occasional carton of American cigarettes for Otto. This was a life-or-death crime. This was murder.

The Russian's? Or Anna's?

One of them would not walk out of this room alive.

Kuznetsov jerked to his feet and spun round to face Anna, his face taut with fury. She hopped backwards out of his reach and pointed the gun straight at his chest, the biggest target, one she couldn't possibly miss. All she had to do was squeeze the trigger.

Squeeze it, Anna, damn it. Squeeze.

But Anna didn't.

'I am going to ask you the question one more time,' Anna stated in a flat voice. 'After that, every time you make me ask it again, I will put a bullet in a part of your body.' She lowered the barrel till it was aimed at his thigh in its elegant fawn jodhpurs. 'Where is my mother?'

'Oh, Anna Wolff,' he said with icy disdain, 'did you really think it would be so easy?'

The metallic click of a gun being cocked in the room was unmistakable. Anna swung round, startled, and froze. She was staring round-eyed at the small revolver in Ingrid's hand. It was pointed at Anna.

'Put the gun on the floor and sit down,' Ingrid ordered.

She didn't trust Anna. She was liable to do something stupid, so Ingrid's finger tightened a fraction, but Anna obediently placed Major Voronin's TT-33 on the polished parquet and walked across the room to sit perched right on the edge of the plush velvet of the chaise longue.

'So talk,' Anna said.

Ingrid had no wish to talk. That was Kuznetsov's job. Ingrid remained unmoving in the centre of the burnished room with its lavish furnishings and its overpowering scent of privilege and with the Russian in his fancy clothes, knowing that this was where it had all started and this was where it would end. Ingrid stood there, gun in hand, missing Otto so cripplingly that she was tempted to point its dainty little barrel at her own head and squeeze.

CHAPTER SIXTY-ONE

◆ ◆ ◆

ANNA

Ingrid. No, not you too.

I sat, stunned. Not moving a muscle. Ingrid was my friend. Timur's last words echoed in my head. *Trust no one.*

I'd trusted Ingrid. I'd taken her into my basement refuge after Otto's death, hadn't I? I'd comforted her, held her, spooned warm broth between her lifeless lips, believed her. And in return she had led me into a trap and handed me over to Pavel Kuznetsov on a platter, this Russian who claimed to be a school inspector.

The Russian started striding up and down in front of me, ebony cane in hand, tapping it on the wooden floor with each step. A bright show of blood in the shape of what looked like a scarlet paw-mark had appeared on the thigh of his jodhpurs, and it took me a second to realise it wasn't a new wound. It was where he had touched his head and then wiped his fingers on his thigh. Why didn't I pull the trigger when I had the chance? I didn't think that I would hesitate. I know Timur wouldn't have.

'Fräulein Wolff, are you listening to me?'

Kuznetsov's words penetrated. I dragged my gaze from his leg to his face and what I saw there gave me a twist of pleasure. The arrogant sheen on his eyes had vanished and they were now the muddy colour of puddles in the gutter and badly bloodshot. Whether it was anger causing it or the blow to the head, I didn't care. He was rattled. That was a start.

'Where is my mother?' I demanded.

'I have just told you. You will be given the answer to that question only after the swap. Not before.'

'What swap?'

He exhaled a jet of impatience. 'I have just made it clear to you. The exchange of your mother for the child.'

'Child? What child? Poldi?'

'Fräulein Wolff, you are being deliberately obtuse. The child with the tattoo.'

He'd read my pamphlet. He wanted Felix. My Felix.

'But no child with the right tattoo has turned up,' I pointed out. I had told no one, not even Ingrid, about finding Felix. I was determined no harm would come to him. 'And now that you've blown up the refuge, the chances of—'

'Find the child.'

But I knew that whether or not I gave him the child, he intended my mother to die. Kuznetsov would make certain of that and rid himself of me at the same time. He expected to walk away free, but I swore to myself that by the time I'd finished with him he would not be walking at all, let alone walking free. I turned to look at Ingrid, a small unnoticeable presence, easy to forget she was here at all, even with a gun in her hand. Would she really shoot me? Abruptly I stood up and took one step towards Kuznetsov. She didn't shoot. Not yet.

'Why the hell have you been persecuting me and why do you want that child?' I tried to keep my words calm but they got away from me. 'What is one more scrawny kid to you?'

'Look on the wall behind you, Fräulein Wolff.'

I turned and felt my heart pound in my chest. A painting hung there. The room closed in on me, suffocating. I am back in the filthy alleyway with the soldier's hand across my mouth, his fingers stinking of other women. His weight is on me and I can't move. The screams from my mother and the pain and the shame and the hatred rise up once more and they rage through my hand as it slams a brick down on the blond head in the painting and I hear again the crack of his skull and taste the coppery slime of his blood slipping on to my lips and feel him clawing at the torn flesh between my legs.

He's here in the room. With me. I can even smell his brandy breath.

'That fine young man, Fräulein Wolff, is my son.'

Yes, I see it clearly, he is his father's son. When I first walked into the apartment I'd been focused on nothing but Kuznetsov at the piano, so failed to see the grand life-size painting, but yes, the same silvery blue eyes and the Nordic blond hair. The same arrogant thrust of his jaw and the air of entitlement. This is a young man who takes what he wants in life. No, I correct myself. This *was* a young man who *took* what he *wanted* in life. I stare, transfixed, the way you stare at a snake or a scorpion, and I see that like his father he is dressed in riding clothes which emphasise their kinship. But there are differences too. The son's face was broader, his mouth much fuller, his cheekbones less like blades. I studied him fiercely. I couldn't look away.

'How?' I whispered. 'How did you know it was me?'

'The brooch.'

I opened my fingers to reveal the cross of pearls gleaming on my palm. Each pearl a marker of death.

'Your son and his comrade attacked me and my mother,' I told Kuznetsov. 'They were drunken animals, cruel and brutal, they ...'

Raped us. Say it. Say the word.

My body shook. I felt sick. That word still had the power to rip me wide open.

'They deserved to die,' I insisted. I didn't mention Timur's arrival on the scene or the bullet that blew a hole in the comrade's chest.

'Look at the back of the brooch's gold pin.' Kuznetsov treated me to a thin gloating smile. The man was so sure of himself. 'It has the name of the jeweller stamped on it. Eckhaus, a jeweller here in Berlin, and it didn't take much for me to persuade him to search back through his records for the customer's details.'

I bet it didn't.

'Where did you find it?'

'It was sunk deep into my son's neck.' His long fingers curled into fists.

I took a moment to think about that, a father learning that a brooch pin had been jabbed into his beloved son, just before a brick had caved in his skull.

'He deserved worse,' I said. 'Far worse. My mother attacked the bastard with the only weapon she had.'

He ignored me. 'I was finally able to come over here to Berlin three months ago and I extracted your name from the jeweller. Then it was a simple matter to track your movements and discover the private investigator you'd hired to locate a three-year-old child.' He was boasting, brimful of his own cunning. 'The investigator's man sang like a canary with a little persuasion.' He smiled again, the thin gloating one that he had perfected. 'I ordered Otto Keller to leave the pearl cross on the investigator in order to make you realise that you – yes, you, Anna Wolff – are responsible for his death and for all the others that followed too. For all those who died in the explosion as well.'

I felt sick.

'But why kill Klaus Dieleman?'

'As a punishment to you, a punishment you deserved, I intend your life to be hell on earth for murdering my son.' He couldn't hide the tears that glittered in his eyes though he tried. He smacked his cane down on a nearby console table with a terrific crack that shattered a marble ashtray and sent a pair of tan riding gloves flying across the room.

But two can play at that.

I seized a glass of what looked like vodka that was standing neglected on a side table and hurled it at the canvas. The glass exploded and the crystal-clear liquid slid down his son's cheeks like fresh tears, but the impact inflicted no damage.

'Where is my mother?' I snarled at him.

'Where is your child?' he roared back at me.

'Felix is nothing to you.'

'He is *everything* to me. His father was my son. Felix is my grandson.' He drew a long laboured breath, stretching the tight muscles of his chest. Abruptly he dragged himself back under control, and I could feel the desire in him to knock me to the floor with his cane. With a glazed expression in his pale eyes he said, 'The child is mine. He will return with me to Russia.'

CHAPTER SIXTY-TWO

◆ ◆ ◆

TIMUR

Time was tight. Minutes ticked away like heartbeats. A team of six heavily armed Red Army recruits, still wet behind the ears but eager for action after the tedium of months of shuffling their feet at checkpoints, took down the door at Timur's command. They moved fast. Every second could be the last breath for Frau Luisa Wolff.

'*Toropit'sya!*' Timur ordered. 'Hurry!'

Two of the soldiers peeled off and took the stairs at a run, their Tokarev rifles primed. The noise of boots and weaponry rattled off the walls and vibrated floorboards as Timur led the rest of the unit in a rapid sweep through the building and courtyard. Doors behind which people were at work were kicked open, crashing back on their hinges. Occupants were herded into the hall on the ground floor where they were made to stand with foreheads and hands pressed flat against the wall. There were fifteen in all, including three women.

'You,' Timur said to the oldest of the three. She was a middle-aged woman who was apparently unruffled by the noise and bluster of young soldiers throwing their weight around. She'd seen it all too often. 'Turn around,' he instructed, first in Russian, then in German.

She turned to face him. A strong patient face, accustomed to being told what to do by men in uniform. She was dressed in a neat wool dress and cardigan, sensible clothes, sensible shoes, sensible eyes. She would give him no trouble.

'Are you German or Russian?' he asked.

'German.'

'The men here? Are they Russian or German?'

'All are German.'

'What is your job here?'

'I am a stenographer.'

'The other two women?'

'Also stenographers.'

Timur nodded. '*Dankeschön*.'

He flicked a glance down the line of men against the wall. None was in uniform, none wore any kind of insignia, just suit and tie, not well paid either, by the look of their ill-fitting jackets and shiny elbows. Unless it was a cover. One was a short self-important fellow who was all puffed up with anger but wise enough not to remove his forehead from the wall.

'Who are you, Comrade Major?' the man challenged. 'What right do you have to enter this building? I demand to see on whose authority you barge in here with—'

One of Timur's young army bucks jabbed a rifle in the suit's ribs. 'By the authority of the uniform we wear.'

'Your name?' Timur demanded.

'Jürgen Beck.'

'Hold your tongue, Herr Beck. Speak only when spoken to.' Timur turned back to the woman and softened his voice. 'What work is it that is done in this building?'

Her sensible hazel eyes regarded him in silence. He waited. It took her three breaths to decide to choose between what were obviously her German masters and this Russian major who held all the cards.

'We collect information and pass it on to K-5.'

Kommissariat 5, otherwise known as K-5, was the political arm of the German police authorities in the Soviet zone. But its lord and master were MVD and MGB, the brutal Soviet security services. Timur was well aware that K-5 frequently carried out specific secret missions for the Soviet military government in Germany. He was on thin political ice here.

A growl of rebuke came from a tall thin suit who earned himself a soldier's metal toecap in the back of his knee. His leg buckled and he made no further sound.

Timur addressed the woman again. 'So it's a K-5 outfit here.'

'Yes.'

'Under the control of Comrade Pavel Kuznetsov?'

'Yes.'

'I'm looking for a woman who I believe may have been brought here, a Frau Luisa Wolff. Do you have a record of her?'

She didn't hesitate. 'Yes.'

'Where is she? My men have searched the building and there are no women in the basement cells.'

'No. She's gone.'

'Where?'

'I don't know. I wasn't told. She was removed.'

Timur paused, but there were no tell-tale signs of a lie, no tightening of lips or ducking of eye contact, no fidgeting fingers or touching of face.

'Do you have paperwork on her?'

'Only her name, Herr Major. She only arrived today.'

'Was she questioned?'

'Yes.'

'By whom?'

Silence. For the first time she looked away towards the door that led down to the basement. Timur pictured the bird-like figure of Anna's mother being dragged down the stairs, white with fear. Blood on her wrists from handcuffs, a bruise on her eggshell cheek from a fist. But she would give them nothing, he was sure of that. She'd spit in their faces and take another slap, just as she had in her apartment. Anger pumped through him and he turned to the row of men lined up against the walls.

'Who questioned Frau Wolff? Which one of you?'

Silence.

Timur walked up to the short puffed-up figure, towering over him for an intimate view of the freckles on his pink pate. Timur stood very close behind him, intimidatingly close, close enough to smell his fear and the sweat sliding like grease down the back of his neck.

'You,' Timur said in an acid tone. 'Who questioned Frau Wolff?' The man's hand was quivering against the wall, soft plump fingers leaving damp round patches on the green paint. 'Herr Beck, give me the name of the person who questioned her or I will assume it was you.'

Nothing.

'Come with me, Herr Beck.' Timur strode towards the basement door and two of his eager soldiers followed with Beck gripped between them.

'No!' Beck squealed. 'I didn't even see her. It was Aldinger.'

'Aldinger? Which of you is Aldinger?' Timur asked with deceptive calm.

A youngish man turned to face him. 'That's me.'

Instantly Timur recognised the kind of man he was. It was written in the iron grey of his eyes. A man who would back himself against anyone. Tall, muscular though not heavy, the straight back of an ex-military man, with quick intelligent eyes that would enjoy prising fingernails from a woman's hand. Timur guessed he was missing his smart black Nazi SS uniform with its shiny *Totenkopf*, the death's head insignia, the one that marked him out as a member of Himmler's devoted Gestapo under Hitler. Another ambitious young *Untersturmführer*. He must have been quick on his feet to evade the denazification process that the Allies put in place to purge Germany of Nazi ideology. And now he'd rolled up here. Quick to get his hands on the pincers again.

'Come,' Timur commanded.

Timur led the way down the narrow stairs to the basement with Aldinger and the two Red Army recruits in tow. The corridor was dim and cold. He ordered all the cell doors to be thrown open and seven men were dragged from them in various states of despair and suffering.

'Out! Get your sorry hides out of here.'

The wretched prisoners needed no second bidding. Supporting the one whose feet were broken, they scuttled up the stairs to freedom.

'Which cell, Aldinger? Which cell was she in?'

'Number two.'

Timur entered the grim room that reeked of tears. The walls were white and naked and the cell contained a table and chair for the interrogator, another seat for the victim with fixed iron fastenings for wrists and ankles, and old blood stains on the cement floor beneath it. Timur summoned Aldinger inside the cell, closed the door after him and turned to address him with cold politeness.

'Sit down, Aldinger.'

'I'd rather stand,' he paused a beat, then added, 'Herr Major.'

'Sit down.' Less polite.

The German glanced at the closed door and sat. He chose the chair by the table. Timur didn't argue the point.

'Did you interrogate Frau Luisa Wolff?' Timur asked.

'Only to check her name and details.'

To check her details. That covered a multitude of sins.

'Who brought her here?'

'I cannot divulge that, Herr Major.'

Timur placed his hands on the table and leaned closer. 'I advise you to reconsider your answer.' His voice stayed low.

The man didn't blink; he held Timur's gaze, and for ten seconds the silence between them pulsed with tension.

'One more time, Herr Aldinger. Who brought her here?'

'I cannot divulge—'

The man didn't see it coming. The hard edge of Timur's hand snapped out in a blow to his throat. He screamed and fell forward. Timur seized a handful of his blond hair and smashed his face into the table. He heard the nose crack. In blind fury Aldinger went for him with a right hook just under the ribs which Timur had to admit was the work of an expert, as pain rocketed through his spine right up to his skull. Yet he neatly sidestepped the next blow and landed a punch on the point of Aldinger's bloodied jaw that laid him out cold. When the German blundered back to some kind of consciousness four minutes later, he found himself seated in the victim's chair, hands chained to its arms.

Timur was propped against the edge of the table, smoking a cigarette and waiting with apparent patience.

'We can do this the easy way, Aldinger, or the hard way. Your choice. But may I suggest the easy way? I am in a hurry and need the information fast, do you understand me?'

A grunt.

'Good. I'm glad we understand each other,' Timur said. 'The information I require from you is this: who brought Frau Luisa Wolff in here, who removed her, and where has she been taken?' He exhaled a long skein of smoke in his prisoner's direction. 'Simple questions that deserve simple answers, I'm sure you agree.'

Another grunt. A headshake and a look of hatred. Aldinger's face was a mask of blood.

'Who are you?' he spat through a spray of scarlet.

'Herr Aldinger.' Timur stubbed out his cigarette on the table top and threw the butt with impatience to the floor to join the bloodstains, 'I ask the questions. You give the answers. For the final time, who brought Luisa Wolff here?' He drew his replacement TT-30 from its holster and laid it in full view on the table.

The German was no fool. Timur watched him work it out. The man wanted to make it out the door alive and that came at a cost. He spat more blood from his mouth along with a sliver of tooth.

'She was hauled in here from a Mercedes by two big MGB bulls—your people.'

'In uniform?'

'No.'

'Was Pavel Kuznetsov with them?'

The bloodied lips clamped shut.

'I'm waiting, Aldinger, but beware, my patience is wearing thin.'

Silence. Laboured breathing. The cell grew smaller. Aldinger had tied his allegiance to Kuznetsov, which made him more of a fool than Timur would have reckoned. He thought of Anna locked in the abandoned factory, desperate for news of her mother, and his patience ran out. He pulled the trigger.

The sound exploded in the tiny cell with an ear-splitting roar. The back leg of the chair shattered in a volley of splinters as the steel-cased 7.62mm cartridge smacked into it. The chair and its occupant slammed to the ground on its side. Timur dropped on one knee next to it.

'The next bullet will be in your leg, not the chair's,' he warned.

This brutality gave him no pleasure, but he'd been trained and this man was scum. He rested the tip of the gun's barrel on Aldinger's smashed nose and let the weight of the weapon do its work. The man didn't twitch a muscle.

'Again,' Timur said quietly, 'was Pavel Kuznetsov with the men who brought Luisa Wolff here today?'

'No.'

'Did he come here alone?'

'Yes.'

'Better, much better.'

He lifted the gun from the broken nose and the man grimaced, revealing bright pink teeth. He was trapped awkwardly on his side in the chair, his head twisted round to glare at Timur through swollen lids.

'Was it Kuznetsov who removed her from here?'

A nod. Another baring of teeth.

'Where did he take her?'

'I don't know.'

'I think you can do better than that, Herr Aldinger.'

'He didn't inform me.'

The man's eyes squeezed to blackened slits and his hands bunched into fists held in place by chains, but Timur was careful to position himself away from the heavy black boots which could snap forward to crack a bone.

'You have family, Herr Aldinger. You wear a wedding ring.' Timur prodded it with the gun barrel. 'I hope your wife is well.'

Aldinger froze.

'Where,' Timur repeated softly, 'did he take Frau Wolff?'

'I swear I don't know.'

Timur rose to his feet. He could taste the man's fear and it sickened his stomach. 'I'm afraid I don't believe you.'

'I swear it. On my life.' His voice was shaking.

'But do you swear it on your wife's life? That is the question now.'

'Yes.' It came out as a scream. 'I do.'

'I'm afraid I still don't believe you, Aldinger. Which is unfortunate for your—'

'No, wait, you Soviet bastard. Wait.' He lay there, panting heavily, the air bubbling scarlet with each breath. 'He took her to an apartment in Kirchestrasse.'

'Number?'

'Number 83 Kirchestrasse.'

Timur nodded. '*Danke*.'

He left the man lying there and headed for the door, but stopped abruptly and turned. 'If you have anything more to tell me, now is the time. I would hate to have to come back here to finish our conversation.'

Aldinger didn't hesitate this time. 'He said he would hide her in a secret room there. Behind the wardrobe in the main bedroom. Now swear to me you'll leave my wife alone.'

Timur was already out the door.

CHAPTER SIXTY-THREE

◆ ◆ ◆

ANNA

It was a stand-off.

I could barely look at him. The murderous rage I felt towards this man, Pavel Kuznetsov, for wanting to steal both my mother and my son burned in me. I wanted to tear him limb from limb. He was evil.

And yet ...

And yet I looked at the beautiful painting of his dearly beloved son, with his horse and his dog and his whole golden future stretching out ahead of him, and something within me wept for Kuznetsov the father. To lose a son is like having a fist plunge into your chest and gouge your heart out. The pain of it never stops. Had grief driven him out of his mind to the point where he could order the blowing up of a basement full of children? It was unthinkable.

We stood face to face, Kuznetsov and I, neither giving an inch, the only sound the incessant tapping of his cane. It was Ingrid who broke the stand-off. Suddenly she was there next to us, two large glasses of cognac in her hands, proffering them.

'Here,' she said. 'Drink.'

'Ah, my Ingrid, always at my side when I need you,' Kuznetsov said in an attempt at his usual smoothness, but the edges of his words were ragged and he knocked back the cognac in one rapid swig. His nerves must be on fire.

I accepted the glass, took a sip and stepped away from the Russian. I sat down again on the chaise longue and presented Kuznetsov with a calm controlled face. I forced myself to keep my eyes off Timur's pistol which still lay on the floor where I had placed it.

'Herr Kuznetsov, even if I were prepared to swap the child you mention for my mother, I'm not able to do so because I don't have the child.'

The child. As if he were not mine, *my* child, *my* Felix. I nursed the balloon glass between my hands to stop their tremor. 'But if you release my mother, I will continue my search for the child and inform you when—'

'Don't take me for a fool.'

'Not a fool, no. You are a man out for revenge, a man blindly obsessed. You give no thought to the violence and violation your brutal son did to me and to my mother. Like father, like son. Both savage.'

The bastard smiled, as if I had complimented him and his son. I wanted to tear the skin off his face but instead I took a mouthful of the cognac and felt it scald its way down through me.

'Where is my mother?'

'Your mother is where she belongs.'

'And where is that?'

'On her way to Hoheneck,' he said.

A groan of despair escaped me. The notorious Hoheneck Prison was a women's forced labour detention centre, or correctional facility, as they liked to call it. A hell on earth.

'It's in Stollberg,' he elaborated. 'Three hundred kilometres south of here. You know of it? A bit crowded these days, I'm told, because it was built for six hundred prisoners but these days it holds sixteen hundred. Sixteen hundred and one now.' He flicked his tongue across his lips with amusement, savouring the tang of the cognac. Or was he savouring the image of my mother in a cell up to her neck in water, one of the favoured *correctional* punishments used there? A sentence of twenty-five years in the name of the Union of Soviet Socialist Republics was not uncommon.

'She has committed no crime,' I insisted.

'Luisa Wolff has committed the abhorrent crime of abandoning my grandson on a doorstep.'

'What?'

How could he know? How could he possibly know?

Abruptly he was on the move again, prowling the room as though driven by demons, his cane tapping tapping tapping till I longed to snatch it from his hand and beat him over the head with it. But I remained seated, my calm face in place.

'Who told you that?' I asked.

'Your mother.'

'That's a lie.'

He laughed, such an easy laugh. 'You're right. It was your friend Klaus Dieleman who informed me.' For a moment he stood still and regarded me with keen interest. 'How does that feel?'

It felt obscene. Klaus was one of the few people in the city who knew about the abandonment of Felix and it was why the friendship between him and my mother had ended so abruptly after thirty years. But the worst part was imagining what this man must have done to Klaus to make him betray us like that, and I knew then that that was why Klaus had thrown his own cane in the drain – as a warning to me. It was a message. Beware the man with a cane. I knocked back the last of my drink, rose to my feet with empty glass in hand and walked over to the painting.

'Sit down,' Kuznetsov ordered.

I chinked the rim of my glass against the wall, a quick strike, and watched a section of the crystalline glass crack off and flutter to the floor, leaving a jagged spur behind. It glittered in my hand, lit by the wall lamp angled above the painting.

'Sit down, Fräulein Wolff,' Kuznetsov roared at me, 'or I will—'

I slashed the canvas. Again and again and again. Ripping and rending and stabbing. The noise of the fibres parting, like muscles tearing, was deeply satisfying. Hacking and lacerating the young man who violated two German women who had been innocently heading home after a day's hard work, laughing. Yes, we were laughing. In the days when we still knew how, before our laughter was stolen from us.

'Stop,' bellowed the young man's father to protect his wounded son from me.

But he forgot to protect himself. He came for me, swinging wildly with his cane. He stripped the ebony covering from the stiletto sword inside, revealing a gleaming shard of steel. He lashed out at me with the blade just as fiercely as I'd been slashing at his son, but I ducked low to knee level and threw myself at him, driving my broken glass into his handsome fawn thigh. He went down with a crash and a ferocious curse, and I stamped on his wrist, snatching the sword. I darted away with it.

The battle was over. Done in seconds. Both of us heaving air into our lungs, eyes fixed on each other. Off to one side, Ingrid gave a low chuckle that startled me and scrambled its way through the thrashing pulse in my ears. I was shaking. The lethal tip of the steel blade in my hand danced in the air, I couldn't keep it still, sending darts of light tumbling over the ruins of the painting. I held the sword at arm's length, pointed directly at Kuznetsov on the floor but out of his reach.

'Ingrid,' he groaned. 'Pull the trigger on the bitch.'

Oddly, I had forgotten the guns, hers and Timur's. Oddly, I no longer felt an overpowering need to see Kuznetsov cut into shreds the way I had cut his son, because something changed in me with each slash of the painting. It was as if I was slashing myself wide open. It was why I couldn't stop. Every single incision in the body of Kuznetsov's son – in his stomach, down his legs, through his lungs, slicing off his offending hands and the proud bulk inside his pants – felt like an incision in myself. Lancing the pain. Cutting it out. I had been rotting inside without knowing it. The pain spilled out of me on to the polished floor like Kuznetsov's blood was doing now from his thigh and I longed for my mother to be here to witness it. To spill her own paralysing pain if I put the silver sword in her hand.

Kuznetsov had untied his white silk stock from around his neck and was fastening it around his thigh, knotting it tight to stem the flow, but still the blood kept coming.

'Ingrid, don't just stand there,' he snapped at her. 'Telephone for an ambulance, for God's sake.'

Ingrid walked over to the telephone on a stand by the door but failed to pick up the receiver.

'Pull the fucking trigger on her,' Kuznetsov bellowed.

I moved closer to him. 'Kuznetsov, I'm ordering you to telephone Hoheneck Prison right now and demand that my mother is returned here immediately or I will stick your own sword into you.'

He looked up from the floor and I could see so much hatred of me in his eyes. Or was it fear? Or pain? I couldn't tell. 'What made you Wolff women dump my grandson in the street to be devoured by starving dogs? You are both cold-hearted whores.'

'The answer is obvious,' Ingrid replied ahead of me. 'Because he was your son's hated bastard.'

'No,' I said, to myself more than to them, 'I loved Felix. I still love him.'

'Like I still love Otto,' she said.

'Otto was an inconvenience.' Kuznetsov grimaced and struggled to his feet, hauling himself up by gripping a chair. He grunted with pain as his jodhpurs flooded scarlet.

I threw down the sword, afraid I would be tempted to use it, but Ingrid darted forward and scooped it up. For one bizarre moment she whirled the blade through the air in aerial ballet like one of the sword dancers I'd seen at Traunstein and I recalled that she used to perform in a circus. Kuznetsov shouted something at her and I felt a sudden dread.

'Ingrid,' I called, 'put it down before …'

She spun round in a circle twice, building momentum, the sword extended, faster and faster.

'No, Ingrid, no, I …'

It was so neat. So tidy. So precise. One strike. The blade sliced clean through Kuznetsov's throat. His eyes grew huge, his hands scrabbled at the wound, seeking air, but all they found was blood before he fell to the floor, face down.

'No,' I screamed and knelt at his side, searching in vain for a pulse. 'He was my only chance of getting my mother back.'

'Oh, Anna,' Ingrid said, 'he would never have given her back to you except in a box.'

I looked up at her. Her eyes gleamed bright and triumphant, and she knew she was visible now. 'I promised Otto,' she stated, as she wiped the blade on Kuznetsov's riding jacket and slid it carefully back inside the cane.

I stood staring down at the pool of blood that harboured such darkness at its heart and at the man who had brought so much heartache into my family's life.

'It's time to finish this,' I said.

I snatched the decanter of cognac from the table, emptied it over his body and spattered it over the immaculate polished floor of the apartment, then seized the solid silver table lighter that was sitting on top of the grand piano. I struck a flame and lit one of the sheets of piano music. It caught immediately, filling the room with the acrid scent of burning paper as a spiral of flame consumed the music, and with a nod of satisfaction I let it float down on to the spilled alcohol. A blue flame leapt up, eager and alive, twisting and writhing, and raced towards the dead body.

We stood outside in the biting wind and watched the building burn.

The residents of the other apartments had escaped. They'd come pouring out of the building with a flurry of weeping and wailing, shouting and shrieking, women clutching jewellery boxes and furs and men with coats wrapped tight around briefcases bursting with secret documents. One elderly military man knelt with a small white dog in his arms and tears on his face. They all gazed, transfixed by the violence of the flames, and thought their private thoughts.

Fire hoses snaked. Fire engines pumped. Water drenched the air while ash fluttered down like black snow and caught in our throats. Men in uniform yelled orders as tongues of vivid flame leapt through the roof and blew out windows. I had no idea a fire could be so loud. The roaring, cracking, spitting and raging. So much fury. So much smoke. There were sudden crashes that sent sparks shooting like fireworks up into the darkening sky.

'Ingrid.' I placed a hand on her shoulder. 'Come.'

But she didn't move. She couldn't tear her gaze away from the flames.

'It's best if we aren't seen here,' I muttered in her ear, 'and I have to find Timur. If my mother is truly in Hoheneck Prison, then I need him to try to get her out now that her accuser is dead.'

I looked up for one last time at the apartment where Felix's grandfather had so nearly ended my life. *Pull the trigger on the bitch.*

'Ingrid,' I murmured, 'why did you point the gun at me? Did you plan on killing me all along? On Kuznetsov's orders?'

A twitch flicked at the corner of her mouth but she didn't turn her head. Her pale cheek had flecks of black ash on it. Or was it blood?

'It was always a possibility,' she said. 'He would have rewarded me well.'

'But you didn't.'

'No, I didn't.'

For a long moment in this strange swirling world of fire and destruction, we both considered that fact.

'Thank you, Ingrid,' I said and pulled her arm to set her in motion. 'Come. Leave it to burn. I must find Timur.'

CHAPTER SIXTY-FOUR

◆ ◆ ◆

INGRID

'Come,' Anna said, and Ingrid felt an urgent tug on her arm.
The easterly wind had picked up and Ingrid was mesmerised by
the way it flung the plumes of flame across the roof. She felt a breathless
excitement. She had killed the man who had put a bullet into Otto's brain
and she felt exhilarated, exonerated, but inside her chest lay a hard stone
of bitter regret that she hadn't done it earlier. If she had killed the murdering bastard the first time she met him in the Kirchestrasse apartment,
Otto would be alive. That thought choked her.

'Leave it to burn,' Anna urged. 'I must find Timur.'

Ingrid started to move, but it was as if Anna had conjured up her
Russian major just by voicing his name. Suddenly Timur Voronin
was right there in the street, blurred by smoke, fifty metres away and
in a huge hurry. They both spotted him at the same moment, a tall
and determined figure in his thick Red Army greatcoat, forcing his
way through the gathered crowd and running straight towards the
burning building.

'Timur!' Anna shouted.

But her shout was swallowed by the crackle and roar of the flames. Daylight was draining from the sky, shutting down the city, leaving behind
only the light of the fire and the tortured shadows creeping into corners.

'Timur, wait!' Anna cried out.

He didn't hear. They pushed forward to try to reach him, but a cordon of blue police uniforms had other ideas. The VoPo were allowing
no one through, unless you happened to be a Red Army officer, of
course, in which case you could do whatever the hell you liked.

Ingrid saw Timur duck under the cordon and get snagged in an altercation with a fireman in full protective gear who tried to block him, but it was brief. No surprise there. You didn't get to be an officer in the Soviet Red Army by taking no for an answer. She wondered if Anna realised what she was getting into, mixing oil and water. Yet there was something about Anna that lived life on her own terms, the same way Otto used to. To hell with anyone else's opinion of her. That's how they got things done.

'No, Timur, no!' Anna screamed.

But they could do nothing except watch helplessly as Timur swept off his peaked cap and yanked his heavy coat up over his head. He plunged inside the burning building.

'You have to breathe,' Ingrid instructed Anna.

They were standing in the street and it felt to Ingrid that each minute was a lifetime. A low moan was coming from Anna, incessant and relentless. Ingrid held on tight to Anna's hand, unwilling to lose her to the flames in pursuit of Timur. Police uniforms had formed a barricade that prevented any other fool from hurling themselves into the inferno.

'There's hope,' Ingrid murmured.

Beside her, Anna stood rigid. Of course there wasn't hope.

'It's a miracle,' screamed the woman next to Ingrid, shaking her husband's arm hard enough to rip it off. '*Mein Vater im Himmel*. Look! A miracle!'

Ingrid didn't believe in miracles. She didn't believe that God reached down and touched a human being with His divine finger just to please the puny creatures on earth. And yet a bulky figure engulfed in flames and concealed in a shroud of smoke staggered from the building and was immediately smothered in blankets to extinguish the blaze.

No, Ingrid didn't believe in miracles. She believed in strength of will and force of conviction to work such wonders. She'd seen Otto swing himself to safety when a trapeze wire snapped twenty metres up in the air and seen her father withdraw his head from a lion's mouth after it had disobediently clamped its jaws shut on him. Neither was a miracle, as people had claimed at the time. Both were achieved through strength of will and years of training. So now she viewed that crazy burning figure with new respect. Major Timur Voronin had created his own miracle.

From under his scorched and blackened greatcoat emerged Luisa Wolff.

Luisa Wolff was in an ambulance. It was the first time Ingrid had met Anna's mother. She was nothing like her daughter. Fair and fragile-boned, sitting poker straight and proud like a queen, sweeping aside the attentions of a medic. She seemed undamaged by the fire except for a heaviness in her breathing. But her eyes, *mein Gott*, her eyes, so wounded by life, it hurt to look at them.

'Stop fussing, Anna,' Frau Wolff said dismissively. 'I'm alright.'

That was it. No tears, not even from her daughter, but the way they looked at each other was the way a flier looks at a catcher on a trapeze, intense and watchful of every tic in every muscle. Needing each other.

'What happened?' Anna asked her. She was holding her mother's hand.

'I was dragged from our apartment and driven to this place by two Soviet bastards.' She spat on the ambulance floor in disgust and her spittle came out black. For a moment she stared at her daughter in tense silence. 'From their car I saw the explosion blow out our apartment's windows. So that's it, we're homeless and will starve.'

'Did Kuznetsov interrogate you?' Ingrid asked.

Frau Wolff looked at her in surprise, as if she hadn't previously noticed this stranger in the ambulance. But Ingrid was used to that.

'Who are you?'

'A friend. Of your daughter.'

'No, no interrogation. What could he possibly want from me? He immediately locked me in a tiny godforsaken room. Its door was hidden behind a wardrobe, no windows and no light.'

Anna made an odd harsh sound but said nothing.

'After a while I smelled smoke.' Luisa Wolff lifted her hand to her nose and dragged in a long breath. 'I stink of it.' She shrugged. 'Then the flames, the roar of burning. Things crashing down. My door on fire. Don't look at me like that, Anna. I survived, thanks to your Russian bear. He burst in, swept me under his greatcoat with him and charged back down stairs that were burning under our feet.'

Ingrid and Anna both stared at her feet. Her ankles were raw and blistered.

'They're fine,' Luisa Wolff said quickly. 'What about your Red Army major, Anna? Is he … ?' For the first time the emotion broke her and tears shimmered in her huge blue eyes. 'Is he alive, Anna?'

'They say he has smoke and toxic gases jammed in his airways, so he's receiving oxygen. But yes, Timur is alive. Scorched, but alive.'

'That's twice that your Russian has saved my life.'

Earlier, jealousy had gripped Ingrid by the throat. It had twisted her tongue in her mouth till she couldn't speak. It was an emotion she'd never experienced before, she'd never had reason to with Otto, but now it was different. When she saw Anna wrap her arms around Timur where he had collapsed on the ground, such a tender loving embrace, she saw a yawning chasm of loneliness open up in front of her. Her grief for Otto was suffocating her.

Timur wouldn't let go of Anna, even though his gloves were still smoking and he could barely breathe for coughing. Anna's arms cradled him and her lips whispered words for his ears only while her tears streamed down his cheeks. Ingrid didn't look away. She wanted to remember what love looked like.

Anna slid an arm around her mother's narrow shoulders and held her. 'Mutti,' she said in a voice that had changed in a way that Ingrid couldn't pinpoint. Something deeper and warmer within it. 'Mutti, I've found him.'

'Found who?'

'I've found Felix.'

CHAPTER SIXTY-FIVE

◆ ◆ ◆

INGRID

A different nightclub. But the same throbbing strident jazz as before, the same loose-tongued laughter, the same stink of sexual desire. The same men entwined with men, and women dancing lip-close with women. There was a heat here in the club, a fever that licked Ingrid's skin and burned right through to the pain inside, numbing it.

She knocked back her shot of Johnnie Walker and instantly another one materialised on the little round scarlet table in front of her. On the walls there were purples and crimsons and great splashes of sunflower yellow that made her heart beat faster. Outside in the rest of the city there was only endless greyness to be had; even death was grey out there in Berlin, grey and wretched and unrelenting. Here to her astonishment she found herself laughing.

She raised her glass. 'To a future without Pavel Kuznetsov,' she declared to Noah Maynard who was sitting opposite her.

Her American pilot was relaxed and smiling, clearly pleased to be trading drinks with her again and to have discarded his USAF uniform for a few hours in favour of stylish loose trousers and an open-necked shirt. She could have put on her posh frock but Kuznetsov had bought it for her, so she intended to burn it. Anyway, Noah didn't seem to care what she wore.

Noah clinked his glass to hers. 'You are a force to be reckoned with, Ingrid Keller, and Kuznetsov reckoned you all wrong.'

She laughed and it felt good.

He leaned across the table, close as a lover. 'You're sure he's dead?'

'Yes. Dead and burned to a crisp.'

Noah raised a dark eyebrow. 'Anything to connect him to you?'

'No, there's no trace of me in the apartment, nothing to connect me with him in any way. But I've killed the golden goose, haven't I, so we're both out of pocket.' She took a good swig of her drink and gathered her next words on her tongue. This was it. The reason she'd asked him to meet her. 'Noah, we make a good team, you and I, too good to let slip through our fingers.' She drew a quick nervy breath. 'There must be someone else out there in the east who wants what we have to sell.'

'Of course there is.' In his dark eyes flickered the reflection of the candle flame on their table like an invitation.

'Do you know the name of anyone who would be interested?' Ingrid asked.

'Yes, I know a couple of names who work in the Soviet shadows.'

'Names we can trust?'

'I am very careful.'

He leaned so close his forehead was touching hers and she caught the smoky aroma of Lucky Strikes on his breath which instantly made her think of Otto, and she felt the room black out for a moment.

Noah must have seen something of the turmoil within her but he misinterpreted it. He said gently, 'Don't worry, Ingrid. The Soviet MGB will pay you well, I'll make certain of that.'

'So we'll continue as we are, doing what we're doing out at Tempelhof? But reporting to someone else.'

'That's right. We have to. You and I know, Ingrid, that communism is the only truly just system, the only way forward that will give ordinary people like you and me a life worth living, and there's so much more we can do to help this become a reality for—'

She pressed a finger to his lips. 'Hush. One step at a time. You make the arrangements to introduce me to a new ... what do you call them? ... a new handler. We'll take it from there.'

He sat back in his chair, satisfied, and signalled for a new round of drinks. 'Leave the bottle,' he told the young German waiter, who smiled from under long slinky false eyelashes when he saw the size of the tip Noah dropped on his tray. Noah's gaze lingered on his tight leather trousers as he threaded his way back to the mirrored bar.

They discussed whether the airlift could possibly make it through the winter when the weather deteriorated, which many experts doubted. Or whether the inhabitants of Berlin would be driven to the brink of starvation by January and the Allies would have to withdraw from the city, abandoning it to Stalin's authority. Ingrid loved Noah's passion, loved his belief in a glorious future for a communist Europe once the Allies were forced out of a reunited Germany and above all she loved his conviction that he could help make it happen.

'You have to destroy before you can rebuild,' he told her.

Ingrid didn't believe that was true. You can always build on what you already have. With Otto gone, she could take the small sliver of her life that remained – the thrill of stepping out on to the high-wire of being a Soviet agent – and build on that. That thought turned over and over in her head as they talked and drank, and drank and talked, so it was two hours and numerous shots later that Ingrid took hold of the American's shirt collar and purposefully drew him closer. Noah was a good-looking man, easy on the eye, and if he had a liking for slim-hipped waiters and nightclubs that stank of leather, so what? She could think of worse things. A lot worse.

'Noah, will you marry me?'

His jaw dropped wide open before his glossy white American teeth came together again with an audible snap.

'Ingrid, my crazy young *Fräulein*, you've got the wrong guy here, remember?' By way of explanation he waved his hand in the general direction of the two young men wrapped in an embrace on the dance floor. 'I know America's War Bride Act allows for foreign military marriages, but believe me, it's the scotch talking, not you.'

'No, Noah, I'm serious. Listen to me. It would be good cover for you. And I'll never want any man except Otto, so don't worry about that side of the arrangement. It would mean we could continue as an undercover intelligence team for the Soviet Union wherever you are posted when all this is over – until our communist dream becomes a reality. We could work in any of the Allied airbases in West Germany. Or eventually back in America, maybe even at the Pentagon. It could work well. Think about it.'

Noah's dark eyes gleamed as he thought about it for all of one and a half minutes, and his whole face grew deadly serious. The place was thrumming with noise but she heard none of it, except his sombre voice.

'Ingrid Keller, I accept.'

'Your answer is yes? You'll marry me?'

'It sure is.' And then he grinned at her, eyes shining. 'You bet your sweet life it is.' He raised his glass. 'To the future Mrs Maynard.'

Ingrid chinked her glass against his. 'To a future full of secrets.'

CHAPTER SIXTY-SIX

• • •

ANNA

'How is your Russian this morning?' my mother asked.

'Call him by his name,' I told her. 'You owe him that much respect.'

She sighed. 'How is Major Timur Voronin this morning?'

'Not good.'

'He needs to go to hospital.'

I regarded my mother where she sat in a feathery patch of sunlight in the factory yard. I'd honestly thought I would never see the day. It was the presence of Felix that had tempted her outside. He was playing in the dirt with Poldi and she was watching from a safe distance, her mouth slowly losing its sharp edge.

'He won't let a doctor near him,' I explained, 'because the authorities will be searching for him after he refused to obey military orders. He knows they will put him up against a wall and shoot him.'

'Who will?'

'The Red Army military police, the Soviet Intelligence State Security officers, the MGB, the MVD, informers, the VoPos, their spies, their tracker dogs, take your pick. Even the unit he worked with, they'll all be hunting him down. You can't be an officer in the Soviet Army and just walk away.'

My words stop. My throat closes.

I look at Felix. My mother looks at me.

More gently she says, 'Tell Timur to get himself through one of the checkpoints immediately, before they roll up here with their tanks.'

'He can't. The moment they check his papers he will be arrested.'

'So? What now?'

'They'll come for him here. We have to leave.'

'And go where?' My mother gave a bitter laugh.

At the sound of it, Felix looked up from his game, saw me watching him and came scampering over. He leaned the weight of his small body against my legs and tipped his head back to gaze up at me, as if to reassure himself I really existed. Everything inside me melted and I find it hard to put into words what I saw behind the startling blue of his eyes. Because what I saw hurt. There were too many layers for one so young, layers of fear and suspicion and pain and anger, and always the desperate desire to love and be loved. It's what we all want.

I scooped him up with a laugh and gathered him into my arms, where he nestled into my neck like a puppy. My nose was in his hair, breathing in every scrap of him, his fingers twined around my ears. I wanted so badly to know him inside and out, this feral little boy of mine, but it would take time, for both of us. Time and tears and love. I would be patient. My hand wrapped itself around his right ankle where the letter A was imprinted on his skin.

'So,' my mother said again, 'what now?'

I kissed Felix's flawless forehead. 'I'll get us out.'

CHAPTER SIXTY-SEVEN

◆ ◆ ◆

ANNA

A circus parade came tumbling out of the west.
'You look ridiculous,' I said.
'Look who's talking,' Timur laughed. 'Clowns are supposed to look ridiculous.' He was wearing a fuzzy orange wig.

'Is the pain bad?'

'Hardly anything.'

He was lying. He had a raging fever and his eyes inside their huge painted white clown circles kept glazing over. The outrageous clown face paint disguised his burns and bruises.

'We'll make it,' he said.

'Of course we will. Who would arrest anyone who looked this silly?'
He smiled, making it seem easy.

I was clad in a baggy lurid yellow romper suit with huge white daisies on it and an amethyst ruff at my neck, a bobbing sunflower on my head over a long rainbow-coloured wig. Timur was in a giant check suit of purple and lime green, both of us unrecognisable. It was all down to Ingrid.

A big bass drum sounded nearby.

'Hear that?' I said. 'That's our cue.'

With a great outburst of noise and a flood of colour that swept away the city's greyness, the circus was drawing closer to where we were tucked out of sight on the eastern side of Pariser Platz. The parade dazzled with its sequins and trumpets and pounding oom-pa-pa music. People stopped whatever they were doing, poured out of their houses and stared, lifting children on to their shoulders, entranced.

A huge drum with plumes and ribbons was booming out their arrival. Clowns frolicked, a whole mass of them, the refuge children dressed up in costumes, all of them being wonderfully silly. One clown in a bright scarlet costume was pushing another in a wheelbarrow while throwing balloons to the gathering crowd, and I watched those two closely because under the face paint and clown costumes were Yvo and Leah. A stilt-walker in long striped trousers and a tall top hat played a wheezy accordion and a troupe of acrobats performed leaps and cartwheels while tossing each other into the air with death-defying spins. One handsome young man made a dramatic show of juggling peacock-blue balls, while another wiry older man with only one ear and dressed like a cowboy – Fridolf was his name, according to Ingrid – juggled throwing knives with razor-sharp blades that glinted in the sun.

Timur and I forgot we were clowns. We gazed in awe.

Six white poodles danced in pink tutus and four cheeky miniature ponies with bows in their manes tried to eat everything in sight. A unicycle was ridden by a slender woman with an eyepatch, dressed up as a pirate with a parrot on her shoulder and boots halfway up her thighs. Even the Allied soldiers were applauding.

All good so far.

But there was one major barrier. Between us and freedom stood a Soviet checkpoint. The circus parade was marching down Charlottenburger Chaussee in the British sector on the other side of the checkpoint. It was in the west. Timur and I were in the east. In front of us in the shadow of the massive Brandenburg Gate stood four Soviet guards with rifles on their shoulders. Two were young, smooth-chinned, barely more than eighteen or nineteen, and they were standing with their backs to us, transfixed by the circus antics on the other side of the divide. The other two, older and warier, also watched the circus performances but with one eye on the crowd that was gathering eagerly in the wide public expanse on our side of the checkpoint. A massive poster of Stalin looked on with a stern eye.

'Leave me,' Timur whispered. 'Leave me here and go.'

He tried to step away but I wrapped an arm around his waist and held him fast. 'It'll work, Timur. Look at it, look at the parade.'

At its head trotted a magnificent ice-white high-stepping horse, so fine-boned I thought its legs might snap as it pranced and twirled in response to the beautiful young acrobat on its back. It was Ingrid. Ingrid as I'd never seen her before, a glorious shining Ingrid who attracted all eyes. She glittered and sparkled in a golden leotard covered in sequins as she swung up to a standing position on the horse's back. Effortlessly she performed an array of handstands and back-springs, while the animal slowly trotted in a wide circle and a British Army truck moved out of its way. Neither missed a step. The grace of rider and horse was mesmerising.

'Come on,' I muttered to Timur. 'Now.'

Together we pushed our way forward, laughing and clapping and waving to the crowd, making fools of ourselves. Timur hurt. I could feel his pain. I tried to take it slow, pretending he was drunk by making drinking signs to the spectators and rolling my clown eyes, to explain his unsteady progress. When one of the crowd slapped him boisterously on the back and shouted encouragement, I thought he would die right there in my arms. I was desperate for the wheelbarrow.

We'd timed it right. Just then an emerald green cart pulled by two gigantic draught horses horses drew up to join the acrobats on the west side of the checkpoint barrier. The horses were sisters, Ingrid had told me, the Polish Sokolsky breed with hearts of oak and blond manes as glamorous as Jean Harlow's. They were old hands at parades and blinked their silvery eyelashes patiently in the sun. But the arrival of the cart brought a rush of oohs and aahs and an overspill of excited energy as onlookers pressed forward to catch a better view.

On the flatbed of the cart stood the barrel-chested ringmaster. He was resplendent in scarlet tailcoat and cracking his whip in the air with the noise of a gunshot. But it was the creature beside him on the cart that caused the gasp of amazement. A huge magnificent brown bear. Delighted shivers of fear ran through the spectators when the powerful animal raised itself on its hind legs, rattling the chain that tethered it and stretching up to over three metres tall. It raked the air with massive paws, wielding claws like scythes. Even the older guards were spellbound.

Ingrid looked beyond the checkpoint, scanned the crowd in the east and spotted us. We were hard to miss in our bright clown costumes. I nodded and in response she slid smoothly into a seated position on her Arab stallion's back and spun him out of his circle to trot right up to the Soviet guards at the checkpoint. She gave them a sparkling smile. This was a seductive Ingrid, an Ingrid wearing glamorous make-up and a flowing auburn wig. I saw her lean her head down to speak to the guards with an intimate laugh and I saw them nod. I saw her blow them a kiss.

That's all it took.

They waved her and her horse through the checkpoint into East Berlin without asking to see papers, two clowns scuttling behind her, one doing cartwheels and the other pushing the barrow. Much closer now. Ingrid threw herself into a series of dramatic jumps on and off the horse as it cantered around at speed in front of this new Soviet-sector audience. The stallion reared up on its hind legs with Ingrid still on its back, pumping up the crowd till they roared and cheered and clapped. Her act ended with a final flourish as she rose up to standing on the horse's rump and waved goodbye as it cantered back through the checkpoint with the clowns in tow.

The crowd cheered. Dazzled. Awed. Bewitched.

Who would notice that four clowns were hurrying along behind her instead of two? Who would be remotely interested in the biggest one in the garish floppy suit lying slumped inside the wheelbarrow or in the other two clowns pushing it?

The bear was roaring. The drum was pounding. The horse's hooves were striking the cobblestones. The laughter of the crowd was sweeping down Charlottenburger Chaussee and the whip cracked over their heads, distracting their senses. In all that noise and spectacle, who would notice?

Who?

'Halt!' the oldest guard called.

He reached out and seized Timur's wide floppy sleeve as I tried to hurry the wheelbarrow in the wake of the horse. The guard's grip slowed the wheelbarrow. It skewed. Started to tip. I slid my hand into my clown costume's pocket where Timur's gun lay. My eyes feasted on Timur in his ginger wig for what I knew would be the last time. A shoot-out with a Soviet guard? We all knew how that would end. But I would not let them take him, not now, not ever. Half a dozen more steps were all we needed. If I could gain one half-minute for him … my finger found the trigger.

Timur's clown sleeve was stretched to ripping point. The guard refused to release it though Yvo and I kept trying to force the barrow forward. A taut scrap of check cotton was all that stood between us and freedom.

'Halt!' the guard shouted again. Louder this time to rise above the noise.

I drew the gun.

Timur turned his head, eyes glazed with fever. 'No, Anna!'

From nowhere a razor-edged throwing knife came spinning through the air from Fridolf's hand on the other side of the checkpoint and sliced clean through that treacherous scrap of cotton sleeve. Released, the wheelbarrow lurched forward. We raced after the horse and plunged into the parade. Behind us the guard was left standing with a piece of check cloth in his hand. Even he could not open fire into a crowd of children.

CHAPTER SIXTY-EIGHT

◆ ◆ ◆

ANNA

Timur didn't open his eyes. I willed him to, but he didn't. Nevertheless I held his hand wrapped in mine and talked to him quietly as if he could hear me because I wasn't willing to let him creep away. So I lifted his hand to my lips in the hope that he could feel my words, even if he couldn't hear them.

The hospital was an Allied military one, all starched white caps and tight bed-corners, and a constant stream of kind pink-cheeked nurses coming to check on him, to take his blood pressure or his temperature, or inject God-knows-what into him. Their smiles grew more fragile, as if they were preparing themselves – and me – for what was to come. But they didn't know Timur like I knew him. They didn't know Russians like I knew them.

He had been installed in this single isolation room in a military hospital because he'd been conscious enough initially to inform them that he was a Red Army officer who wished to defect to the west. The Allied military authorities had gathered him into their waiting arms and eyed each other gleefully in anticipation of gleaning valuable intelligence when he was ready to be questioned. As I said, they didn't know Timur like I did.

So the nurses kept coming, hovering, injecting, supplying oxygen, bandaging with their iodoform and bismuth gauzes. He'd lain unconscious for two days, two knife-edge days, every breath a struggle, a hoarse effort to drag air into his scorched lungs, and I inhaled each breath with him. The nurses had given up trying to throw me out.

'Anna.'

I looked up. On the other side of the bed stood Ingrid. Not in her glittering gold sequins and flame-coloured wig, though that's how I pictured her now. I knew that somewhere deep under her drab coat and brown headscarf, she still shimmered.

'Hello, Ingrid.'

'How is he?'

'Improving.'

She raised a sceptical eyebrow. She had most likely already spoken to a nurse and been told otherwise. In her hand sat a sugared doughnut – from the Tempelhof food wagon – which she placed on the bedside cabinet.

'Thank you,' I said, though those two simple words would never be enough. 'You were wonderful. I will spend the rest of my life thanking you. Timur too when he's well again.'

She looked down at the bandaged face and shrugged. 'I didn't do it for him.'

'So who did you do it for?'

'For Otto. I knew he'd be watching from wherever the hell he is now and I wanted him to remember me when I was ...'

'Spectacular,' I said.

'Yes.' Her eyes shone.

'He'd have been very proud of you.'

Again a shrug. 'I don't want his pride.'

'What is it you want then?'

'I want him to lust after me, as much now as he did in life.' She laughed and said again, 'I did it for Otto.'

Did I believe her? I don't know. Ingrid was not an easy person to read. Did she do it for Otto or for me or for the circus performers or to give the Soviets a kick in the teeth or a million other reasons? I'll never know but I'll always be grateful.

'Anyway, it worked out well,' she said with a smile.

I stood, walked round to Ingrid and removed the necklace I wore around my neck under my jumper. It was the one of beaten gold that Timur had sent me as a gift from Siberia, the one I'd believed I would wear for a lifetime.

'This is for you, Ingrid, from Timur and from myself. We will forever be in your debt.'

Her face brightened and she let me fasten the gold snake chain around her neck. She didn't say thank you because there was no need, but her fingers caressed it against her skin with sensuous pleasure.

'So what now?' she asked. 'Will you be coming back to work at Tempelhof?'

'I will if I can because I need the money. But they've probably given the job to someone else by now.'

'I'll speak to Captain Maynard to arrange it. You know he has a soft spot for you.' Her gaze switched back to the still figure in the bed. 'Do you think your Russian might end up working with the Allied military here if – I mean, *when* – he gets better? As an adviser or something? He has so much inside knowledge. And I'm sure Captain Maynard would be interested in talking to him,' she added.

I frowned. I was telling no one, not even Ingrid, Timur's future plans.

She changed the subject. 'Where are you living now?'

'Here in West Berlin with Martha Dieleman on Ku'damm. My mother, Felix and I are staying with her for now in her large apartment. She has taken us all in while we register with the Allied authorities for new ration books and identity papers to allow us to live permanently in the west. Martha is a dear kind soul. We couldn't go before because my mother would never go outside our apartment and I couldn't leave because ...' I paused.

'Because of Felix?'

'Yes, I had to find him first.'

She nodded. 'I understand.'

Did she? I doubted it. Because what I didn't say was how would Timur ever have been able to find me if he'd come back from Russia and I was gone?

'Let's hope you haven't escaped from East Berlin only to starve with us in West Berlin because of the Soviet blockade.'

'Not while the airlift continues. It is our lifeline.'

She shook her head uncertainly. 'It can't go on forever.'

'Oh, Ingrid, you must trust the Allies,' I said. 'They are brave men. Men like Captain Maynard, men who have proved themselves loyal to us Germans.'

Ingrid gave me a strange look. 'Maybe.'

'And you?' I asked.

'Oh.' She shrugged in her usual offhand manner. 'I'll carry on pouring out coffee in my food wagon over at Tempelhof.' She smiled. 'But not forever.'

'Things are bound to change, Ingrid, for all of us. For good or bad, I don't know which, but they can't go on like this. That's why I still want to help the children while I can. A few of the kids will be staying with us at Martha's too. Poldi and Leah and Lars.'

'Not Yvo?'

'No, not Yvo. He'd rather live in his lairs where no one tells him to wash his hands or wipe his feet or put out that cigarette. But as soon as I can I intend to set up another refuge for the kids.'

Ingrid nodded softly to herself. 'Of course you do.'

'One thing more, Ingrid. I'd like to come out to your stables to thank your knife thrower myself. Such quick thinking and amazing accuracy. He saved us. Please thank Fridolf from us both until we can do it ourselves.'

'I'll tell him.'

'Thank you.'

Our eyes met and for a moment nothing was said but much was understood. I took her in my arms, gathered her close and held her for a long time. I could sense a desperate need in her for closeness.

'Anna, I'm glad you found your Felix. He's such a sweet kid.' She stepped back. 'But he doesn't look at all like you, you so dark and him so fair.'

I breathed carefully. 'Felix's father was white-blond, if you remember Kuznetsov's painting.'

'I remember.' Her eyes fixed on mine. 'But the person he looks most like is ...'

I knew what was coming.

'Your mother,' she finished.

'She is his bloodline, so of course he looks like her.'

But Ingrid wasn't going to give this up. 'Are you sure that's all?'

'Oh, Ingrid, you are sharp-eyed. You'd make a good spy.' I laughed. And it was a laugh of relief. To voice the truth at last. 'Yes, you're right, Felix was born to my mother after the attack on us in the alleyway, but she hated him from the first moment he drew breath. So I took him as mine.'

The memory of it pierces me. In the bedroom. Sliding the tiny slippery being out of my mother's body, the blood, the tears, the pain, and the overpowering love that gripped my heart as I held newborn Felix in my arms.

Ingrid nodded. 'Be happy, Anna. With your son and your Russian.'

We parted and I walked to the door with her. 'Thank you,' I said. 'See you at the food truck.'

She gave me a shy smile as though my words bonded a friendship she hadn't expected.

'Stay safe,' she said, pressed my hand, and was gone.

Alone with Timur again, I turned back to the bed, slid into my chair and lifted his hand to my lips once more. His chest continued its fight to rise and fall.

What will happen to you, Timur? What will happen to us?

We can't stay in Berlin, I know that, it's too dangerous for you, my love. Even in the western sector of Berlin the Russian machine is too close, too eager to track you down anywhere in the city and snatch you off the street. Our only hope for a future lies a hundred and sixty kilometres away in West Germany. The Allies will want to whisk you away to Munich or Bonn or some such city where they will try to dredge every Soviet secret out of you.

I bend close and kiss your blistered lips. I listen to your rasping intake of air. They don't know what a good chess player you are, but they will learn that you only play on your terms. Very softly I whisper the future I see. A new life, you and me. And yes, my mother and Felix will join us to help build a fine new productive Germany that we can be proud of. But first, Timur, you must come back to me.

I sat upright again. 'Enough sleeping,' I said sternly. 'Time to wake up. We can't laze around here all day with so much to do. I have children to feed now.'

A touch. So slight, I was imagining it. But no, there was a faint pressure against my fingers and I felt a shudder of relief sweep through me. Timur's eyes opened a crack, a thin flint-grey line that allowed my mind to believe in a future.

'Welcome back,' I said.

THE END

AUTHOR'S NOTE ON
THE BERLIN AIRLIFT

The **Berlin Airlift** (called *Berliner Luftbrücke* in German, meaning 'Berlin Air Bridge') took place from 26 June 1948 to 30 September 1949 and was a turning point in European history. It set down a marker. A vital wake-up call to the ambitions of Stalin's communist Soviet Union.

In 1945, at the end of World War II, Germany had been divided into four zones by the victorious Allies. The American, British and French zones occupied the west of the country, the Soviet zone occupied the east. Berlin, the country's capital, lay marooned deep in the communist Soviet zone.

The city was also divided into four sectors, each one administered by one of the four Allies. But immediately after the war the relationship between the Western Allies and the Soviets deteriorated to such an extent that the Soviets withdrew from the Allied Control Council that had previously governed Berlin with a degree of cooperation. It soon became clear that Stalin had plans to oust the Western powers from the city. Bent on further domination of Europe, he had already seized control of Czechoslovakia in February 1948. If Berlin also fell, the Western Allies were convinced that Stalin's expansion plans would press forward to take over the whole of Germany.

British Prime Minister Winston Churchill had declared that 'an iron curtain' had fallen across Europe and nowhere was this more evident than in Berlin. The balance of power was on a knife edge. The threat of World War III was real. East against West, capitalism against communism. This was a turning point in our history that needs to be remembered.

Stalin was no longer willing to tolerate the existence of the capitalist sectors of Berlin isolated within his huge swathe of communist territory, a thorn in his side, so when on Friday 18 June the Americans, British and French collectively launched the Deutsche Mark to replace the Reichsmark, the Soviets took it as their chance to strike back hard. They gambled that the Western powers would have no stomach for another war. They closed access to the Western sectors of Berlin. Checkpoints were erected in the streets and all rail and water routes were closed off. The Berlin Blockade had begun.

The two million inhabitants of West Berlin would be left without the electricity, food, and fuel needed for survival and they would starve if nothing was done to help them.

So the Western Allies resorted to the air routes. At the Potsdam Conference in 1945 when the war ended, three air corridors into Berlin, each 20 miles wide, had been agreed by the Soviets. It was to these corridors that the Americans and British now turned. They realised that a massive unprecedented airlift was the only alternative to war or withdrawal. They had no wish to enter into another war but Allied withdrawal from Berlin would open the door to the Soviets to push deeper into Germany. American President Truman stood firm against further expansion of Soviet territory and in June 1948 the Berlin Airlift - named *Operation Vittles* - began, in order to keep a city supplied with food, fuel and essentials by air transport alone. It had never been done before and by many it was believed to be an impossible task.

On 28 June, the first American and British planes landed in Berlin at the US airport of Tempelhof and at the British RAF airbase of Gatow. During the next ten months it was a constant battle to keep the aircraft flying into Berlin with their life-saving cargo, two-thirds of which was coal, non-stop day and night through all weathers. In the winter of 1948/49, freezing conditions and fog often made flying conditions difficult and dangerous, so that tragically there were 101 fatalities during the operation. Nevertheless the Berlin Airlift delivered 2.3 million tonnes of cargo to the city, transported by more than 275,000 Allied flights. Of these flights, 75% were American, covering over 92 million miles. One US pilot, Gail Halvorsen, even found time repeatedly to collect and drop candy to the children of Berlin in a wonderful gesture of friendship, and became known as the well-loved Candy Bomber.

The Airlift, under the command of US Generals Lucius D Clay and William H Tunner, became so efficient at keeping the inhabitants supplied with the basics needed for life that after ten months the Soviets recognised that despite the hardship the inhabitants were undoubtedly suffering, Stalin's strategy to drive the Western powers out of Berlin had failed. On 12 May 1949, the Soviets conceded defeat, lifted the Blockade and reopened land and water access to Berlin. The Airlift continued until 30 September to ensure the build up of a stockpile of supplies in the city in case the Blockade was reintroduced by the Soviets, but this didn't occur.

Twelve years later in 1961, to the West's horror the city was further divided by the construction of the notorious wall, but in 1989 it was torn down and the two halves of Berlin were finally reunited in freedom. It was the Airlift, *Operation Vittles*, that laid the foundation to make this possible.

The Berlin Airlift was an astounding feat of dedication, skill and immense bravery, as well as of political foresight for which we in the West should today be grateful.

ACKNOWLEDGEMENTS

I love Berlin. It is a city that possesses a unique energy, one that is young and vibrant, and which gives me an abundance of inspiration the moment I set foot there. It is a city that oozes culture from every pore and yet is surrounded by lakes and woods where the stresses of urban life can be sloughed off and clean air brings clarity of thought. A trip to the top of the magnificent Fernsehturm, the television tower that dominates the skyline, is a must if you want a bird's eye view of just how green this wonderful city is. Yet it is a city that has been through terrible heartbreaking trauma and division, with a history that fascinates me and triggers a fierce desire to delve deeper through the stories of my books. For this inspiration I thank Berlin.

This book has taken me longer to write than any of my previous books though it is far from being my longest. But I was writing it at a time when the world was turning itself upside down on many fronts and I found it hard to draw together any creative flow. So it is with immense pleasure that I finally view it in book form. For its safe journey and arrival at this stage I have numerous people to whom I am deeply grateful.

First and foremost, I want to thank my exceptional publisher Jo Dickinson for her unswerving faith in me and in this book. She is the best of the best. Always able to see to the heart of a story and to guide me with grace and insight. Thanks, Jo. My thanks also to all the brilliant team at Hodder for bringing this book to life and producing a beautiful cover. Huge hugs to you all.

As always, my mega agent, Teresa Chris, has been my rock and an eternal source of encouragement during this process, using every one of the many wiles in her armoury to get me to the end of the book. Thank you, Teresa. You are awesome. My gratitude also goes to Anne

ACKNOWLEDGEMENTS

Menke for her ever-enthusiastic help in building up a picture of the life of Berliners in a post-war world and for providing a vital map of the divided city. Thank you, Anne.

My thanks again to Marian Churchward - I missed you! As for my fabulous gang of Brixham Writers, your never-flagging enthusiasm, laughter, wisdom, and cake kept me going when the going got tough.

Lastly and most profoundly, my love and thanks to Norman for being as passionate about this story as I am and for providing a wealth of knowledge about the aircraft involved. You made them come alive for me and walked with me down the unlit streets of Berlin 1948. It was always an adventure together.

THRILLINGLY GOOD BOOKS
FROM CRIMINALLY
GOOD WRITERS

CRIME FILES BRINGS YOU THE LATEST RELEASES FROM
TOP CRIME AND THRILLER AUTHORS.

N UP ONLINE FOR OUR MONTHLY NEWSLETTER AND BE THE FIRST
TO KNOW ABOUT OUR COMPETITIONS, NEW BOOKS AND MORE.